"Jennifer Pearson weaves the threads of this slick thriller
with such mastery; it seems almost effortless. Full of twists,
turns and characters you can't help fall in love with,
it kept me up way past my bedtime."
Cynthia Murphy, author of *Win Lose Kill Die*

"Pearson's YA debut sparkles with wit and heart, and its satisfying
twists and reveals will keep you on the edge of your seat. With its
layered, compelling characters and one of my new favourite
YA detective duos, *Drop Dead Famous* stands out from the
crowd. I can't wait to see what Pearson writes next."
Kathryn Foxfield, author of *Good Girls Die First*

"Fast paced, full of twists and turns."
Anne Cassidy, author of *Looking for JJ*

"Jennifer Pearson has written a compelling and utterly
unputdownable YA thriller. I raced through it because I had
to know what happened, and the twists blew me away. Full of
mystery and heart, with complex family dynamics, a fantastic
friend duo determined to solve the crime no matter what it takes,
and even a sprinkling of romance, this is a book for any YA thriller
fan or YA contemporary reader. *Drop Dead Famous* proves that
Jennifer Pearson, already known for her brilliant middle-grade
novels, is bound to be a breakout star in the YA world."
Katherine Webber, co-author of *Twin Crowns*

"A tense thriller that grips the reader throughout,
Drop Dead Famous is Pearson at the top of her game."
Benjamin Dean, author of *How to Die Famous*

"Engrossing and entertaining."
Kirkus Review

DROP DEAD

DE AD

Famous

JENNIFER PEARSON

SIMON & SCHUSTER

London   New York   Amsterdam/Antwerp   Sydney/Melbourne   Toronto   New Delhi

First published in Great Britain in 2026 by Simon & Schuster UK Ltd

1 3 5 7 9 10 8 6 4 2

Simon & Schuster UK Ltd
1st Floor, 222 Gray's Inn Road
London
WC1X 8HB

www.simonandschuster.co.uk
www.simonandschuster.com.au
www.simonandschuster.co.in

Simon & Schuster Australia, Sydney
Simon & Schuster India, New Delhi

The authorised representative in the EEA is Simon & Schuster Netherlands BV, Herculesplein 96, 3584 AA Utrecht, Netherlands. info@simonandschuster.nl

A CIP catalogue record for this book is available from the British Library.

ISBN 978-1-3985-5335-4
eBook ISBN 978-1-3985-5340-8
eAudio ISBN 978-1-3985-5341-5

Printed and bound by CPI Group (UK) Ltd, Croydon, CR0 4YY

For my brilliant and very clever sister,
Caroline—if I were ever murdered,
I know you'd be the one to hunt
down whoever did it.

One

Stevie Baker stopped in the parking lot of her high school's football stadium and looked up at her sister. All twenty feet of her. It had been over a year since she'd seen Blair, and now here she was, looming over her. A beautiful, two-dimensional giant.

The billboard of the blond-haired, platinum-album selling, Grammy-winning, international *music phenomenon* could probably be seen from the other side of town. Blair—Honeyville's most famous export since, well, honey—was dressed in the Honeyville High band uniform, though a much glitzier version, with thigh-high boots and a rhinestone-encrusted military-style hat towering atop her head. The words *Homecoming Tour* were lit up around her. Her shiny red mouth was open—pink tongue sticking out.

It was all *very* Blair. Stevie's dad, Frank Baker, clapped his hand on her shoulder and gave her a vigorous shake. "This is quite something, isn't it, Little Bear?"

It was *something*, all right.

Five years ago, just before she turned sixteen, Blair and her guitar had stepped onto the stage of *America's Next Icon* and were catapulted from obscurity—aka Honeyville—into the national spotlight. Starting this homecoming tour in her hometown was an obvious PR stunt, Stevie thought, but a good one. Blair was about to turn twenty-one—become an adult—and this concert was her party. Three days, from June 1 to 3.

Everyone was invited—for the cost of a ticket.

Frank gave Stevie's shoulder a squeeze. "Mia would have loved this."

Stevie pushed back a sudden swell of emotion. "She really would've."

Just then, Marnie Baker marched toward them and threw her manicured hands in the air. "Always with the tongue. Why can't she just smile? Blair has a lovely smile. Who wants to see *tongue*?"

"The tongue's her *thing*, Mom," Stevie said.

It was a valid point though. Stevie was no fan of seeing her sister's tongue. Especially now with it looming above her, bigger than a pool float.

A group of freshman girls clattered past them, shrieking as they raced to join the steadily growing line of fans waiting to get through the stadium turnstiles. They were all wearing variations of the same outfit—sequined skirts, cowboy boots, arms covered in friendship bracelets and glitter. A shit ton of glitter. Someone in the line had brought a speaker, and after squeals of delight, an impromptu singalong of Blair's biggest song, "Broken Roots and Burnt Bridges," started up.

Frank's eyes widened with concern. Marnie was not a fan of that particular hit. In fact, all playing or mention of it had been banned in the Baker household on account of it being about a drunk and overbearing mother. True, Marnie liked a glass of wine or a margarita from time to time, but she wasn't an alcoholic. At least not one who would shout at cats from the porch, as the song suggested. Blair had insisted the woman in the song was imagined, but Marnie still took offense. And Stevie liked to blast the track out at full volume over the house speakers whenever she and Marnie were arguing. Which, these days, was often.

Marnie flipped open her compact and teased her blowout with a comb. "Frank, where's the VIP entrance?" Then, before he could answer, she continued: "You should have let Blair send us a car, Frank. Why didn't you let her send a car?" Then: "Does this trouser suit look all right? Should I have worn the blue? I should have worn the blue. Why didn't you tell me to wear the blue?"

Frank looked unsure as to which question to attempt to answer first, but was saved by a shout of "Mr. and Mrs. Baker?"

It was Hilton Moore, one of Hollywood's top celebrity reporters. Stevie recognized him immediately: the dark, shoulder-length, wavy hair; the tight suit; the strong jaw. He was objectively handsome, Stevie admitted, though he was older. He had to be pushing forty.

Hilton strode toward them, teeth first, with a megawatt smile and microphone in hand and a cameraman behind, who was struggling to keep up. Stevie let out an involuntary snarl. Hilton was a jerk. He had been the one who had written that shitty story about Hal.

Marnie forced a huge smile and murmured, "Charm offensive, people. Don't give him *anything* but 'Happy Family.'"

Stevie looked at her doubtfully.

"Just smile!" Marnie hissed. Her eyes ran over Stevie, then slipped toward Frank. "Didn't I tell you there'd be cameras? I told you both to dress smart—why don't you ever listen?"

Stevie's dad smoothed down the front of his shirt. "But we like the plaid." Frank winked at Stevie. "Matchy-matchy!"

Stevie gave her dad a weak smile. It was true—she was also wearing plaid. She would have avoided *matchy-matchy*, but she'd walked over straight from the gym and that was all she'd brought with her.

"Mr. Moore!" Marnie cried.

Stevie hung back, hovering behind her dad so she wouldn't have to talk to him.

"Mrs. Baker, you look positively radiant," Hilton said, leaning in to kiss the air on either side of Marnie's cheeks. "That yellow—it's outstanding on you!"

"It's Pantone twelve, resplendent canary," Stevie whispered.

Frank snorted, coughed to cover it up.

"Oh, you," Marnie said, slapping Hilton's arm playfully. "How are you finding South Carolina?"

"Absolutely charming, the whole town smells like fried dough and lake water. I had the best shrimp and grits I've ever eaten in my hotel last night," Hilton said, then offered his hand to Frank. "Mr. Baker."

Frank shook Hilton's hand, though it was clear he didn't want to. "And may I just say that you look positively radiant too!"

It was Stevie's turn to snort.

Radiant was not the word she would have chosen to describe her father. He was more . . . dependable. Sturdy. One hundred percent dadlike, maybe.

Frank looked mildly horrified. "'Radiant'?"

"It's the plaid," Stevie whispered.

"Well, apart from the eye," Hilton said, tilting his head to the side. "Is that a shiner I see there, Mr. Baker? What *have* you been up to?"

"Frank helps out at the Aaron Taylor Community Center," Marnie said quickly, clearly worried that Hilton would intimate to his readers that Blair Baker's dad was some kind of street fighter.

"Aaron Taylor . . . why does that name ring a bell?" Hilton asked.

Stevie flashed a concerned look at her dad. This was a difficult subject for him—he'd been one of the first officers on the scene.

Marnie placed her hand over her heart. "He was the poor boy who was killed on Independence Day four years ago. After he retired, Frank wanted to give back to the community, so he started volunteering at the center."

"And someone at the center is responsible for the black eye?" Hilton asked.

Frank waved a hand dismissively. "It was nothing. I got in the way of a couple of kids roughhousing. Some of the boys can get a bit boisterous at times."

Hilton smiled. "Oh, I bet they can! But I'm not here to talk about troubled teens—"

"I think they're just regular teens, actually," Stevie interjected.

Hilton swung to look at her.

Oh great. Now she might have to speak to him. She should have kept her mouth shut.

"Oh goodness! I didn't see you there!" Hilton clutched his hand to his chest, a look of genuine surprise on his face. Sure, she was short, especially compared to Blair. But she wasn't *transparent*. "And who might *you* be?" he asked, thrusting the microphone at her.

She was eighteen and he was talking to her like she was a preschooler.

Her eyes shifted from the microphone to Hilton. "*I* might be Stevie." Her voice purposefully bright, not matching her scowl.

"The sister!" Hilton threw his arms in the air. "Of course!"

"Yup, the sister."

Not a person in her own right, or anything like that.

"I didn't recognize you!" Hilton shook his head and laughed. "It's extraordinary how very different you look from Blair!"

Stevie got this a lot. Blair was five foot ten, slim, blond. Stevie was five foot three, built like a gymnast, and dark-haired.

But they had the same bright blue eyes.

"You three must be very excited to see Blair kick off her new tour tonight. And back at her old school, in her hometown!"

Marnie nodded enthusiastically—too enthusiastically, Stevie thought. "We're hugely, *hugely* excited, like everybody else in Honeyville. The concert has been the talk of the town for months. We're extremely proud of her."

Proud wasn't one of the many words Marnie had used to

describe how she felt about her daughter the last time Blair had graced them with her company. Exhausting, demanding, chaotic . . . Blair's visits had always had the potential for tears, tantrums, and family drama. It was true what people said about fame changing a person. But fame hadn't only changed Blair; it had stolen her away from them, too.

So, yes, Marnie was right—they were proud of Blair. But their pride was tinged with sadness.

"It's wonderful to see her back performing after *another* one of her breaks!"

Annoyingly, Hilton emphasized the word *another*. Six months earlier, Blair had *checked into a clinic*. The party line, and one Marnie had desperately tried to swallow, was that she was going to a health spa for some rest and relaxation, but the rumor was that she was in rehab again.

Hilton lowered his voice. "An emotional time though, I would imagine?" Hilton's smile was replaced by a look of concerned interest. "Have family relations been . . . difficult?"

Stevie's eyes moved from her dad to her mom. How were they going to field this one? She actually jumped when Marnie let out a very loud, forced laugh.

"What family doesn't have their little disagreements? But we're fine. Completely fine. Better than fine!"

It wasn't the most convincing performance.

"That's great to hear." Hilton clearly didn't believe a word of it. "So Hal is coming to see the show?" He looked around as if to say, *Because I don't see him.*

"Of course!" Marnie's voice pitched up. She cleared her throat, found a lower tone. "He wouldn't miss it for the world!"

Not what Stevie's half brother had told her.

"I'm sorry, Hilton—we'd better be going," Frank said, placing his hand on Marnie's back, ready to guide her away.

Good old Frank. He was the expert at maneuvering Stevie's mom out of all sorts of situations. Frank had prevented many a public showdown, including the time Marnie had confronted Stevie's school counselor in the seasonal aisle in Target. Mr. Hassell had no idea how close he was to getting beaned by an ornamental pumpkin.

"I think that's Bex Lyons over there," Frank continued. "We're meeting her so she can take us to our seats."

"Oh yes!" Marnie said, eyeing her escape route. "That's Ms. Lyons! Ms. Lyons!"

Bex was Blair's manager's assistant. At least, that's who Stevie thought she was. It was possible she doubled as a bodyguard, too. She was a short, stocky woman, with pale skin and hair cut close to her scalp and a *don't mess with me* aura. Now she was watching them from behind sunglasses, her face completely still, unmoved by the sight of a woman in a billowing yellow trouser suit hollering at her.

"Must dash!" Marnie marched off, leaving Hilton and his microphone in her wake.

"*Is* Hal coming, Dad?" Stevie asked as they started after her.

"Not sure. I thought I saw his truck earlier, but I guess that was wishful thinking," Frank said. "Your mother tried to persuade him. He said he was too old for a concert."

Stevie raised her eyebrows. Hal was only thirty-three, so they both knew that wasn't the reason. The truth was, Hal had never completely forgiven Blair for the story she'd leaked to the press about him a few years ago.

"Annie might have talked him around. She said even if Hal refuses, she might still come," Frank said.

Hal wouldn't show. Not after the disastrous *Welcome Home, Blair* dinner that was supposed to happen the night before. When a huge bouquet of flowers arrived in Blair's place with a message saying she had to work, Hal had been more than a bit pissed. Annie had tried to calm him down, but even her usually super-effective wifely influence hadn't worked. Stevie understood his reaction—Hal had gone, ready to finally set things right with Blair, and he was hurt that she hadn't bothered to show.

Blair had sent Stevie a message, the first in four months according to her phone, clearly trying to get her to smooth things over.

Please don't hate me. Tell everyone I'm sorry. But this is super, super important. Can't explain but believe me I have a reason.

Typically overdramatic and probably bullshit. *I have a really good reason but can't come up with one right now, so just take this word salad as an excuse.*

Stevie had sent back a quick response.

Sure. No problem.

She didn't see the point in getting into it.

"Mr. and Mrs. Baker . . ." Bex pulled down her sunglasses a fraction of an inch and looked at Stevie. "And the *sister?*"

Again, with the surprise—and Bex had met Stevie at least twice before. Although she supposed that was a while ago now.

Music started up from inside the stadium—the support act, Dime a Dozen. A murmur of impatience rolled through the people still queuing up to get inside.

"Do you have your lanyards?" Bex barked.

Stevie flinched.

Wow. Bex Lyons was a real charmer.

Marnie frantically rummaged through her purse, handing Stevie an enormous can of hair spray, a fistful of receipts, and a Saran-Wrapped turkey sandwich before finally producing the three VIP lanyards with a triumphant "Ta-dah!"

Bex remained stony-faced. "If you wouldn't mind putting them on, I'll take you through security and show you to your seats."

Bex led them right to the front of the lines, where the security guard was looking on with indifference as an overemotional Blair Baker fan begged to be let backstage.

"Heavens! Is that girl wearing a bathing suit?" Marnie whispered, loud enough for anyone in a thirty-foot radius to hear.

It was quite the outfit. A purple one-piece, with tassels running down the front and arms, and silver cowboy boots.

Stevie knew her—Colby Green—with her bouncy blond hair and too much lip gloss. Just over two years ago, Colby had transferred from East Side High to Honeyville midway through freshman year. When Colby had discovered that she was in the same year as Blair Baker's sister, she'd spent an entire semester hassling her. Stevie had tried her best to avoid her, but when Colby had accosted her while she was in the bathroom stall one lunch break, Stevie had decided enough was enough. Mid-flow was not the time to discuss whether Blair would do a live chat on Colby's Blair Baker fan page. Stevie told her to back off or she'd have her banned from all Blair's concerts for all eternity. Colby had left her alone after that.

Colby didn't look like she was about to give up this time though. The fringing of her bodysuit flapped about wildly as she waved her phone in the security guy's face. "I'm her number one fan! Look! I literally run the Blairites fan page! I—"

"I don't care if you have her name tattooed on your ass—you're not going backstage."

Stevie tried not to look too pleased when she cut past Colby. But it did make her feel a little bit important; maybe there were some benefits to being a superstar's sister.

Stevie and her parents flashed their VIP passes to a woman in a high-visibility vest who fired at them, "Names."

"Mrs. Marnie with an *ie*, Baker." Stevie's mom spoke loudly and with an air of importance that got a few people waiting in the queue whispering, "Is that Blair's mom?!"

Stevie's dad leaned in, cleared his throat. "Frank Baker."

The woman checked off their names on her clipboard, then frowned after Stevie gave hers. "*Stevie Baker?* Huh." She tapped the clipboard with her pen. "Do you have your ID?"

"It's in the car." Stevie's cheeks burned. Was she *actually* about to be turned away from her own sister's concert? This was karma for feeling all pleased with herself.

Bex stepped in. "Is there a problem here, Janie? These people are Blair's family."

Janie fumbled her clipboard. "No, no problem, Ms. Lyons."

Bex gestured inside. "If you'd like to follow me."

Marnie nodded curtly—a *screwed up there, didn't you, Janie?* look on her face.

Stevie heard a shout from behind. Sheesh. Colby and her tassels were getting increasingly animated.

"What if I got on my knees and begged?" Colby was asking.

Marnie tutted. "What a scene!"

"Might get you one of those purple numbers, Marnie," Frank said, giving her a playful pat on the bottom.

Ugh. Stevie did not need to hear that.

Marnie rolled her eyes. "Behave yourself, Frank."

Bex led them out onto the field, and Stevie took a breath, trying to take it all in. The stands were almost full. She'd heard there were ten thousand tickets sold, and looking around now, she believed it.

The inside of the stadium was unrecognizable. The Blair Baker production machine had rolled into town the moment Honeyville High had let out for summer. In under two weeks they'd constructed an enormous stage on the north end zone, directly in front of the sports center. Several covered walkways had been erected to allow access to the stage. Heavy-duty flooring had been laid over the turf and extra stands had been added to the bleachers to allow for more seating.

Marnie was loving life. She was nodding and waving and yoo-hooing when she spotted someone she knew in general admission seats, and reminding Frank who they were along the way.

Some of Stevie's former classmates were there too. The concert was the start of their graduation celebrations. Tomorrow, they were heading to Folly Beach for beach week. She'd been invited but didn't feel she could go. She wasn't graduating and didn't feel she had the right to celebrate. She'd gone to kindergarten, elementary, and middle school with them, but after what had happened with Mia, she'd fallen behind in her studies, and had to repeat her freshman year. She'd drifted apart from them—all her fault—she knew that—still, she wished things could have been different.

"The whole of Honeyville is out in force tonight!" Frank said as Stevie watched her classmates heading toward the east stand.

He put his hand on her shoulder. "You okay, Little Bear? You can go with them if you want."

Stevie forced a smile. "What, and ditch my matching plaid partner?" she said, nudging his arm. She glanced toward the others, then back at him, and smiled properly when she saw the concern in his eyes. "Honestly, I'm good here."

Bex Lyons led them to the front of the stadium and up the steps of the stand right next to the stage. They shuffled along the row to their seats, Marnie oblivious to the fact that she was managing to hit everyone in the row with her purse as she passed. The place was almost full, a sea of sequin-clad fans largely ignoring the support act, who were valiantly battling through their set despite the disinterest. Concert mascots, dressed up as giant teddy bears in the Honeyville High football uniforms, were clapping their paws together, trying to drum up some enthusiasm.

"Prime position!" Frank declared, rubbing his hands together as they reached the middle of the row.

"You'd hope so," Marnie said, lowering herself into her seat in a queenly manner, as she nodded and smiled at people she didn't know and who clearly had no idea who she was.

Stevie looked at the empty seat next to her, then glanced at Bex. Was she going to have to sit next to her for the whole concert? That would make for a cheery experience . . .

"That's for Gunner Trip," Bex said.

Oh, thank god. Wait. The *Gunner Trip?*

"He'll be along later," Bex said, already looking elsewhere. "I'll give you my number in case you need to contact me." Stevie handed Bex her phone and she punched the number in. "I need to get backstage. Lots to do. Enjoy the show. We're pushing the limits with this new tour. You're going to see a whole new, grown-up Blair."

Pushing limits was something Blair was an expert at. Pushing people to their limit, and then straight over the edge, in Hal's case.

Marnie elbowed Stevie in the side and mouthed, *Gunner Trip*, eyes flashing with wild excitement. Stevie tried to play it cool. But it was a bit exciting that he was going to be there, sitting right next to them.

Gunner Trip was a linebacker for the Titans. National hero after his stint on *Dancing with the Stars*. And Blair's boyfriend, apparently. *Apparently* because, according to the laws of Marnie Baker, boyfriend status could not be confirmed just yet, as no one in the family had ever met him. Although it looked like that was about to change.

"Did you hear that, Frank? Gunner Trip!" Marnie cried, pushing herself to her feet, then swatting Stevie's knees. "Stevie, swap seats with me!"

Stevie had only just managed to move out the way when

Marnie launched herself into her space.

"Gunner Trip!" Marnie said again, bouncing her shoulders up and down and rubbing her hands together.

Stevie had never met the guy, but she already felt sorry for him.

She settled into her new seat and had a discreet look around. Maybe there were some other celebs in the VIP box. There was some old guy in the section below with someone who was probably his daughter. Stevie thought she recognized him—an actor, maybe? It wasn't until he turned around that she realized who he was—Kirk Tyler, Blair's manager. Stevie had never met him in person, but she had decided he may be a bit of a douche when Blair had missed Mia's thirteenth birthday because Kirk had made Blair perform at some shopping mall. His douche status was fully confirmed when Blair hadn't shown up for any of Mia's vigils last year due to *work commitments*.

His eyes fell on Stevie, then drifted to Frank and Marnie. He held up his hand. Marnie waved back. Frank managed a curt nod.

Stevie turned around, wondering if there was anyone else she'd recognize. Two rows back, the actor Todd Richards sat next to the supermodel Asha Deacon. She was scrolling through her phone, looking pretty cheerless. Probably because Honeyville local Weatherman Stan was on her other side, and obviously beyond excited—Stevie tilted her head—and, yeah, possibly a little drunk. Down the row from him were the members of the K-pop band KP1, and Roddy Ripper, recently retired Ultimate Fighting Champ.

Incredible, really, that they'd all made the trip to little old Honeyville, population five thousand.

By the time the support act left the stage, Gunner Trip had still not materialized. Marnie only stopped sighing with disappointment when the lights went off and the arena was plunged into darkness.

Then two faces appeared on the huge screen under the words

Honoring Those We've Lost.

Stevie sucked in a breath so fast, she almost choked, and a weighted silence fell around the stadium.

Aaron Taylor and Mia.

What the hell was this?

Aaron wore a serious expression and an East Side High varsity jacket. His dirty blond hair was cut short at the sides but left slightly messy on top. His face was angular, almost hard-looking, and his intense green eyes stared out at the crowd. Stevie had never met him, though she had met his foster parents, Marvin and Gloria Thompson, a couple of times at the community center with her dad. Aaron was a good-looking guy, but there was a sadness behind his eyes.

In contrast, Mia's smile was luminous. Her photo was one Hal had taken on a Baker family vacation the summer after she turned twelve. Just before snapping it, he had said something corny—*The sun called, said you're outshining it*—and her smile was wide and completely unguarded. She was wearing a white dress and her charm bracelet. Her sandy blond hair was tied back in a ponytail and her usually pale complexion had taken on a soft bronze glow. This was a private family photo—one that Stevie knew hadn't been released to the press.

Blair's voice came blasting through the speakers. "Honeyville has been struck by tragedy twice. Today, as a community, we lift Aaron and Mia up in our hearts."

Stevie turned to her mom and whispered, "Did you know about this?"

Marnie, eyes filling with tears, shook her head.

Stevie turned to her dad—he looked shaken too. "I'm sure your sister is trying to do a nice thing . . ."

Nice? She was exploiting the town's pain.

Thank god Hal hadn't come.

The fireworks started, shooting high into the night sky, exploding loudly in yellows and reds—the colors of Honeyville High. The crowd oohed and aahed, and then a voice echoed through the bleachers.

But Stevie couldn't move on from what she'd just witnessed.

Blair should have warned them. Should have *asked*.

The final firework exploded with a dramatic boom. The stadium fell silent, anticipation thrumming in the air.

"I'M BACK, BITCHES!" Blair's voice rolled over the crowd.

"Your sister, polite as always," Frank said to Stevie, trying to lighten the mood.

Screams and cheers rose. Everyone was on their feet. Smoke filled the stage. Lights flashed. Then a strum of an electric guitar so loud, it vibrated through Stevie's rib cage.

More screams, bordering on the hysterical now.

"HO-HO-HOMECOMING!" came Blair's voice again.

The lights flashed faster, and a platform climbed upward through the smoke.

Lying on top of it, bronzed legs draped over the edge, was Stevie's sister. She was wearing the outfit from the billboard, except her hat lay next to her, the stage lights bouncing off the rhinestones.

Stevie tried to push Mia's face from her mind—tried to let go and enjoy the show as the screams of the crowd intensified and the platform rose higher.

Her heart began to race. Blair certainly knew how to make an entrance.

"I hope she's strapped onto that thing," Marnie said, grimacing. "It's very high."

The guitar strummed again. The crowd whooped, recognizing the song. Stevie grinned. Blair was opening with "Broken Roots and Burnt Bridges." Marnie bristled beside her. A group of fans in the standing section grabbed one another and jumped up and down, screaming. There were girls in the crowd who had already started crying. One shouted, "I love you, Blair!"—as though loving Blair was easy. Phones were raised, ready to capture the first song of Blair's homecoming tour.

The guitar sounded again, settling into the song. The shouts died down, quieting to let Blair come in for the first verse.

"Four albums, over eighty songs to her name, and she chooses this one," Marnie muttered.

"It's a crowd favorite, Mom," Stevie said.

"Why couldn't she sing the one about her first love? That one's lovely."

A loud *shhh* came from behind them. Stevie swung around to see Todd Richards glaring at them.

Marnie turned around, waved, and smiled, while muttering angrily, "Who does he think he is, shushing me at my own daughter's concert? The nerve of the man!" She quieted down after that though, ready for Blair's vocals. But when the band played the opening verse, the lyrics went unsung.

"Isn't that the part where she starts singing?" Marnie said.

"Usually," Stevie said. "Probably part of the buildup."

The lead guitar opened the verse for a second time, and the whole crowd seemed to lean forward as one, ready for Blair to sing the words *a queen of her own kingdom with a bottle in her hand*, but again, there was nothing.

"Do you think her microphone's not working?" Marnie said, elbowing Stevie. "Go and tell someone you think her microphone might be broken."

"I'm sure her massive team will be all over it if it is, Mom. She's just maximizing the tension."

"Well, I wish she wouldn't," Marnie said.

"She looks very still up there—do you think she's okay?" Frank said.

"I'm sure she's fine. It's just Blair being Blair—milking the moment," Stevie said, but she thought she clocked a quick look of confusion on the faces of the band before they looped back to the intro again.

The verse started for a third time, the guitar louder, more urgent, like the guitarist was getting a little irritated. Stevie didn't blame her. Marnie was right—Blair should just stop dicking around and sing.

But again, there was silence.

Murmurs rumbled through the arena as the band cycled back to the opening for a fourth try.

Weatherman Stan waved his hip flask in the air and bellowed, "Get on with it!"

Marnie turned around and snapped, "She's building the tension, you fool!"

Stevie tilted her head. Frank was right—Blair did look awfully still up there. A creeping sense of unease spread through her.

Something felt off. Wrong.

The whole arena seemed to hold its breath when it was time for Blair to come in with her vocals.

Surely, this time, she'd sing.

It was only when somebody screamed that Stevie noticed the blood.

Two

Blood? Was it blood?

Stevie leaned over the railing. Below the platform, a pool of something dark and thick glistened in the stage lights. It couldn't be blood. It was something else—a spillage of some kind. Oil, maybe? A drop fell from above, disturbing the surface. Stevie's eyes traveled upward, to the source. To Blair.

Her dad was right—she *was* so still. Why was she so still?

A few whoops and cheers rose from the crowd, like they were still trying to encourage Blair to sing. Did they know this was all part of the act? Stevie's mind whirled, then latched on to what Bex had said about Blair pushing limits. It was an act. This was all choreographed. An artistic choice—a grim one after the tribute—but Blair would jump up any second, reborn in front of a hometown or some creative shit like that. Stevie shook her head, relieved but pissed, too. That wasn't blood, not *real* blood. Of course it wasn't. There was too much of it, for a start.

Blair was just messing with everybody . . . though maybe she should have told her band. They didn't look like they had a clue what was going on. They were still playing, although a critic might have said with little conviction. Stevie swallowed, unease rising again. Surely, if something bad had happened, they'd stop? Someone would do something—

Bex Lyons suddenly raced onto the stage, one hand on her earpiece, shouting words Stevie couldn't hear, the other hand waving at the platform. Stevie's stomach lurched—her skin prickled. What if . . . No. It could still all be part of the show. Just Blair screwing with everybody.

The music stopped, the bass guitar taking a little longer, its low notes resonating across the crowd of stock-still fans. Shit. Something was wrong. Really wrong. The platform began to lower and a team of paramedics ran onto the stage. Security next, escorting the band off. A wave of confusion rolled through the arena. Through Stevie.

"Frank?" Marnie said, eyes wild.

Stevie looked to her dad too, searching his face for reassurance. Frank was pale, his jaw stiff.

"Dad?" Stevie heard the desperation in her voice.

Frank put his hand on Stevie's shoulder. Looked her in the eyes. "Wait here. I'll find out what the hell's going on." His voice was steady, commanding, but his pupils flared with concern.

Stevie nodded dumbly as Frank made his way along the row. Reverting to cop mode.

The platform, Blair's motionless body draped like a rag doll on top of it, was still making its descent. Bex Lyons was shouting, pacing the stage, throwing her arms up in frustration while paramedics snapped on white plastic gloves.

Thousands of anxious voices rose and rumbled around the arena. A woman clutched two little girls in Blair Baker T-shirts close to her as she ushered them through the seats, her coat held up to shield their eyes from the stage.

Static crackled—the PA system shrieked—then a booming voice sent the crowd silent.

"Attention, everyone. Due to an unforeseen medical emergency, we need to ask everyone to calmly and safely exit the arena. Please follow the instructions of the event staff and use the nearest exits. Satellite Entertainment would like to apologize for the inconvenience and appreciate your cooperation. Thank you."

For a moment everything was quiet. Except the sound of blood pounding in Stevie's head. Then the whole place gasped as one—made the air contract, tighten around her. There was a wail. Then another. Then more and more rising up all over the place. Stevie wanted to put her hands over her ears. Tell them all to shut up.

The ground shifted under her feet. Stevie steadied herself on the railing. A hand clasped onto hers. She turned around, her body heavy, the world spinning.

"Stevie?" Marnie said, eyes searching, chin trembling. "Stevie, what's happening?"

The platform reached the stage floor. Three paramedics swarmed around it—around Blair. Bex, hands on hips, eyes cast downward, was talking to a man in a suit who was gesticulating wildly. A stagehand brought out a screen, began to unfold it, but not quickly enough to stop Stevie seeing her sister's face. Or the way her head lolled back. Jaw open. Eyes glassy. Or the shake of the paramedic's head, after he'd placed his fingers on Blair's neck.

A girl screamed, "Oh my god! Is she dead?! Is Blair Baker dead?!"

Shut up. Shut up. Shut up.

Marnie clutched at Stevie's wrist. "What's going on? What did she say? Why did that girl just say that?"

Stevie pushed the picture of her sister out of her mind. Didn't want to believe it. "I . . . I don't know. Dad—let's find Dad." She took her mom's hand, but Marnie batted it away.

"Stevie! What did she just say about Blair?!"

Stevie cried, "I don't know!" A lie—but she couldn't repeat the words.

"Is she unwell? A medical emergency? What kind of *medical emergency*?" Marnie said, frantically gathering up her bag. "Take me to Blair. I want to see my daughter."

Stevie grabbed her mom's hand, pulled her toward the steps

among the bodyguards guiding their celebrities out of the VIP area. She needed to find her dad—he'd know what to do.

She reached the bottom of the steps. The arena was emptying. People shaking their heads in disbelief, others sobbing. Hands clasped over mouths or wrapped around friends. All rushing to get out of there as soon as possible. She pulled out her phone, tried calling Bex. No answer.

Stevie stood on her tiptoes, spotted the sign for backstage. She pushed forward—held her mom's hand tighter as she battled against the flow.

"I need to see Blair!" Marnie said, pulling back. "Are you taking me to see Blair?"

Blair's face in her mind again. The pool of blood. Stevie's breath hitched in her throat and her legs hollowed. No—keep moving. She sucked in a breath. "This way." She pulled Marnie forward, tried to shield her from the jostles and knocks of the crowd. She took an elbow to the ribs, then another. Anger rose in her and burst out when someone clattered into Marnie.

Stevie turned on them. "Watch where you're going!"

Colby didn't register her. Her mascara-stained face blinking at her phone, too focused on giving a running commentary. "It's chaos here. I don't know what's happening!" Her voice charged, frantic. "I'll try and keep you all updated."

Stevie's insides curled with disgust. Colby was filming content for her fan site. She disappeared into the crowd, still talking to her phone. Her sister had just died, and Colby was reporting it live.

Because that was what had happened, wasn't it? Blair was dead. Her sister was dead.

"Stevie!"

A voice pulled her out of her thoughts, into the now.

"Stevie, over here!" A cop was striding toward her. His face clear among a sea of blurred faces.

"Uncle Jimmy?" Stevie's resolve wavered—she only just managed to stop herself from bursting into tears. She swallowed, fought for her voice. "Mom, look, it's Uncle Jimmy."

Marnie clutched his hands. "Oh, Jimmy! I think something awful has happened!"

"I just got the call. Got here as soon as I could." His eyes moved from Marnie to Stevie, assessing them. "How much do you know?"

The shake of the paramedic's head—that small final motion lodged in her mind. Stevie couldn't say it. Not in front of her mom. "Only that there's a medical emergency."

He nodded. From his eyes, Stevie sensed he knew more. "Frank with you?"

"Dad went to find out what was happening."

Jimmy sniffed, shook his head. "Always the cop, huh? Let's get you two somewhere private and I'll find out what's going on." He led them to a door with the words *Green Room* on the outside. His radio buzzed at his hip. A voice crackled: *"Unit forty-six, in attendance at incident at Honeyville High Stadium. Victim is a twenty-year-old female, confirmed to be dece—"*

Jimmy turned it off before the voice announced what Stevie already suspected. But she wouldn't believe it, couldn't believe it.

Jimmy pushed the door open, looked around, seemed satisfied. "In here. Officer Dean will wait with you. I'll be back as soon as I can."

Stevie frowned. "Officer who?"

The young cop who was hanging back from them took a step forward. "Officer Dean," he said with a nod.

Stevie barely registered the name. Her eyes passed over him without really seeing—just broad shoulders beneath a neatly pressed uniform; brown hair clipped close at the sides, longer on top; and a face shaped by gentle angles.

"Find out what's going on," Marnie said, grabbing hold of

Jimmy's hand, eyes urgent. "Then you come back and tell me my baby's okay, you hear me?"

Uncle Jimmy didn't meet her eyes. "I'll be back as soon as I can."

The door closed and the room grew quiet. Stevie stood there trying to make sense of the incomprehensible.

The walls of the green room were plastered with posters of Blair. Her face smiling at them from every side. That tongue again. It was perverse, waiting for news of her sister while she winked, and grinned, and laughed at them. So many Blairs. But where was *her* Blair? She had to be okay. That paramedic had gotten it wrong. Stevie had gotten it wrong. Blair wasn't dead. She couldn't be dead. Not her sister. Not her Blair. Stevie's heart raced in her chest—her breathing too shallow. Her mind was unraveling, her insides, too. There was so much blood. A sob burst from her mouth.

"Don't," Marnie said, heat in her voice. "She's going to be fine."

Stevie nodded, tugged the threads of herself back together, wished she could believe it.

Marnie swayed, felt for the wall.

Stevie grabbed hold of her. "You should sit down."

"I don't want to talk," Marnie said. "Not until I've heard Blair is okay. I just can't talk."

Stevie guided her mom onto one of the two massive, bright pink couches shaped like lips. Marnie sat bolt upright, twisting her wedding band around and around. She looked so small sitting on that giant pink mouth. She was small, like Stevie, but usually she came across as taller. Probably because of the way she conducted herself—how her presence filled the room, squeezed everyone into the corners.

But not now.

The resplendent canary long gone, Marnie waited, gray-faced, eyes fixed on the door. There was so much hope in them, Stevie had to turn away, because that door was going to open, and when it did, the truth was going to walk right in and destroy them.

No. No. No. Blair wasn't dead. Uncle Jimmy would come back and say Blair was okay.

Stevie got to her feet and began pacing the room. She didn't know what to do with herself. The striplights too bright. The room too hot. She opened a can of Diet Coke. Left it on the table untouched. She sat down on the couch, feet tapping. She knew this restlessness. The restlessness that came from not knowing what the hell was going on. She'd had the same itch in her bones for over a year after Mia had disappeared. It had driven her to distraction, and beyond. To a point where her mind was always spinning, and Stevie had started to wonder whether she was disappearing too.

"She's going to be fine," Marnie said fiercely, eyes still on the door. "Blair is going to be fine."

Stevie swallowed. Couldn't respond. She stood up. Paced some more. Chewed her fingernails. Stopped when she saw Officer Dean sitting on the other mouth couch, watching her with his solemn face—eyes too full of pity. She'd forgotten he was there. A rush of irritation swept through her that he was. "How old are you anyway?"

"Twenty-one, ma'am."

Three years older than her and fresh out of training, then. How would he be any help? He looked ridiculous, sitting on those giant lips. And he'd just called her *ma'am*. The whole thing was ridiculous. None of this should be happening.

"I'm sure Chief Baker will be back with news very soon," he said, a hopeful glance at the door.

"*Good* news," Marnie said. "He'll be back with good news."

Officer Dean opened his mouth. Shut it again. Sniffed. Settled for an unconvincing half-nod. Looked relieved at the sounds of voices outside.

Stevie came to a stop and Marnie sat forward, right on the edge of the sofa. They waited for the door to open, for the truth to be let in, but when it didn't, Marnie looked at her and nodded.

Stevie took a shuddering breath, and with shaking hands stood and opened the door, then closed it behind her. Outside, she found her dad sobbing on his brother's shoulder. She locked eyes with Jimmy. And she knew.

Blair was gone.

"Frank," Jimmy said quietly, "Stevie's here."

Frank lifted his head quickly. Straightened himself up—the tears stopping, his eyes still red.

"Let's go inside." Jimmy ushered Frank through the Green Room door, jerked his head at Officer Dean to tell him to leave. He passed Stevie and she turned away, couldn't bear to look at his pitying eyes.

Marnie got to her feet, face hopeful. "Frank?"

Frank's jaw tightened.

"Well, how is she? How's Blair?" Her voice clipped with impatience, an anger borne solely from fear.

Frank breathed in deep. Shook his head. The same way the paramedic had.

"Don't you shake your head at me, Frank Baker. Don't you *dare* shake your head." Marnie jabbed a finger at him. Left it in the air, trembling.

Frank took a step toward her. "Marnie—"

"Don't you 'Marnie' me. You get back out there and go and bring me my daughter!"

Her chest was heaving, that trembling finger now pointing toward the door. Stevie wanted to shout at her to stop. To stop making everything worse.

But didn't she want to shout at her dad too? Tell him to go and get Blair? Tell him to make everything better. Like he was supposed to. Her mind whirled, faster and faster, latching on to thought after thought until she couldn't bear it anymore. She dropped into a chair, buried her face in her hands. Tried to wish it all away. But there was her mom's voice again. "Frank?"

Frank closed his eyes. Swallowed. Shook his head again.

"Say it," Marnie said, her voice a low rumble now.

Frank hung his head, heaved in a breath. He couldn't do it.

"Say it!" Marnie shouted.

Stevie lifted her head, shouted back louder, "She's dead!"

Marnie turned to her, disbelief in her eyes.

"Blair's dead, Mom." Stevie spoke more gently this time. Her voice distant, not her own. "Blair's dead."

Marnie blinked at her, like she couldn't comprehend a word she was saying. Stevie reached out to take her hand, but Marnie drew back. "No! I won't have you say that!"

"Mom, I—"

Marnie let out a deep, guttural moan and clutched her hand to her mouth as she doubled over. "Hasn't this family suffered enough!"

Frank crossed the room in three strides, pulled his wife into him. She fought against him, thumping her fists on his chest. Frank waited, took the blows, then held her as she cried in his arms. He rested his chin on her head, eyes closed against his tears. Stevie had witnessed a scene like this before—her mother unraveling, her dad trying his best to hold her together.

A scene just like this.

After Mia.

When Mia had gone missing, Frank and Marnie had lost their granddaughter, Hal and Annie had lost their daughter, and Stevie had shattered into pieces. Losing her niece had thrown her emotions too far apart, spread them too wide, and Stevie had lost herself. Coming up on three years later, she was still trying to put the shards of that hurt back together. They all were. And Stevie could feel herself splintering again. She couldn't let that happen. Wouldn't let it happen. She had to block herself off from the pain. Push it deep down into herself. With Mia, so many questions went unanswered. That couldn't happen with Blair.

She turned to Jimmy. He was leaning against the wall, rubbing the bridge of his nose. "How? Did she . . . ?" Stevie looked at her mom—her chin wobbled, couldn't say the words.

Jimmy looked over at her, jaw tensing. "She was shot, kiddo. I'm so sorry. Somebody shot her."

Three

"She was murdered?" Stevie said.

If she was honest, a tiny part of her had wondered if Blair had done it herself. She hadn't been in a great place when she'd last rolled into Honeyville a year ago. *Volatile*—that was the word Annie had used. *A total freaking mess* had been Hal's description.

Like the rest of the world, Stevie had seen her sister break and rebuild herself time and time again. She knew the cycle. Blair's partying would get harder. Photos of her falling out of clubs would appear online. She'd clap back at her critics. Then disappear. After that would come the articles about her checking into rehab. Then she'd come out a changed person just in time for the next platinum album, and everyone, including Blair, seemingly, would convince themselves that things were all right. Until they weren't.

Marnie doubled over, one hand grabbing for Frank. "Murdered?" she said, the word almost incoherent, tugged apart by her sobs.

"That's our current line of thinking," Jimmy said.

Marnie shook her head. "No! Who could do such a thing?! Who would want to murder Blair? Everybody loved Blair!"

Stevie nodded . . . but did they? Did everybody love Blair? Stevie tried not to read the press about her sister, or comments online, but she knew that while Blair had legions of fans, she had her haters, too.

"Whoever did it, I'm going to find them," Jimmy said, placing one hand on Frank's shoulder, the other on Marnie's. "I promise you."

Stevie wanted to believe him—wanted to trust that Jimmy would catch Blair's killer and bring them to justice—but it wasn't like Honeyville PD had a great track record. Jimmy had promised to find someone before and never delivered. The police had never found Mia. And that wasn't the only example. They hadn't solved the Fourth of July murder of Aaron Taylor in the lumberyard the year before either.

"We've secured the area around the stage, including the dressing rooms—forensics are running over the crime scene now. From the condition of the b—" Jimmy stopped, remembered who he was talking to. "We're working under the assumption that Blair was . . . that she was killed just before the concert. We'll check over the security-tape footage. We haven't managed to locate her phone, and I've got all the men I have out looking for the gun."

"Any idea of the make? Model?" Frank said, then seemed to catch himself. This was his daughter's murder they were discussing. He exhaled heavily, then looked up at the ceiling, desperately trying to blink back the tears. The muscles in his jaw clenched at the effort it took to not cry.

"Dad?" Stevie said gently, placing her hand on his arm.

He looked at her, eyes red, and choked in a breath. "I'm okay, Little Bear." He tried something like a smile, but it wouldn't settle on his face, so he pulled Stevie toward him, and she buried her face into his chest. The pain broke through, and her tears fell again.

Jimmy's voice broke into her safe space. "We may get some information from the bullet, after the autop—"

Stevie flinched. *Autopsy. He was going to say* autopsy.

Jimmy moved on quickly. "We've started taking statements from the crew already—we're hoping one of them saw something."

Stevie pulled away from Frank's chest. "But there were literally thousands of people in the arena—"

"And I'll talk to each and every one of them if I have to."

"But you let them all go!" Stevie's words came out in a rush at the realization.

Jimmy rubbed the back of his neck. "Blair's management team put the announcement out. I guess they thought it was best—to protect her dignity and prevent fan hysteria."

A screwup, then. Panic rose in Stevie's chest. "The killer could have gotten away."

"Stevie, we'll find whoever did this. We can track who was in attendance via the ticket vendor, and I'm sure if one of Blair's fans saw something suspicious, they'll contact us."

Stevie shook her head in disbelief. The case was being bungled already.

"I want to help," Frank said. His hands were trembling and there was a wild, desperate look in his eyes. "I could come back on a temporary basis until we track down the son of a bitch that did this."

"I've got this, Frank. You handed in your badge, and there's no way you should be working this case even if you hadn't."

"But you're her uncle," Frank said.

"And the most experienced cop in Honeyville PD. You have to trust me to handle this."

"But—"

"No, Frank," Marnie said, her voice trembling with concern. Frank opened his mouth to argue again, but Marnie sniffed, and more tears flowed down her cheeks. "Think of your health."

Marnie had forced Frank to retire not long after the Aaron Taylor case. Pericarditis—an inflammation of the thin sac around the heart that can worsen with stress—that's what WebMD had told Stevie when her parents had sidestepped her questions.

"Marnie's right," Jimmy said. "I'll keep you informed every step of the way."

Frank gestured at Officer Dean. "You've got a kid for a partner! What is he, in his first week of field training?"

"Two months, actually," Officer Dean said.

Stevie gave him a sideways look—a whole two months—how reassuring.

Frank pinched the bridge of his nose and shook his head. "Jimmy—"

"He's sharp, Frank, graduated basic training at the top of his class; he's practically ready for solo patrol, but I'll be running the investigation—there will be a big team working on this."

Before Frank could argue, there was a knock on the door.

"Yes?" Jimmy said.

A plainclothes police officer poked her head in. "I've got Kirk Tyler here—wants to know if he can speak to the Bakers."

Jimmy looked to Frank. "It's up to you."

Frank nodded. "Yeah, let him in. I want to hear what he has to say."

Kirk entered the room, face solemn, jaw set. His shirt was buttoned low, showing *way* too much chest, given the circumstance. Actually, for any circumstance.

"Mr. and Mrs. Baker"—he turned to Stevie, searched for her name, failed to find it—"Blair's sister, please accept my sincerest condolences. Blair was like a daughter to me—"

"She is—*was* a daughter to me," Frank said, flint in his eyes. "And five years ago, back in your fancy office in LA when she was only fifteen, you told me you'd look after her. Protect her."

"And I have. Mr. Baker, I understand that this is a difficult t—"

"*Difficult?* You don't understand anything. Look after her? Last time she came back here, she was a mess. *You* did that to her.

31

And where was your protection tonight?"

"Frank," Jimmy said, "this isn't helping. Hasn't Mr. Tyler always done right by this family?"

Her dad had a point though, didn't he? How had someone managed to kill Blair with all the Satellite Entertainment security around?

"We are fully cooperating with the police department."

"And? You want a medal?" Frank seethed. "No, a trophy. Bet you'd like one of those to add to your collection."

"Enough, Frank!" Marnie shouted, voice wobbling. "I can't bear this!"

Frank directed his answer at Kirk. "I'm just trying to work out how my daughter died under his watch!"

"Save your anger for the guy who actually killed her," Kirk said, anger flaring in his own eyes.

"Stop it! Both of you!" Marnie sat back down on the lip couch and dissolved into sobs, her shoulders rising and falling.

Stevie looked away. It was too much, seeing her mom like that. It made her own pain too real, too massive. She couldn't let it grow. She couldn't let it tear her apart again.

"Emotions are understandably running high, but I don't think this is helping anyone," Officer Dean said, stepping forward, then immediately shrinking back when everyone turned to look at him.

Kind of bold for a rookie to comment—but something needed to be said.

"Officer Dean is right," Jimmy said. "We need to work together. We'll take formal statements later, but for now, do any of you know of anyone who might have wanted to hurt Blair?"

Officer Dean took out a small notepad. He triple-clicked his pen and looked up, expectant.

"No!" Marnie cried. "I do not!"

"Anybody else?" Dean pressed.

Kirk ran his hand through his hair, sighed. "I don't know. Could be a crazed fan. She's had stalkers in the past. There's one guy who's been pretty persistent."

"Okay, we'll look into that," Dean said, tapping his notepad with the pen. "We're going to need any information you have on him, as well as all of Blair's correspondence, emails, phone records."

"I'll get Bex on it," Kirk said.

"Possible stalker," Dean said out loud, as he wrote the words on his notepad. Then he looked up again. "Anyone closer to home? Most murder victims know their killers."

Stevie blinked. Had he actually said that like it might be some unknown fact?

"My Blair isn't *most* murder victims," Marnie said, venom in her mouth. "She's special, and you had better remember that."

"Of course, I didn't mean . . ." Dean's cheeks flushed as he stumbled over his words, then clicked his pen again, eyes fixed on Marnie. He spoke gently. "Still . . . was there anybody? Anybody she fought with? Anyone who had a problem with her?"

"No, nobody," Marnie snapped.

"You're sure?" Dean said, pen hovering over the page. "Take a moment to think."

Stevie and her parents exchanged glances. They were all thinking the same thing, weren't they? She could almost feel his name in the air.

Hal.

But that was ridiculous. Hal wouldn't kill his own sister. All that stuff that happened in the press was ages ago.

"Gunner Trip," Stevie blurted out, forcing the thought of her brother away.

Dean tilted his head. "The Titans' linebacker?"

"Blair's boyfriend," Stevie said, then added, "apparently," because maybe Marnie's rules about these things mattered in murder investigations.

"And he and Blair had had a falling-out?" Dean said, interested.

"I . . . I don't know. I've never met him. He was supposed to come to the concert, but he never showed."

"Stevie's right! He never showed!" Marnie wailed. "Oh god, it was him, wasn't it? It was Gunner Trip."

"You may well be correct, ma'am," Dean said. "It's often a disgruntled, vengeful lover in cases like these."

Stevie looked at him, incredulous. Was he for real?

"Officer Dean! Not the time to speculate," Jimmy said, clearly as unimpressed as Stevie.

"I'll kill him," Frank snarled.

"Dad, I know I mentioned Gunner, but I could be wrong," Stevie said.

"Stevie's right," Marnie said, then her eyes turned wild and dangerous. "Wait until we know for sure—then you can kill him."

"No one's killing anyone," Jimmy said, "but Gunner Trip is definitely one line of inquiry. Let's get him brought in for questioning. Put a call out for all units to be on the lookout for a white male, about six foot—"

"It's okay, Chief—I think they'll know who he is," Officer Dean said. "In the meantime, can you all let me know when you last saw Blair?"

"Over a year ago," Stevie said.

"She's been busy," Marnie added quickly. "She was supposed to come for dinner last night, but she couldn't make it."

Jimmy's eyes flicked up. "Did she say why?"

Frank glared at Kirk. "Had to work."

Kirk held up his hands. "Not for me, she didn't. Last she told me she was all set for her welcome-home meal. Insisted she needed the night off. She left here after the rehearsal yesterday morning. Didn't see her until she got back before noon today."

Stevie studied Kirk's face carefully. She couldn't work out if he was lying. Who else would Blair be working for?

"And did she say where she'd been?" Officer Dean pressed.

"No, I assumed she'd been at her folks'."

"So when did you last see her?"

Marnie let out a sob.

"In her dressing room, around an hour or so before she was due onstage. She likes to be left alone right before a performance."

"And how did she seem to you?" Dean asked.

Kirk shrugged. "Fine—she seemed fine. Pre-performance nerves, but nothing unusual about that. This concert meant a lot to her."

Officer Dean scribbled some more in his notebook, then looked up at Stevie. "Did Blair say anything to you? As her sister, did she confide in you about her relationship with Gunner Trip or anyone else she had any disagreements with?"

Officer Dean was staring right at her—Kirk Tyler and Uncle Jimmy, too. It wasn't an unreasonable question—she *was* Blair's sister after all. And once that had meant something. Stevie would have been able to tell them exactly who had upset Blair. Which of her friends she was annoyed with. Which boys she'd left heartbroken. But now, she could tell them nothing. In all honesty, she didn't know who her sister was anymore.

"Anything at all? The better we know Blair and what was going on in her life, the better chance we have of finding the killer."

Stevie kept her eyes on the floor. "No. She didn't tell me anything about her life. She was really busy, you know, being famous. We didn't really speak that much anymore."

When she looked up, Dean's eyes met hers and she could see the pity in them.

"Shame," he said quietly.

Yeah. It really fucking was.

Jimmy checked his watch, straightened his uniform. "Look, it's late. It's been a traumatic evening for everyone. I think we should get you all home and we can start going over this place with a fine-tooth comb tonight. We may have more to tell you in the morning."

"I'll be in touch tomorrow too," Kirk said. "Work out how we're going to manage this."

Frank spluttered. "You want to *manage* my daughter's death?"

"I'm sorry, Mr. Baker, but someone needs to. The press will be all over it. All over *you*. There's already TV crews camped out in the parking lot. No doubt they'll be at your place too."

Frank tensed. "I can manage this myself. We don't need your help."

"Frank, be smart. You know you need me," Kirk said.

Frank glared at Kirk for a second—then his shoulders dropped slightly. "Fine."

Jimmy stepped forward, gestured to the door. "I'll take you out the back—see if we can avoid the reporters."

Stevie leaned her head against the window of Uncle Jimmy's car while her mother cried silently in the back. The glass was cool—welcome—against Stevie's skin. She blinked, her vision still blotchy from the camera flashes. Jimmy's route out the back of the arena hadn't fooled the press. They'd had to fight through a mass of lenses and microphones and bodies, and a wall of questions, just to get to the car. Frank had lost it: shoved one guy, thrown a camera, then tried to snap a boom microphone over his knee. When it proved indestructible, he'd sent it flying like a furry-tipped javelin. Now he sat with his arm around his wife, staring forward, eyes vacant.

No one spoke as the town passed by in a blur of lights and memories. The pet store where an eight-year-old Blair had sobbed with happiness when she and Stevie had picked out two Russian Blue kittens to take home. Blair had named them both after her favorite singers—Dolly Purrton and Catsy Cline—and Stevie had gone along with it because even she knew her suggestion of *Fluffy* was a bit boring. Founder's Park where Stevie and Blair would sit on the swings, talking about making it as a girl band, while Stevie would try to make her swing do a three-sixty. The pool where Blair choreographed dance routines in the water, dishing out instructions that Stevie largely ignored, but that Mia had followed dutifully because Blair was always pulling out the *I'm five years older and your aunt* card. Wes's Diner, with its sun-bleached awning, where Blair had kneed Josh Wright in the crotch after he had told everyone Stevie was a terrible kisser. Which was an outrageous lie. She was a phenomenal kisser.

Officer Dean's words, how it had been a shame that she didn't know Blair, came back to her. But she had known her sister once. *Really* known her. Stevie had thought she always would. When Blair looked like she was about to make it big, she'd promised Stevie that things wouldn't change—they'd still be each other's favorite person. But somewhere along the way, their lives became too different. Blair wasn't just Stevie's anymore—she belonged to everyone. If Stevie was honest, she had never forgiven her for that. And Blair was always angry that Stevie didn't understand what she was going through—the cost of fame and all that.

The fights they'd had when they were young were fierce and hot and charged with emotion, the reasons for them clear and bellowed into each other's faces. They'd say the worst things they could think of, aiming at sensitive parts and creating wounds only sisters could. But they spoke the truth, and they could find a way through that. The fights they'd had later, when they were older, simmered quietly, angrily—things left unsaid, the expectation being that the other one should just know what was wrong. Despite the distance. Despite not knowing who the other had become. Blair had expected Stevie's forgiveness for what she'd done to Hal even though she would never give an explanation for why she sold him out. She never explained any of her actions. And there was no way through the unknown.

Stevie would give anything to try to find a path to her sister now. She couldn't accept that she would never have that chance again.

She should have reached out. Should have tried harder. Why hadn't she?

The better we know Blair and what was going on in her life, the better chance we have of finding the killer.

Stevie played the words over in her mind. What if it wasn't too late? What if she could find out who her sister had become?

She sat up, stared out the window. When Mia had gone missing, it was the not knowing that had consumed her. The pain of unanswered questions was a pain that refused to take shape, a pain that couldn't be caught hold of or examined. And yet it existed everywhere—in every cell of her body, in every breath of air. Ever present—insurmountable.

Stevie couldn't go through that with Blair, too. She couldn't watch her family go through it.

She had to find a path back to her sister.

She couldn't live not knowing.

She was going to find Blair's killer.

Four

Jimmy killed the engine outside 9 Clover Lane and let out a sigh. They'd had to circle the block for half an hour while Honeyville PD had removed the TV crews from outside their house. Some had followed them from the arena—others were there before they'd arrived. Stevie realized then that Kirk was right—they did need help managing this.

It was after midnight, but the downstairs lights were on in the house. Annie appeared in the front doorway, hugging her cardigan around herself, tears coursing silently down her face. Hal was hanging back in the hall, face in the shadows. Someone must have told them. Jimmy, probably. He got out, opened the rear door, and helped Marnie to her feet. Stevie didn't move for a moment, stayed in the front seat as her dad and Jimmy shepherded Marnie up the steps to the porch, where Annie enveloped her in a hug.

Annie and Marnie had gotten along well from the start. Marnie was always grateful to her for helping straighten Hal out. Annie had met Hal a few months after his accident. He was in a really dark place, but she brought the light back and showed him there was more to life than football. Without her, there was no way he would be running a successful landscaping business. And also, Marnie knew what it was like to have a kid so young. Hal's dad hadn't stuck around when Marnie had become pregnant with him at seventeen, and Annie found out she and Hal were having Mia at the exact same age. Annie's family had kicked her out and the Bakers had taken her in. Stevie was three when Mia had been born—more a sister than a niece. And despite the age gap, Hal had always felt more like a full brother to Stevie than half.

Annie nodded as words were exchanged under the porch light. Uncle Jimmy was probably telling her what he knew—what little he knew—repeating promises to catch whoever did it.

They all glanced over at the car. Stevie took a breath, unbuckled her seat belt, and stepped out into the warm June night. She couldn't hide forever. Annie waited for her on the porch while the others went inside.

"I'm so sorry, Stevie." Annie reached out, her face twisted in grief, and pulled Stevie into a hug. Annie was one of the few people who could slip past the walls Stevie kept so carefully in place, and to stop herself from crumbling in her sister-in-law's arms, she bit her lip and focused on the moths flitting about the porch light.

"I'm so sorry you have to go through this. Mia"—Annie's voice caught and broke mid-sentence—"and now Blair. It's not fair. It's just not fair."

Stevie pulled away from the mass of her sister-in-law's blond curls. She didn't want to think about the unfairness of it, or for Annie's sympathy to soften her so her feelings could find a way out.

Annie kept hold of Stevie's arms, her grip light but sure. She searched Stevie's face. "I've been so worried about you. How are you holding up?"

Stevie let out a puff of air. How was she supposed to answer that? "Not sure, really."

Annie's gaze lingered on her for a moment, as if weighing whether to press, and seemed to decide against it. "We came straight over when we heard. And the reporters were already here and Hal had an argument with one of them. I was worried he was going to hit him. Thankfully, the police showed up." She rubbed the mascara smears from under her eyes with the heel of her hand. "Jimmy said it might have been Gunner Trip. Some of the reporters were asking about him too. Do you think it's possible?"

"I don't know." Stevie had thrown his name out without thinking before, but yes, if she thought about it, it was possible. He'd skipped the concert, and as that Officer Dean had said, it was often someone close to the victim.

"Come on," Annie said, guiding Stevie inside, "we'd better join the others."

Everyone was sitting around the kitchen table, Blair's massive apology bouquet plonked right in the middle. Hal was leaning against the wall in the corner of the room, hands stuffed in the pockets of his shorts, head down, dark brown fringe covering his eyes.

Marnie's face was buried in her hands, her shoulders rising and falling as she sobbed and asked, "What has this family done to deserve so much pain?"

Nobody answered.

Frank pulled the lid off a bottle of scotch and, with unsteady hands, poured four glasses. Stevie took a seat at the table and looked at him hopefully. "One there for me?"

Frank looked at Marnie, but she shook her head. Seemed even one dead sister wasn't going to be enough to bend the strict *over twenty-one only* rule of the Baker household.

Annie brought the tumbler to her mouth and knocked it back in one gulp. Impressive for her—she wasn't much of a drinker— probably out of support for Hal, who hadn't touched a drop since his accident. Stevie would have commented, if the circumstances had been different. Annie placed the empty glass on the table with trembling hands, shook her head. "We should have been there."

"You mustn't think like that." Marnie squeezed her hand, then broke down in tears again.

"What could we have done if we had been?" Hal said. He didn't look up when he spoke. There was a bitterness to his voice.

There always was when he spoke about Blair. Seemed her death hadn't changed that.

Jimmy leaned forward. "So you weren't there, then—at the concert?" He spoke casually, but it was obvious what he was driving at.

Frank thumped his glass down, liquor sloshing over the side. "Hell, Jimmy! He said he wasn't!"

"You know I have to ask."

Did he though? Now, only hours after Blair's death? Stevie glared at her uncle. Why was he here questioning Hal and not out looking for Gunner Trip?

Hal tilted his head, fixed his green eyes on Jimmy. "You're asking if I killed Blair? Really, Jimmy?"

It sounded ludicrous. Of course he hadn't. Hal doted on Blair when they were young. Sure, their relationship had been strained, but, frankly, that was understandable. Four years ago, when Blair, for who knows what reason, had told the world about the drunk-driving Hal had been charged with when he was seventeen, she had shattered Hal—the family, too—especially when Blair point-blank refused to explain why she'd done it. Stevie could only imagine it was some horrible attempt to get more attention from the public. But for Hal to *kill* her over it? There was no way it was possible. No way.

"Oh, Jimmy, don't. Please don't!" Marnie bawled. "Don't treat him like a suspect in his sister's murder. He used to help change her diapers, for crying out loud!"

"I don't think he did it, Marn. I just want to find out if he knows anything that could help."

Marnie's voice grew louder. "Of course he didn't do it! And what would help is you bringing in that Gunner Trip!"

Stevie caught hold of her mom's fire. "She's right." She pointed at the door. "Shouldn't you be out there looking for him?"

"I've got people on it. If it was him, we'll nail him. But I just need to rule this line of inquiry out officially. There are already people on the internet suggesting Hal might be responsible."

"Oh, people from the internet! I'm so glad you're consulting them in your inquiries," Marnie said.

"He *is* on record saying he'd kill her."

Hal snorted, contempt in his eyes. "Well, obviously, that means I did it."

"Don't even joke!" Marnie snapped, then set her sights on Jimmy again. "He said that years ago, when Blair gave that story to Hilton Moore!"

"And he didn't mean it!" Stevie added—definitely the more important thing to be noted.

Jimmy kept his voice even. "I know all this, but I need to be seen doing my job properly, Marn."

"*Seen* doing or *actually* doing it properly?" Hal said.

"Both. This is a high-profile case—eyes are going to be all over Honeyville PD. We're going to throw everything we have at this," Jimmy said.

He'd said that about Mia and the Aaron Taylor murder too. Everything the police department had thrown then hadn't worked. Mia had never been found, and the person who had put a bullet in Aaron's stomach in that lumberyard had never been caught. Perhaps Jimmy and his pals were throwing the wrong things.

"We have to look at everybody. Her team, the fans, the stalker, the boyfriend, and also the family. And I'm very eager to rule out the family straightaway. So, Hal"—Jimmy cleared his throat—"I've got to ask, bud. Where were you from seven this evening?"

"He didn't go to the concert," Annie said, before Hal could answer. "Neither of us did. We didn't even take the VIP passes, so we couldn't have gotten in. I was considering it, but after Blair's no-show last night, there was no way Hal could be persuaded, and I didn't want to go without him. We stayed home. Together."

"Is that right?" Jimmy said, eyes on Hal. "I just need you to confirm it."

Hal looked from Annie to Jimmy, then down to the floor, and shifted his weight ever so slightly. "Yeah, that's right."

Shit. He was lying. A wave of nausea rolled through Stevie. It was that shift of weight. She'd seen him do it hundreds of times before. When he was getting a dressing-down from Marnie or Annie for some small misdemeanor, he'd look down at the ground, shift from foot to foot, and swear to god he hadn't done what he was accused of. About bigger things too.

Stevie caught his eye—he held her gaze for a moment and looked away.

Jimmy smiled. Tapped his hands on the table twice. "That's all I needed to hear."

Frank stood up, eyes glowering. "I think it's time you left."

"Come on—don't be like that."

Frank choked back a sob. "I'm not being like anything. Our daughter died tonight, Jimmy."

"And I'm going to make every effort to find out who killed her."

Hal gave a hollow laugh. "Forgive me for my lack of faith."

Marnie started sobbing again and Annie jumped up, knelt by her chair, and took her hands. "I don't understand how someone could have walked into the arena and shot my daughter with all those people and her security team around. Explain how something like that could happen, Jimmy!" Marnie stared at him, eyes flaring with desperate anger.

"We're still in the very early stages of the investigation," Jimmy said.

Stevie leaned forward. "But you must have a theory?"

Jimmy screwed up his mouth. "It's too—"

"If you've got something, we want to hear it," Frank said, cutting him off.

Jimmy held his brother's gaze for a moment, then cleared his throat. "Okay, here's what I've got. Constructed below the stage, there's this holding room, a little like a metal cage, that contains the platform that rises up into the arena. It's away from the dressing rooms and the tech areas. Before every concert, Blair insists on half an hour of alone time to enable her to get in the zone."

Stevie nodded as an image of a nervous ten-year-old Blair locking herself away in the restrooms before a dance recital flashed in her mind. Stevie was the only one who used to be able to get her to speak before a performance when she was younger. Despite her talent, Blair was never really equipped to deal with fame. When her first single had gone viral when she was just fifteen, and she immediately started pulling in huge crowds, a doctor had prescribed her Xanax to deal with the stress. That was the first drug she'd become addicted to—cocaine was the next. Stevie had always worried about what the future might hold for Blair. But it had never been this.

"So she goes into this room, shuts the door, and her security team of three wait outside. We're thinking that somebody must have already been waiting in there."

Stevie's heart, blood, organs—everything—turned to ice.

Marnie gasped. "Someone was in there?"

"The platform was last checked in a tech rehearsal around three p.m.—Blair's entrance was at eight thirty, which leaves a substantial window where someone could have snuck in."

Five and a half hours substantial.

"I believe that the shot was fired when the fireworks went off, to mask the sound."

"But she was alive after that. We heard her voice," Stevie said.

"Prerecorded audio."

"But if security were outside that room, how did they not see who did it?" Stevie pressed.

"Once that platform had risen, Blair's security detail went upstairs to the wings of the stage. Nobody realized anything was wrong for a few minutes. By the time anyone thought to check the room below, whoever had shot Blair had already gone."

Hal thumped his fist against the wall. "Do they have to train to be that damn incompetent?"

"Clearly, mistakes were made," Jimmy said evenly.

"You think?" Hal shot back.

"What about CCTV?" Frank asked. "There must be something?"

"Not in that area, apparently. The only CCTV is what was already installed in the field house. There's nothing covering the walkways, or the area under the stage. Still, I promise we'll trawl through the footage to see if we can find anything."

Stevie rubbed her temples, trying to make sense of what she was hearing. "Wouldn't she have been miked up? If someone was in that room, why didn't she say anything? Why didn't she just open the door—call out for help?"

"That we don't know. Her audio was turned off—either by her or whoever killed her. Production was talking to her, giving her the countdown. Apparently, it's not that unusual for her not to respond when she's meditating before her act, so they didn't realize anything was wrong."

The kitchen fell silent.

Stevie wrestled in her mind with all the *what-ifs*. What if just one of those security guards had checked that room? What if Satellite Entertainment had bothered to set up adequate CCTV? What if she had gone to see Blair before the concert? Spoken to her, wished her luck like a sister should do, instead of hiding at the gym.

Frank broke the silence with a long, heavy sigh. "It's late and we should all try to get some sleep so we have some strength to face this all again in the morning. There will be the funeral to sort out." His face grayed and he looked at the bottom of his glass. "How do you arrange a funeral for a superstar?"

Stevie's stomach twisted at the thought of it—of all the people, the cameras. Blair's final performance—their pain for the world's entertainment.

Jimmy drained his scotch and stood up. "I'll let you know when I can release the body, but you know how long these things can take. A patrol will stay outside to try and keep the hacks away for you tonight. We appealed to their better nature, and they've granted you a night's grace, but there's not much we can do about them showing up tomorrow. There are no laws against them being on public property."

"Granted us? That's big of them." Hal sneered.

Jimmy ignored him. "I'll drop by first thing—let you know if we've made any progress overnight. In the meantime, stay off the internet. People are saying all sorts of things and coming up with wild theories that you don't need to hear."

Stevie resisted the urge to get her phone out and start looking right there and then. If people had theories about who killed Blair, she wanted to know what they were.

Nobody else moved, so Stevie got to her feet. "I'll see you out." Maybe ask some questions on the way.

Outside, the night felt too humid, too heavy. As Jimmy opened his car door, Stevie said, "You really think you're going to catch who killed her?"

Jimmy paused, hand on the roof. Somewhere a tree frog began to chirrup.

"I really do. That place was packed. Someone will have seen

something. No way could someone walk in, kill one of the world's biggest stars, and walk out again unnoticed."

Stevie nodded. But that was exactly what had happened, wasn't it?

"And if it wasn't Gunner Trip, who's your next prime suspect— the stalker?"

"Stevie, do me a favor?"

"Yeah?"

"I'm saying this in the nicest way possible, but don't get all Nancy Drew on me again." He was smiling, but his eyes were serious.

Her cheeks flushed with anger, embarrassment, maybe both. Was she so obvious? *"What?"*

"With Mia—it didn't do you any good, did it? All that time you spent trying to figure out what happened made you sick."

"Someone had to try."

"You ran around town accusing innocent people! And lots of people were trying, Stevie. Lots of people who had a far better chance of finding out what happened to her than you."

Stevie's cheeks burned hotter. "And yet you didn't find anything. It's been almost three years, and you have nothing."

"We will this time. This case is different."

"How?" she said, eyes blazing.

"We have a body, for a start. And a crime scene."

Stevie flinched, but if Jimmy thought he could put her off by mentioning Blair's body, he was wrong. She came back at him. "You had both of those with the Aaron Taylor case."

"Stevie, this is not like the Aaron Taylor case."

"Why?"

"Aaron Taylor was just some kid with a difficult past who made a few poor decisions and died because of them. Blair . . . well, the world cares about what happened to Blair."

"The world should have cared what happened to Aaron Taylor, too!"

Jimmy sniffed, irritated. Guess he didn't like being reminded of his failures. "I'm not going to stand here arguing with you. I think it's best if I go. But remember what I said, no investigating."

Jimmy slammed the car door, then reversed out of the driveway. Stevie raised her hand to say goodbye, then swapped it for the middle finger when he was far enough away. Thanks for the concern, but yeah, she absolutely was going to get all Nancy Drew again. She hadn't found out what had happened to Mia. She'd jumped to conclusions, made error after error. But this time would be different. She was older now—she'd learned from her mistakes—and she wouldn't make them again.

When she got back inside, Hal and Annie looked like they were ready to leave. Under the hall light, the dark shadows and lines on Hal's face were so much more apparent. He looked far older than his thirty-three years. Understandable, after everything he'd been through.

"When did Uncle Jimmy turn into such a jerk?" Stevie asked.

"Oh, I think he may always have been one," Hal said. "Mom's in bed—Dad gave her a Valium to knock her out."

"Standard night," Stevie said. "Mom loves the benzos." A joke—to try to lift the mood. But she shouldn't have said it.

Hal tried a smile, didn't quite manage it. "You going to be okay, Stevie? If you need anything . . ." His voice trailed off, the offer of support hanging in the air.

Stevie saw it as an opportunity and blurted out, "You were at home tonight, then?"

Hal exhaled, looked at the ceiling. "Not you, too."

"Oh, Stevie, you can't think Hal was involved," Annie said. "He was at home all evening."

"I don't think he killed her," Stevie said. She turned to Hal and her words spilled out. "Of course I don't. It's just, you did that thing with your feet when Jimmy asked—you know, like when you aren't telling the truth, and I wondered why that was. Why would you lie? Because you can't have killed Blair, so I thought maybe there was something else—"

Hal put his hands on her shoulders and looked her square in the eye. "Stevie, calm down. I promise you—I was at home all day and all night. I did not sneak into the concert and kill my own sister, okay?"

Stevie kept her eyes on him, then quickly glanced down at his feet. Stock-still. "Yeah, okay."

He shook his head. "My feet? I never knew I did that."

"So that's your tell." Annie squeezed his arm and gave him a smile.

Stevie flung her arms around her brother, gripped him tight. He squeezed her back tighter. "I'm sorry for asking." She hated that she had. "I know you loved Blair. That you'd never do anything to hurt her."

When she pulled away, Hal was crying.

Guilt tugged at Stevie's chest. That he was so tall and strong made him look even more vulnerable. "Oh, Hal, I am so, so sorry."

Hal's breath hitched. "I can't believe she's gone. I think I did hurt her."

Stevie's brow arched, waiting for him to explain.

"I never made things right with her . . ." His voice caught in his throat. "And now . . ." He stopped, tried to hold back his sobs.

"She loved you, Hal, and she knew you loved her," Stevie said.

"You think?"

"I know."

Hal rubbed at his eyes, drew in two long breaths. "I guess I'll have to keep telling myself that's true."

"You cannot blame yourself for how things were between you

and Blair—she was troubled," Annie said, voice bordering on stern.

"Annie's right," Stevie said. Although wasn't she blaming herself too? She'd let Blair disappear from her life and now it was too late to get her back.

Annie placed her hand on Hal's arm. "Let's go home, baby." She turned to Stevie. "Are you going to be okay?"

Okay? No. She wasn't. Of course she wasn't. And the only chance she had of ever being okay again was if she found out who had killed Blair. "Do you think it could've been Gunner Trip? It's odd that he didn't show up at the concert, right?"

Annie tilted her head, surprised at Stevie's sudden question. "You're not going to try and investigate Blair's murder, are you?" Her voice was laced with concern.

Stevie looked away. "You sound like Jimmy."

"Stevie, think about what happened last time," Annie pleaded. "Hal, tell her."

"It's not that we didn't appreciate your efforts, but it wasn't good for you. Mia's disappearance . . ." He swallowed, a fresh sheet of tears slipping down his face. Annie reached for his hand, her eyes filling too. Hal took a breath. "Losing our daughter was so painfully hard, but watching you fall apart just made it even harder."

"I didn't fall apart . . ." Stevie's words died on her lips. Forgetting about everything else in her life, losing fifteen pounds, and missing so much school the year after Mia disappeared that she was now a year behind were pretty strong evidence she had. But it was the *not knowing* that had caused that. Not her investigating.

Annie shot Hal a worried look.

Hal placed his hands on either side of Stevie's face, looked her in the eyes, imploring. "Promise me you're not going to get all obsessive and investigatory again."

"Hal, I promise, I'm not going to get 'all obsessive and investigatory.'" It would be the perfect amount of obsession and investigation. "Besides, Jimmy seems confident he's going to find whoever did this. Gunner Trip could confess by the morning. *If* it was him. He may have an alibi. What then? Kirk Tyler mentioned a stalker. They might be harder to find. She does have legions of fans—"

"Stevie, stop. You're starting already," Annie said gently. "You need to process your grief, work through what has happened."

She thought she was working through what had happened. But okay.

Annie put her bag down on the hall table. "You know what—you should go to bed. We'll tidy up here. Get some sleep."

Hal bent down and kissed the top of Stevie's head. "No investigating. Sleep."

Stevie leaned her head against his chest for a moment. "I hear you, Hal." Then she headed off to her room above the garage.

She flicked on her bedroom light, kicked off her shoes, and sat down on her bed next to Catsy Cline. Catsy stirred, a stretch rippling through her body, paws extending, toes splayed wide. Her eyes half open, her pink nose twitching slightly, she rubbed her cheek against Stevie's hand.

"Hey, there, little loaf." Stevie stroked her soft gray fur and Catsy's eyes melted shut. The events of the evening weighed heavy and Stevie's eyes started to close too. She blinked them back open. Sleep would have to wait. She pulled her laptop toward her—the screen lit up, displaying her screen saver: a picture of her and Blair when they'd first brought Catsy and Dolly Purrton home. They were outside the front of the house, tiny kittens in their hands, huge smiles on their faces.

"There's only two of us left now," Stevie whispered.

She felt herself start to crumble and took a deep, shaky breath to steel herself. *So, then, people of the internet—what do you all have to say about the killing of Blair Baker?*

Five

Blair was the lead story on all the news channels. Every major newspaper had put out a breaking news headline. So had all the celebrity pages. Those were really something else. The editors' excitement leaping from the screen.

Homecoming Heartbreak!
Princess of Pop Unplugged Forever!
Blair Baker Silenced for Good!
No Final Bow for Blair Baker!
At Night with the Stars *Postponed Following Blair Baker Murder!*

Since when were exclamation points a respectful way to announce a death? Who signed off on those? The perverse joy some journalists seemed to be taking in writing about her sister's murder turned Stevie's stomach.

Other headlines were more personal. The *State* had led with *Baker Family Double Heartbreak* and included Mia's middle-school photo alongside an image of Blair. The *News* ran with *One Girl Missing, Another Lost Forever.*

On reflection, maybe the exclamation points were better.

The *Post and Courier*—the main South Carolina paper—had gone with *Honeyville Horror: Star's Murder Is Third Tragedy to Hit Town in Almost Half a Decade.* The article cast doubt on whether Jimmy Baker was capable of investigating his own niece's murder and finished up by asking the question: *Is Honeyville PD up to the task?* It was clear, like Stevie, they thought the answer was probably fucking not.

Stevie read everything she could find. Every single word of every single article, just in case there was some tiny scrap of new information about what had happened. Some lead. Some small clue. But none of them told her anything she didn't already know. Blair was dead when she came onstage. Single gunshot wound to the chest. Police were undertaking inquiries.

A car door slammed outside, then somebody shouted. Catsy raised her head and Stevie's eyes lifted from the screen.

"What's that, do you think?" Stevie asked, stroking Catsy's head.

Catsy hopped from the bed and padded over to the window. Stevie followed and pulled the curtain back. Outside, Officer Dean was dragging a reporter off the front lawn. The other guy was putting up a fight—shouting about the public having a right to know, that he wasn't breaking any laws. Officer Dean didn't respond, just opened the door to the guy's car and pushed him in.

"Huh," Stevie said, looking at Catsy, "he handled that better than expected."

Officer Dean looked up at her window and raised a hand.

Stevie gasped.

Oh, good god, he'd seen her.

"Oh no, Catsy," Stevie hissed.

Casty looked disinterested, jumped down from the window ledge, and curled back up on the bed.

Stevie tried to duck out of view, got caught up in the curtains. Cheeks flushing, she waved back.

He saluted, stuck his hands in his belt loops, started to swagger back to his car, then tripped off the curb and tried to style it out by breaking into a little jog and running his hand through his dark brown hair. Stevie snorted.

She went to turn around, but her gaze snagged on something outside. She drew closer to the window. Further down the street, a man was standing completely still, bleached in the moonlight. He was tall, with a heftiness to his form. His hands in the pockets of a long overcoat that swelled at his middle. A baseball cap was pulled low over his eyes, obscuring his face. What was his deal? A reporter? He didn't look like a reporter. But it was odd to be out there at this time if he wasn't.

Unease swept through her, settled in her bones, and hardened into understanding—something wasn't right about this guy.

How long had he been there? Minutes? *Hours?* His size made him seem so permanent—a tree planted on the sidewalk.

Slowly, he raised his head, face washing into nothingness by the shadows, eyes solid black. Stevie drew a breath. He was staring right at the house. No, at her window—at *her*. Her heart lurched in her chest, sent blood pounding to her ears. He'd be able to see her clearly—him out there in the dark, her lit up in her room. She lunged at the light switch and paused a moment before she dragged her eyes back to the window. Would he still be there? Or had he vanished now he knew he'd been seen? Her mind raced. Maybe he hadn't been there at all. A figment of her imagination. A person formed from trauma. Like all those times she thought she'd spotted Mia or thought she'd seen someone watching the house.

But he was there, head still lifted to her window. He reached inside his coat, pulled something from the inside pocket, like he knew she was watching him. Like he wanted her to see. Stevie stiffened, hairs lifting on her neck.

A flash of something in the moonlight. Metal? A gun? No . . . a blade.

Her heart tripped again, started up birdlike in her chest. Why was she just standing, watching? She should do something—

Do something!

Throw open the window and shout for Officer Dean. Scream

that Blair's killer was right outside. Because that was who he must be—surely?

The man lowered his arm—let it hang long and loose at his side.

Open the window and shout!

Her limbs were too slack, too hollowed out to move. And those black holes were still fixed on her . . .

Then, slowly, he turned away. Walked off down the street, coat flapping, arm hanging at his side, clutching the knife—it was a knife, wasn't it? Stevie's eyes stayed trapped on him until he disappeared around the back of the houses. Then finally, *finally*, her body jolted into action. Hands on the latch, she threw the window open. Voice fracturing, she cried out, "Officer Dean!"

The door to the cruiser swung open and he was out of his car, then under her window, concerned eyes looking up at her. "Stevie, what is it?"

"A man . . . there was a man!"

"A man?"

"He was watching the house." Her voice sticking in her throat. "I think he had a knife."

"When?"

"Just now!"

Officer Dean's eyes widened. "Are you sure?"

Was she sure? Irritation flared in her. "Yes, I'm sure. He disappeared around the back of those houses."

It was too late. She'd been too slow reacting. He'd be gone. He'd be gone and it would be her fault.

Officer Dean looked down the road, back at her, then turned and ran in the direction she was pointing, arms pumping at his sides. Her eyes were fixed on him as he reached the end of the road, then disappeared out of view.

Thoughts crowded Stevie's mind. What if the man hadn't gone?

What if he was there? Waiting—knife ready to strike. Would Officer Dean be able to fend off an attack? He had a gun—but what if he was taken by surprise? A blade across his neck before his hand could find his weapon? Stevie's throat tightened. She tried to shake the image away. Would that be her fault?

She bit her lip. No. He was doing his job. He was a police officer. Well, almost a police officer. He wouldn't be there if Jimmy didn't think he was up to it. But *was* Officer Dean up to it? Should he have been left alone? He should have been watching. Why hadn't he seen? God . . . if the man was still there . . .

She fixed her eyes on the end of the road, lungs frozen on the inhale, and waited. He'd be back soon.

Soon.

She leaned farther out the window. Listened. The street lay in silent shadows below her.

She felt Catsy's warm body slink around her legs. She picked her up and buried her face into her fur. "How long does it take to see that someone isn't there, girl?"

Not this long, surely?

The sound of footsteps at the end of the street.

Her eyes found him—running toward her. She let out a gasp of relief.

Officer Dean didn't stop until he stood under her window. Hands on hips, bent over, his shirt stretching over his pecs as he tried to catch his breath. "No sign of him, I'm afraid."

"He was there." She sounded brusque—she hadn't meant to.

"I believe you, Stevie."

She put Catsy on the floor. "It's just . . . I was too slow. I kind of froze . . ." Her voice trailed off. Why was she admitting this? He should have seen him. Wasn't that why he was there?

"Completely understandable. Seeing some guy in your street, holding a knife, would make anyone freeze."

Was it a knife? Already Stevie's mind struggled to hook on to the details of what she'd seen, what she thought she'd seen.

"Have you ever seen him before?"

"No. Never. Do you think he might have something to do with Blair? Some sicko fan? Her stalker?"

"It is possible. Of course, it could be a coincidence—he could just be an opportunist creeper."

"What, and he just happened to like the vibe of our street?"

Officer Dean sighed. "I mean, maybe? He could have been attracted by all the activity. But this needs to be taken seriously. Can I come in and take a statement?"

"No, I'll come down."

Marnie and Frank didn't need to hear this tonight on top of everything.

Stevie closed the front door quietly. Her hands were still shaking, so she stuck them in her back pockets. Officer Dean was ready and waiting on the porch with his notepad and pen. Her eyes snatched a glance down the road.

"I won't keep you long. I can write up what happened later, but I just need a few more details from you."

"Okay, sure."

"Can you remember what he looked like?"

"I don't know . . . like a creepy-ass weirdo." She shook her head. *Super helpful, Stevie. Get the E-FIT drawn up immediately.*

"'Creepy-ass weirdo,'" he repeated.

Sweet that he was writing it down—not making her feel stupid.

He looked up   the porch light was casting a soft glow across his face, illuminating the freckles on his nose and cheeks. His eyes were steady, encouraging. "Anything else?"

Stevie sucked in a breath. "He was tall. Like, over six feet. And a little heavy—like he was maybe out of shape. Soft around the edges. He was wearing a long coat and a baseball cap."

"Okay, this is good. You're doing great."

Was she?

"Hair color? Eye color?" His pen on the pad again.

"It was too dark. I couldn't see. Sorry; I'm not being much help."

He closed his notepad, stuck it in his back pocket. "I'll be honest—it's not a huge amount to go on. But a big guy like that should be fairly obvious to spot if he shows up again. I'll make sure everyone is aware. As I said, it could just be a passing prowler, but we can't rule out a link to Blair."

"You think maybe her stalker showed up to be . . . close to her or something? See the impact of what he had done?" It was humid out still, but a chill ran through her. She hugged her arms around herself. "You hear about it, don't you? Whack jobs who get off on killing people."

"People like that are much rarer than the movies would have you believe, but we can't rule it out as a line of inquiry. Especially with Blair being as famous as she was. I don't want to worry you unnecessarily, but if it is the case, a stalker may take an unhealthy interest in you, as her sister."

Stevie pressed her lips together. "Right. Hard not to worry about that."

"I think you just need to be sensible. Don't go out on your own, especially at night. Keep your windows and doors locked. Be vigilant. Be cautious."

She rubbed at a knot in her neck. This was serious. "You think he might come back?"

"I don't want to speculate, but if he does, you can be reassured that there will be a police presence outside at all times."

Stevie nodded—didn't want to point out that he *had* been right outside.

"It may not be this guy, Stevie. Gunner Trip is still our prime suspect and he's yet to be located—"

"And 'it's often a disgruntled, vengeful lover in cases like these' . . ." Stevie let her words—the words, his words—hang. A joke? A dig? She wasn't sure.

Either way, he didn't bite. "I'll speak to your folks tomorrow and speak to all the neighbors, ask them if they've seen anything and tell them to keep an eye out."

"Okay, thanks."

"So . . . I think we're all done here. Try to sleep—I'll be right outside if you need anything." He took a step back, tripped down the porch steps.

Stevie raised her eyebrows. Not exactly reassuring . . . but . . . was he shaken by what had happened and trying not to show it? "Shouldn't you have had someone with you tonight?"

"I thought I'd be okay for an hour. We didn't think anything would happen."

"Well, you got that wrong."

He put his hands on his hips and nodded, a half-smile on his lips. "Yup, we sure did."

Thinking about it now, Stevie couldn't decide if he'd been brave or reckless to chase after a possible murderer.

"Don't worry—Officer Dwight will be here soon, so it won't just be me."

Stevie nodded and turned to leave. Officer Dean cleared his throat, then looked at the ground.

"I just wanted to say that I am very sorry about what happened to your sister."

He raised his eyes to meet hers and looked so genuine that a lump formed in Stevie's throat. She didn't trust herself to speak, so she nodded again and hurried back inside.

Stevie cast a quick look down at Officer Dean's car before she drew her curtains. He was sitting in the front seat, staring up at the roof, his chest rising and falling in slow, measured breaths—like he was trying to steady himself. She had an impulse to open the window and shout down to ask if he was okay. But that would have just been weird.

Her eyes fell on Catsy—she was curled in a soft little ball, breathing slowly and rhythmically. Stevie should have been tired too, and maybe she was, but her mind was too loud, too busy, too frayed. Her sister was dead. Her body seen by thousands—millions now, thanks to the internet.

Seen by her.

She was so very still.

The shake of the paramedic's head.

She climbed under the sheets, trying not to disturb Catsy, and pulled her laptop toward herself again.

Six

Stevie clicked on Google and typed her sister's name into the search engine. It threw up a ton of hits. Blair's face again and again.

There was nothing new left to read on mainstream media, so socials it was, then—that's where she'd find the theories.

They were buzzing with the story of the murder of America's Singing Sweetheart. Celebrities expressing their condolences, posting pictures of themselves with Blair, saying how much she meant to them, like it was some kind of competition. Even the president had quoted one of Blair's songs as a tribute.

Video after video of fans crying into their cameras—sharing their devastation with the world. *"Blair meant so much to me. Blair was there when I needed her. Blair felt like my best friend. Blair, Blair, blah blah blah."* They didn't even know her. They were stealing Stevie's grief for likes.

Stevie blinked and rubbed her eyes. They were dry, her contacts fused onto her eyeballs. She peeled them off, put her glasses on, took a moment for her vision to settle, then kept scrolling until she found some videos of the concert. People had posted shaky camera footage from various seats around the arena. What if someone had captured something? The man in the coat? Officer Dean had said he should be fairly obvious to spot—maybe she'd see him in the crowd. Maybe she'd see Gunner—or someone else . . .

But to see it again—watch it play out? Stevie hesitated before clicking on the first video. Her finger trembling above the touch pad.

It won't be worse than being there.

She hit Play.

The faces of two girls filled the screen. Smiles wide—they stuck out their tongues, screamed when the music started. Now the stage. The camera bouncing up and down. The band. The mascots. Then Blair. Rising up on the platform. Legs not moving. Arms resting at her sides. Her body emerging to a crescendo of cheers. A sacrifice at the altar of entertainment.

So still. So very still.

Stevie swallowed. How hadn't she realized? How could she have sat there with all the others and not known? Her throat tightened, bile rising in her stomach too fast. She scrambled to press Pause, dived off her bed, hand over her mouth, and threw up in her wastebasket. She placed her hand against the wall and tried to stop the room from spinning. Her heart pounded in her ears. Blair's broken body in her mind and Hal's warning ringing in her ears—*it wasn't good for you.* Why was she putting herself through this?

She heaved in a breath. Spat away the drool.

Then she wiped her mouth, took a drink of water, forced herself to sit back down. She knew why she was doing it. Someone might have captured something.

Just detach. Focus on the details. Block out the emotion. Push the pain away.

She brought her eyes to the screen.

Finger steady this time, she hit Play.

And she focused on the details. The faces in the crowd. The people on the stage—behind the stage. Security and merchandise vendors. She zoomed in on every shot, trying to look past heads that were blocking her view. She relived it all. Frame by frame. Blair's entrance. The missed cues. Bex Lyons running onto the stage. The screams. The panic. The announcement. That paramedic. Again and again, angle after angle. But there was nothing she hadn't seen herself in the flesh. Doubt crept in. Then anger. What was she hoping to find? Some guy tiptoeing out with a gun in his hand and an *I Murdered Blair Baker* T-shirt?

But she kept scrolling. And scrolling. Reel after reel replaying her sister's murder. Her desperation growing, her mind slipping— letting go of the details, leaving a path for her pain. Blair was dead. Her sister was dead. It tore through her—carved her open. She dropped her eyes from the screen. Sobs racked her body, shook her from the inside out.

She gave in to it—cried violently and uncontrollably. She didn't think she'd ever stop, but then she felt the lick of a rough tongue on her cheek, a nose nudging her.

Stevie sniffed, blotted her eyes on the sheet. "I'm okay, I'm okay."

She curled herself around Catsy, kept repeating that she was okay into her fur. But she wasn't okay. Annie was right. It wasn't fair. She'd lost Mia, now Blair. And she might never find out what had happened to either of them.

Stevie pushed herself upright, the movement heavy and reluctant. She should turn out the light. Try to sleep. Maybe she'd have more success in the morning after some rest. A faint chatter was still coming from her laptop—one reel merging into the next. Her sister's name over and over.

Stop. Just stop.

She reached out, ready to slam the screen down, but paused at the sight of a familiar face.

Colby Green—sobbing, cheeks covered in rivers of mascara. Of course she'd have something to say.

"I'm devastated. We are all devastated. We lost a star, but heaven has gained an angel." Disgust coiled thick in Stevie's throat. Colby could shut right up about heaven and angels. She reached for the lid again, but then Colby said something else.

"After tonight's traumatizing events, I feel that I have to share

something with you all. I will be uploading a video of my experience of what happened before Blair's homecoming concert on the Blair Baker fan page. I know this is a very painful time for everybody and I hope you are all practicing self-care right now. But I have some important information as to what might have happened to Blair and I want you, her loyal fans, to see it first."

Stevie's heart leapt. *Important information?* What the actual . . . ? She glared at the frozen image of Colby. What did she mean, what happened *before* the concert? Colby couldn't know anything about Blair's murder, surely? Still, a rush of adrenaline sent prickles over Stevie's scalp and made her rush to click the link to the fan site home page.

And there was Blair, dressed as a cowgirl, riding a horse that had been dressed up to look like a unicorn. Colby had captioned it with the words *Dear Blair, thank you for everything, may you ride unicorns in heaven.*

Ride unicorns? Stevie grimaced, clicked the blog link.

Wow. Stevie leaned back, rubbed her forehead. Colby was a *dedicated* poster—there were over a thousand blog and vlog entries. She quickly found the video that had been added that night. It had only been up an hour but already had eighty thousand views, sixty-two thousand likes, and seventeen thousand comments.

Stevie hit Play.

Come on, then, Colby Green—let's see what important information you have for me.

Colby's face loomed into view, lips downturned, purposefully solemn. Colby spoke more about how devastated she was, talked about her favorite Blair moments, lit a candle, said a prayer. Hardly important information. More like clickbait. But then she cleared her throat, and her eyes narrowed. *"As some of you will know, following the disappointment of Blair pulling out of our preconcert party the evening before the concert, she got in contact with me to meet with her on the afternoon of opening night."*

Stevie paused the video and frowned. Blair wouldn't go to some fan party. And she definitely wouldn't meet with a random fan—would she? Colby had to be lying. Mind you, Blair had also agreed to the homecoming meal chez Baker. She might have said to Colby she'd go but had no intention of following through. Maybe Colby had been really pissed at Blair for standing her up. Crazed fan decides to kill? Stevie shook her head. It was too much of a reach. She was jumping to conclusions. Colby was annoying, but a *killer*? She pressed Play again.

"While waiting for her outside her dressing room, at around three p.m., I was filming content for my channel when . . . something disturbing happened. I'm going to play this for you now. You may need to turn your volume up, as the audio isn't great."

She was outside Blair's dressing room? How did she get back there? Maybe Colby *did* know something. Stevie's pulse picked up as she turned the computer volume to max and leaned in close to the screen. Colby's face came into view again, cheeks flushed with excitement. She was talking quickly and quietly, eyes darting everywhere.

"That's Blair's dressing room just down the corridor. I'm waiting to be called in. I think she has someone in there with her at the moment. I'm not sure who it is, but it could be Gunner Trip!" Colby then let out a little squeal of excitement, but a noise in the background caused her to stop and turn around.

The sound on the video was quiet, but it must have been loud enough in real life to get Colby's attention. She turned back to the camera and whispered, *"I think something's going on! I can hear raised voices. I'm going to get closer, see if I can find out what is happening."*

Stevie's adrenaline spiked again. Colby hotfooted it toward

her sister's dressing-room door, the camera pointed directly up her nose. Not her best angle. She stopped outside. Stevie leaned in and caught the sound of voices, but the audio was way too muffled to make out what was being said.

"Okay, Blair's shouting, 'But I do know!'" Colby said, her face puzzled, then concerned. *"She sounds distressed. I think I should go in and check she's all right—"*

The camera suddenly swung downward and there was a *"Hey! What are you doing in here?!"* Then the screen went blank before cutting back to Colby sitting in her bedroom.

"As you can see, something was definitely going down in Blair's dressing room on the afternoon of her unaliving. I don't know who was in the room with her, but I think it could have been her murderer! Unfortunately, there was a little confusion as to who I was and a member of Blair's staff moved me on before I could discover what was going on with Blair. You can imagine the guilt I feel at not having done more." Colby swallowed, then looked upward. *"Blair, I want you to know that I am so sorry, and I love you. We all love you."*

Stevie slumped back against the headboard, the laptop hot on her legs. What on earth had she just seen? Colby, for all her dramatics, might be right. Whoever was in that room arguing with Blair could have been the one who killed her. This could be an actual lead—Stevie clasped her hands together but couldn't stop the tremor that was running through them.

First thing in the morning, she'd pay Colby Green a visit and ask her some questions about the preconcert party Blair had apparently said she'd attend. And about who the hell was in Blair's dressing room.

Seven

Colby Green answered the door dressed head to toe in black. Stevie gave her a slow once-over. Black skirt, black top, black nail polish with little pink *BB* details on each finger, and black friendship bracelets on her wrists with *RIP BB* printed on the plastic beads. Someone was serious about their mourning.

It was early. Too early to be knocking on somebody's door. Stevie hadn't slept well and had woken up just before five crying. She'd woken up in the same way for a year after Mia had vanished. She was better at keeping her feelings reined in during the day, but in that time between awake and asleep, she was always defenseless.

She'd wanted to stay in bed. Maybe forever. Visions of Blair—of the man with the long coat and baseball cap, pinning her down. But when Catsy had kept pushing that concerned, insistent nose of hers into Stevie's side, she made herself get up, reminding herself she had a job to do—a lead to follow. She busied herself texting acquaintances to find Colby's address, then writing down notes about suspects, placing Gunner Trip and the stalker at the top of the list and Colby Green at the bottom. Not because she really thought Colby was the murderer, but because a suspect list of two seemed a bit weak. Besides, Colby had been in the concert venue the day Blair had been killed, and Blair hadn't gone to her party, so there was a possibility she was involved.

She'd also checked the Blair Baker fan page again and saw that Colby had posted about a candlelight vigil for Blair in two days, which she'd organized. Maybe Stevie should have thought about doing something like that—Blair was *her* sister—but to be honest, she just couldn't face another vigil. Could someone be vigiled out? *Yes*, she thought, *they could.* There had been three for Mia—one after she had gone missing, then again on the first and second anniversary of her disappearance, and she'd never drawn any comfort from them.

At six a.m., she slipped out the house, leaving her mom crying in her room upstairs and her dad trying his best to comfort her. She couldn't stay with all that pain—couldn't let it keep tugging at her own. She stepped out the back door and breathed in a lungful of air. The sun was just rising, casting a soft golden light across the dew-covered lawn. It was already warm, and the sky was clear. Wrong, really, for the world to carry on being so beautiful.

She'd climb over the garden wall to avoid the paparazzi out front. Jimmy was right that they'd be back—they'd arrived just after she had woken up. Vans of them, with their cameras and mics, hungry for a story. Officer Dean had been replaced and now three cop cars were stationed outside the front yard.

She ignored Dean's advice about being out alone and walked to Colby's, rather than drive, to kill some time. No one would be stupid enough to attack her in the daylight, out in the open. Still, she jumped when a man and his dog passed her on a morning run.

She loitered on the path outside Colby's house, planning what to say, until she convinced herself that seven was a reasonable enough time to knock—she was conducting a murder investigation after all.

Stevie turned her phone to silent and waited.

A few minutes later, Colby answered the door with a yawn. "Hi?" Then her eyes flew open when she recognized who was on her doorstep. She pointed a finger at Stevie. "You're . . . you're Stevie Baker."

"I am," Stevie said. Ugh, she was going to get all ridiculous because she was Blair's sister, wasn't she? Better not to give her a chance. "Look, I wondered if—"

Colby cut her off. "Oh my god!" Then she burst into tears and flung her arms around her. "I am so sorry for your loss. I'm so, so sorry. I don't know what to say. It's all so awful."

Stevie stood motionless, her hands in her pockets—a sobbing Colby clamped on to her. A lump formed in her throat. No. She would not think about her loss. And she wouldn't allow Colby Green's unexpected kindness to make her cry. She was there to ask questions—she didn't want sympathy.

She leaned backward, tapped Colby on the back twice. So awkward. Surely, she'd get the message?

Colby gave her a squeeze, then pulled away, her face wet and puffy. "I can't believe it's real. I saw it all happen, I was right there, but I keep thinking that it's some terrible dream." She seemed genuinely upset. Definitely more genuine than in her videos.

Stevie cleared her throat. "I'm looking into what happened. I'm not prepared to leave it up to Honeyville PD to work out who killed Blair. I saw your vlog post. I have a few questions I'd like to ask you about what you saw and what you knew about Blair."

"Oh my god, of course! You can ask me anything." Colby put her arm around Stevie. "Come inside."

Colby's place had a new, almost unlived-in feel to it. The walls were white and bare, the carpet a functional gray. There were no photos or pictures or plants . . . or much sign of any life, really. None of the general clutter of stuff that a family usually accumulates. Unlike the Baker house, which was crammed full of the trinkets and ornaments that Marnie—the whole family—had collected over the years. The walls in Stevie's home were plastered with photos—of her and Hal and Blair at various ages, of Marnie and Frank's wedding, of dead grandparents. Of Mia. You could walk into the Baker residence and get a pretty good handle on the whole family. Colby's house offered up nothing.

"This is nice. Very minimalist," Stevie said, because she should probably say something.

Colby smiled. "Thanks. Mom's not big on décor. She won the lottery a few years ago and she bought this house. We haven't ever really done much with it though. But it's a *lot* better than our last place."

"The lottery? Wow. I didn't think anyone won that."

"Apparently, they do." Colby pointed to a photo frame on a windowsill at the top of the stairs, the one photo in the whole house, by the looks of it. A woman, who had made some exceptionally bold make-up choices, was holding a large bank check made out to Faith Green for eight hundred thousand dollars and smiling maniacally. "Mom insisted on me taking a picture—she said no one would believe her otherwise."

"Wow," Stevie repeated.

Colby pushed open a door. "This is me."

Stevie braced herself to walk into some Blair Baker shrine, but Colby's room did not have the psycho-fan aesthetic that Stevie was expecting. There wasn't a single poster of Blair on the walls, just one framed photo on the nightstand of Blair and Colby—Blair on a red carpet and Colby leaning across the rope toward her. There was a bulletin board of old Blair Baker concert tickets and a desk pushed up against the back wall, a laptop with a ring light attached. Lastly, there were piles of little black beads on the carpet.

"So, this is where you make your death merch," Stevie said.

"My what?" Colby looked at her, confused.

Too blunt, too mean—she didn't know why she'd said it. She gestured at Colby's wrist. "Your bracelets."

Colby looked at her wrist. "I stayed up making them last night. I was home on my own and I just didn't know what else to do."

"That and organizing a vigil. Busy night for you."

"Blair deserves to be remembered. She meant so much to so many people." A tear ran down Colby's face as she took hold of Stevie's hands and slipped a Blair death bracelet onto her wrist. "You should have one."

Stevie glanced down at her wrist. Yup. She would not be keeping that on for long.

"You should speak at the vigil!" Colby said, like it was the best idea in the world.

Stevie pulled a face—no way was that going to happen. All those people looking at her . . .

"Or not, if you think it would be too hard."

"Could we maybe get to your video?" Stevie was not about to go soul-searching with Colby.

"Of course. Take a seat." Colby sat down on her bed and gestured toward a pink beanbag chair. Stevie lowered herself into it, rustled about trying to get comfortable. Not the optimal position to conduct a murder interrogation, but it would have to do.

"So you were outside Blair's dressing room on the day she was murdered. I was wondering if you could tell me about what you saw, what you heard."

"It's pretty much like you saw on the vlog. I heard Blair arguing with someone." Colby looked at the wall behind Stevie. "I won't ever forgive myself for not going in there and helping her. Maybe if—"

"It wasn't your fault," Stevie said quickly. *If*s were the route to madness. "Did you recognize the voice? Could it have been Gunner Trip?"

"It was a man. I think. Maybe. I'm not sure. It *could* have been Gunner Trip. That's who I first thought, but I'm not one hundred percent certain. Maybe fifty percent. No, like, forty-six percent."

Stevie raised an eyebrow. "'Forty-six percent certain'?"

"Something like that. But it doesn't make sense. Gunner loved her. He said so in his interview in *Stars Align*. They were the perfect couple. He can't have killed her."

"Well, if that's what *Stars Align* said, he definitely didn't do it."

Stevie was being sarcastic, but Colby took it at face value. "That's what I thought!"

"He wasn't at the concert though," Stevie said.

"What? Really?"

"The police are looking for him to see if he has an alibi."

Colby's mouth dropped open. "Oh. My. *God!*"

"Which is why I think it's important to work out if he was the one Blair was arguing with. But forty-six percent certain doesn't really cut it. In your video, you said Blair was shouting the words 'But I do know.' What do you think she meant by that?"

Colby exhaled. "I've been thinking about that. I'm not sure. Maybe she was telling whoever was in there that she knew something about them."

"And if that something was bad, that could be a motive to kill her," Stevie said, thinking out loud. "You didn't hear anything else?"

Colby shook her head. "Sorry, no."

"Did you see anything else? Anyone going into her dressing room? Anyone hanging around, looking suspicious?"

Colby shook her head. "No, I don't think so."

"A man in a long coat and a baseball cap? Big guy."

Colby's eyes widened, confused and searching. "A man in a coat and baseball cap?"

Stevie's jaw tightened. "Yes, did you see him?"

"No, no one like that. Who are you talking about? Do you think that's who killed her?"

"I don't know, but he was watching my house last night."

"What the hell?" Colby said, eyes unblinking.

"Could I watch the footage you took? I'm assuming there's more than what you posted?"

Colby held her breath for a second, then let the air out in one puff. "Errr . . ."

"What is it?" Stevie tried to lean forward, but the stupid beanbag fought against her.

Colby clapped her hands together, then steepled them under her chin. "Right. Well. Yes. You can. But you have to promise me that what I show you stays between us."

"I'm not sure if I can do that. What if you show me something that incriminates someone? I can't keep that to myself."

"The only person it incriminates is me."

Stevie frowned. "What do you mean, *incriminates you*?"

Colby shifted in her seat. "It's just that I might not have been completely, one hundred percent truthful about how I came to be outside Blair's dressing room."

Stevie raised an eyebrow. Oh boy, what now? "So, what, you were, like, forty-six percent truthful?"

"Ooh, maybe a little lower than that. Look, the thing is, when I said I was invited to see Blair, that wasn't strictly true."

Stevie tilted her head, stayed silent, waited for her to go on.

"It wasn't strictly true in that it was a lie. Blair didn't invite me. I snuck into the arena. But in my defense, I couldn't not try to see her, not when she was right here in my hometown."

"But you told your followers that she'd asked you, for a bit of social media clout?"

"I had to do something after Blair didn't come to the preconcert party I'd planned. Let's just say I'd gotten a fair bit of online backlash. I thought that a video of me and Blair at the arena would shut the trolls up."

"You must have been pretty disappointed that Blair didn't show at the party." Stevie tried to sound sympathetic so Colby wouldn't realize that she was trying to figure out whether Colby had a motive.

Colby saw right through her. "Not upset enough to kill her, if that's what you mean. I'm not insane."

"I didn't think you had." Little bit of a lie.

"Look, I'll show you on the condition that you don't post anything about me making the invite up."

"Sure. Don't worry about it. I don't post on social media anyway."

Colby looked at her, askance. "Really?"

"Yeah, really." Stevie nodded at the laptop. "Now, show me what you've got."

Colby went over to her MacBook and brought up the video while Stevie struggled her way out of the beanbag.

Her eyes widened when she saw Colby's image on the screen. "What the hell are you wearing? Are you dressed up as a teddy bear?"

Colby's cheeks pinked. "I dressed up as a mascot so I could sneak in."

Stevie grinned. "I can see how that would work, very inconspicuous. I didn't notice the costume in the video you posted though."

"That's because I took the bear head off as soon as I was in and I was careful to only film my face."

"Honestly, I admire your dedication to your content creation." Stevie pressed Play on the video and watched the footage that she'd seen the night before, but this time it didn't end when security moved Colby on. Instead, the camera waved about furiously, swinging between shots of Colby's furry teddy bear legs and torso, and the corridor behind her, as she tried to outrun the security guard.

"There!" Stevie said. She stopped the video. "Look!"

On the screen behind Colby's frozen face was Blair's dressing-room door.

And someone coming out of it.

Eight

"Are you sure you can't zoom in any closer?" Stevie asked.

Colby scrunched up her nose. "I don't think closer is going to help. I can't even see what you're looking at now—it's just a load of pixels. It could be anyone."

Stevie flopped down on Colby's bed. "You're right. The video quality is garbage. It could be someone from the crew, her manager, the guy delivering sandwiches."

"Yup, but I honestly don't think that's Gunner," Colby said. "He doesn't look big enough. Gunner Trip is really big. You know, gladiator big. Look."

Colby waved her phone in front of Stevie's face. There was a photo of Gunner Trip, shirtless and carrying a bale of hay on each shoulder, and looking exceedingly happy about it.

"You just have that on your phone, ready to go like that?"

"No! I searched!"

"Sure you did."

Colby waggled her eyebrows. "But lucky Blair, right?"

Lucky Blair? Stevie raised her eyebrows, and Colby, realizing what she'd just said, clapped her hands to her cheeks.

"I can't believe I just said that! Not lucky Blair. Not lucky Blair at all! Stevie, I am *so* sorry!"

"It's okay." Stevie looked down, picked at her fingernails.

"No, it's really not!" Colby looked properly horrified. "I. Am. Mortified."

"Your mortification is noted," Stevie said, eager to move on.

"And I think you're right."

Colby looked back at her phone and sighed. "I mean, yeah, Gunner is one fine piece of ass."

"Get your head out the gutter, Colby." Stevie pointed at the computer screen. "I meant you're right about him. I'm not exactly getting 'carries around hay bales for fun' from whoever that guy is. He doesn't look tall enough." Not the guy in the long coat or baseball cap either, then.

Colby fell backward onto the bed and covered her face with the pillow, let out a muffled "What is wrong with me?"

Less than Stevie had expected, actually. Colby wasn't quite the crazed fan she thought she'd be. Okay, so she was a little bit crazy, but she was also kind of *nice*. Stevie pulled Colby up by her hands. "I should probably send your footage to the police."

"Ugh. God. Yes. Okay. They can all have a good laugh at me dressed as the Honey Grizz."

"It's for the greater good."

"If it isn't Gunner Trip, do you think it could be that guy in the long coat?" Colby asked.

"He was second on my list, but he was big too. I guess it's likely Blair had more than one stalker."

"Stalkers are the worst!" Colby said.

A smile flickered on Stevie's lips. *Stalkers are the worst?* Had she seriously just said that?

"And third on your list?" Colby continued.

"I don't think I have a third anymore," Stevie said airily, her cheeks reddening. Colby might have been able to sneak into the arena disguised as a bear, but she was not giving off murderer vibes. And she was arguing with the security guard when Stevie went into the stadium—she couldn't have had time to sneak in and shoot Blair. Besides, there was no way she would have been able to hide a gun in that purple outfit Stevie saw her wearing later.

A door slammed downstairs. Stevie jumped, her heart lurching before her brain caught up. She let out a slow breath. Clearly, she was still on edge from the night before.

"Colby!"

Colby closed her eyes briefly. "Oh no. That's my mom."

"Your mom," Stevie repeated. It annoyed her how her nerves were too close to the surface.

A moment later, the bedroom door flew open and Colby's mom swung into the room, holding on to the doorframe like she might topple over if she didn't. She was wearing tight jeans and a black lace-up top and swaying ever so slightly. Her updo looked like it was trying incredibly hard not to become a downdo. "Colby, Mommy needs a coffee. Mommy needs a lot of coffee!" Her eyes fell on Stevie, and she pointed a wavering finger at her. "Who are you?"

Colby's mom was drunk, or had been drunk very recently.

"She's a friend, Mom," Colby said, her voice stoney.

Stevie did not want to be around for this. She got up from the bed. "I should probably go. Colby, thanks—"

"Where've you been?" Colby said, her eyes fixed on her mom.

"I've been out." The words all ran into each other like a smudge.

"You went out three days ago," Colby said, jaw tense.

Stevie's eyes ping-ponged between them. She and Marnie had their spats, but nothing like this. And it was Marnie doing the questioning.

"What can I say—I lose track of time when I'm with Mike. I tell you, that man!"

"You didn't answer my messages. You could have picked up the phone."

Well, this was awkward. Stevie hovered by the bed, desperate to leave, but not quite sure how to. Could she squeeze around Colby's mom? Would that be rude? Did it matter? All she knew was that she did not want to be in the middle of some family argument.

"You're seventeen! Old enough to look after yourself! I was out having a life, Colly-boo! You should try it sometime. I don't know, maybe get yourself a boyfriend rather than obsessing over that damn Blair Baker." Colby's mom cupped her hand next to her mouth and whispered loudly at Stevie, "I think my daughter might be a *les-bi-an*."

A waft of stale wine breath hit Stevie square in the face. God, this woman was a piece of work. Stevie's eyes flicked to Colby—her cheeks were flushed with embarrassment and she looked like she might cry.

Stevie turned to Colby's mom and said brightly, "I think you mentioned coffee. Let's get you some coffee."

Faith Green was asleep on the couch before the kettle had even boiled. Colby hadn't said much since they'd helped her mom down the stairs. It was actually impressive that she'd managed to get up them by herself in the first place.

"She'll be out for ages now," Colby said, both hands around a cup of coffee that was meant for her mom. "You won't tell anyone, will you?" Her eyes didn't meet Stevie's.

"No. Of course not." Stevie would never—she knew how it cut to have family business spread around.

"Thank you," Colby said. Then she sighed. "I bet you get along great with your mom, don't you?"

Stevie bit her lip, not quite sure how to answer. People said that parents weren't supposed to have favorites, but Marnie had never quite managed to hide the fact she favored Blair. Stevie resented her for that, and maybe Marnie resented the fact that Blair was never around and Stevie was. Maybe it was why they often rubbed each other the wrong way.

"Yeah, we get along great." Stevie checked the time on her phone. It was coming up on ten o'clock. "I should probably go. Got a murder to solve and all." She sounded casual, but the words tugged at her chest.

Colby looked up now. "I want to help."

"Oh . . . I don't know." Did she want Colby hanging around while she was trying to conduct a murder investigation? Probably not the best idea.

"I have, like, zero plans for summer break . . . other than hanging out at the mall or the beach."

"Those sound great—you should do those." Stevie didn't have any plans either. Other than a study group Marnie had signed her up for, but that probably wouldn't be happening now.

Colby spread her hands. "Hear me out. I literally know everything there is to know about Blair Baker. You need me. I run the fan page, and I get all sorts of weirdos posting crap. If a stalker did kill her, maybe they've visited my site. I can take a look through the comments, see if anything stands out."

Oh god. That actually wasn't a bad thought. And it was probable that Colby did know more about parts of her sister's life than she did.

"It may take a while, but I can go through all her past boyfriends, find out where they all were last night. Look into all the rumors of secret lovers."

"Secret lovers? Blair didn't have a secret lover, did she? She was dating Gunner Trip." Stevie hadn't ever been able to bring herself to read any of the salacious stories that were written about her sister. But if Blair did have a secret lover, they'd be a suspect.

Colby shrugged. "Who knows? There's always been rumors. I could see if I can find anything out. And besides, don't you think Stevie and Colby has that detective-duo ring to it?"

Stevie blinked twice. She did not think that at all.

"Please, let me do something to help." Colby glanced at her mom flat out on the couch. "I really think I'd be useful."

"Fine, you can help." Stevie could always cut her loose if she turned into a problem.

Colby leapt up and flung her arms around her neck. "Stevie and Colby, the detective duo!"

"If you say that again," Stevie said, pulling Colby's arms away, "you're out."

Nine

Stevie turned the corner at the end of Colby's road and pulled out her phone. Her heart tripped—there were a bunch of missed calls from her dad. He must have news. She took a breath before calling back.

"Little Bear, thank goodness—"

The concern in his voice was cut off by Marnie shouting in the background. "Is that her? Where is she?"

"I went for a walk. I'm heading back now."

"She went for a walk," Frank relayed back.

"A walk?!" came Marnie's incredulous response. "Tell her we've been worried sick!"

"Where are you? I'll come and pick you up," Frank said.

"It's okay—I'm not far away."

"I don't want you out on your own. Jimmy just filled us in about what happened last night—the man in the street. Oh, Stevie, why didn't you wake us?"

He sounded so broken.

Guilt twinged in Stevie's stomach. "I'm sorry. I didn't want to worry you—not on top of everything. Honestly, I'm fine—I'll be home soon."

"Stevie, we're your parents—worrying is just what we do."

"Is she okay?" Marnie again, loud, voice shaking with emotion.

"Your mother wants to know if you're okay."

No, not really. "I'm fine." They were such meaningless words, but she didn't want to address how she was actually feeling because if she did, she risked being swallowed up by grief. "Has Jimmy found out who he was?"

"He's looking into it. But it was likely just some ghoul—a 'tragedy tourist,' Jimmy called him. Still, I want you to be careful."

"I will. Did Jimmy have any other news?" Stevie said.

"Lord knows what they're doing down at the station, but they still haven't located Gunner Trip."

"Have they put out a public announcement?"

"Oh, believe me, I pressed Jimmy on that. He doesn't want to turn the investigation into a media circus. He's been talking to Gunner's agent—thinks he can get ahold of him that way. But I told Jimmy, if Gunner doesn't show up soon, I'll go to the papers myself. The longer Gunner Trip's AWOL, the more guilty he looks."

Stevie nodded to herself in agreement.

"Are you going to be long? Kirk Tyler is sending a car around. He wants to have a 'crisis meeting.' I'm not saying you have to come, but I wanted to let you know where we are."

"I'll come. I'll be home in ten." Stevie wanted to be there. Kirk *was* Blair's manager. Maybe he knew something. Hell, maybe he even did it. Though that seemed unlikely—Blair was too valuable to him. Still, she could show him the video of the man leaving Blair's dressing room and see how he reacted. Maybe he'd be able to identify him. And she could also ask him why his security team had been so bad at their jobs.

Stevie weaved her way through the crowd of reporters, head down. Nobody noticed her, all too busy pointing their cameras at a blacked-out SUV parked in the driveway.

She made it to the edge of her front lawn just as her parents, flanked by Jimmy and Officer Dean, emerged from the house. The shouts and camera flashes started up immediately. Frank and

Marnie held their hands to their eyes, shielding themselves from the glare. Jimmy shouted at everyone to back away as he steered her parents toward the SUV. Stevie tried to push her way through the throng, but someone grabbed her arm.

She swung around, eyes blazing. Hilton-asshat-Moore.

She tore her arm out of his grip. "What do you want?"

He pressed a card into her hand. "If you want to speak."

Stevie glared at him. She'd rather cut her tongue out than speak to anybody from the press. She stuffed the card in her pocket, turned away, and elbowed her way through the bodies.

She was shoved from side to side as everyone clamored to get closer to the car. A woman in a red suit moved, and through the gap, Stevie saw him again—the man she'd seen the night before, this time standing among the reporters. No coat this time, no baseball cap. A shirt and slacks. Dark hair in a center part. But his size—the way he held himself. She froze. Ice pricked at her neck. He was just standing there, a few feet away, no mic in his hand, no cameraman nearby. Just standing and watching. So still. Like he had been the night before. It was him. It had to be him.

Someone knocked her, propelling her into action. She had to get to him—find out who he was. She pushed herself forward, trying to force a path through, but there were too many people! *Get out the way. Get out the way!* Where was he? She spun around, trying to get eyes on him. Had he gone? Too many freaking bodies! Too small to see over them. She made for the front lawn, away from the car, where there weren't so many reporters. She burst free of the throng, lost her footing. The grass rushed up at her and she landed face-first, right next to one of Marnie's ornamental roosters.

"I've got you!" A pair of strong hands scooped her up under the armpits, turned her around, and for some inexplicable reason presented her to the lenses.

The camera flashes went crazy—the lawn diver was one of the Bakers! The sister!

"Don't worry—I'll get you out of here!" Officer Dean was half dragging, half carrying her toward the car.

"No! Stop! You need to listen! The man! The man!" Her voice was swallowed up in all the noise. "The man!"

She was thrown in the back of the car, the door slamming shut behind her. Outside the window, Officer Dean was saluting her from the driveway. Yeah, technically, he had helped her out, but hadn't he heard what she'd said?! The man was right there!

"Stevie, did you fall?" Marnie was looking at her, bewildered, her eyes still red and puffy.

Well, yes, she had, but that wasn't important. "I saw him! I saw the man!" The words tumbled out of her.

"What man, Little Bear?" Frank said.

"The man from last night. The one I saw watching our house."

Marnie gasped, a tremble in her chin. "He was out there?"

"Yes!" Obviously.

Frank took out his phone, voice serious. "Jimmy? Stevie thinks that guy she saw outside the house last night is out there with the reporters. Can you see if you can get eyes on him?" Frank nodded his head—Jimmy's voice tinny on the other end of the phone.

"Uh-huh. I know. But just check it out for me, won't you?"

Frank hung up.

"What did he say?" Stevie asked.

"He said they've been keeping a close eye—doesn't think there's anyone that matches his description. But if he's there, they'll find him."

No one matching his description? How could they not have seen him?

"He was there," Stevie said, certain now.

Frank's phone rang again. "Okay. Yes . . . I'll show her now—hang on."

"Show me what?" Stevie asked.

A message pinged through. Frank held up his phone. "Is this him? Is this the man you just saw?"

Stevie grabbed the phone from Frank's hands. "Yes, that's him!"

Frank pursed his lips and watched her. "Stevie, that's Declan MacGregor from Channel Fourteen News."

She shook her head. "What? He didn't have a mic . . . a camera . . ."

"If he's the man you saw last night, we don't think he's involved in Blair's death. He wasn't even in the state when she was killed. Got here early this morning." Frank's voice was gentle, like he was worried he might break her.

It took a moment for the information to settle. For her to understand what it meant. "Then the person I saw was someone different."

"Yes, maybe, Little Bear."

What did he mean, *maybe*?

Frank raised the phone to his ear. "Okay, Stevie thinks it may be someone else she saw. I know . . . I know . . . So is there any news on Gunner Trip? Okay . . . I know you are. Keep in touch."

Frank hung up, shot Marnie a look. Stevie knew what it meant. All those times she'd sworn she'd seen Mia. And hadn't she believed someone was watching the house then, too? But it wasn't like that now. Her mind hadn't broken like it had then.

"I saw a man watching the house last night. I know I did."

A look from Frank to Marnie again. "I believe you, Stevie, but even if there was someone outside the house, he might just be someone awful who takes delight in watching this sort of thing. Jimmy will look into it, but right now his priority has to be locating Gunner Trip."

Stevie turned away, looked out the window. Her nerves, still too close to the surface, had caused her to make a mistake. And now her parents doubted what she'd seen the night before.

But she knew she hadn't gotten this wrong.

Kirk Tyler was staying at Sable and Stone Manor, an upscale inn on the outskirts of town with views of the lake. It claimed to be five-star, and maybe it was thirty years ago, but it was a little tired now. Still, it was the best Honeyville had to offer, and Kirk Tyler had taken the largest room on the top floor.

Bex Lyons opened the door, spoke formally. "Thank you for coming. I'll take you through to Mr. Tyler."

Kirk was sitting on a couch, laptop in front of him. He snapped the lid shut when he saw the Bakers but addressed Bex first.

"Any press outside?"

"Two TV crews, by the looks of it. They must have followed the car."

"The driver did their best to lose them," Stevie said.

"He certainly did," Marnie muttered. The drive had been a little intense. Marnie had interspersed her sobs with cries of fear and had made her way through an entire pack of tissues. Frank seemed oblivious to the erratic driving—too focused on cussing out Jimmy for failing to find Gunner Trip. Stevie had spent the journey thinking about the man in the coat—he *was* real; she had seen him—and about the person who Blair had been arguing with in her dressing room. If Kirk Tyler knew who he was, then she might be close to finding her sister's killer.

Kirk gestured at the couch opposite him. "Please, take a seat."

Stevie sat, squashed between her parents, while Kirk leaned back, arm draped over the side of his own couch.

"This is an extremely challenging time for us all," he began.

Stevie's lip curled at the oily lilt of his voice. In that moment she hated him. He had taken Blair away from them. And it was his security team who hadn't done their jobs. Hadn't protected Blair.

"How could you let this happen?" Her words came out hot and angry.

"I am as devastated as you are about Blair's death."

Frank rounded on him. "That wasn't what she asked. And I'd like to know the answer too. How, with all your security, did someone get into that room below the stage and murder my daughter?"

Kirk leaned forward, fingertips pressed together. "The security team followed protocol. Undoubtedly, there were some lapses in judgment, and all I can do is offer my sincerest apology for—"

"I'm not here for an apology," Frank snarled. "I'm here for answers."

"And as I said before, Satellite Entertainment is doing everything we can to help the police with the investigation. If it transpires that we are at fault in any way, we will accept the consequences."

Frank ground his teeth together, turned his head like he couldn't stand to look at the man.

"The reason I wanted to bring you here is to offer my assistance. I want us all to be clear about the best way to proceed. Dealing with the public interest is going to require thought and consideration."

Marnie clawed at the crumpled tissue she was holding. "I don't want to think about the public."

"I'm here to do the thinking for you, and I think you should issue a statement . . . and quickly. Get some of the hacks off your back. I've taken the liberty of getting a draft written up." He gestured to Bex, and she handed a piece of paper to Frank.

"It's very standard. A bit about Blair and how heartbroken you are. Then some stuff about people respecting your need for privacy at this difficult time."

"Nothing about this is standard," Frank muttered.

"No. Of course it's not." Kirk looked sincere for a moment. "But please do not mistake my professionalism for a lack of concern for you all. Everything I'm doing is in your best interest. Let me handle the press—you have enough to worry about already."

"The things they're saying about Hal," Marnie said, her voice wobbling. "Can you do something about that?"

"We can add something to the statement about the whole family standing together, supporting the police to help find Blair's killer. Send me some photos of Hal and Blair when they were kids—any videos, too. Does he have socials?"

Marnie and Frank both looked confused so Stevie said, "He does, but he doesn't really use them."

"We can sort something out. He should post his own statement too. I'll get someone to write it for him."

"I don't know about this," Frank said. "It feels wrong to do this without Hal."

"He can check over what we've written. We won't post anything without his blessing."

Frank ran his hand over his chin. "I don't know—"

Marnie leaned across Stevie and grabbed his hand. "Please, Frank, Kirk knows what he's doing. Hal needs protecting."

Frank sighed heavily. "Fine. You write your statements."

A faint smile played on Kirk's lips. He nodded at Bex, and she got out her phone and started typing.

"Any news on the investigation? I hear Gunner Trip hasn't been found," Kirk said. "I suppose that makes him the number one suspect."

"I suppose it does," Frank said, noncommittal.

Stevie saw her chance. "Unless there was someone else who might have had a reason to kill Blair. You mentioned Blair had a stalker."

"She's had a lot of stalkers, some more persistent than others."

Stevie pulled out her phone. There were five messages from Colby on the screen. All starting, Oh. My. God! Stevie swiped them away—she'd look at them later. "Here's a video, see, taken on the afternoon of Blair's murder. It shows someone coming out of Blair's dressing room after they'd had an argument."

"Where did you get that?" Marnie said, eyes wide.

"On the internet," Stevie said, quickly pushing herself up to show Kirk.

She watched him carefully as she handed her phone over. "I wondered if you recognized them?"

Kirk studied the picture, and Stevie studied him, to see if there was a glimmer of recognition, or if he made a *crap, that's me* face. There was neither. He just looked up and said, "It's very blurry. That could be anyone."

"Have you shown Jimmy that?" Frank asked.

"Yes. No. I mean, I meant to but got distracted. I'll do it ASAP." Stevie turned back to Kirk. "Do you think it could be Blair's stalker?"

Marnie sniffed into her tissue. "Do we have to talk about this right now?"

"Please, Mr. Tyler, do you think it could be her stalker?" Stevie pressed.

"I suppose it's possible, but security was very tight that day. I doubt anyone we didn't know could have gotten in."

Anyone, apart from a fan in a Honey Grizz mascot suit and a murderer.

"And what about a man in a baseball cap and coat? A big guy."

Out the corner of her eye: a quick look from Frank to Marnie.

"I'm sorry, not that I'm aware of. I've sent all correspondence from Blair's stalker to the police already. Not light reading, I'm afraid."

"Did you know that Blair had an argument with someone the

91

day she died, likely the person in that video?" Stevie pressed.

"Blair had an argument?" Marnie said, dabbing her eyes with her crumpled tissue. "Stevie, how do you know all this?"

Stevie kept her focus on Kirk. "Did anyone tell you they heard Blair arguing with a man in her dressing room? A security guard, maybe?"

"No, I didn't get any reports of anything like that. Bex, did you hear anything?"

Bex shook her head. "No, Mr. Tyler." Her face was blank—gave away nothing.

Stevie studied Kirk carefully, trying to see if he looked uncomfortable, if he could be hiding anything, but he seemed to take Stevie's concerns seriously.

"Bex, do me a favor. Speak to the crew. See if anyone heard anything. I know you've given a copy to the police already, but take a look at the sign-in sheet, see who was in the arena that afternoon."

He handed the phone back to Stevie. There was another message from Colby. Sheesh, she was persistent.

"Send that video to your uncle now," Frank said.

Stevie typed out a message, attached the video, and held the phone up so he could hear the message-sent ping.

Kirk lounged back on the couch. "Stevie, I can understand why you want to look into this. Of course, it may be nothing, but if I find anything out about an unexpected visitor or an argument, I will be sure to let the police know. Please believe me when I say that everyone here at Satellite Entertainment is committed to fully cooperating with the investigation. Honeyville PD has asked us to stay in town for a few days so we're here to answer any questions. Blair was family, and family sticks together. If there's anything you need, anything at all, don't hesitate to call me."

"That's very kind of you," Marnie said.

Frank said, "Yes," which was about as much as Kirk was going to get from him.

Kirk got to his feet. "I'll have a car take you back home." He shook Frank's and Marnie's hands, then Stevie's. He held on to hers longer, noticing her bracelet.

"Yeah, it's like an RIP bracelet thing," Stevie said, a little embarrassed.

Kirk nodded, muttered quietly to himself, "Very marketable." He lifted Stevie's wrist. "Bex, look at this—we should do these— add them to the official merchandise."

Stevie snatched her hand away.

Kirk turned back to Frank and Marnie. "You know Blair's albums are all doing incredible sales at the moment. I know it doesn't bring her back, but it's a real demonstration of how loved she was."

"No," Stevie said, "it doesn't bring her back."

In the elevator down to the foyer, Stevie read through her messages from Colby.

Oh. My. God! Call me.

Oh. My. God! Call me NOW!

Oh. My. God! Where are you?!

Oh. My. God!!!! Did you fall on your face? Who's the cute cop that scooped you up? Actually, that is not top priority right now! CALL ME!

Oh. My. God! I know where you are. I'm coming to get you!

OK! I'm outside!

A blast of the horn sounded as Stevie finished reading the last message. Colby was leaning out of her car—a beat-up Honda Civic covered in dents—waving like crazy at her across the hotel parking lot.

"Do you know her?" Marnie said.

Stevie hesitated, a small, awkward smile tugging at her lips. "Yeah . . . I'm gonna see what she wants."

Stevie poked her head in through the window. "How did you know I was here?"

Colby beamed at her. "From Hilton's *Got Moore News* TikTok. There's a video of you falling face down on the lawn outside your house. I saw the SUV, figured someone from Satellite Entertainment came to get you. Then I drove here, because where else would a top music exec stay in Honeyville?"

"There's a video of me on TikTok?"

"That is what you take from all my excellent detective work?"

"Sorry, yeah. Well, good job on finding me."

"If you're impressed by that, you're going to be even more impressed by what I tell you next."

"Go on."

"I know where Gunner Trip is."

Ten

Kirk Tyler's SUV driver could be considered cautious in comparison to Colby. She was an actual maniac behind the wheel.

"How the hell did you pass your driver's license test?" Stevie asked as Colby ran her third stop sign.

"Fluttered my eyelashes, showed a bit of leg."

"And set the feminist movement back a couple of years in the process?"

Colby laughed and shrugged. "Maybe! But I'm sure your protest against make-up cancels that out."

"I am not protesting against make-up—I just don't wear much. And, for your information, feminists believe you can do whatever you want to your own face."

"Cool. Sign me up as a feminist, then!"

Stevie rolled her eyes. "So how did you find out that Gunner was at the Rising Sun Motel?"

"BBfankittygalore told me."

"Excuse me?"

"She's a member of the Blair Baker fan site. I put the question out about Gunner Trip's whereabouts on the blog and she answered. I figured if Gunner Trip was somewhere around town, someone would have noticed. BBfankittygalore's brother works in the gas station opposite the motel—he saw Gunner Trip go in there after he bought a slushie. An ICEE."

"He didn't tell the police?"

"About the drink?"

"That he'd seen Gunner!"

"I know. I was joking. There's been no public announcement that the police want to talk to him, so why would he? We know though, so maybe we should phone the cops."

"We will. Just after we've spoken to him first." Stevie shook her head. "I can't believe you managed to do what Honeyville PD couldn't."

"It wasn't hard."

"It wasn't hard for *you*. Thanks."

Colby smiled. "You're welcome."

Stevie grabbed her seat as Colby took a bend too sharply. "It is a bit weird that he's staying in some run-down motel though. Wouldn't a star NFL player stay somewhere fancy? It's not like he's short for cash."

"Maybe he's in hiding!" Colby turned to look at Stevie, the car swerving with her. "You know, if he did it, we're essentially delivering ourselves into the hands of a murderer."

Stevie hadn't really considered that—wasn't sure if she actually cared. She just wanted to find out what had happened to her sister.

"Roadside motels are prime spots for killing!" Colby said, eyes lighting up.

"And yet, you seem excited by that?"

"Not excited, exactly, but it beats staying at home, feeling miserable and making bracelets—that's for sure."

Stevie's lips pulled into a brief smile. "True, but let's be serious for a moment. Are we doing the right thing? What if he does get all murder-y on us?"

"It's the middle of the day. There's two of us. He's not going to try anything. Besides, I never travel without my rape alarm and pepper spray. So don't worry; I'll protect you."

"You weigh, like, a hundred and ten pounds, and I can't see you fending off an attack in those." Stevie pointed at Colby's black-heeled cowboy boots.

"These? These are my fast boots. One time, when I forgot running shoes, Coach Tranmore made me wear these babies. I beat Alison Garcia over four hundred meters *and* she's on the track team."

"Her fast boots," Stevie said to herself. "Right."

Colby pulled into the Rising Sun Motel, or "sin Motel," according to the letters that were still lit up on the neon sign. She made no real effort to actually position her car in a parking space and left it straddling two. They got out and Stevie put her hands on her hips and looked around. It was a two-story building, set in a U shape with the parking lot in the center. There must have been at least eighty rooms.

"How do we know which one is his?" Stevie said.

Colby's nose scrunched up, her freckles contracting. "We could ask at the office?"

"You think they'd tell us?"

"Probably not," Colby said. "Ooooh! How about I create a distraction, and you could sneak behind the desk and look Gunner up on the computer system?"

"Or," Stevie said, pointing toward the metal staircase, "we could just follow him?"

Colby grabbed hold of Stevie's hand. "Oh. My. God. It's Gunner Trip!"

He was making his way up the metal staircase, large ICEE cup in hand.

Stevie and Colby stood outside room 47, Colby's purse hanging over her shoulder, the alarm and pepper spray that Stevie hoped they wouldn't need hidden inside. They waited a few minutes after Gunner had gone in, and now Stevie was building up the courage to knock.

She took a breath. "Okay, I'm doing it. Once we're in, let me do the talking, okay?"

Colby nodded, then took a breath spray out of her bag and pumped it twice into her mouth.

"Seriously?" Stevie said. "We're interrogating him about Blair's murder. Do you *need* icy-mint breath?"

"I think it's better than *not* having icy-mint breath."

"Fine." Stevie grabbed the pump and sprayed it in her mouth—she wasn't going to be the only one without freshly minted breath. Then she knocked on the door, took a step back, and waited, trying to ignore the slightly sick feeling in her stomach.

Colby gave her hand a little squeeze. "You've got this."

Stevie nodded. She could do this. She was just going to ask some questions. Find out if Gunner shot Blair in cold blood. Simple. He would have to answer the door first though . . .

Stevie knocked again, a bit harder this time.

"He's not answering," Colby said.

"Yes, I can see that."

Stevie moved to the window, pushed her face up against it, tried to peer through the gap in the curtains.

Colby leaned over her. "Do you see him?"

"I'm not sure. Quit leaning on me. Jeez, the place is a mess. The guy's a total slob."

Colby wiggled in next to her. "Let me look—he's got to be in there somewhere! We saw him go in!"

"I'm telling you, I don't see him."

"What the hell do you think you're doing?"

Oh crap.

Stevie straightened and turned slowly. Gunner Trip, all six foot six of him, was standing behind them, arms folded, a furious expression on his face.

Eleven

"Do you want to tell me why you were violating my right to privacy and looking through my window?" Gunner said.

Stevie gulped—a bead of sweat trickled down her back. "Right. Yeah. Sorry. We did try knocking."

"I heard."

"You didn't answer," Colby said in a slightly more accusatory tone than Stevie would have selected.

"Because I didn't want to. Now get out of here before I call the cops."

"Call them," Stevie said, aiming to sound commanding, not sure if she'd pulled it off. "Because I think they'd be *very* interested in talking to you."

Gunner glared down at her. "What's that supposed to mean?"

Stevie swallowed. "Look, could we come inside? We can explain."

"Inside? No, you can't come inside. I just want to be left alone." He thumped his fist against the wall. He didn't look great. Well, he did look great, if the *muscly, blond-haired, blue-eyed, chiseled-jaw Adonis* type was your thing. Which Stevie didn't think it was. Usually. But under his undeniably godlike exterior, Gunner looked tired—tired and sad.

Colby shook her head. "Someone is not okay, are they?"

Stevie threw her a look—didn't think patronizing him was the way to go.

But Gunner's face softened. "Sorry, I don't mean to be angry. It's just . . ." He swallowed, then covered his face and started crying.

Colby seemed to take this as a sign she should finish his sentence for him. "The love of your life was just murdered!" She leaned forward and touched his arm.

Stevie batted Colby away and whispered, "Stop molesting the suspect!"

Colby rolled her eyes and whispered back, "That was hardly molesting, but fine."

Stevie cleared her throat. "That's why we're here, actually. See, Blair is—*was*—my sister. And I want you to help me find out what happened to her."

Gunner's hands dropped from his face. "You're Blair's sister? You don't look anything like her."

"I get that a lot," Stevie said. Then, seizing on his moment of weakness, she took him by the arm and steered him toward his room. "Why don't we get inside, into the AC?"

Colby followed behind, muttering, "So it's all right for *you* to touch the handsome football player."

Stevie flicked on the light. Gunner's room was littered with ICEE cups and pizza boxes. The smell of sweat mingled with expensive cologne.

Colby put her hands on her hips, eyes sweeping around. "Whoa. You really like iced drinks."

"What I would like to do is chug a few bottles of beer. But Coach has a strict no-alcohol policy."

Colby looked him up and down. "Your body *is* a temple, after all."

Stevie cut her off. "Gunner, we're here because the police are looking for you."

"I thought they might be." Gunner sat down on his bed and put his head in his hands. "I can't believe this is happening."

Colby went to sit next to him, but Stevie pulled out the desk chair and pointed at it. Colby sighed but did as she was instructed.

Stevie leaned against the wall, eyes on Gunner, ready to see how he reacted. "They think you might have something to do with Blair's murder. You didn't show up on her opening night and there's been radio silence from you since. People have been trying to contact you."

"Me? They think I had something to do with it? I'd never hurt Blair!" His eyes widened in disbelief. "I turned off my phone after I saw the news. I couldn't face speaking to anybody. I came here to hide from the press. I didn't think anyone would think to look for me in a motel. I just wanted to hole up here for a bit. Deal with it in my own time. I was going to go to the cops once I got my head straight."

"Okay, right, but it also makes you look mega guilty," Colby said. "An angry husband or boyfriend is always the first person the cops look at. You know, a 'crime of passion' type thing."

"But I wasn't angry with Blair. It wasn't like that with us."

"What do you mean?" Stevie asked.

"We weren't a *couple* couple. We were friends. Good friends. But there was no passion between us. No romance."

Stevie frowned. Was that true? Blair had certainly let the world believe there was romance.

"That is *not* what you said in *Stars Align*," Colby said indignantly.

"None of that was real. Blair had a good business head on her, said it made sense for us to pretend to be together. And she was right. We got exposure individually, but together it was another level." He paused. "To tell you the truth, Blair was a little too messed up to be in a proper relationship."

"Messed up? In what way?" Stevie asked. "Was she using again?"

"No, she got clean, and this time she'd stayed clean. But there was something . . ." Gunner looked thoughtful. "I don't know, something . . . sad about her. I don't think she liked herself very much."

"That doesn't sound like Blair." Stevie hesitated. Was she being unfair? Maybe there was something more going on underneath all that confidence and showbiz sparkle. It wasn't like Stevie would know if there had been. Blair was good at putting on a show. The best in the world, in fact. Perhaps there *was* more to it than dealing with the pressures of fame. Maybe Blair had problems she didn't know about. It would take some effort to get behind that façade—to work out the reason behind Blair's pattern of self-destruction. Effort that Stevie hadn't put in. Stevie felt a lump forming in her throat. It was too late to do anything about that now. What she *could* do was find out who killed her.

"So if you two weren't a *couple* couple, do you know if she was seeing anyone else?" Stevie asked.

Gunner ran his hand over his jaw. "I don't think so. I think she would have told me if she was. Besides, she had a punishing schedule. Fitting an actual romance in with a pretend one? Nah, don't see it. But then again, anything is possible with Blair."

"Show him the video," Colby said.

Stevie took out her phone. "It's not a great picture, but do you recognize this man?"

Gunner watched intently, a frown creeping onto his face. When the video ended, he shook his head. "No, sorry. You think this could be some boyfriend of hers?"

"That, or maybe her stalker. Kirk Tyler told us she had a few."

"She did. I think it messed with her head. Made her paranoid. She was always hypervigilant. One guy in particular was sending a lot of messages."

"A big guy? Might wear a long coat and a baseball cap?" Stevie asked.

Gunner ran his hand over his chin. "No idea about that. Hell! How could I forget? There's something you need to listen to." He took his phone from his pocket and turned it on. It immediately started buzzing as message after message came through. "Man, people really have been trying to get ahold of me." He took a moment scrolling, his eyes widening and jaw becoming more and more tense. He looked up. "I need to go. The lawyer from the Titans has told me I need to go turn myself in to the police for questioning. I can't put it off any longer."

"Could we listen to that thing we need to listen to first though?" Stevie said, voice pleading, eyes fixed on his phone. Gunner's eyes flashed to the door. "Please."

"Okay, fine, sure." He placed his phone on the desk. "It's a voicemail from Blair."

There was a hiss of static, then—

"Hi, Trippy-Top!" Her sister's voice. Clear. Alive. Stevie's insides dropped. *"Babe, I think I've worked out who my stalker is, and you are not going to believe it! Gotta run now but will tell ALL later!"*

"Oh. My. God!" Colby said, eyes rising from the phone to Gunner. "Who was it?"

"I don't know. I flew in the day of the concert—we'd arranged to meet and she was going to spill then—but she canceled on me for Kirk Tyler. Said she'd had enough and was going to have it out with him about a few things."

Have it out with him? "About what?" Stevie asked.

"It could have been anything. Her schedule, the songs, her outfits, where she was staying, the food. She was always having it out with him. They both had strong personalities, and let's just say their relationship was a roller coaster. She'd threaten to leave Kirk and Satellite Entertainment one week, then tell me she would never leave the next."

"What time were you supposed to meet her?" Colby asked.

"Three p.m."

Stevie and Colby exchanged glances.

"That's the same time the video we showed you was filmed. So maybe it was Kirk who Blair was arguing with. Do you think she told Kirk she wanted to leave Satellite?" Stevie said.

"If she was serious, that would *so* give Kirk a motive to kill her," Colby said.

Gunner held up his hands. "Look, maybe. She mentioned some fresh, young producer she was thinking about working with. So if Kirk found out, I guess it could have been him. Or it could have been the stalker. All I do know is that it wasn't me." Gunner's voice cracked. He grabbed his phone, stood, and made for the door. "And the sooner I speak to the cops to prove that, the better."

"Just one more question," Stevie said.

Gunner turned around.

"You didn't actually say—where were you on the night of the concert?"

His shoulders stiffened. Maybe he was annoyed she was asking for his alibi. Or maybe he had something to hide.

"I was at the Sable and Stone in my hotel room. I took a nap, overslept. Missed the start. By the time I woke up, Blair's murder was all over the news."

Took a nap? He traveled all the way to Honeyville and missed the concert? Something wasn't adding up. For a moment Stevie stared at him. "Anyone there who can confirm that?"

Gunner hesitated. "In my hotel room? No. Maybe the concierge saw me. I'm sure there's security footage from the hotel lobby to prove what I'm saying. I need to go, so you two can let yourselves out. It was nice to meet you, Stevie. I'm sorry about Blair. Truly I am." His voice caught. "She was a sweetheart, underneath it all."

A weight pressed down on Stevie's chest, caused her voice to wobble. "Thank you. And, Gunner?"

"Yup?"

"Would you not mention to the police that we came to speak to you? My uncle Jimmy is leading the investigation, and he won't like it if he finds out I've been asking questions."

Gunner shrugged. "Sure."

Colby stood next to her at the window, watching Gunner jog over to his rental car. "I don't think he did it. He doesn't have a motive, and if he was the killer, it would be a pretty weird move to leave us alone in his motel room, right?"

"Yeah, I'm not convinced he killed Blair either, but I don't think we can rule him out," Stevie conceded. "I get the feeling he's hiding something."

Colby raised an eyebrow. "We're so going to root around in here, aren't we?"

"We certainly are, Colby. Get rooting."

Stevie closed the door to the motel room and hurried after Colby. "You cannot steal his boxers, Colby!"

"We need something to show for all our effort!"

The search of Gunner's room had turned up absolutely nothing, but Stevie hadn't really expected it to. He'd hardly have left the gun there for them to find if he was Blair's killer.

Colby had opened the door to the car and Stevie had one foot inside when someone called down from the balcony.

"You girls been visiting that football player?"

Stevie shielded her eyes from the sun. There was a guy in a dirty white tanktop, briefs, socks, and slides hanging over the railing. He laughed but it sounded more like a hoot. "He's had company the past four nights!"

Stevie took a step toward him. "He's been here the last four nights? You sure?"

He scratched his beard, stretched his arms as he yawned. "Four nights. I know everything that goes on here."

"Right . . . thanks." Stevie turned around and got into the car, ignoring the vest guy's offer to stay and party. She pulled on her seat belt, mind racing. "Gunner's been here four nights. But he told us he only came yesterday *after* he heard about Blair's death."

Colby turned the key in the ignition. "Why would he lie about that?"

"I don't know, but there's definitely no way we can rule him out as a suspect now."

Twelve

Colby pulled out of the parking lot, then looked at Stevie. "Where are we heading?"

"Back to my place to plan our next move."

Colby hit the blinker. "Clover Lane here we come."

Stevie tilted her head slightly. "You know where I live?"

"It's a small town," Colby said, and turned too sharply, causing the tires to screech. She pressed her foot on the gas. "So, what's the plan?"

"I guess to see if my uncle Jimmy has had any updates on the case. Although I suppose his biggest update will be that Gunner has turned himself in for questioning."

"*If* he turns himself in. He might not."

"True, but I don't think someone like Gunner Trip could stay in hiding forever. The whole world knows who he is. He's clearly lying about how long he was at the motel, but I'm not sure if he's lying about killing Blair."

"I agree. He genuinely seemed to care about her."

"But it doesn't mean he didn't do it." Stevie shrugged. "Maybe the guy can act. But if it's not Gunner, I guess that bumps the stalker to the top of the suspect list."

"Yup! My money's on him!"

"As you said, stalkers are the worst. If Blair had found out who he was and threatened to go to the police, that could be a motive to kill her. It would be good if we could get our eyes on the correspondence that Kirk sent the police. I'll think about how we could do that."

"And then there's Kirk," Colby said. "Gunner said Blair was meeting him at three p.m."

"I'm less certain of him. He's made a lot of money from Blair, which makes me think he wouldn't want to kill her. But if it was Kirk who she was arguing with in the dressing room, he's a person of interest."

"Agreed. Anyone else?"

"There's the possible secret love interest."

"So that gives us three main suspects."

"Four—we're not ruling out Gunner Trip."

"More than happy to interrogate him again if you need me to," Colby said.

Stevie rolled her eyes. "I'll bear that in mind."

"So the stalker is officially our prime suspect." Colby arched an eyebrow. "And I'm betting this stalker might be the 'long coat, baseball hat wearing' type?"

"Possibly. The police think he might just like to be around the drama of a celebrity murder."

"Yeah, but it could also be something. I'll get back online later—see if I can find anyone who needs looking into."

Stevie took her phone out, opened the Blair Baker fan site. "No time like the present." She scrolled up through the reams of condolence messages, searching for anything that didn't quite look right. It was all broken-heart emojis and expressions of devastation, so she clicked back to the day before the murder and looked through the posts there. "This person, QueenBB, posts an unnerving amount . . . like, they're commenting on *everything*."

"That's not the stalker."

"How do you know? The sheer number of posts they've made looks stalkerish to me. I mean, talk about obsessive."

"Stevie, that's me. On my second account. It says 'mod' under the username."

Stevie fought back a smile. "Oh, right, sorry." Then she said, "Why do you have a second account?"

"Just to help the conversation."

"So, here, this is you having a conversation with yourself?"

"Yup."

"And that's not weird at all."

Colby elbowed her. "Nothing wrong with being seen as a bit weird."

Stevie laughed and shook her head. She hadn't seen it coming, but being with Colby was a welcome—no—a needed distraction from the pain of her sister's death. She couldn't remember the last time she'd actually hung out with someone like this. Before Mia, probably.

Stevie kept scrolling but stopped when she saw a screenshot of one of Blair's social media accounts. Colby had messaged her saying, *Holding a preconcert party at Wes's Diner in your honor! 6pm night before the concert. Would love it if you could come. Even created a special Blair Baker Burger!*

Surprisingly, Blair had responded.

Sounds great Bx

It didn't seem like a definite yes to Stevie. Blair had probably answered tons of messages without thinking anything of it. But she could see how an overexcited Colby would read it like an acceptance. Poor Colby. A lot of fans seemed to want to believe it too—many of them were *screaming, crying, throwing up.*

Stevie carried on scrolling, then paused. A post had been deleted, but the comments underneath it were still visible.

OTT much?
Think that's a bit harsh.
Don't blame Blair, blame her manager.

Like she ever agreed to come in the first place.

Can't believe I fell for your lies. Don't blame Blair!

"You deleted a post," Stevie said quickly. "You said something about Blair not turning up to your preconcert party and then you deleted it."

Colby chewed her lip, kept her eyes on the road. "I was upset. I posted without thinking. It was stupid."

Stevie's heartbeat ticked up. She tried not to let it show in her voice. "What did you say?"

"Nothing, really. That I was let down. Hurt that Blair didn't care about her most loyal fans. That I didn't know what I was going to do."

Stevie shifted in her seat, hands clammy on her phone. "Didn't know what you were going to *do*?"

"Yeah, I meant about how I was going to get to see Blair. What I was going to do to make it right with the Blair fans who come to me for content."

"Right." Stevie put her phone back in her pocket. She didn't say anything for a moment, while her heart thundered in her chest. Colby was silent too, but she was definitely gripping the steering wheel tighter.

Stevie kept her eyes fixed on the road. "It's just . . . that could sound like you were thinking about doing something about Blair."

"Like what?"

Stevie didn't answer.

Colby slammed her foot on the brake and swerved to the side of the road. "Stevie, I didn't shoot your sister. I was at the concert with a load of other Blair Baker fans most of the day. I legitimately have thirty legitimate alibis! I don't even know how to shoot a gun! And even if I did, I'd never be able to shoot someone. I don't like loud noises."

"You don't like loud noises?" Stevie said slowly.

"I'm not even good around fireworks! Yes, I was upset Blair didn't show, but I wouldn't have killed her for it."

Stevie studied Colby's face. Ran the facts through her mind. *Legitimately have thirty legitimate alibis.* An actual killer would never say that. And Colby had been outside the arena when Stevie went in—she wouldn't have had time to get to Blair underneath the stage before the show. Stevie took a breath. She'd been like this before when she was investigating what happened to Mia. Suspicious of everyone. Fixating on the wrong people. Throwing around accusations instead of focusing on the facts.

"Okay!" Stevie held up her hands. "I'm sorry."

Colby held Stevie's gaze, her eyes intense. "You promise you believe me?"

Did she think Colby could have done it? Maybe there was the tiniest part of her that thought it was a possibility. The part of her that struggled to trust anybody. But her rational mind? No, she didn't think Colby had killed Blair. "Yeah, I promise," Stevie whispered.

Colby nodded. "Good."

She pulled into the road without looking. A car honked and swerved past them. They drove in silence for a couple of miles until Colby said, "You know that film, *The Bodyguard*?"

Stevie gave her a sideways glance. "Uh-huh." Where was she going with this?

"Whitney Houston's stalker turned out to be a hitman hired by her sister."

Stevie snorted. Oh. She was going there. "Colby, I did not kill my sister."

"Yeah, I know you didn't."

"Okay, good. And as we are officially ruling us both out of the suspect list, let's focus on the four we do have—the stalker, Kirk, a love interest, and Gunner."

"And there isn't anyone else who had a grudge against Blair that we haven't considered yet?"

Hal's face flashed in Stevie's mind. She pushed it away. "I think that's it. Take a right down here, then a left on Ashgrove—it's a shortcut to my house. Let's find out if the police department have made any progress in their investigation, besides us tracking down Gunner Trip for them."

Thirteen

Colby nudged her car through the TV crews that had camped out on Clover Lane, knocking over a couple of chairs and bumping into some sort of food station before finally coming to a stop on the front lawn. She put the car in park, then grinned at Stevie.

"Didn't I say I could get through?"

"You did. Ready to make a run for the front door?"

"I told you—these are my fast boots. Just try not to fall on your face this time."

Stevie grabbed the door handle. "Okay, let's go!"

The shouting started up immediately.

"It's the sister!"

"Stevie, how are you feeling?"

"Any update on Blair's murder?"

"Blond girl? Who are you?"

"How are you connected to the Baker family?"

Stevie let the questions bounce off her, charged up the steps to the porch, unlocked the door, and threw it open. "Made it!" she gasped out, but then she turned around to see Colby had not, in fact, made it.

Colby was standing on the path just below the steps, fingers split into peace-sign Vs, posing for the cameras.

Hilton Moore was at the front of a baying crowd, his mic pointed at her.

Oh, good lord, no.

"All I'll say is that whoever the monster is that killed Blair,

Stevie and I are going to find him!"

What the actual hell! Stevie's eyes widened. She couldn't believe what she was seeing. "Colby," she hissed, "shut your mouth and get your butt inside!"

Hilton's lips twisted into a smirk. "Are you telling me that you two"—he gestured over at Stevie and she could have slid down the doorframe with shame—"are investigating Blair's murder?"

"We are," Colby said, her chest puffing up.

"No, we're not! We are absolutely, categorically not," Stevie yelled.

"We are," Colby repeated, "so you can put that in your column and say that the murderer better know we're coming for him."

Stevie felt the panic rush through her. "Colby, if you don't shut up right now, I swear to you there's going to be another murder!"

"She doesn't mean that," Colby said, rolling her eyes. "Oh, and I should also tell you that, as the person in charge of the world's largest unofficial Blair Baker fan site, I am, with the blessing of the Baker family, holding a candlelight vigil two nights from now, in honor of Blair. Seven p.m. June 4, in the parking lot of the Honeyville High Stadium. Go, Honey Bears!"

The blessing of the Baker family? This time, Stevie did slide down the doorframe until she was sitting half in and half out of the house. Colby had just invited the whole of America to her sister's vigil.

"We'd love for anyone who was a fan of Blair's to come and join us in a celebration of her life." Colby struck a few more poses before finally making it up the steps to the porch. She looked down at Stevie. "Why are you sitting on the ground?"

Stevie looked up at her and said, very slowly, her voice trembling with anger, "What did you just do?"

"Something to help us solve the murder, obvs!" Colby said.

"If you want to talk more privately," Hilton yelled over, "you have my card!"

"Cold day in hell!" Stevie yelled back.

"Stevie? Is that you?" Marnie emerged from the living room. She looked exhausted, shadows ringing her red eyes. Her face fell. "For heaven's sake, get up and close the door!"

Stevie dragged herself to her feet and closed the door behind her.

"Where have you been?" Marnie said, then became distracted by Colby. "Weren't you outside the Sable and Stone hotel earlier?"

"Mom, this is Colby."

"Colby, I'm Marnie. Stevie hasn't mentioned you before."

"We've only really just become best friends."

"Best friends?" Stevie and Marnie said at the same time.

"I definitely see that as a strong possibility."

Marnie turned to Stevie. "But I didn't think you liked people anymore."

"Of course I like people, Mom!" Just not *all* people . . .

"What's going on?" Hal stepped into the hallway. He was wearing the same shirt and shorts he had on last night, except his shirt looked like he'd slept in it. He set his eyes on Colby, then Stevie. "I don't think this is a good time to be bringing home visitors, Stevie."

Even though Stevie was pretty sure she had made a massive mistake bringing Colby to the house too, she wasn't about to let her brother tell her what she could and couldn't do. "Colby gave me a ride, and this is my home, Hal, not yours. I'll invite who I like."

"For god's sake, Stevie. Mom and Dad have just come back from the morgue."

"Stop it, both of you! I can't bear it!" Marnie swallowed, tears pushing at the corners of her eyes. "This is a very difficult time; could you please not fight?"

"The morgue?" Stevie said, heart leaden.

Hal nodded, looked at the floor, the muscles in his jaw tightening. "To formally identify Blair."

"They called to say we could see her after we left the hotel and you'd left with . . . Colby."

"I . . . I . . . didn't know. Mom, are you okay?"

"I couldn't do it," Marnie said quietly. "I couldn't see her. Not like that. Your father had to . . ." Marnie heaved a breath, her chest shuddering.

Hal pulled her into him, placed a kiss on top of her head, and rubbed his hand up and down her arm. "No parent should have to."

Stevie didn't know what to say, didn't have the words to make any of this better.

"I should go," Colby said, throwing a desperate look at the door. "I'm intruding. Mrs. Baker, I'm so sorry for your loss." She squeezed Stevie's hand, then opened the door to a flurry of camera flashes and shouts.

Stevie quickly shut it again before Colby could step outside. "We can't let her out there now. Not with *them* out there."

"I can just wait here, in the hallway," Colby said, "and make a dash for it if I see a chance."

Marnie gripped hold of Hal's arm, stared up at him. "Go and get your father to call Jimmy again about removing those vultures from our front lawn."

Hal nodded. Then paused before he left and looked at Stevie. "Sorry, I didn't mean to lose it with you." He ran a hand through his dark hair and suddenly looked exhausted. "It's just . . . all this is bringing back a lot of painful memories."

"You don't need to apologize. I'm the one who should be sorry—I was awful to you just now."

"I've been pretty awful too. When Dad phoned to say they were going to view Blair's body, do you know how I felt?"

Stevie shook her head.

"Honestly, a little jealous." Hal looked down at the floor. "How's that for awful?"

"Oh, Hal," Marnie said, reaching out for him.

Hal looked up and, blinking back tears, took Marnie's hand. "I would have done anything to see Mia one last time."

"We know you would have," Marnie said, "and I am so sorry you didn't get to."

Stevie's chest ached with the weight of seeing her brother's pain. She took hold of Hal's other hand and he squeezed it back. Then he cleared his throat and said, "I'll go see about those reporters."

Marnie placed her hand on her forehead. "This is all so dreadful. Grief piled upon grief. I don't know what to do with myself. I can't bear to be in this house and I can't bear to leave and no one's telling us anything and I feel so lost . . ." She trailed off. Seemed so utterly devastated.

Stevie put her arm around her and guided her through to the kitchen. "Come and sit down, Mom. I'll fix you some iced tea."

"Iced tea?" Marnie said, like it was the most ridiculous suggestion in the world. Maybe it was.

"I'm trying here, Mom," Stevie said, her voice cracking. "I don't know what to do either. I'm feeling just as lost as you are. So, please, let me make you some iced tea and maybe we can talk. Or we can just sit together in silence if you prefer. Or we could just stand here by the front door."

Marnie's chin trembled. She reached forward, placed her hand on Stevie's cheek. "I'd love some iced tea." Then she turned to Colby, who was still hovering by the door, looking a little awkward. "Come on—it will be a while before it's safe to leave, and I can't have you there, making my entryway look untidy."

Stevie placed a glass of iced tea down in front of Marnie and one in front of Colby. There was another bouquet of flowers next to the ones Blair had sent.

"Those are nice," Stevie said.

"From the ladies in my book club—they sent a lovely card, too." Marnie's chin trembled, and she took a sip of her drink to calm herself. "So, how do you two know each other?"

Stevie could tell she wasn't really interested—she was just going through the motions, trying to ask the questions she'd normally ask if her daughter hadn't just died.

"Colby runs the Blair Baker fan page. She's organizing a candlelight vigil for Blair. She came over to discuss the arrangements." Stevie held her breath, waiting to see how her mom would react.

Marnie tilted her head, face softening. "You are?"

"Blair was important to so many people. I just wanted to do something to show how much she was loved."

Marnie sniffed, placed one hand over her heart. She seemed genuinely moved. Which was a relief. "That's very lovely of you, Colby. We'll all come, of course."

Marnie took another sip of her tea, stared blankly out the window. "They handed me a brown envelope."

"An envelope? Who did?" Stevie said, not following.

"Of Blair's things. All Blair's beautiful things in a brown envelope." Marnie nodded toward the sideboard. "I put it there, behind her high-school photo. She always was so photogenic. So beautiful."

Blair's blue eyes shone from behind the glass. Her hair was plaited into two French braids. Stevie had once asked for the same hairstyle, but hers had fallen out before she'd even made it off the school bus. She'd grown annoyed and sulky, but then Blair had told her she looked beautiful and wild with her hair down, and Stevie had managed to smile when the photographer said *Cheese.*

Stevie got up before she started to cry. She went over to the sideboard, hesitated before picking up the envelope. "Can I look?"

"Of course," Marnie said.

Stevie peered inside. There were half a dozen little plastic baggies containing the jewelry Blair wore for the show.

Carefully, she placed each piece onto the table. Large diamond earrings. Gemstone rings. Several sparkling bracelets that caught the afternoon sun streaming in through the kitchen window and sent out little bursts of light like cascading stars. And a delicate necklace with a little silver feather pendant.

"Would you like something?" Marnie asked. "I'm sure Blair would've wanted you to have something of hers."

Most of it was far too much for Stevie's taste, but the necklace . . . Her eyes fell on it again. "The necklace is beautiful. But . . . wouldn't you like it?"

Marnie smiled. "It suits you better." She stood, opened up the baggie, and poured the necklace into her hand. "I'll put it on for you." She moved Stevie's hair out the way and fastened it. "There. Now you can carry a little part of your sister with you." She kissed the back of Stevie's head and whispered, "I'm trying too."

Stevie's fingers found the feather. She turned it over—on the back, the letter *B* was engraved in swirling calligraphy. She swallowed down the lump that was rising in her throat.

"Mom, thank—"

"Marnie, love! Get in here!" It was Frank, shouting from the living room. "I've got a message from Jimmy! Gunner Trip's handed himself in."

Stevie and Colby exchanged looks and Marnie stopped short, placed her hand on the table to steady herself. "Oh, thank god."

Fourteen

Stevie followed her mom into the living room, Colby hanging back in the hallway. Frank was pacing the carpet, phone still in his hand. His eyes were ringed with dark circles, hair sticking up in all directions.

"Has he confessed?" Marnie asked, breathless, face hopeful.

Frank shrugged. "I don't know yet. Jimmy's just taken him to the interview room for questioning. He said he'll call as soon as he has an update."

Marnie leaned on the back of the couch, closed her eyes. "Dear god, please say he has. Please let this be over."

Stevie didn't know what to say. She knew the message that Jimmy would send back. *Gunner Trip is saying he's innocent. Checking his alibi. May have to look at someone else.*

Frank continued pacing, his face looked a sickly gray. Stevie worried that all this stress would take its toll on his heart. "Dad, why don't you take a seat?"

Frank sat down, but his legs continued to bounce.

"How long will it take, do you think?" Hal was sitting in the window seat, curtain inched back, looking out at the TV crews.

Frank sighed. "Depends how cooperative he is. Could be an hour, could be five."

Hal jumped up. "Annie's here—I better go help her get through that pack of hyenas out there."

Stevie took up Hal's position at the window and watched as he pushed his way through to Annie. A loud whirring sound passed over the house—Stevie looked up above the houses across the street. "That's a helicopter! They're circling the house in a helicopter!"

"I wish they'd just leave us alone!" Marnie cried.

Outside, Hal put a protective arm around Annie and tried to guide her inside, but the reporters were swarming around them. Crap. It looked like they were in trouble. Stevie was about to run out, but then the reporters started moving back. Officer Dean emerged through the melee, shouting and ushering Hal and Annie through.

Stevie ran and opened the front door to a flustered-looking Annie, a slightly disheveled-looking Officer Dean, and the sound of Hal shouting a few choice words at the reporters. Stevie slammed the door and leaned against it.

"It's a little wild out there," Officer Dean said, straightening his shirt. He gave Stevie a quick smile, which for some reason she was absolutely not willing to dwell on made her feel a little flustered.

"If they're on our property, it's your job to remove them!" Hal stormed straight past Stevie into the living room, Annie running after him, casting an apologetic look at Officer Dean.

"I told you not to say anything to anyone outside!" Frank called from the other room.

"I didn't!" Hal yelled back.

Stevie screwed up her eyes. Hal could find his way to anger so quickly. She glanced over at Officer Dean. "Sorry, things are a bit difficult—"

Officer Dean held up his hands. "No need to apologize. I'm going to call for backup to see if we can get those reporters a bit farther back from the house. Don't want anyone falling over them again."

"Okay," Stevie said. "Great."

Officer Dean gave her a little nod, then stood there looking at her like he was waiting for something.

What more did he want? A round of applause? Oh god, did

he want her to thank him for scooping her up off the lawn this morning? She *really* didn't want to—would rather pretend the whole thing had never happened. The words came out of her mouth before she could fully vet them. "Yes. The lawn. I fell. Thank you kindly."

A little smile flickered across his lips. "You're welcome." Then he nodded again at the doorknob.

AT. THE. DOORKNOB.

He didn't want thanks. The guy wanted to leave!

Stevie jumped out the way. "Sorry, yes, you want to get out."

He was still smiling a little as he closed the door behind him.

Stevie turned around to see Colby looking at her from where she was sitting on the bottom step of the stairs, an eyebrow raised. "Wow."

"Do *not* say anything," Stevie warned.

"Is it me," Colby mused, "or is that cop kind of attractive?"

"It's you. And he's a rookie, not an actual cop."

"Great jawline and he has those big soulful eyes—you know what I mean? The kind that really draw you in."

"I don't know what you're talking about," Stevie said. She'd barely looked at his eyes. And if anything, they were more kind than soulful.

"And those freckles . . ."

"You really shouldn't objectify a member of law enforcement!" Stevie snapped, and headed into the living room.

Annie was sitting next to Marnie on the couch, holding her hand. "Stevie," she said, sitting upright, "how are you? Hal told me you saw someone watching the house last night. You must have been so scared."

She had been scared, but she didn't want Annie to worry. "I'm honestly fine. Officer Dean was there, and he said it could have been some sick fan attracted by the drama."

Annie's mouth fell open. "How awful."

Stevie nodded. But . . . had anyone actually followed that up further? Sure, she'd messed up with the Channel Fourteen reporter, but it didn't mean she'd fabricated an entire guy with a knife. Surely? She turned to her dad. "Did Jimmy speak to the neighbors—get any sightings or any leads?"

"Sorry, Little Bear, no. If there was someone here, nobody saw him."

What did he mean, *if* he was there?

"And Jimmy agrees with Officer Dean—if there was someone like you described, watching the house, he was probably attracted by the TV crews. Some people are just nosy."

"Some people are just dicks," Hal added, eyes flicking towards the window.

"They'll still keep a lookout though, right?" Colby said from the doorway, drawing everyone's attention. "Because, in my opinion, he is totally sus."

"Who the hell are you?" Frank said, the crease between his brow deepening.

"That's *Colby*. Stevie's friend," Marnie said, like Frank really should have known. "Lovely Colby here is organizing a candlelight vigil for Blair."

Hal glanced out the window, exhaled loudly. "And I expect we will all have to attend. Even though Blair didn't bother to come to the ones we held for Mia."

Marnie stiffened and Stevie wondered why he had to bring up old wounds. Things were hard enough.

Annie clasped her hands together. "Hal"—she spoke like a parent trying to soothe a child—"your sister had her reasons. And no one here is going to make you do anything you don't want to do."

The *SportsCenter* theme song blared. Frank frantically rummaged in his pockets.

"Frank, your phone!" Marnie said.

"I know it's my phone," he said as he fumbled, trying to swipe to answer.

"Quickly!" Marnie said. "It might be something important! News on Gunner Trip?"

Frank finally managed to answer and held the phone to his ear. "Jimmy." He started pacing the room, face serious.

Marnie clutched the back of the sofa, her knuckles whitening.

"Uh-huh. Uh-huh. And it checks out?" Frank ran his free hand through his hair. All eyes were on him. "Okay. I guess it is what it is. Yup. You too. Stay in touch."

"Frank?" Marnie said.

Frank shook his head and slipped his phone back into his pocket. "Sorry, love. Gunner Trip has an alibi. Security cameras have him at his hotel at the time of the concert."

So he wasn't lying about that—but why lie about when he arrived in Honeyville?

Marnie closed her eyes, swallowed.

"This is exactly why they need to keep looking for that creep Stevie saw," Colby replied.

"My god, why is Little Miss Marple here?" Hal said under his breath.

"Hal!" Marnie snapped. "Colby is a guest in our house!"

"So what happens now?" Annie pushed a blond curl behind her ear. "Do they have any other suspects?"

Frank puffed air out of his lips. "They're still interviewing everyone who was working at the concert, going through security footage."

"Do they think it might be Blair's stalker?" Stevie asked. "Did Jimmy look at that video I sent?"

"That's one line of inquiry. Jimmy says he's got a team of people going over the correspondence Kirk Tyler sent through too. They're hoping to get an ID on the guy in the video ASAP."

"Did he say anything else?" Stevie asked.

"Only that Blair's phone is missing. They have her laptop and have sent that off for the tech guys to go over."

"Her phone is missing? Does Jimmy think the killer took it?" Stevie asked.

"It's a possibility for sure. But she could have just left it somewhere before she performed and we haven't found it yet. Other than that, Jimmy says they're working through all the messages from people who have phoned in to claim they did it."

"There are people who are claiming to have shot Blair?" Stevie asked. "Why would they do that if they didn't do it?"

Frank shrugged. "I don't know, Little Bear. Not right in the head, is my guess, but every claim has to be looked into."

"So they have nothing." Hal let out a slow breath. "Somebody shot Blair at her own concert, and they have no idea who did it."

"Your uncle is working on it," Frank said.

Hal stood and started to walk out of the room. "How reassuring."

"He's hurting." Annie, always quick to provide an excuse for her husband's behavior, even if it was obvious to everyone.

"Jimmy will find who did it, won't he, Frank?" Marnie looked at her husband, desperation in her eyes.

Quiet.

Then Frank nodded. "'Course he will, love."

But there was too much of a pause to be convincing.

Stevie chewed her lip. Jimmy hadn't even been able to find Gunner Trip, something that had only taken Colby a matter of hours. What chance did he have of finding Blair's killer?

"I'm going to go to my room with Colby," Stevie said, hooking her arm through Colby's as she swept past. "We've got a lot of . . . preparation to get started."

Fifteen

Stevie sat on her bed and opened her laptop. Colby plonked herself down next to her and exclaimed, "Let the stalker hunt commence!"

"No fast boots on the sheets." Stevie kicked Colby's feet off. "And before we do anything, I think we need to discuss what the hell you thought you were doing speaking to Hilton earlier?"

"I was thinking it would be useful for our investigation. People might prefer to come to us, rather than the police, if they have information."

"I guess—that might be true."

"Besides, it will be good for the murderer to know we're looking for them. They'll feel the pressure of being hunted, and when criminals are under pressure, they make mistakes."

Stevie took a very deep breath. "You think whoever did it is going to be worried about *us* searching for him?"

"He should be!" Catsy slinked in through the door and Colby swooped to pick her up.

"Who's a beautiful kitty cat?!" she said, holding Catsy up in front of her face. "What's its name?"

"Catsy Cline—after the singer," Stevie said distractedly.

"Great name. Hello there, Catsy Cline, aren't you a gorgeous fluff lump?!" Colby tilted her head at Stevie. "Speaking of names, why does your dad call you Little Bear?"

Stevie smiled; she always did when she told this story. It was one of those warm, precious memories. "When I was little, like three or four—something like that—I used to follow Blair around. I'd dress like her, copy her—her hair, her movements, even the way she spoke. I just thought she was the best person ever and all I wanted in the world was to be like her. People even started calling me Little Blair. They thought the copying was really cute, and I got all this attention for it. Mom even started buying us matching outfits on purpose."

"Aww, that is quite cute."

"But I remember one night, Dad comes into my room, and he sits at the end of my bed and says to me, 'Stevie,' and before he can say anything else, I say, 'No, Daddy, I'm Little Blair.' And he just smiles and kisses me on the nose and says, 'You can't be Little Blair, because you're Stevie. And you might not understand this now, but you can't be anybody but yourself. You shouldn't want to be anyone but yourself. Your wild, wonderful, perfect self.' And I say to him, 'Am I wild like a bear, Daddy?' And he says, 'Yes, just like a bear! So, what do you say, kiddo? You can be Stevie for everyone else, but you can be Little Bear to me.' I screwed up my nose—not quite sure. So he says, 'It even sounds like Little Blair!' And I guess something in me just wanted to be special to someone, so I became his Little Bear."

"Your dad is very wise. Blair was like this totally phenomenal person, but you are too, Stevie—in your own way."

Stevie rolled her eyes. "Flattery is not going to get you out of explaining to me why you thought announcing the vigil to those reporters was a good idea."

"It's not a good idea—it's an excellent idea! Criminals always return to the scene of the crime!"

"Do they?"

"Yes!"

Catsy turned her head toward Stevie and meowed.

"See, Catsy agrees. It's an actual established fact! Criminals are always showing up at the scene of their wrongdoings. So I think there's a very good chance the criminal may show up at Blair's vigil."

"Colby, are you getting this intel of yours fully from movies?"

"*All* movies are based on real life!" Colby sat back down on the bed, Catsy on her lap.

Stevie raised her eyebrows. "*Finding Nemo, Dune, Avengers: Endgame . . .*"

"Okay, not those movies, but my reasoning is solid. I figure, if Blair was killed by some crazy who was obsessed with her, they're going to want to show up at her vigil so they can soak in the aftermath of their actions. They get off on that sort of thing. Your man in the long coat might even show up. And if he—or whoever the scumbag was that was stalking Blair—is there, we also have a chance of spotting them. But for us to do that, they're going to need to know that the vigil is happening, and let's just say I haven't made a great deal of progress on the advertisement front."

Ugh. She had a point. "So, how far have you gotten with organizing it?"

"Well, I just made a massive step forward, telling all of those reporters."

"Has Principal Mathers agreed you can hold it in the parking lot?"

"Not exactly, but I don't see how he can stop it from going ahead now. Don't worry about it—it will all be fine! Damn it! I should have told people to bring their own candles."

Stevie pinched the bridge of her nose. She had a headache coming on and she was tired, which was making it harder to push down the sadness that was suddenly fighting its way up through her again. She realized she was very close to tears.

"It will all be fiiiiine!" Colby said, giving her a nudge. "Now, let's do some investigating!"

Stevie exhaled heavily, gave herself a shake. There was no time to be sad when Blair's killer was still out there. "Okay, let's do it."

"It looks like we can scratch Gunner off the suspect list as his alibi checks out."

"He still lied about when he got here, but I guess he's not our guy."

"So let's start with our prime suspect, the psycho stalker. Want to help us find a killer, Catsy?" Colby said, scratching Catsy's head. Catsy blinked slowly, then jumped off Colby's lap, giving them a cursory glance as she left the room. "I guess that's a no."

Stevie brought up the fan site, but Colby grabbed the computer from her.

"I'll log in as admin. Look, I have a blocklist. We should start here."

Stevie flung her head back and groaned. "There are hundreds."

"I don't think that is a very detectivelike attitude."

"Sorry. Yay, there are hundreds!"

Colby ignored her, squinted at the screen. "Most of them are bots, so we can rule a good chunk out. Then we can see if what they posted rings any alarm bells." She reached over and clicked on the first one: @Ashley_pashley. "Hmmm. Thirty comments . . . Ah, this is the one that got them reported."

Stevie leaned in. "'Blair Baker's second album is overrated garbage. Should have left it at one.'" She looked at Colby. "You blocked them for that?"

"We don't tolerate haters." Colby moved to the next one. "Hotdog Hunter. Oh, I remember this guy! All he did was post pictures of hot dogs. It was too annoying, and he clearly wasn't a genuine Blair Baker fan."

"Probably not our killer," Stevie said.

The next user, @Mira4Eva, had been blocked by Colby because she was posting love about Mira Parker and not Blair.

"I think she was a bit confused. I sent her a link to the Mira fan page, then blocked her as a kindness."

"And Foot Fan Friday?" Stevie asked.

"Oh, he was really strange. Every Friday he'd post a picture of Blair's feet. I just didn't think it was appropriate."

For the next hour, they analyzed the blocked posts—nothing really jumped out as being written by a potential murderer, but when they got to @BBWill_be_mine, Stevie and Colby exchanged a look.

"It's quite a stalkerish username," Stevie said.

"I remember this guy too! Assuming it's a guy. I kicked him off because he was harassing another member." Colby brought up the past messages. "Yes, here, see? They were writing some really weird crap to a DollyPurrton-underscore-fourteen."

Stevie's heart thudded against her rib cage. "Dolly Purrton?" She swung the laptop to face her. "That's Blair—it's got to be!"

"What?" Colby said, eyes wide, voice breathy. "Why?"

"Dolly Purrton was her cat. We got her and Catsy in 2014! Only Blair, or someone very close to Blair, would know that!"

"Oh. My. God!" Colby covered her face with her hands. "You are not seriously telling me that *the* Blair Baker was a member of my fan site!"

"I think I am."

Colby dropped her hands from her face. "Holy crap on a cracker! You are kidding me right now!"

"Maybe she liked seeing all the praise—liked knowing what her fans were saying about her?" Stevie said, because Blair absolutely would enjoy that. Who could blame her? Stevie sat up straighter, tightened her ponytail. "We need to read everything she posted, and everything this BB-will-be-mine character said to her."

"The *actual* Blair Baker was on *my* fan page!" Colby said, a far-off look in her eyes.

"Colby, that is really *not* the biggest thing right now."

"How didn't I realize?"

"I'll tell you what, you just take your time to process, and I'll go through the posts."

Stevie started with Dolly Purrton. Surely, she'd be able to figure out if it really was her sister. When @DollyPurrton_14 first joined, she was mainly liking comments that were positive about Blair. Not really saying anything, just lurking. She made her first actual comment when a @kitty_katrainbowlove said that Blair's darker blonde didn't suit her. To that Dolly Purrton had replied, *Maybe she didn't have a choice, maybe it was a management decision.* Seemed very like a Blair response to Stevie.

The next comment she posted was about the duet Blair had sung with Tayt Grover on *Saturday Night Live.* @GingerQueen had suggested that they'd lip-synced, and Dolly Purrton had replied: *Maybe that was because Tayt doesn't have the vocal talent to sing live. I'm sure if Blair had her way she wouldn't choose to lip-sync. She probably didn't even want to perform with him in the first place.*

Then a comment was posted by @Icklepickle19 asking whether Blair had her eyelids done. To this Dolly Purrton had replied, *Why would Blair have her eyelids done? There's nothing wrong with her eyelids. I've just looked at her recent photo shoot with* Rolling Stone *and her eyelids look fine. But comments like this might give a person a complex about their eyelids.*

"You know, I really think this could be Blair. It *sounds* like Blair. Can you show me how to see what this BB-will-be-mine guy said to her?"

Colby leaned over Stevie, clicked through until the posts came up.

The first interaction between them was sixteen months ago.

Dolly Purrton had posted something about Blair's new single being her best yet and @BBWill_be_mine had replied with *You would say that @BB.*

Stevie swallowed. "I think this guy knew Dolly was Blair."

After that, @BBWill_be_mine posted seventy-three posts that were all exactly the same.

@DollyPurrton_14 @BB. @DollyPurrton_14 @BB. @DollyPurrton_14 @BB . . .

"He's telling her he knows who she is," Stevie said, scrolling down the page. "And look here—this is where she starts responding."

October 21
@DollyPurrton_14:
who are you? @BBWill_be_mine
@BBWill_be_mine:
Blair's biggest fan @BB

October 22
@BBWill_be_mine:
Blair Baker looked so good today.
Gym shorts suit her @DollyPurrton_14
@DollyPurrton_14:
how do you know BB wore gym shorts?
@BBWill_be_mine
@BBWill_be_mine:
I'm her biggest fan @DollyPurrton_14

October 23
@BBWill_be_mine:
Chanel smells better on BB than anyone
else @DollyPurrton_14

@DollyPurrton_14:
Blair doesn't wear Chanel @BBWill_be_mine
@BBWill_be_mine:
It smelled like Chanel @DollyPurrton_14
@DollyPurrton_14:
Who are you? @BBWill_be_mine
@BBWill_be_mine:
Blair's biggest fan @DollyPurrton_14 @BB

"Okay, this guy is as creepy as hell." Stevie said. "It took you a while to block him."

"There are so many posts—it can be hard to manage. I might not see something until someone makes a report."

"And did Blair—I mean, Dolly Purrton, report him?"

Stevie clicked through to another screen. "Yeah, she did, I blocked him straight after."

"If that is Blair, it sounds like BB-will-be-mine knew stuff about her. Can you find out who he is?"

"Users do need to register an email . . ." Colby stuck her tongue between her teeth as she clicked through some back pages of the site. "BB-will-be-mine registered under wbm12345@buzzmail.com."

"Whoever it is clearly set up that account just to register. Is there a way we can find out who it belongs to?"

"I'll ask ChatGPT if it knows how."

Colby's painted fingernails clattered away on the keyboard.

"Not that promising," Stevie said, reading the response. "Looks like we can try typing it into the search bar on social media and see if it gets a hit, but I can't see someone being stupid enough to use the same email for stalking purposes. Or we can pay some email lookup service—but it does say results aren't always accurate. Or we can send them a polite email and see if they reply. I can't see that working." Stevie put on a fancy British accent. "Terribly sorry to bother you, but you didn't by chance happen to murder my sister?"

Colby tilted her head, nose scrunching. "It couldn't do any harm. Personally, I think you should try it all."

"And what will you be doing while—"

She was cut off by shouts coming from outside.

Colby gasped. "Something must be going on with those reporters!" She scrambled over Stevie, all knees and elbows, to get to the window first. She turned around, mouth open. "Your brother's outside and he looks like he's about to knock out Hilton Moore on your front lawn."

Sixteen

Stevie pulled back the curtain and shoved Colby to the side. There was Hal, all six foot three of him, holding Hilton Moore by the lapels of his too-shiny jacket. Hilton stood on his tiptoes, eyes wide with shock. The other reporters were crowding around, some shouting at Hal to stop, most with their cameras rolling.

"What the hell is he doing?" Stevie said, although she knew the answer was losing his shit.

Marnie, Frank, and Annie came bursting out the front door, Frank shouting, "Hal, this isn't helping anybody!" and Annie crying, "Hal, please don't," and Marnie producing a high-pitched wailing noise.

Frank got to Hal first, put his hand on his shoulder. "Hal, enough!"

Hal didn't react, just kept his eyes fixed on Hilton.

"I said, enough!" Frank shouted, face reddening.

Hal registered him this time and shoved Hilton backward with both hands. Hilton fell onto the lawn, narrowly missing one of Marnie's ornamental roosters. Shame. A beak up the ass seemed deserved when it came to Hilton.

Hal jabbed his finger at Hilton. "Stay away from me and stay away from my family."

Annie grabbed Hal, pulled him back by his arm. She put her hands on his face, started talking to him, trying to calm him down. Whatever she was saying seemed to be working. Hal's shoulders loosened—then he nodded and handed her the car keys. They pushed through the reporters and Hal got into the passenger seat, still glowering.

Stevie watched their pickup all the way to the end of the street.

"What the hell got your brother so riled up?" Colby said, moving away from the window. Then she pulled a face, spoke apologetically. "I mean, other than your sister being killed?"

"Hilton Moore, I would imagine. He wrote a pretty nasty article about him."

Colby narrowed her eyes. "Didn't he get caught drunk-driving? Did I read something about that?"

Stevie closed the curtains, sat back down on the bed. "Yup. When he was seventeen, he hit a tree on the bend of Westville Drive. Smashed up his knee and his chances of getting a football scholarship. Then, four years ago, Blair told Hilton all about it. God knows why. Attention, maybe? But she totally sold him out. 'Blair Baker's Loser Brother.' I think that was the headline. He was furious . . . and devastated. Couldn't believe Blair had done it to him. Didn't want Mia knowing about it, which is understandable, but he could hardly hide it from her when it was all over the internet. He wanted Mom to pick a side. She wouldn't. I guess she was worried about Blair—probably because Mom knew she already had an issue with drugs. And Mom blamed herself for that, as she'd agreed that Blair could take something to help her with her anxiety when she first started performing. It was all a total shit show. Hal refused to come around for months. But then Frank spoke to him, reminded him that people weren't perfect. And things started to improve . . . for a while at least."

"Mia—she's your niece, right?" Colby spoke gently, cautiously. "She went missing after a party?"

"Yeah, that's right." Stevie looked down, picked her nails. She wasn't sure if she wanted to talk about it, but the words came streaming out of her mouth anyway. "It was the evening of my sixteenth birthday, and things between Hal and Mom and Blair were better. Shaky, but better. Mom was anxious before Blair even showed up—worried about how Blair would act. There'd been a few photos online of her coming out of clubs, looking wasted. An hour after the party was supposed to start, Blair hadn't arrived, and Hal started grumbling about her being selfish. Mom didn't want to hear it. She kept telling him that she was a superstar and she was probably just busy working, and she'd be there as soon as she could. No one believed it. Dad suggested we should just get going and eat without her, but Mia wanted to wait, as she was so excited to see her famous aunt. But as the minutes ticked by, Mia's hopes started to fade. Mom got more irritable—Hal could barely contain his fury. Annie, Dad, and I tried our best to keep a party atmosphere, mainly for Mia, but when Blair finally showed up three hours late, drunk— high, too, probably—everyone was already on edge. Hal lost it. Really lost it. Mia was there, and he didn't want her to see her beloved aunt wasted, but he was also just so mad at Blair still. Mom started crying. Annie, god love her, was trying to calm everyone down, but she was making everything worse because she always sides with Hal. Blair pushed over the cake, then stormed out. There was this huge fight—everyone disagreeing about what needed to be done about Blair. Then, when things quieted down, we realized Mia wasn't in the house."

Colby let out a long puff of air. "Whoa."

Stevie kept picking her nails while she spoke. "Mia wasn't answering her phone, so we went out searching for her. We didn't think she could have gotten far, but we couldn't find her anywhere. We were out all night. We checked the doorcam footage and saw her leave around nine fifteen p.m.—she must have been trying to get away from all the fighting."

Colby sat down beside her. Stared at the wall. "Stevie, that's awful. And the police? They didn't find anything? No clues?"

"They said they had evidence that she was in the alleyway that runs alongside Founder's Park and the side of Millbrook Street—the one the garbage trucks use as a shortcut. Stevie swallowed. "They found traces of her blood. Some tire tracks. But other than that, nothing. They never found her, never found a body."

Colby swallowed. "I can't imagine how that must have been for you all. I heard you disappeared for a while after it happened."

"My parents were worried that I was having a mental breakdown. I was conducting my own investigation, and I was just so completely convinced I would find her, but in reality, I didn't get close. After they found me searching the alleyway with a flashlight and a magnifying glass at three in the morning, good old Frank and Marnie decided my obsession with discovering what happened was unhealthy."

Colby exhaled heavily. "I mean, they weren't wrong."

Stevie managed a half-smile. "I guess not. They staged an intervention, organized some intense therapy, and I started to find my way through."

"I salute your determination, but you've got to look after yourself."

Stevie looked up, stared at the wall. "It's been almost three years since she disappeared. I think about her every day. It's our fault she's not here. It's Mia we should have been looking after that night."

"Every family has arguments, Stevie."

"Not ones that lead to someone being murdered."

"You think she was murdered?"

"I used to believe she was still alive. I still want to. But I think we would have found her by now if she was. Blair offered up a million dollars for anyone who came forward with information; if Mia had ever been seen again, we would have heard about it."

"I remember the reward, Blair's pleas for help. Kids from school were out combing the streets for months."

"She felt guilty. And to start with, Hal blamed Blair, of course, told her it was all her fault. But he knows that really our whole screwed-up family is responsible."

"And you don't think Hal . . ." Colby trailed off, left the question unsaid.

"Killed Blair because of it?" The question sat uncomfortably in Stevie's chest. She shook her head. "Honestly, I've thought about it and I don't believe he could do it." She paused. Had she though? Had she thought about it deeply? Hal was short-tempered, sure, and had been through so much. But she still couldn't get to a place where it was possible. "Hal's relationship with Blair was strained, to say the least, but she was still his sister, and he loved her."

Stevie waited, expecting Colby to push her more. But she only said, "Okay, then, if that's what you believe, we focus our efforts on the stalker, the secret lover, and Kirk Tyler. Agreed?"

Stevie looked down, touched the feather hanging from her neck. Blair's necklace. "I have to find out who killed Blair, Colby. I failed with Mia, and I can't fail again. I just can't."

"And that is why we're going to kick the ass out of this investigation." Colby brought up a new document on the laptop. "Let's write out all the suspects we have so far."

@BBWill_be_mine—online stalker
Long coat and cap guy—could he be @BBWill_be_mine?
Gunner Trip—why did he lie?
Kirk Tyler—was Blair going to leave him for another manager?
Did Blair have a secret lover?
Who argued with Blair in the dressing room? Kirk? One of
the above, or someone else?

"There," Colby said with a triumphant nod. "That is an excellent start."

Stevie ran her eyes down the list. "I don't know where to even begin."

Colby rolled off the bed and started putting on her boots. "And that is why you're lucky to have me here to tell you what to do. You are going to look into that email address and I'm going to head home and see what info I can find about Blair, and I'll do a deep dive into her love life—see if I can find out if she really did have a secret boyfriend."

Stevie sighed heavily. Blair's killer was out there, and she was just playing around online. Running down dead ends. Getting no closer. Was she just kidding herself that she could do this, like she had with Mia?

"Is any of this going to work?"

"Honestly, I don't know, Stevie, but surely it's better than not trying. And just so you know, I'll be keeping a close eye on your emotional well-being throughout this investigation. Can't have my new best friend losing her grip again."

Stevie rolled her eyes, then became serious. "Thank you, I've dumped a lot on you tonight."

She'd never been able to share so much of what had happened to her with anyone before, but Colby had made it feel okay. Other than Annie, she hadn't really let herself get close to anyone since Mia disappeared and she and Blair had drifted apart. Sure, Colby was unlike anyone else she knew, and it felt kind of nice to be called someone's new best friend. And maybe, with Colby's help, she might have a better chance of finding out who had killed her sister.

"I'm glad you did. I'll be here anytime you need me. I'll message if I find anything. And I'll meet you tomorrow?"

"Sure."

Colby paused in the doorway, turned around. "Oh, before I go, I want to ask you about something your brother said."

Stevie raised her eyebrows.

"Who the fuck is Miss Marple?"

"A detective."

"She'd better be hot."

Stevie grinned. "She's a total babe."

Colby nodded. "Thought so."

Seventeen

Stevie was woken by Catsy licking her face. She blinked her eyes open—they were so dry. *Crap.* She'd fallen asleep with her contacts in. The laptop was still open beside her. It was almost eleven—she'd slept in because she'd been up till the early hours trying to get a hit on the email address. She'd posted it into every social media site search bar, but no one, as she suspected, had registered for an account using wbm12345@buzzmail.com. She'd also spent twenty dollars on web pages that claimed to be able to link email addresses to individuals, but that had turned out to be a total waste of money. Only then, reluctantly, had she sent an email to wbm12345@buzzmail.com. It had taken her over an hour to work out what to say. In the end, she'd kept it brief: *Would like to discuss Blair Baker. It's important. Please email back.*

Her phone started ringing on her nightstand. She stretched an arm over Catsy, hit the loudspeaker, and placed her phone on the pillow beside her head.

"Yup?" she said, rubbing Catsy's belly.

"Stevie? Oh Stevie . . ." Her mom's voice gave way to sobs, then the rustling sound of the phone changing hands.

Oh god, what now?

Stevie sat up in bed, put the phone to her ear.

"Hi, Stevie, it's Ronald Bryant from Gilbert and Greens. I've got your mom here in the store. I'm afraid we have a bit of a situation—nothing alarming—but I was hoping you could come down here."

What was her mom doing at the store? It was only two days after Blair had been killed. Surely, she wasn't up to shopping—being out in public yet—with all the reporters around.

"What happened? Is she okay?" Stupid question. Her daughter had just died.

"She came to shop, but I'm afraid her card was declined. I've taken her into the office, and I've told her it's no big deal, especially with what you're going through at the moment. We can sort it out later, of course, but I don't think she's in a fit state to drive."

"I'll be right there."

She hung up and jumped out of bed. Catsy looked at her questioningly. "Sorry, girl, I've got to go."

Stevie ran up to the store entrance as Annie and Marnie were coming out of it. Ronald was wheeling the shopping cart behind them and Annie had her arm around Marnie.

"Mom?" Stevie said. "Are you okay?"

Marnie looked up, mascara blotched on her cheeks. "I'm sorry—I didn't mean to make all this fuss. I shouldn't have gotten so upset over my card being declined."

"I think it's probably over a bit more than that, Mom," Stevie said.

"Little things can seem like a lot when you're grieving," Annie said. "I remember, a month after Mia disappeared, breaking down and crying at a parking meter when I didn't have any cash on me."

"I thought I could just step out and grab a few things for lunch—I didn't mean to cause such a scene."

"You should have told me," Annie said. "I would have shopped for you."

"How did you get here before me?" Stevie asked.

"I was just picking up some things myself when Ronald ran over and told me Marnie was in the office. I'm going to drive her home. Hal can pick up her car later."

"I brought my card," Stevie said. "I can settle up here."

"Already done," Annie said.

"You're a star," Stevie said, then helped her mom into the front seat of Annie's car. She squeezed her mom's hand, then closed the door.

"Do you think she's going to be okay?"

Annie closed the trunk and walked closer to Stevie. "She's going to have ups and downs. It's all part of the grieving process. I imagine the visit to the morgue has affected her. She was so upset when I found her in the office."

Stevie nodded. She knew it was true—but it didn't make it any easier to witness.

Annie gave her a hug. "I'll see you back at your place?"

Stevie's phone buzzed in her back pocket. There was a message from Colby: OMG! Boy, have I found some STUFF!

Stevie's heart picked up—then she pursed her lips. Was it bad if she left Annie to take her mom home by herself? It probably wouldn't win her *daughter of the year* award, but Colby had found some stuff. And *stuff* was written in caps.

"Do you think you'd be able to stay with Mom for a bit?" Annie was so much better at that sort of thing anyway.

"Sure, honey," Annie said. "I can take her home."

She didn't ask for a reason, but Stevie gave her one. "I need to go and help Colby with the vigil." A half-lie. Not a full one—they *might* do that too.

Stevie glanced at her mom. She was staring out the windscreen, blotting her eyes with a tissue, waiting patiently to be driven home. "I'll be home as soon as I can."

"And are you doing okay?" Annie asked. "I worry about you, you know."

"I'm doing okay," Stevie said.

"Remember, I'm always here if you need to talk." Annie gave her another hug, then opened the door and climbed into the driver's seat.

Stevie waited until Annie's car had pulled out of the parking lot, then messaged Colby.

On my way.

Stevie pulled into Colby's driveway and killed the engine. She opened the rear door to grab her bag. Then she reached out, but stopped, her eyes catching on something else. A package on the back seat—the size of a shoebox and wrapped in brown paper. She tilted her head. It wasn't hers, and she didn't think she'd ever seen it before. Her heart fluttered. Had she locked her car? Officer Dean had told her to keep things locked. Did she lock it at the store? She was hurrying, so maybe not. Was it even locked when she left the house? She gave herself a shake. *Stop it.* She was spiraling. It might be nothing. Maybe her parents had put it there.

She picked it up. It was light.

She was about to open it when her car door swung open. She jumped, heart in throat.

"Jesus, Colby!"

Colby's face loomed in at her. "Whatcha doing?"

"This was in my car." Stevie held the package out to Colby like an offering.

"For me?" Colby asked, taking hold of it. "What is it?" Colby gave it a vigorous shake, whatever was inside was sliding along the bottom.

"Hopefully not something fragile. It just appeared in the back of my car."

"Really?!" Colby eyed the box intently. "That's a bit strange, don't you think?"

Yes, she really did, but she refused to freak out about it. "Could just be my mom or dad's. Maybe they put it in there for some reason." She didn't sound convincing.

"Here's an idea," Colby said, "how about we go inside and open it?"

Stevie and Colby sat cross-legged on the floor of Colby's bedroom, the package on the carpet in front of them.

"I'll do it," Colby said. "And in exchange, I'll tell you what I've found out about Blair's love life through my internet sleuthing."

Stevie gestured toward the box. She tried to sound casual. It was going to turn out to be nothing anyway. "Be my guest. It's probably something my dad ordered for his woodshop at the center."

Colby pulled the box toward her, then looked up. "I hope it isn't a finger or something like that. Murderers like to send digits, don't they?"

Stevie swallowed. No . . . it wouldn't be a finger. Whose finger would it even be? She sighed, annoyed that Colby had made her think, even for a split second, that it might be. "I don't think it's a finger."

Colby shrugged. "Probably right." She tore open the paper and lifted the lid. Inside was a tiara embellished with rhinestones.

Stevie frowned. A tiara. Not exactly threatening. Still weird though.

"Ooooh, pretty!" Colby turned it over in her hands. "Don't think it's your dad's, somehow."

It was gaudy and awful, and, yes, it clearly wasn't Frank's. Stevie had no idea where it had come from. And she couldn't shake the growing feeling in her gut that it was something bad. But at least it wasn't *finger* bad.

And Colby didn't seem concerned. She placed it on her head,

pouted, and fluttered her eyelashes. "How do I look?"

"Is the correct answer, like a beauty queen?"

"It is! You know, I think I would have killed the pageant scene." Colby got to her feet, clutched her hands together. "Becoming Miss America is a dream come true! I would like to thank my ass—it's always been behind me, looking exceptional."

Stevie rolled her eyes, smirked, but she still felt uneasy. Why would someone leave a package with a tiara in her car?

Colby went to the mirror, started striking poses, which morphed from being quite model-like to her goofing around. She turned to Stevie, head pulled back to create an impressive number of double chins, mouth pulled down at the edges. "Tell me I'm pretty?"

"You, Colby Green, are a stunner." Stevie picked up the box. Perhaps there might be another clue as to where it came from inside. The bottom was covered in black paper—no, not paper—an envelope. Stevie's pulse quickened. "There's a note!"

She ripped it open, her heart stopping dead as she read the words, the hairs rising on the back of her neck.

For my princess, Blair, to wear when she is laid to rest.

"What is it? What does it say?" Colby said.

"Take it off," Stevie said, voice low. "Take the tiara off."

"What's wrong?" Colby stared at her, confused.

Stevie leapt to her feet, holding up the note. Why hadn't she realized sooner—trusted her gut? Packages don't just show up out of nowhere. "It's evidence! Take it off!"

"Evidence?" Colby snatched the note from her hand, her eyes scanning the print before meeting Stevie's gaze. "It's a death crown! I'm wearing a death crown." She ripped it off, hurled it at the bed, and shuddered. "The stalker, right? It's from Blair's stalker?"

Who else? Stevie paced the room, hand on her head. "The guy

in the long coat—he knows where I live—he could have put it in my car."

"Don't you lock your car?"

She did. Mostly. "I might have forgotten."

Colby looked down at the note, shuddered again. "'My princess'? That is totally creepy."

Stevie pulled her phone from her pocket, dialed her uncle's number. This was proof there had been someone outside their house. "We need to get this to the police. Hopefully, we haven't contaminated it."

Colby placed the note back in the box. "My fingerprints are going to be all over everything!"

Stevie's call went straight to Jimmy's voicemail. "Hi, Jimmy, I think I've got some evidence. That stalker guy—the one I told you was watching the house—I think he left a tiara in the back of my car for Blair. He sent a note with it. Anyway, I think you should see it. Call me back."

"What do we do now?" Colby asked, then glanced back at the tiara and shuddered again.

Stevie shrugged. She wasn't sure. "I guess we just wait until he calls."

They sat in silence staring at Stevie's phone until Colby said, "How about I fix us some lunch, then present to you the findings of my internet detective work?"

"I don't think I'm hungry."

"It's after one, I'm starving, and you need to eat. Besides, it might take our minds off the death crown."

"Guess we may as well."

"Good, because I have found some STUFF!"

Colby disappeared downstairs and returned with a couple of cheese sandwiches—one in her mouth and one in her hand. She passed one to Stevie, then picked up a stack of paper from her table and started laying the sheets out on the floor. "I was going to tack it to the wall, link it all up with string, like they do in the movies, but I didn't have any sticky tack or string."

She must have been up all night. She'd printed out blurry paparazzi photos and even blurrier fan photos of Blair in various locations, and lists and lists of dates, some crossed out, some circled.

"Blair," Colby said, moving the photos into an order, "came back to Honeyville on all the dates I've circled."

That couldn't be right. Stevie took a bite of her sandwich and scanned the dates. "Blair was here all those times?"

"Yes, I think so," Colby said around a mouthful of bread. "I'm, like, ninety-three percent certain."

"That high?"

"Uh-huh."

"And those dates are all accurate?"

"I think so—I cross-referenced them from what I could find of her schedule and when they were posted. I trawled the internet for fan sightings of her. Found a load of pictures—some gave her location, others I could figure out from various landmarks. See this one?"

Stevie nodded—it was a photo of Blair wearing a headscarf and sunglasses. "Is that Founder's Park?"

"Exactly right. If you look behind her, way in the distance you can see King Harry on the bench."

King Harry was a local legend—all the kids knew him. He'd gotten the name because he was never seen without his plastic crown. He was friendly enough—liked to dance and share peanuts with the birds, flipped out if he ever saw a dog.

"It *is* King Harry!" Stevie said. "I love that guy!"

"Me too! I'm pretty sure he keeps a pet squirrel in a grocery bag, but the reason he's of interest is that he enabled me to confirm that Blair was in Honeyville on"—Colby turned the picture over where a date had been written in swirly handwriting—"the seventh of November last year."

Stevie shook her head. The day after her birthday, and the second anniversary of Mia's disappearance. "That can't be right. That was the day of Mia's vigil. Blair couldn't come because she had work."

"It's right. She was here. She might not have shown up at the vigil, but she was definitely in town. King Harry doesn't lie."

Stevie looked at the photo, the date it was posted. Her stomach dropped. Colby was right. How could Blair have been in Honeyville on the day of the vigil and not bothered to go?

"And look," Colby said, pointing to another photo, "I think this is her inside the coffee shop the same day."

It was a blurry picture, but Blair was wearing the same headscarf and glasses. She was talking to someone. A woman. She had her back to the camera, but Stevie thought she recognized the blond curls.

Stevie's stomach dropped. "I think that might be Annie."

Colby licked her finger clean, picked up the photo, and held it close to her face. "Maybe Blair came to Honeyville to personally apologize to Annie for missing the vigil because she had to work. If that *is* Annie. It's only the back of someone's head."

"That makes no sense—if she had to work, she would have saved herself the trip and made her excuses over the phone. But if Blair *was* in Honeyville, the whole work thing was an excuse."

"From what you've told me, Blair and Hal didn't get along great—maybe she couldn't face seeing him. Maybe she blamed herself for what happened on your birthday."

"Things were getting better between them by then. We were trying to pull together as a family. Blair had offered rewards. She was supportive. It's only when she skipped the vigil that the rift between them opened up again."

"Okay, so maybe she was telling the truth, and she did have to work the evening of Mia's vigil. But she feels so bad that she flies in especially to explain that to Annie in person, then flies out again. Annie doesn't mention Blair was in Honeyville because she knows no one is going to understand why Blair can be in Honeyville but has to leave right before the vigil."

"If Blair had explained to us all in person, we would have understood."

Colby arched an eyebrow. "You're telling me that no one would have given her a hard time about flying out the evening of Mia's vigil?"

Stevie sighed. Colby was right. Still, would Blair have gone to that much effort to apologize? Something felt off. Stevie looked at the list of dates again. "But all these other times . . . How could I not know she was in town? There must be fifteen visits here."

"Seventeen in the past year and a half, actually."

"So who else was she meeting up with? It wouldn't have been Annie. No way. She would have said something."

"Then maybe Blair did have a secret lover, and maybe that lover was from Honeyville! And maybe I'm wrong about her working. Maybe she skipped the vigil for him."

"That would be a shitty thing to do." Stevie shook her head, trying to take it all in. Blair wouldn't do that. Would she? But Blair *had* been in Honeyville all those times, and for whatever reason, while she was there, she hadn't bothered to see her or check in with their mom and dad. It was a punch in the gut.

"My parents can never find out about this. It would kill them to know she was here and didn't take the time to visit."

"Hard for you, too, I would imagine," Colby said gently.

Stevie shook her head. Shook it too hard to be convincing. "It's fine. Blair and I weren't that close in the end." She forced a smile, gave Colby a little punch on the shoulder. "But look at you, Miss Marple. You did a great job finding all this out."

"This was not my first rodeo. Scouring the internet to find someone's whereabouts is well within my skill set," Colby said, clearly recognizing Stevie's need to change the subject and running with it. "When Greg Chambers and I were dating, he told me he was going upstate to visit his grandparents. After a bit of internet investigating, I discovered he'd gone to Coachella with Lucy Bridges. He thought he'd managed to avoid getting his photo on the internet. It took me a while but, in the end, I found him in a crowd shot that some random guy had posted."

Stevie smiled, grateful. "Sheesh, sorry about that, but kudos to you for finding out through your 'not at all stalkerish' behavior."

Colby shrugged. "A girl's gotta do what a girl's gotta do to find out who the pricks are."

Stevie's phone started ringing.

"The police?" Colby asked.

"No, my dad. I should take this." Stevie put the phone to her ear. "Hello?"

"Stevie, you need to come home right now."

Crap. He sounded angry. Could it be about the tiara? Did he know she was investigating?

"Is everything okay?" Stevie kept her tone light.

"Just get yourself here. We need to talk."

Eighteen

The *New York Times* was laid out on the kitchen table—Frank, Marnie and Jimmy sitting around it.

'Two Nancy Drews?' was the caption under the photo, which was taking up most of the front page. The image was of Colby standing, hip cocked, finger Vs in the air, with Stevie behind her, sitting on the porch, a leg on either side of the front door.

Stevie's mouth dropped open. "What the shuddering fu—"

"Is this true?" Marnie cut in. There was a tremor in her hands, but she looked better—more with it—than she'd been at the store. "Are you looking into Blair's murder?"

Before Stevie could answer, Jimmy said, "I expressly told you to stay out of it, Stevie! How do you think this makes me look?"

"I . . . I don't know," Stevie said, unable to tear her eyes from the front page. However it made him look, Stevie thought it was much worse for her. She looked like some sad rag doll slumped on the porch. She put the tiara box on the table and grabbed the paper, scanned the first few lines.

Blair Baker's sister and a mega fan named Colby Green, are on the hunt for the singing sensation's killer.

Her eyes leapt to the end of the article to see who'd written it. Hilton-flaming-Moore.

Jimmy thumped his fist on the table, making Stevie jump. "It looks like you have no faith in the police department—that's how it looks!"

"Hey! Go easy on the kid," Frank said. "We're all trying to

find ways to work through this."

Jimmy closed his eyes. Exhaled. Opened them again—looked a little less furious. "Please, Stevie, leave the investigating to the professionals, okay?"

Stevie did a half-nod, made a noncommittal grunt, hoped he'd take it as a yes. Then looked at the box—how was she going to bring up the tiara now? *Here's some potentially crucial evidence I may have ruined, Uncle Jimmy—you are welcome?* Yeah, that would go down well.

"Honestly, if you and your brother could stay out of the news, that would make my job a whole lot easier."

"Hal?"

"Yes, Hal." Jimmy let out a weary sigh. "Hilton Moore posted a story on his site about him, too."

Stevie took out her phone to have a look. 'Baker Brother Loses It' was written above a GIF of Hal repeatedly grabbing Hilton, shoving him to the ground. The camera had zoomed right in on Hal's face, eyes full of fury, veins bulging in his neck. He looked like a psycho. Stevie scrolled down to the comments section, a chill running through her.

The brother totally did it.

He's got the eyes of a killer.

Something not right about that guy.

They were wrong.

They *had* to be wrong.

"Put it away! I don't want to see it!" Marnie said.

Stevie put her phone in her pocket, tried to close her mind off to what she had read and push away the doubt. She glanced at the hallway, suddenly desperate to leave, but Frank said, "Sit down, Stevie. Jimmy needs to talk to you."

There was *more*? Oh hell.

Stevie pulled out a chair, its legs scraping on the tiles. Marnie flinched. Stevie huffed when she sat down. What the heck was this going to be about?

"Now, that video you sent to me," Jimmy began. "The girl in it, the one dressed as a bear, is this Colby person, right?"

Stevie nodded. "She's organizing the vigil for Blair."

"I know—I've had Principal Mathers on the phone this morning ranting about it. He said no one had asked his permission. Wants to pull the plug on the whole thing."

"He can't!"

"He knows he can't. Thanks to your little friend, every damn Blair Baker fan in the country knows about it. It'll happen. But we'll make sure there's police presence there."

"That's reassuring, thank you, Jimmy," Marnie said, clutching his hand.

"The video, Uncle Jimmy—did you work out who was in Blair's dressing room? The person she was having an argument with?" Stevie pressed.

"The thing is, Stevie, that's the other reason I'm here. We've gone over the footage and this Colby friend of yours? She never left the arena on the day of Blair's murder."

Stevie blinked. Couldn't quite catch on to what he was saying. "What do you mean? A security guard kicked her out. She told me."

"We've spoken to him. She gave him the slip before he could get her out the door. We've looked through the footage from that day and we don't see her again until much later, when she'd joined the queue outside."

"So, if she was outside, she must have left at some point after the dressing-room incident."

"Yes, we're just not exactly sure when."

Stevie's voice lodged in her throat. "I . . . I . . . don't understand. Are you saying Colby is a suspect?"

"We're working under the assumption that she may have been inside the stadium at the time of Blair's shooting."

Stevie's head was whirring, the kitchen a blur around her. Jimmy had to be wrong. Colby was committed to solving the case. She'd spent all night working on it. Had she done all that just to divert attention away from herself? It was possible. But to kill someone because they didn't show up at a party? Colby wasn't capable of that, was she? Stevie's head pounded, her pulse loud in her ears. "No, I saw her arguing with a security guard when we went into the stadium. She wouldn't have had time to get through security and kill Blair."

Stevie's mind turned. If Colby had hidden the gun earlier . . . maybe then she'd have had time.

"You're right. Considering the time line, it's unlikely, but not impossible." Jimmy placed his hands flat on the table, leaned forward. "We're not treating her as a suspect *yet*, but we're going to interview her to see if she saw anything."

"If she saw something, she would have told me." Stevie caught the uncertainty in her voice.

"Still, we need to speak with her anyway," Jimmy said.

Stevie rubbed her temples. What did she really know about Colby Green? Enough to be confident that she wasn't a killer? Had she trusted her too quickly? Colby had straight-out lied to her about when she left the stadium.

"I was sent a tiara," Stevie blurted out, desperate to move the conversation and thoughts away from Colby.

"What?" Jimmy said.

"Somebody left a tiara in my car with a note. I think it's from Blair's stalker."

Marnie gasped as Stevie opened the box and handed the envelope to Jimmy.

Frank leaned forward. "A note? What does it say?"

"It says that the tiara's a gift for Blair." Stevie left out the other details. She didn't want to upset her mom.

"So you were right—there was someone outside?" Marnie's words sounded apologetic. Her family really hadn't believed her, then.

Jimmy read the note, then closed his eyes and pinched the bridge of his nose and sighed. "Stevie, why didn't you leave it in the car and call me as soon as you found it? You've probably destroyed any chance we could have had of pulling DNA evidence from it."

"I didn't know what it was until I opened it, and I did leave you a voicemail as soon as I realized what it was!"

Jimmy took out his phone. "So you did. I haven't had a chance to listen to it yet—been a bit busy."

Stevie supposed that was fair enough. But he must have seen she'd called. She wasn't expecting a personal hotline or anything, but it would be nice if he placed a little importance on her calls.

Jimmy put the phone back in his pocket. "Where were you parked? Close enough for the doorcam to capture who put it there?"

"No—I was a little farther down the street."

"I'll ask the neighbors and the reporters—see if anyone saw anything." Jimmy inclined his head. "Does this Colby have access to your car?"

"I don't think so. Maybe. I might not have locked it," Stevie said.

"Oh, Stevie!" Marnie closed her eyes, shook her head in disbelief. "After you saw that man outside?"

"In my defense, I hadn't driven it since before the concert. And just a heads up, you will probably find Colby's fingerprints all over the tiara."

Jimmy sighed again, wearier than the last one. "Why?"

"She might have tried it on."

"She tried it on?" Jimmy said flatly. He looked up at the ceiling. "Give me strength."

"We didn't know what it was!"

157

"It could be seen as convenient that she touched it in front of you," Jimmy said.

"What do you mean?" Stevie said, though she knew exactly what he was getting at.

"Gives a plausible reason as to why her fingerprints were on there."

"No . . . she didn't know . . ." Stevie faltered. Her doubt was building, making her trip over her words. Could Jimmy be right? She had told Colby about the stalker . . . but she couldn't believe that she was *that* good of an actor. "She had no idea what it was before we opened it. And, if you haven't forgotten, there was a man watching the house, holding a knife, two nights ago!"

A phone started ringing. Jimmy pulled it out of his pocket. "It's Officer Dean. I need to take this."

He stood up and moved into the corridor, giving Stevie a disappointed look on his way past.

Marnie put her face in her hands, shaking her head slightly like she still couldn't believe it was all happening. Frank placed his hand on her back and rubbed it gently. Neither of them spoke.

Stevie strained to hear Jimmy's conversation. He sounded angry. "How the hell did Hilton Moore get ahold of them?"

Stevie went over and casually hovered by the door. Jimmy had his back to her. One hand massaging his temple, the other holding the phone.

"If there's a leak from inside, we need to find out who!" He swung around, locked eyes with Stevie, and continued. "I've got to go. I'll come down to the station after I've finished up here."

Jimmy hung up the phone.

"What is it?" Stevie asked.

Jimmy tugged at his collar. "Not good news, I'm afraid." He walked back into the kitchen, but didn't sit down. "There's been . . . a development."

"Have you gotten news back from ballistics on the bullet?" Frank asked.

"No. Should come through soon though. This is something else. Somehow the press has gotten ahold of the emails that Blair was sent by her stalker. There are extracts up on the Hilton Moore news site. We're issuing a takedown notice, but—"

"How did Hilton Moore get his hands on them?" Marnie said.

"Most likely, someone at Satellite Entertainment," Jimmy said.

"But it could've been someone in Honeyville PD, too, right?" Stevie said.

Jimmy narrowed his eyes. "We're looking into it, but I trust my team. What would any of them have to gain?"

"I imagine a ton of money," Stevie said.

Jimmy picked up the tiara box. "As I said, I trust my team. They're *professionals*." Pointed, aimed at Stevie. "I need to get down there, see what's going on. If you want my advice though, don't look at what Hilton's put up. Trust me—it's unsettling reading."

Marnie put her elbows on the table, covered her face with her hands. "Why are they doing this to us?" Her shoulders started shaking. "I just want to be able to grieve for my daughter."

Frank got up, put his hand on her back, nodded a goodbye to Jimmy. "Marnie, love, don't cry. Hilton Moore's a schmuck. He doesn't care who he hurts and we can't let him get to us."

Jimmy held up his hand and left, giving Stevie a stern look on the way out. "Remember what I said. Stay out of it. And if you get anything else like this"—he held the box up—"you bring it straight to me."

Stevie glared at his back—then, when she heard the front door click shut, she pulled the card Hilton Moore had given her and texted the number. If he had the stalker's emails, he might be a route to finding out who had sent them.

It's Blair's sister. I'm ready to talk.

Nineteen

By the time Stevie had gotten to her room, Hilton had texted back.

Name the time and the place.

She lay back on her pillow, Catsy curled up like a hot-water bottle on her feet. Where was a good place to meet a journalist to grill them about a stalker? She couldn't do it at home. She dragged her laptop toward her and typed into the search bar, *where's best place to meet for a clandestine meeting in Honeyville?*

The Rising Sun Motel? No chance. She was not meeting Hilton Moore there.

Her phone started buzzing on her nightstand. It was Colby. She thought about ignoring it, but she needed to know if what Jimmy had told her was true. She hit the Answer button, ready to ask her why she'd lied about when she left the stadium.

"Hey there, are you *the* Stevie from the *New York Times*?!"

"So you saw the article?" Stevie's voice was clipped, cold.

"I sure did!"

"I'm sure the killer is quaking in their boots now they know we're on the case."

"Exactly!" Colby said, too excited. Stevie's sarcastic tone was lost on her. "There's something I need to tell you . . ."

"Good, because there's something I need to ask you."

They ended up speaking over each other.

"Did you give the security guard the slip and stay in the arena on the day of the concert?"

"There are stalker letters on Hilton Moore's site."

"I know about the letters," Stevie said as Colby said, "Who told you I was in the arena?"

Stevie spoke first, wanting to pin Colby down on an answer. "The police say you gave the security guard the slip."

Silence.

Stevie's heart raced, loud in her ears.

"Colby?"

"I did. I hid in a janitor's closet for, like, fifteen minutes, then went to try Blair's dressing room again. But there was no answer."

"Then what?" Stevie snapped.

"I thought I was risking it if I stayed any longer, so I snuck out. I didn't hide there all day and then murder your sister, if that's what you're asking."

"I'm not suggesting that." But she clearly was, wasn't she? The last time the room containing the platform was checked was at three p.m., so Colby could have hidden there after she'd filmed that video.

"I dumped the mascot costume, left the stadium, and then went home to prep for the concert. It took me, like, two hours to get ready."

"Two hours?!"

Colby shrugged. "Yeah—I had to shower, exfoliate, do my nails, hair—"

"Okay, I get the picture." Stevie sighed. "I don't understand why you didn't just tell me the truth."

"I don't know why I didn't come clean. I should have."

Stevie fell silent. She wanted to believe Colby. Really wanted to believe her.

"Stevie, you must know how committed I am to finding out who did this."

"Why *are* you so committed?" Grit in her words.

"To help you, and because I loved Blair."

"You didn't *know* Blair. I don't get it."

"What don't you *get*?"

"The whole fan thing. How can someone you didn't know mean so much to you?"

"Don't shame me for liking her."

"I'm not shaming you—I just don't understand."

"Blair—her music—she just got me. Have you listened to the lyrics of her songs? It's like she knew all my secrets, my hopes, my fears. I felt seen. Blair was just like me. And she became this megastar, and she made me think that anything was possible. I don't have many close friends, Stevie, but Blair? She was always there for me. You know 'Broken Roots and Burnt Bridges'? It was like she was singing about me and my mom."

"Your mom?"

"Oh my god, completely. Mom is always out on the porch, bottle in hand, shouting at neighborhood cats for crapping on the lawn."

Stevie smiled, despite herself, gave a sleeping Catsy a quick stroke.

"I should have told you that I didn't leave the arena immediately, but I didn't think it was important."

Stevie snorted. "You didn't think it was important?"

"It's not important because it has nothing to do with what happened to Blair. I swear on my life, I didn't have anything to do with Blair's murder."

"And the tiara had nothing to do with you either?"

"Why would you think that? Of course it didn't!"

Stevie looked up at the ceiling and sighed. Could she picture Colby as a murderer? Her mind just couldn't make it fit. Colby's explanation seemed far more likely, and she could definitely picture her taking two hours to get ready. And if she'd been in the stadium longer, maybe she'd seen something.

"Did you see anything, *anybody*, that looked suspicious while you were hiding out?"

"From the closet? I would have told you if I had."

Stevie exhaled slowly. "You're going to have to tell all this to the police. Uncle Jimmy wants to speak to you now."

"I'll tell the police everything I told you. I promise I'm telling the truth." Colby's voice cracked a little, like she was begging Stevie to believe her.

They were both silent for a moment. Stevie wasn't quite sure how to start the conversation again. How to make the creeping doubt disappear.

Eventually, Colby spoke. "Shall we move on to my point of business? The stalker letters . . ."

Stevie wasn't sure if she wanted to. If she was ready to trust Colby again.

"Have you read them?"

"No."

"Maybe don't."

"I'm going to meet Hilton Moore and ask him where the hell he got them from." Should she be telling her this? Stevie swallowed.

"You think he'll tell you?"

Stevie's mind looped. *Colby didn't kill Blair. Of course she didn't. There was a man on your street with a knife!*

"Stevie, are you still there?"

"Yes, sorry." Stevie forced herself back to the conversation. "He might, if I give him what he wants."

"What he wants?"

"An exposé on the Baker family's grief. It's how reporters work, isn't it—trading information?"

"Ooooooh. Risky. But smart."

"I was looking for a good place to meet when you called."

Stevie turned back to her laptop, noticed there was a new message in her inbox. "Hang on a sec." She put her phone down.

It was from wbm12345@buzzmail.com, sent ten minutes earlier at 4:48. Her heart skipped, then rapped hard against her ribs.

She clicked on it, her fingers trembling. Her eyes ran over the words three times before they would sink in. And when they did, the world blurred around her.

Stop digging into Blair's affairs. Or do you want to die like your sister?

Twenty

Colby had wanted to head straight to Stevie's after she'd read the message to her, offering to stay over. But Stevie put her off—said that she was fine—that she'd prefer to drive to her place in the morning. What with Jimmy telling her parents that Colby could be a witness or even a suspect, she didn't want to have to navigate through the questions they may have.

She didn't know what to do with the email. She'd stared at it for ages, wondering if she should reply, but didn't know what to say. Even though it would have been the right thing, she didn't want to tell her uncle—not after he'd warned her to stop investigating. So, when the front doorbell rang, she left it sitting in her inbox—evidence for later, when she knew more.

Cindy Fogle, one of the neighbors and Marnie's friend, was at the door, brandishing a peach cobbler. She hugged Stevie, expressed her condolences, said, "No, I couldn't come in," then fought her way back through the reporters.

Cindy must have put the word out that the Bakers were accepting food, because the doorbell rang four more times, and that evening Stevie, Frank, and Marnie had a choice of mac and cheese, chicken casserole, potato salad, banana pudding, and Cindy's peach cobbler. Marnie had cried at the dinner table about how caring everyone was, but later commented that Mary River's potatoes were a bit overcooked.

After they'd eaten, Stevie went to her room to phone Annie, to ask about her meeting with Blair on the day of Mia's vigil.

She took a breath, not quite sure how to bring it up. Probably best to be direct.

"Stevie? Everything okay?" It was Hal's voice on the end of the line.

"Hi, Hal, everything's fine. Is Annie there?"

"She's fallen asleep on the couch. Neither of us have been sleeping that well."

"Don't wake her—it's not important."

"Anything I can help you with?"

For a moment Stevie wondered if she should ask Hal if he knew that Annie had met Blair. But she didn't want to cause any problems. "It's nothing—I just wanted to thank her for looking after Mom today at the store."

"I'll pass that on. You doing okay?"

Stevie leaned against her bedroom wall. "Yeah. You?"

"Yeah."

Neither of them sounded convincing.

"I love you, Hal."

"Love you, too."

Stevie hung up and went over to the window. Outside, the moon hung like a porch light and fireflies blinked across the front yard. She looked down the street at the spot she'd seen the man. Was it him? Was he the one sending her emails and packages? A flash of movement caught her eye—her heart lurched upward, then quickly descended when she realized it was just Mr. Ramone putting his trash cans out. Freaking hell, she was jumpy.

She closed the curtains, sat down at her desk—there was something she needed to do, which she'd been subconsciously putting off—reading through the emails Hilton Moore had published on his site. The sick ones that had been sent to Blair. Maybe she could find something that could link them to the email she received and the posts on Colby's web page by @BBWill_be_mine or the note that came with the tiara.

Stevie found the post and scanned through. The sender's information had been redacted, so Stevie tried to look for any similarities in language used.

Hilton had said that he had only published a small handful of the messages sent to Blair. Some, he said, were too depraved, too awful, for public consumption.

We're meant to be together. I know you know it. I can see it in your eyes when I watch you on TV.

You ignore me? You think you're too good for me? I'll make sure you notice me, one way or another.

You used to be real, but now you've let fame go to your head. You think you got where you did by yourself?

I love you, but sometimes I think about breaking into your house and cutting your throat while you sleep. If I can't have you, then the world shouldn't have you either.

I watched you today. Working out. You train so hard. You don't need to. You are already perfect.

Do you like prostituting yourself? Selling your soul to the world? You're a talentless whore.

They were clearly the rantings of a mad man. Or *men*—Stevie supposed there could be more than one. Did the messages sound like @BBWill_be_mine? It was possible, but then maybe all stalkers sounded alike with their declarations of love and threats of violence. The message about watching Blair work out caught her attention though. Hadn't @BBWill_be_mine posted about Blair's gym shorts? Maybe it *was* the same guy.

Do you want to die, like your sister? The thought of him standing outside her house with that knife caused her to break out in a cold sweat.

Stevie pressed her temples, tried to push out the words she'd just read. Poor Blair—dealing with stuff like this all the time. Gunner had said it had made her paranoid, hypervigilant. Stevie understood why, and yet Blair had never spoken about it. The image of Blair showing up at her sixteenth birthday party clawed its way into Stevie's mind. Or *had* she tried to talk to them? She saw Blair's manic eyes, remembered her erratic behavior, the rambling words—the dramatic exit.

I'll just head off into the night, then. If I'm murdered, then you'll all be sorry!

That's what Blair had said before she slammed the door.

It had been Mia who had gone missing though, not Blair.

Stevie had thought her sister had just been messed up on drugs, imagined she was playing for sympathy. But maybe Blair *had* been scared. Perhaps it wasn't mania she'd seen in her sister's eyes. Perhaps it was true fear. Stevie's heart pounded a faulty beat. Had Blair's stalker been there that night, watching? Another thought made her stomach drop, stone heavy—could he have something to do with Mia's disappearance? She ran the possibility over and over in her mind. Pictured the man in the long coat following Mia down the street, knife in hand . . .

The sound of a gate slamming outside caused Stevie to jump again, her heart leaping high in her chest. Catsy raised her head, gave Stevie an inquisitive look, then jumped off the bed.

Stevie went over to the window, pulled back the curtain, expecting to see the man in the long coat—almost certain she would.

Stevie turned to Catsy. "It's only Silvia Miller from across the street, taking out her trash." Garbage day was not great for a girl on the edge, but Catsy seemed unbothered and disappeared out of the room. She probably had nighttime prowling to do.

"Be careful out there," Stevie called after her.

She looked back out the window and shook her head. How

must it have been for Blair—to be scared all the time? The terror she must have felt when that gun was pointed at her . . .

Stevie's fear twisted into anger. She wasn't going to let someone frighten her off from finding Blair's murderer.

It was only an email. Words on a screen. And the fact that someone had sent it meant she was getting closer.

Stevie checked the time—it was past midnight. She needed to get some sleep if she was going to be able to think straight in the morning and press Hilton for information.

Stevie turned off her laptop and climbed into bed. She couldn't turn off her mind so easily and at three in the morning, with only her own spiraling thoughts for company, she even began to regret not letting Colby stay, even though a good deal of her thoughts were about Colby's lie. She considered waking up her dad, or even calling Jimmy and telling them about the email, the possible link to Mia's disappearance, but she knew they'd chew her out for investigating the case. They'd think she was losing it again.

Stevie must have fallen asleep at some point, because at nine she was woken by her alarm. She crawled out of bed, looked in the mirror. Jeez—she looked a mess. She splashed some cold water on her face, then paused at her reflection, her eyes catching on Blair's feather necklace. She felt a rush of pain. Blair had only been gone three days, and the thought of days piling endlessly on without her was unbearable.

Stevie forced herself to turn away. She changed, and threw her hair into a messy bun, then went down to make a coffee to have in the car on the way to Colby's.

She found Annie in the kitchen, holding a stack of envelopes. She could ask her now about the meeting she had with Blair on the day of Mia's vigil. Maybe even tell her about the email, too. They were close, weren't they?

Annie looked up, eyes immediately filling with pity. "You look—"

"Like crap?"

"I was going to say tired. Oh, sweetie, how are you doing?"

"I'll be better when I have some caffeine in my system."

Annie placed her hands on the countertop, leaned forward, wasn't going to let her get away with it. "How are you *really* doing?"

Stevie wasn't sure how to answer that, so she said, "I'd probably feel better if my picture hadn't been plastered on the front of the *New York Times*."

"About that—you're not investigating, are you?"

She wouldn't be telling Annie about the email, either, then. "Before you say anything more, Jimmy has already had a stern word with me about it, so you don't need to as well."

"Okay," Annie said, clearly sensing Stevie wasn't prepared to have that conversation again.

"I'm sorry—I don't mean to sound snappy, I'm just tired."

"You don't need to apologize."

"I do, especially when you were so good with Mom at the store yesterday."

"We're family, Stevie. But if you really want to apologize, you can make me a coffee too."

Stevie smiled and opened a cabinet, hoping to find the coffee pods among the boxes and boxes of herbal teas that Marnie insisted on buying but never drank. Her mom had a secret stash of pods hidden away somewhere—she usually only brought them out for guests.

Annie put some envelopes on the kitchen table. "All these cards were on the mat when I arrived. People are so kind. Cindy Fogle brought us a peach cobbler. Hal had it for breakfast."

"She gave us one too. What time did you get here?"

"Thought I'd come around early and do some cleaning. I want

to do something to help, but it all seems so meaningless." Annie gestured at the massive apology bouquet Blair had sent, a look of genuine concern on her face. "I was wondering what to do about these."

Stevie stopped rummaging for a moment. The flowers were wilting, heads heavy on their stems, colors fading.

"Ah, I see. Yeah, Mom probably doesn't need to see those shrivel up and die." Annie winced, but Stevie could picture how that scene would play out quite clearly—Marnie sobbing among the drooping petals. "Maybe throw them out?"

"I was thinking I might press them, so Marnie could have them as a keepsake. Maybe I could frame them or put them in a book."

That seemed like a lot of work. But then Annie looked like someone who was in need of something to do. "I think a book of pressed flowers would be lovely."

Annie's face split into a smile. "Okay, that's what I'll do, then." She started pulling the stems out of the vase. Stevie leaned on the counter, took out a pink zinnia. "How's Hal doing—he said he was having trouble sleeping?"

Annie's face tightened. "It's been hard for him. All those awful things people are saying about him online."

The image of Hal's face, full of fury, flashed in Stevie's mind. "He was at home, during the concert, wasn't he?"

Annie's face fell. "Really? You're asking that again?"

Shame rushed through her. "I know it's awful of me—I don't even know why I'm asking when I know he didn't do it, but he can get so riled up sometimes and—"

"Stevie, I swear to you, your brother was home the entire time." Annie looked Stevie in the eye, held her gaze. "I wouldn't lie to you."

Stevie nodded. She knew Annie was telling the truth. "I need to ask you about something else."

"Go on."

"Does Hal know you went to meet Blair in the coffee shop on the day of Mia's vigil last year?"

Annie paused, flower in hand. "No, he doesn't. I didn't mention it to anyone. How do you know about that?"

Stevie sidestepped the question. "Why didn't you tell anyone she was in town?"

"She didn't want anyone to know, and I didn't see the point in upsetting everybody." Annie's chin started to tremble; she suddenly looked on the verge of tears. "I'm sorry—it's a painful memory now. I wasn't very kind to Blair. She came to me because she was concerned about coming to the vigil and turning it into a paparazzi circus. She was talking about all the security she needed because of a stalker." She placed the stem on the countertop, pulled another one from the vase. "I didn't handle it well. I was trying to organize Mia's vigil and I didn't have the capacity to deal with her worries. I realize now that she was right to be concerned. She was thinking of us, but at the time I couldn't see it. I thought she was being selfish."

"I understand—I would have felt the same. What did you say . . . about her coming to the vigil?"

"I think I was a bit blunt. I told her it was up to her what she did; my only concern was finding my daughter." Annie closed her eyes briefly. "I should have been kinder."

"Blair understood, I'm sure." A knot of guilt twisted in Stevie's stomach. She'd thought Blair had chosen to work, or worse, that she'd been off seeing a secret boyfriend. Either way, she'd thought that Blair hadn't seen Mia's vigil as important. But maybe she really was being considerate. Maybe she really had wanted to go.

A thought bubbled up in her again. What if Mia's disappearance *was* connected to Blair?

"Annie, do you think the person who killed Blair could also be responsible for Mia's disappearance?" The words surged out before she had a chance to think—of their impact, of whether it was right to say them at all.

Annie looked up through her wet eyelashes, mouth open. "Why would you say that?"

"What if the person who killed Blair was here watching her at the house the night Mia went missing? What if he took Mia to get to Blair?"

Annie placed a flower down on the countertop. "If that was the case, wouldn't they have contacted Blair? Made a demand? Asked for a ransom?"

Stevie swallowed. Of course they would have. She was doing it again, letting her mind race down the wrong tracks.

"Stevie, honey, I know Blair's murder is stirring up all sorts of feelings, but I don't see how it can be linked to Mia's death. Please don't do this to yourself. Not again. I understand you have all these questions, but it's not up to you to work out what happened."

It was the first time Stevie had heard Annie say what Stevie had felt for a while now. "You think Mia's dead?"

"It's been almost three years, Stevie. If I'm honest, I think I knew the night she went missing that she was gone. A mother's instinct, maybe—but I tried so hard to ignore it." A fat tear, then another, rolled down her face and landed on the flowers. "I guess Blair's death has shown all over again how easy it is for a life to be taken. How those that kill can get away with it."

"But they shouldn't get away with it!" Stevie said. It sounded like Annie had given up on ever finding who had harmed Mia. Stevie couldn't understand it. How could she live with no answers?

"I don't want to keep chasing. I want to grieve my daughter. Finding out who killed her isn't going to bring her back. And you'll see that finding out who killed Blair won't bring her back either. You're not grieving, Stevie. You're running from your grief.

And I don't want to see it break you again."

Stevie didn't want to hear it. She couldn't listen to Annie's words, but she wouldn't argue with her. Not with Annie. She'd been through so much, and here Stevie was, pressing and opening up old wounds.

Stevie turned back to the cabinet, changed the subject, her voice wobbling a little. "Why is there so much herbal tea? There are six packets of unopened Bigelow Lean and Fit green." She turned to face Annie. "Looks like we're going to have to settle for instant coffee."

Annie looked like she wanted to say something else, like she wanted Stevie to admit that she wasn't dealing with things, but she sniffed, opened the cabinet above the stove, and forced a smile. "Marnie hides the good coffee pods up here. Don't tell her I told you."

"You're a lifesaver." Stevie popped the pod in the machine, filled a cup for Annie first.

She poured in some half-and-half and handed it to Annie.

Annie took it, placed it on the counter. "Stevie, I really need you to tell me if you're struggling again. You're like a sister to me, and I care about you."

"I care about you, too. But I'm okay—I promise." Stevie looked her sister-in-law in the eye, so Annie would know she really meant it.

And maybe to convince herself it was true as well.

Twenty-One

"So it said, 'Stop digging into Blair's *affairs*.'" Colby lay sprawled across the couch, in what she called her thinking pose. This consisted of her closing her eyes and pinching the bridge of her nose. "Hmmm. Do you think it means 'affairs' like romantic ones, or her business dealings, or what? Could it be the same person who sent the tiara? The man in the long coat? Someone else?"

"I have no idea," Stevie said, more abruptly than she'd meant.

Colby arched an eyebrow. "Are you sure you're okay? Getting an email like that must have been pretty scary."

Stevie had been scared when she'd first read it. To be honest, she still was. But her fear had quickly twisted, wrapped itself up with something else. Anger, definitely. And determination. Yes, she was scared shitless, but she wasn't going to let that stop her from finding Blair's murderer.

But now, after talking to Annie and trying to force a link to Mia that probably wasn't there, and now listening to Colby, she realized how little they actually knew, and that she'd let her fear and frustration spill over. "I'm fine, just didn't sleep well last night—keep going."

Colby studied her face a moment longer. "No mental breakdown on the horizon? Because I'm here for it if there is. Sorry, 'here for it' sounds like I'm encouraging it. I mean, I'm here for *you*."

"I'm fine—I promise," Stevie said.

"And we're okay? I really am so sorry that I wasn't completely straight with you."

"We're okay." Being in Colby's company, listening to her go over the case, made it much easier to silence the doubts. Stevie almost felt stupid for having them in the first place.

"Good." Colby returned to her thinking position, then suddenly bolted upright, raising her arm like she was in class.

"Ooh! Could BB-will-be-mine be the same person who Blair was arguing with in her dressing room? I heard her telling them she knew something, and that person did not seem happy about it. BB-will-be-mine's charming email certainly suggests that he doesn't want you digging into Blair's *affairs*. So maybe Blair knew something about this BB-will-be-mine that got her killed."

"I guess it's the strongest hypothesis we have," Stevie admitted.

"And it's the same guy who left the tiara?"

"I don't know. BB-will's message was a warning for me. The tiara was a gift for Blair."

"Both creepy though," Colby said.

"But they *feel* different."

Colby tapped her lip with her finger. "So we're thinking two different people?"

"Possibly. The guy Blair was arguing with doesn't look big enough to be the guy in the long coat I saw outside. And we still have Kirk Tyler to look into. I know Blair met Annie one time she came back to town, but we still don't know if she was seeing a secret boyfriend the other times she was here. And we can't forget that Gunner Trip lied." Stevie clutched her head with both hands—there was just so much to think about.

"You should ask Hilton Moore if he knew about a boyfriend and if he knew anything about the issues between Blair and Kirk—he's a celebrity reporter—he should know about these things. I'll try asking around online again."

"Don't worry—I've got a *looooong* list of questions for Hilton Moore."

"How long until you meet him?"

Stevie checked her phone. "At one; I should probably get going." She rolled herself off the couch and grabbed her bag.

Colby bounded over to her. "And I definitely can't come?"

"He wants to talk to me. Besides, haven't you got a vigil to organize? It starts in seven hours."

"All in hand. I was up crafting most of last night."

"'Crafting'?" Stevie said, then held up a hand before Colby could speak. "Never mind—don't have time for a full rundown now. I'm sure whatever you've been creating will be *very* Blair."

Colby's eyes found hers. "You're one hundred percent sure you should be doing this?"

"Meeting Hilton?"

"Looking into Blair's affairs. Stevie, this BB-will threatened to kill you. And there's some hulk of a man roaming the streets with a knife."

The word *knife* hit Stevie like a jolt. But what choice did she have? She forced a smile. "I'm meeting Hilton at Wes's Diner—the only thing that has a chance of killing me in there is the hot dogs Wes leaves out on the roller grills for weeks at a time."

Colby didn't laugh. She grabbed her bag, which was hanging on a hook by the door, rummaged through it, then turned around and pressed the pepper spray and rape alarm into Stevie's hands. "Take these. Don't worry—I have spares. I just want you to be safe."

"I will be." Stevie put them in her bag but wasn't sure if they made her feel any better. "Thank you. I'll see you at the vigil later, okay?"

"And you're sure I can't convince you to say something? I really think a show of emotion from a family member might trigger a reaction from the murderer."

Stevie slung her bag on her back. "I don't do public speaking, and I don't do shows of emotion."

Stevie sat in the booth, watching the door, waiting for Hilton to arrive. She'd ordered a milkshake but felt too sick to drink it. Her knees bounced under the table, nervous energy coursing through her. A guy walked past the diner window wearing a baseball cap and a black T-shirt. She jumped and almost knocked her drink over. She shook her head at her reflection in the window. *Get a grip.* She couldn't always react like that when she saw a guy in a cap.

The bell above the door chimed and Hilton walked in, nose scrunched, eyes full of disgust as he looked around the place.

Stevie held up a hand and he nodded a hello.

He reached the booth, took a purple handkerchief out, laid it on the seat, then gingerly lowered himself onto it.

"This place is really . . . something." He raised his hand, mouthed, *Coffee* at the waitress.

She came over, coffee pot in hand, and filled his cup.

He took a sip and made a show of swallowing it. "I would have paid for a nicer place, you know."

Wes's Diner was hardly fine dining, but it was familiar, and Stevie felt safe there and had a sudden need to defend it. "I like it here," she shot back.

"Really?" Hilton looked around, perplexed. "Well, I'm pleased you decided to talk. The world is waiting to hear how the Baker family is coping. Clearly, some are finding Blair's death harder than others."

He meant Hal. Stevie wouldn't rise to it, jabbed her straw up and down in her shake instead. "Before I say anything to you, I want something in return."

Hilton gave a knowing smile. "Straight down to the money, is it?"

She raised her eyes to meet his. "I don't want money."

Hilton inclined his head. "*Everyone* wants money."

"I want information."

Hilton laughed. A loud laugh that caused the waitress to look over.

Stevie's resolve hardened. "Maybe coming here to talk was a mistake."

"I didn't say no." He smiled and leaned forward, spoke conspiratorially. "What *information* do you want?"

He was enjoying this. He may as well have rubbed his hands together.

She leaned forward, matching his pose, used the same tone back at him. "I want to know who gave you the emails Blair received from her stalker."

His smile faltered for a moment.

She kept her eyes on his.

He raised his eyebrows. "You're serious?"

"My sister was murdered. I want to find out why and who did it. So, yes, I'm serious."

"I'm truly sorry about your sister's death, but as I just told the police, I don't know where the correspondence came from. It just showed up in my inbox late last night. I imagine it was sent from some fake account."

It sounded like a load of bull. "You're telling me you don't know? Nobody asked for payment?"

"No, which I find as puzzling as you. But I say, don't look a gift horse in the mouth."

"I think you do know who sent them but you won't tell me."

"Look, say I did know—I still couldn't reveal my sources. No one would ever speak to me again. A reporter's word is his bond."

He knew. Of course he knew. It was written all over his face.

"That's a shame, Mr. Moore," Stevie said, standing up, "because in that case, I can't speak to you either."

Hilton raised a finger. "I could, however, tell you who *didn't* send them to me. I'm not completely heartless."

A moment of understanding passed between them. Stevie sat back down. If he wanted to play games, she'd play. "So it wasn't someone in Honeyville PD?"

"No, it was not."

"Someone at Satellite Entertainment?"

He inclined his head, said nothing.

Stevie felt her heart quicken. It had to be Kirk Tyler or Bex Lyons. Why would they send Hilton the stalker messages? If it was Kirk, probably for more publicity—to boost the interest in Blair and her album sales. It seemed unlikely that Bex would care about that. Kirk, then, probably. The lowlife.

Stevie got out her phone, showed Hilton the wbm12345@buzzmail.com email address. "Were any of the stalker emails Blair received sent from this address?"

Hilton squinted at the phone. "Possibly . . . whoever it was used a lot of different addresses. Where did you get that?"

Stevie put her phone away. "I can tell you where I didn't get it."

Hilton smiled. "Fair enough."

"And do you know if Blair had a secret boyfriend?" Stevie continued.

"I suppose it's possible. But if she did, I think I would have found out and written about it."

Stevie nodded. That made sense. But if there was no boyfriend, why was Blair taking secret trips to Honeyville? Was she meeting someone else? Or maybe she was better at keeping her love life a secret than Hilton realized.

"It would make an excellent angle though: 'Gunner Trip Kills Blair Baker in a Fit of Jealous Rage.'"

"He has an alibi, apparently," Stevie said.

"So I hear."

"And Blair's relationship with Kirk Tyler. How was that?"

"I was thinking I'd be doing the interviewing," Hilton said.

Stevie worried he was about to shut her down, but he didn't sound impatient, more intrigued. "I've only got a couple more questions—then you can ask me anything you want."

Hilton took a moment before he answered. "Fractious. That's how I would describe them. But a lot of relationships in show business are shaky."

"You don't think Blair wanted to leave Satellite?"

"Honestly? I don't think that was an option for her."

"Why not?"

"I would imagine that Kirk has enough dirt on Blair to end her career for good. It's hardly a secret that she had a few . . . messy years. The drugs, the partying. I'm sure we only know a tiny part of what she got into. It must have been hard for her, catapulted into stardom at such a young age."

"I don't think some of the things you wrote about her helped, Hilton."

Hilton sighed and nodded. "No, probably not." For a moment Stevie thought she saw a flicker of regret in his eyes. "But if it wasn't me, it would have been someone else. And if you look over the stories I did write, you'll see that most of them were positive. You might not believe me, but I liked your sister. I watched her grow up, watched her through the ups and downs. It's hard not to care for someone when you've followed them for so many years, to feel a connection of sorts."

Stevie almost laughed, but it was too sad. "You think there was a connection between you and Blair?"

"Maybe I'm kidding myself, but I like to think so. She contacted me, a month ago, wanting to do a story about 'someone important,' but then she went quiet on me. I guess Kirk might have found out and put a stop to it. He had so much control."

Stevie's heart rate ratcheted up. Blair had contacted Hilton about running a story shortly before she was killed? That had to mean something, surely? "You don't know who the story was about?"

"If I did, I would have investigated and written it."

"What if it was about Kirk? Would you have written about him?"

Hilton considered the question. "It would need to be something explosive for me to ruin the relationship I have with him. But frankly, I don't think Blair would have risked destroying her career. Now, as novel as it is for me to be the one being interviewed, perhaps I could ask you some questions."

"Just one more thing—I promise." Stevie looked at him, eyes pleading.

Hilton nodded for her to continue.

"Four years ago, Blair spoke to you about Hal's DUI. I want to know why she did that." It wasn't to do with her investigation— she just wanted to know. To see if there was a reason why Blair had sold her brother out and shattered the family in the process. To try to understand her sister better.

Hilton steepled his fingers under his chin. "You know, some people think he might have done it."

"He didn't kill Blair," Stevie said quickly, not willing to give that theory air. She'd believed Annie when she swore he was at home. "Why did she speak to you about him? She'd always promised she would protect us from the spotlight—then, out of nowhere, she did *that*."

Hilton gave a lopsided smile. "You already seem to know how reporting works—someone gives a story in exchange for another." He looked at her, like she might understand what he was getting at.

"What do you mean, 'a story in exchange for another'?" Stevie asked.

Hilton took a sip of his coffee, pulled a face. "At that time, Kirk Tyler had found out that I was looking into another story on Blair. I'd had a tip, albeit a sketchy one, and I'd barely started investigating it when he came to me and put forward a deal."

"A deal?"

"He offered up the Hal story and first access to any other salacious celebrity gossip that may come his way *if* I left it alone. I told him that I'd think about it, but Kirk's sudden interest obviously piqued mine. I tried to contact my source, but they ghosted my calls, ignored my emails. Clearly, Kirk had gotten to them. The story was dead. So I took the deal."

Stevie ran it through in her head. Four years ago, something was going to come out about Blair, but she gave up Hal and his DUI to Hilton to save her own ass. "So Blair screwed over Hal to protect herself?"

"She was certainly protecting someone."

"But how could she do that to Hal?"

Hilton shrugged. "Are there any other secrets in the Baker household that she could have offered up?"

"No, of course not," Stevie said, angry at the suggestion.

"Then there's your answer."

"What story was Blair trying to keep quiet?"

"Never found out. I can show you the message I received, but then you would have to comment on it, on the record, if I ever decide to write about this."

Stevie could give a comment. She just wouldn't say much. "Let's see it."

I have a story on Blair Baker that will blow your mind. That family sure thinks they're something, but I know they're nothing but a bunch of criminals. You gotta pay for it though. Believe me, you're gonna want to hear what I have to say.

Hilton was watching her, analyzing her reaction. She wouldn't let the confusion rolling through her play out on her face. Whoever had emailed Hilton sounded like they knew Stevie's family. It sounded personal.

Stevie handed Hilton's phone back. "It's a hoax."

"So you don't know what they're talking about? You're sure about there being no other secrets?"

Stevie's resolve thinned for just a second. "The only criminal things I'm aware of are Hal's drunk driving, which you already know about, and my dad's criminally liberal use of Old Spice."

Hilton put his phone on the table. "Well, I guess we may never know what it's about. Shall we move on to the reason you got me here in the first place?"

She nodded. Anything was better than being asked if her family was a gang of criminals. "Go on, then—ask your questions."

Hilton opened his recorder app. "So, Stevie, can you tell me what it was like growing up in the shadow of one of the world's greatest singers?"

Twenty-Two

Hilton turned off the voice recorder and leaned back in the booth. "I think I have everything I need. But if you wouldn't mind sending a photo of you and Blair—something cute—from when you were young . . . ?"

Stevie stood up, forced her tears back. She wouldn't cry—not in the diner. Not in front of Hilton. She needed to get out of there. She'd talked too much. Shared too much of herself. Of Blair. She hated herself for it.

"I'll email you something," she said, moving to leave.

"Thank you." Hilton reached across the table and surprised Stevie by taking her hand. "I thought I'd be writing about Blair forever. I thought I'd cover her wedding, the birth of her children. This should never have happened, and I am so sorry for your loss."

Stevie nodded, not trusting herself to speak. She hurried out of the booth, knocking over her glass. Milkshake splattered over the table, dripped onto Hilton's lap. He leapt up. She didn't turn around again, just kept running for the door, and burst out of the diner, into the heat of the day.

She stuffed her hands in her pockets, started walking, head down, eyes blurred with tears.

She wasn't sure whether to believe him, but she'd been relieved when Hilton had told her she needn't worry—his intention was to celebrate Blair. Right now, people wanted to remember how wonderful Blair was, and he just needed Stevie to share some personal recollections of Blair as a loving, caring sister. Easier said than done.

She knew she had stories like that, but Blair's last visits were all that came forward in her mind. Blair's behavior at Stevie's disaster of a sixteenth birthday party. The few times she had been home after she'd missed Mia's vigil, and all the drama she always brought with her. But then Hilton had asked some questions about their childhood—he'd talked about how bright and fun Blair had seemed when she was just starting out in the business. That Blair had once told him Stevie was her favorite person, and slowly, Stevie had started talking. She'd surprised herself. She was normally good at keeping herself in check, holding personal things close. But maybe she'd wanted to talk about Blair. Maybe she'd needed it. Because Blair had once been her favorite person too.

She talked about how an eight-year-old Blair would sneak into her bed and sing to her if she'd had a nightmare. About how an eleven-year-old Blair had given Stevie her lunch after she'd left hers on the school bus. About how when Stevie was eleven and she'd fallen out with her best friend, Blair had taken her hands and told her that it didn't matter—she was her best friend and always would be.

The box where Stevie put her pain, the one she had worked so hard to shut, had started to crack open.

Stevie walked along the street, sweat trickling down her back. She didn't know where to go, what to do. Her memories of Blair colliding with that awful message Hilton had shown her about her family. It was ridiculous. Who in her family could be a criminal? It was laughable. Hal had had his brush with the law, but he was young and stupid, and he'd learned his lesson. He wouldn't have done anything else like that again. Would he? She remembered his feet shifting and her heart dipped. What if he had? What if he'd done something worse and Blair knew about it and gave the press the DUI story to protect him? Her heart dipped again. If Hal thought Blair was going to say something about the other thing he'd done . . . Stevie stopped short on the sidewalk. What was she doing? This was *Hal* she was thinking about. Her brain was spiraling out of control. Hal had been pissed at Blair for talking about his DUI. If she was doing it to protect him, he would have understood—been grateful, even. Besides, he was at home when Blair was shot. She needed to get her head straight.

It was just after three, and she had a few hours to kill before the vigil, so she decided to head to the library. She needed somewhere cool and quiet to knit herself back together again. But when she walked in, she found herself heading toward the computers.

She logged in, telling herself that she was only doing it to rule the possibility out. Her fingers hovered over the keys, not sure where to start. But then she saw herself type *Marnie Baker conviction* into Google.

She buried her face in her hands. Was she actually losing it? Was her mind fracturing, like it had done with Mia?

"Are you okay, sweetie?"

Stevie looked up. The librarian, Mrs. Thorne, was standing over her, a worried look on her face.

Oh, I'm wonderful! My sister's been murdered and I'm about to embark on an extensive internet search to find out if someone in my family is a criminal.

"I'm fine, just looking for something," Stevie replied.

Mrs. Thorne's eyes fell on the computer screen, and she did a double take. Stevie quickly closed the tab.

Mrs. Thorne frowned, backed away. "I hope you find whatever you're looking for. Send my condolences to your parents. I've been praying for you all."

Stevie thanked her and waited for Mrs. Thorne to get back to her desk before she started searching again.

Did she expect to find anything? No. Was she prepared to scour every possible corner of the internet anyway, even though she felt like she was way off base, disloyal, a little unhinged? Yes. She had to look, and then she could stop thinking about it.

She typed her mom's name again. Scrolled past the entries about a Marnie Baker who was a watercolor artist and another who was a therapist. Other than her relationship to Blair and her fundraising efforts for different charities, nothing came up about her mom that was of interest. Of course it didn't.

The only things she found about her dad were linked to his career—arresting criminals rather than acting as one. And then his volunteering at the Aaron Taylor Community Center. The woodshop he'd set up, the new audio equipment, the free breakfasts.

There were obviously a whole bunch of articles about Hal and his DUI. Apart from that, there were some local newspaper reports of his high-school football victories.

For Uncle Jimmy, she found an article in the *Honeyville Hive* about his promotion following Frank's early retirement, and then a few news reports about people he had arrested—mainly for petty thefts and fighting outside Lacey's Bar.

The only articles on Annie Baker were about her missing daughter.

Stevie put her head down on the keyboard and groaned. What was she doing? If there was something on the internet about her family, she'd already know about it. Whoever had emailed Hilton calling her family a bunch of criminals had to be making it up. Apart from Hal's DUI and possibly Blair, she couldn't imagine anyone breaking the law—they just weren't capable of it. It was probably someone trying to make a quick buck. Or perhaps someone Frank had arrested in the past was trying to get revenge by smearing the family name. He was protective. But if it was made up, why had Kirk Tyler been so eager for Hilton to drop it? If there was a story, it had to be about Blair—she was clearly the only one he was worried about protecting. *Had* Blair done something awful once? Or was this all a big load of nothing that was distracting her from focusing on the stalker? Whatever it was, the answer wasn't in the library.

A wave of exhaustion rolled over her. She checked the time— she had a couple of hours before she needed to leave for Blair's vigil. A nap suddenly seemed like a very good idea, so she found a quiet corner between the library shelves and set the alarm on her phone.

Colby banged on the window, then shouted, "Are you coming?"

Stevie had been parked for fifteen minutes, trying to build up the courage to get out of her car. The place was heaving with Blair Baker mourners, TV crews, cops, and groups of teenagers dressed in Blair Baker-branded T-shirts and hoodies, their arms laden with black bracelets, ready to remember Blair and capture it all on their social media. There were older fans too, in cowboy boots and black Stetsons. Plenty of Honeyville residents had turned up. Some who knew Blair or were friends of the Baker family, but mostly those who wanted to experience the spectacle. It was a change from bowling or a trip to the movies. Blair was as entertaining dead as she was alive.

Stevie's fingers fidgeted nervously with Blair's feather-pendant necklace as her eyes glided over the crowd. Was the stalker among them? The man in the long coat, or someone else? She'd scanned every face. Posed the same question each time. *Was it you? Did you kill my sister?* Would she know if she saw them?

Colby opened the car door. "Hello? Are you ready?"

Stevie glanced over at a group of ninth graders posing, tongue out, among the mass of flowers and cards and soft toys lying underneath Blair's billboard. Tongues and sad, mournful eyes. What a combo.

Ready? How could anybody be ready for that?

"Do you need me to coax you out with words of kindness and encouragement, or do you want me to go down the tough-love route?"

"Neither. I'm coming," Stevie said, without making any effort to move.

"Frank and Marnie are already here with Annie."

"No Hal?" Stevie kept her eyes on the ninth graders. They were doing one of Blair's viral dances now.

"Didn't like to ask, after the other night." Colby placed her hand on Stevie's shoulder. "Come on—everyone's waiting for you in the VIG area."

Stevie turned to look at her. "'VIG'? Oh . . . Colby . . . please don't tell me that means 'very important grievers.'"

"Well, that's what you are. Here's your lanyard." Colby hung it over Stevie's neck.

Stevie looked at the lanyard, then at Colby, and then back at the lanyard. "Have you really used rhinestones to spell out VIG?"

"Do you like it? Took ages supergluing them on. Managed to get one stuck to my lip." Colby looked at her expectantly.

"I . . . I . . ." Stevie stuttered.

"I wanted tonight to represent Blair, and I think she would appreciate a bit of bling."

Stevie spotted the small red blood blister on Colby's lip, shook her head, then managed a smile. "You know, I think she'd love the bling. This whole thing is *very* Blair. Thanks for going to the effort to organize all this."

Colby smiled back. "I wanted to do it." She leaned farther into the car. "So, are you ready? Because you said you were coming, and yet you are still buckled into your seat."

Stevie swallowed, nodded at the crowd. "Do you think he's out there?"

"I don't know. Maybe. I've been staring at everyone and thinking, 'Do you look like a murderer?'"

"Same," Stevie said. "Any sightings of a guy in a long coat and cap?"

"No, but there was this one kid who had this really dark vibe about him. He had these really murder-y-looking eyebrows, and his skin was super pale—almost translucent. Looked like a gamer—you know the sort? In desperate need of some time outside and a good steak? Anyway, I questioned him and his mom told me they were in San Diego at the time of the concert. She had photo evidence to confirm it."

"Colby, you did not actually interrogate some kid because he had murder-y-looking eyebrows?"

"I am a little bit psychic, and I thought I was picking up something."

Before Stevie could piece together a response to the *little bit psychic* revelation, Colby pulled out her phone and tapped the screen. "We really need to haul ass—it's starting in fifteen."

Stevie unbuckled her seat belt and stepped out of the car. It would all be over in an hour. She'd gotten through vigils before. She could do it again.

Colby hooked her arm around Stevie's, started directing her through the crowd. The VIG area, as Colby called it, was a roped-off area just to the left of the temporary staging that Colby had covered in battery-powered candles and decorated with a black, white, and pink balloon arch and a large cardboard cutout of Blair. Stevie's parents were on the other side with Annie. A few feet from them were Kirk Tyler, in a black suit, and Bex Lyons, who was also wearing a black suit but had chosen to sport a pair of sunglasses even though it was nighttime. Gunner Trip was standing with two sturdy-looking men on either side of him. It seemed even six-foot-six football players needed bodyguards.

Officer Dean unclipped the rope to let Stevie and Colby through. Stevie's cheeks flushed a little. The last time she'd seen Officer Dean, she'd come out with that whole *thank you kindly* thing. Stevie threw him a quick glance, then stared dead ahead. She was so busy *not* looking at him that she didn't notice the step down. His hands were around her waist before she hit the ground.

"Are you all right? You missed the step," Officer Dean said, hands still on her, those eyes of his staring into hers. Damn it. Colby was right. They were quite soulful.

Stevie stepped back, cheeks now an inferno of embarrassment. "Yes, I am well aware that I missed the step. *You* distracted me."

"*I* distracted you?" His lips flickered into a smile. "Then I apologize."

Why the hell had she said that?! She needed to go, and she needed to go now. *Just thank him and split.* "Well, thank you anyway . . . for your service." Oh, good lord above. That was on a par with the whole *thank you kindly* thing.

Colby looked at her like she'd gone mad. Stevie looked at the ground, eyes widening. Ugh. What was wrong with her?

Officer Dean smiled and winked. "Always ready to serve and protect."

Colby elbowed Stevie as they made their way toward her parents. "'Serve and protect,' huh? Is something going on with you and the strangely attractive cop?"

"No! Nothing's going on! This is my sister's vigil, Colby. Show some respect!"

She sounded like Marnie.

"You're the one flirting with a police officer!" Colby said.

"That was not flirting!" Stevie had no idea what *that* was. "And he's *not* strangely attractive."

"Oh, come on! He totally is! He has lovely eyes, and a kind face, and very expressive eyebrows."

"What is it with you and eyebrows today? Can you focus on what we're doing here, please?"

"You're right. I'm speaking soon." Colby pulled out some index cards from her back pocket. "We can discuss Officer Cutie Patootie later."

"We will not be discussing Officer Cutie—I mean Officer *Dean*—later!"

Colby gave her a hug. "Your parents are over there—go be with them. Keep an eye on the crowd, but be ready for me to call you onstage."

"What do you mean, *call me onstage*?"

Twenty-Three

A few minutes later, center stage and squinting against the flash of cameras, Stevie put her hand over the mic and hissed into Colby's ear, "I cannot believe you convinced me this was a good idea."

"It's a great idea," Colby whispered back. "You'll be fine. Just speak from the heart."

Speak from the heart? In front of all these people? She has to be kidding.

Stevie glared at the back of Colby's head as Colby went down the steps from the stage. At the bottom, Marnie and Frank embraced her. Then, eyes brimming with tears and encouragement, they lifted their gaze to Stevie.

Stevie took a breath, turned back to face the crowd. Crap on a cracker, as Colby would say. There were so many people—all staring at her. Waiting for her to speak. And she didn't have the first idea what to say.

She brought the microphone to her lips, trying to stop her hands from shaking. Her "Hello, I'm Stevie Baker" was drowned out by the shriek of static. She winced. The crowd winced too. Could she just make a run for it now? Say it was all too much? But Colby and her parents were there in the wings, all nodding at her to continue.

Beads of sweat collected at the nape of her neck and trickled down her spine. "Sorry, I'm not as familiar with microphones as Blair was." There were so many faces looking at her, all blurring into one. She scanned the crowd. Was the killer there? Watching her?

"I'd like to start by thanking my friend, Colby Green"—she said Colby's name through slightly gritted teeth—"for enabling all of us who loved Blair to gather here today in her memory." Colby smiled at her from the side of the stage.

"Blair was . . . Blair was . . ." Stevie stopped. Not sure what to say next. She was drowning out there—in a sea of expectation.

She threw a desperate look at Colby, who mouthed back, *Speak from the heart.*

Stevie gripped the microphone tighter. "Blair was always so comfortable on the stage—me, not so much." She let out a sigh, looked down at her feet. "I'll be honest with you—I'd rather be anywhere than here. I don't want to be standing in front of you."

She raised her head. Saw all the lights of all the phones pointing at her, recording her, and a surge of emotion coursed through her. Jagged and bitter. "Am I supposed to get some comfort from your presence here today, from your grief? Some comfort that Blair meant something to you?" She paused, shook her head, her voice growing quieter as her anger loosened and was washed away by a crushing sadness. "Because I don't. Not even a tiny bit." Stevie closed her eyes and when she opened them again, she was crying. "You might feel like you've lost something, but you haven't, not really. Blair was never yours to lose. She was mine . . ." She sniffed, blotted her eyes with the heel of her hand. "She was mine . . . and you might feel like you know her because you've watched her interviews, seen her concerts, witnessed her highs and lows. But you didn't know her. And the worst thing is"—Stevie's breath hitched, her words barely holding together—"neither did I. Not in the end. And that's why I'd rather be anywhere than here, because it just reminds me that my sister . . . my beautiful, talented sister, who promised she would always be my best friend, is dead, and I'll never have a chance to know her again. And I'm mad as hell about it." Stevie looked up at the billboard of Blair, a fresh curtain of tears falling. "My sister was a star—she lit up the stage and every room she walked into. She was so fucking dazzling that it could hurt to stand next to her. Blair was brilliant, and I'd do anything to be close to her light again."

A shout. Loud and angry. Crap—maybe she'd lost the crowd with that speech. Perhaps it was a touch too bitter.

Another shout.

Hold on. Stevie blinked. Was it him? The stalker?

Stevie scanned the crowd, heart accelerating. There were too many damn phone lights to see anything. Then movement—

Someone was pushing their way through toward the stage. Toward her.

Shit. Her eyes flashed over to Colby and her parents.

"You're a liar. Blair Baker wasn't brilliant!" A girl burst out in front of her, a cup in her hand and pure hate in her eyes. "She wasn't a good person!" Such venom in her voice.

"What?" Stevie said, her voice almost failing her.

There were more shouts—Jimmy's this time, the crowd parting around him.

"Blair Baker was a liar! A liar who only looked out for herself!"

Stevie didn't have time to react. The cup hit her straight in the face. She heard the gasp of the crowd as she staggered back. She was wet. Covered in something. Acid? My god, was it acid? She blinked furiously, looked down at herself, and felt the rush of relief. It was milkshake. Only a milkshake. Then someone was shouting, grabbing her, pulling her toward the steps. She knew those hands—it was Officer Dean. She tried to get out of his grip, tried to turn around to see who the girl was. But Jimmy and another cop were already bundling her off toward a police van.

Officer Dean practically dragged Stevie down the steps into the VIG area.

"Who was she? I need to speak to her!" Stevie shouted, trying to push past him.

Officer Dean put his hands on her shoulders, fixed his eyes on hers. "Stevie, take a moment. Breathe. You've just been assaulted."

She looked past him, avoided those deep brown eyes. "Only with a milkshake! And I want to know why! Where are they taking her?"

"To the station, I would imagine. Stevie, please, we'll find out what this is all about, but right now you need to calm down— you're in shock."

"I do not need to calm down! I am calm! Look at me! Calm! Calm! Calm!"

Officer Dean raised an eyebrow.

Okay. Fine. He had a point. She was borderline hysterical and covered in milkshake. She took a slow breath.

He pulled out a packet of travel tissues from his inside pocket, handed the remaining one to Stevie. She looked down at herself and sighed. It was going to take more than one flimsy tissue to clean her up.

"Thanks," she said, as the tissue disintegrated into bits on her face.

He leaned forward, tenderly brushed his thumb over her cheek, removing the tissue residue. "There, that's better." Then he pulled back suddenly, as though he'd realized that tender cheek cleaning was probably not very professional.

Stevie blinked up at him, shake dripping from her lashes, heat spreading across her cheeks.

"Stevie! Stevie! Are you okay?" Marnie rushed over, pushing Officer Dean to the side, and pulled Stevie into a hug, covering herself in milkshake in the process.

"Who was that girl?" Frank asked. "Stevie, do you know her?"

Stevie shook her head. She'd never seen her before in her life.

But she was going to find out who she was—and why she thought Blair was a liar.

Principal Mathers opened the door to the stadium field house. Colby had managed to persuade him to let them in so Stevie could hide from the reporters and clean herself up. Officer Dean had insisted on accompanying them to make sure they only used the bathroom and didn't accidentally wander into the crime scene.

Stevie ran the faucet and waited for the water to heat up.

"That went better than expected," Colby said.

Stevie looked down at her sopping-wet clothes. "Are you being serious right now?"

Colby was right though. The vigil had drawn someone out into the open. Stevie just hadn't expected it to be a teenage girl; it didn't fit with the profile she had in her mind of Blair's stalker. They were more the *creepy long coat, baseball cap wearing* type. And Blair had been shot in the chest. Stevie had been hit by a flying milkshake. It was hardly the same MO.

"Do you really think it was her? Do you think she killed Blair?"

Colby leaned against the bathroom stall, face screwed up in thought. "I don't know. I suppose anything's possible."

Stevie took off her top, chucked it in the trash can, then splashed herself with water. "We need to get down to the police station and see if we can find out who she is. What her deal is with Blair."

Colby chucked her a towel. "Sorry, it's not that fresh. It's been in the trunk of my car a while."

Stevie patted herself dry, held out her hand and Colby threw her a clean T-shirt. Stevie sniffed it, wrinkled her nose, and pulled it on. She looked down at herself, then back at Colby. "Really?"

It was a Blair Baker cropped tee that said Turn the Volume up on Your Dreams.

"It's all I had."

Officer Dean was waiting for them outside. Stevie tugged at the bottom of her shirt, trying to make it cover her midriff.

His eyes flitted downward, then flashed back to hers. He cleared his throat, put on a professional-sounding voice. "Jimmy's asked me to take you home. Your parents have already left—had to get away from the cameras."

"It's okay—Colby's offered to drive," Stevie said.

Officer Dean looked like he might argue, but said, "If you're sure?"

"Don't worry—you can give her a ride some other time," Colby said, then winked at Stevie.

Stevie elbowed her in the ribs. Colby had not just said that! Stevie's eyes flicked to Officer Dean. No reaction. If he'd heard—he was ignoring it. Thank god.

"I'll take you through the back exit. We'll avoid most of the TV crews that way." He took out his flashlight and set off through the corridor. Stevie and Colby followed behind, their footsteps echoing off the concrete floor.

They turned a corner, the flashlight beam lighting up a barrier of police tape, blocking off the covered walkway that led below the stage.

Stevie stopped. "Can you show me where Blair died?"

Officer Dean rubbed the back of his head. "I'm not sure that's a good idea."

"Please?" Stevie looked at him, eyes pleading.

"Stevie, there are protocols—"

Stevie ran her fingers over Blair's silver feather. She knew she was asking a lot. "Please, I need to see."

"We're probably going to go down there anyway," Colby said.

Officer Dean held Stevie's gaze for a moment, then nodded and pulled back the tape. "Okay, but you cannot tell anyone I agreed to this. I could fail field training."

"Relax," Colby said, "we're not going to rat you out."

They walked along the makeshift tunnel, Stevie's breathing loud in her ears.

"Here," Officer Dean said. They were below the stage, in front of a metal door—the door to the room containing the platform that had delivered Blair's broken body into the arena.

"This is where it happened," Stevie said, her voice a whisper.

It wasn't a question, but Officer Dean answered anyway. "Yes. The evidence is conclusive."

"How much room is in there?" Colby asked.

"It's bigger than it looks." Officer Dean shined his flashlight at the door but moved it away quickly. But Stevie had seen the dark stain on the floor from where her sister's blood had pooled and spread.

"I want to go in," Stevie said.

Officer Dean chewed his lip. "I don't know . . ."

"I won't touch anything."

"One minute and one minute only." He flicked a switch on, and Stevie followed him. Her eyes went immediately to the dark bloodstain on the platform. There were sequins in it—they twinkled almost mockingly, a grim kind of glitter. She pulled her gaze away, studied the room—more like a metal storage container—the platform right in the middle. Against one wall was a chair and a table of untouched snacks and bottles of water. Against another was a large metal cabinet.

"What's in there?" Stevie asked.

"The electronics for the platform. It's linked to a panel in the control room."

Had the killer hidden behind there? Or had they been sitting in the chair when Blair walked in?

"What a horrible place to die," Stevie said quietly.

"Is there a good place?" Colby said.

Officer Dean looked at the doorway. "Some are worse than others."

Stevie appreciated him saying that. For speaking the truth. Blair had been shot in the chest. She would have seen the gun. Looked into the eyes of her killer and known what was about to happen. She must have felt so scared and alone. And the whole time she was only feet away from thousands of fans. All those people had been right there, and not one had been able to help her. And Stevie had been there too, hadn't she? As far as places to die, this ranked among the worst.

Officer Dean gestured toward the door—he looked eager to get out. "We should go before people start wondering where you are."

Stevie lingered a moment in the doorway, whispered quietly under her breath, "I'm here now, Blair. I'll find out who did this to you."

As they headed down the corridor toward the exit, Stevie fell in step with Officer Dean. "Are you working on any leads?"

He came to a stop at the door. "I'm afraid I can't discuss that— all communication with the family has to come from Jimmy." Something had shifted; he was speaking more formally now, like he was regretting showing them the room.

"But you are looking into the stalker, right? Did you get any evidence from the tiara?"

"It would be reasonable for you to consider that was one of our lines of inquiry," Officer Dean said. "I'm afraid we couldn't draw anything from the tiara."

Stevie nodded. She knew it was her fault. "Have you considered that there's a possibility she may have had a secret boyfriend? She was taking trips back to Honeyville and none of us knew about it. You should look into that, too. And Kirk Tyler. His and Blair's relationship was . . ." She paused, what was the word Hilton had used? "Fractious. Their relationship was fractious. I think she might have wanted to leave Satellite. I think she argued with him in her dressing room about it. And I don't think Gunner Trip was honest about when he got to Honeyville. He came here three days before he said he did—some guy at the Rising Sun Motel saw him. Oh, have you gotten any ballistics back from the bullet?"

Officer Dean came to a stop. "We are looking into every possible lead, Stevie. I promise you that. I shouldn't really tell you this, but we're no longer looking at Gunner Trip. We have nothing to place him at the concert venue—we have footage of him at his hotel at the start of the concert—and he passed a polygraph. I know I said it is most often a jealous lover, but he didn't kill Blair."

"But polygraphs aren't one hundred percent accurate, are they?" Surely, he should know this?

Officer Dean sighed, put his hands on his hips. "Who told you Gunner was at the motel?"

"I didn't get a name, but he seemed pretty certain Gunner had been there."

"He'll be easy to find. He was wearing a white vest and briefs, socks and slides," Colby said.

Stevie's cheeks flushed. Not the most thorough detective work, and *white-briefs guy* hardly sounded like the most reliable witness.

"We're getting pressure from the Titans's lawyers to allow Gunner to leave, but I'll see if we can keep him here a couple more days while we look into it."

"Okay, thanks," Stevie said. "It's not that I think he did it, but I think it does need looking into."

"You have to trust us to handle this investigation, Stevie," Officer Dean said with an almost weary kindness.

Had she annoyed him by telling him how to do his job? Or was she pushing too hard?

"Still, I really think you should listen to my girl—those are some good lines of inquiry she gave you," Colby said.

"And you should both listen to me when I say that we are going over everything." His words were blunt, but he managed to not make them come across that way. "If we make a break in the case, Jimmy will make sure that you know about it."

He could have been giving her the runaround, but there was something about the steadiness of his voice that made Stevie think he was sincere.

Officer Dean opened the side door that led out onto the parking lot and ushered Stevie and Colby through. Stevie snuck a glance at him—his dark hair had fallen across his eyes, and she almost reached up and brushed it away for him. She stared wide-eyed at the asphalt, horrified that the thought had crossed her mind. Somehow, she decided, it was all Colby's fault.

The place had quieted down—the police must have moved most of the mourners on. Only a handful were left, watching a couple of reporters filming in front of Blair's billboard.

"Think we'll be okay from here." Colby pointed at one of the few cars remaining in the lot. "That's me just over there."

Officer Dean didn't look certain. "I really would prefer to see you safely into your automobile."

Stevie rolled her eyes. Who under the age of sixty said *automobile*? She almost smiled. Managed to stop it. She would not find that cute. Not find *him* cute. Whatever his eyes looked like. "Thank you, but we'll be fine."

Officer Dean nodded, turned away, and Stevie set off toward the car with Colby. But then she spun around and called out,

"Officer Dean, what's your actual name?"

"It's Oliver."

"Oliver," Stevie repeated, then turned back around.

Colby looked at her, eyebrows raised.

Stevie put her hands on her hips. "What?"

"You like him."

"I do not."

"I think you two would make a supercute couple. Oliver and Stevie. Oliver and Stevie. Does that sound good? I can't decide."

"Would you knock it—" Stevie broke off, her eyes catching on someone on the other side of the parking lot.

Kirk Tyler. And he looked like he was in the middle of an argument.

"Stevie and Oliver. Is that better? Stevie and Oliver—"

"Oh my god, Colby, will you shut up and look!" Stevie nodded toward two people standing under a streetlight. "Colby, how does your mom know Blair's manager?"

Twenty-Four

Stevie asked again, "Colby, how does your mom know Kirk Tyler?"

Colby turned to her, mouth open. "I don't know. She doesn't. How could she?"

Stevie scrunched up her nose. "She really looks like she does."

Colby's hand flew to her mouth. "Oh hell! Don't tell me she's hitting on him."

"Doesn't she have a boyfriend?"

"Mike Tithe?" Colby sort of spat his name out. Stevie didn't need to ask what she thought of him. "Don't think that would stop her." Colby started striding across the lot.

"What are you doing?" Stevie said, running to keep up.

"Finding out what's going on, *obviously*."

As they drew closer, Colby shouted, "Mom!"

Faith Green looked up, eyes wide, surprised at hearing her daughter's voice. She arranged her mouth into a smile. Kirk clocked Stevie and gave her nod, then glanced at his car like he wanted to get away.

"Colby, baby, you did great out there," Faith drawled. "Sorry that lunatic with the milkshake spoiled it!"

Colby folded her arms. "What are you doing here?"

"I came to support you, honey."

"Support me?" Colby laughed but it was cold. "You said this whole thing was ridiculous. You said *I* was ridiculous."

Faith widened her smile but sharpened her eyes. "You're misremembering and also forgetting your manners in front of Mr. Tyler, young lady."

"You know each other?" Stevie asked.

"We just met," Kirk said quickly. "And I really should be going. I'm sorry about tonight, Stevie."

Stevie arched an eyebrow. "Still, I suppose it will mean there will be more interest in Blair, which will mean more sales for you."

"Believe me," Kirk said, opening the door to his Tesla, "I didn't want tonight to go down like this."

Was he telling the truth? Who knew?

Kirk climbed into the car—Bex Lyons ready in the driver's seat. He turned to her and said, "Anyone ID the girl yet?"

He shut the door before Stevie heard the answer.

"I should get going too," Faith said, checking her watch. "I'm meeting Mike down at Lacey's. Don't want to keep my man waiting."

"Mom," Colby said, "why were you really here? What were you doing with Kirk Tyler?"

Faith patted Colby's cheek. "As I said, I came to support you. Don't make me wonder why I bothered." She turned on her high heels and tottered over to her Chevy Malibu.

"She's lying," Colby said. "There's no way she was here to support me."

Stevie didn't think so either. "You okay?"

Colby brushed her question aside. "We should get going too. We need to get to the police station. See what the deal is with Miss Milkshake."

Twenty-Five

"As I've already said, if you're not next of kin, I can't tell you anything."

Stevie looked at Colby, wondering what to do next. The Honeyville PD desk officer wasn't giving them anything.

Colby leaned on the desk, her eyes falling to the name badge, "Listen here, *Marge*, Stevie was the person who was assaulted with the milkshake—surely she has a right to know *who* assaulted her?"

Marge looked over her glasses, the irritation clear in her eyes. "As I've also said, the girl's a minor. I am not at liberty to pass on her personal information." She turned to Stevie. "Now, Miss Baker, I know your connection to the station. I know both your uncle and your father, and I am very sympathetic as to your situation, but I cannot answer your questions."

She didn't sound the least bit sympathetic.

"Is my uncle here? Can I speak with him?" Stevie asked. Jimmy wouldn't be happy that she was there with her questions, but maybe he'd tell her something. Colby was right—she was the one who'd been assaulted with a cold beverage after all.

Marge rocked back in her chair, a look of disdain in her eyes. "He is not."

"Okay, then . . . Officer Dean? Can you find out if he'll see me?"

"He's not going to tell you anything that I haven't already."

Stevie gave her the big pleading eyes. "Please, Marge, my dad always said how efficient and helpful you are."

Marge looked at her through half-lowered eyelids. "Flattery won't work on me, young lady."

Colby leaned across the desk. "Go on, Marge, give Ollie Boy a buzz. If not, we're just going to stay here chatting with you all evening. Allllllllll evening."

Marge let out a gusty sigh, but she picked up the phone. "I'm telling you, he's not going to say anything to you two."

That might be true. But it was worth a shot.

A few minutes later, Oliver came through the double doors to the waiting room, smoothing down his shirt and finishing off the last mouthful of something.

"Stevie, I thought you'd gone home," he said, a puzzled look on his face.

"We wondered if you had any news about the girl you took into custody?"

"I'm sorry, but I can't tell you about that—not yet."

Marge, who was clacking away on her keyboard, muttered, "That's what I said. Would they listen? Would they heck."

Colby swung around. "All right, Marge. You've made your point."

"Oliver, please?" Stevie grabbed his arm.

He looked down at her hand. Stevie did too. What was she doing touching him? She whipped it away. "Has she said why she did it? Why she hates Blair?"

Oliver shot a look at Marge, then nodded to the corner. Stevie followed him over, Colby practically stuck to her hip.

"What you got for us, Oliver?" Colby said.

"I'd prefer if you'd call me Officer Dean at work," Oliver said.

Colby saluted. "Okay, Officer Dean, what's the milkshake bandit said? Did she kill Blair?"

"Honestly, I don't think that's likely, but as she's only fifteen, we can't speak to her until her stepdad gets here. He should arrive in the morning. He's been beside himself wondering where she was. Apparently, she took the bus down here last night. Must have taken her eight hours."

"Have you arrested her?" Stevie asked.

"That depends on whether you want to press charges."

"I don't," Stevie said quickly. "I just want to speak to her."

"I can't let you back there, I'm afraid."

"Have you got her locked up in a cell?" Colby asked.

"No, she's not locked up. We're looking after her and keeping her safe until her stepdad gets here."

Stevie tried to peer over his shoulder, through the little glass panel in the door. "But that's where she is, right? In the cells?"

"Yes, Stevie. Why?"

"And there's no way you'd let me speak to her, just for five minutes?" She tried her big pleading eyes again.

He shook his head, glanced at Marge, and lowered his voice. "I've already let you in somewhere I shouldn't tonight. And the only people allowed back there are staff and people we've arrested."

"I think you're being quite obstructive," Colby said indignantly.

"You are entitled to your opinion," Oliver replied. "But unless you want me to arrest you, I'm afraid, Stevie, the answer is no."

"Arrest me, then," Stevie said.

Oliver blinked, a tilt to his mouth. "I'm not going to arrest you. Not when you haven't done anything wrong. What I am going to do is insist that you go home." He placed his hand on the small of her back, like he meant to walk her to the door.

Stevie stepped to one side. She wasn't going to let him eject her. She had to speak to that girl and find out what she had against Blair. She had to get into the cells. But to do that, she was going to have to do something wrong, and she could only think of one thing.

"Stevie, you need to go," Oliver said.

She was probably going to regret this. But he hadn't given her much choice. If anything, he'd given her the idea.

"I'm really sorry, Oliver—I wish I didn't have to do this. It's nothing personal."

Oliver's brow furrowed. "What do you mean?"

Stevie brought her arm back, then punched him right in the face.

"Holy shit, Stevie!" Colby said, as Oliver staggered back, hands clutching his nose.

Stevie shook her hand, stuck it between her legs. "I'm sorry, I'm sorry." She was—she really was.

Marge cried out, slammed her fist on the alarm button.

Oliver looked at Stevie, eyes full of disbelief. "What did you do that for?"

"I . . . I . . ."

Two cops burst through the doors. Both tall and dark, so similar looking, they could have been carbon copies.

"Her—that girl there!" Marge said, pointing a finger toward Stevie. "She assaulted an officer."

Oliver wiped at the blood under his nose with his sleeve, kept his eyes on Stevie. "Take her to the cells—put her in 3B. I'll log it and be down in a minute."

The door to her cell squealed on its hinges, then clunked shut. Stevie lowered herself onto the bench. Took a couple of deep breaths. She was in an actual holding cell. One with bars and a stainless-steel toilet like in cop shows. She'd had her prints taken, her phone taken, her statement taken—then her shoelaces. Stevie swallowed. What the hell had she just done? She'd got herself arrested, that's what, and when Marnie and Frank found out, which they would, they were going to be apoplectic. And Oliver—she'd properly clocked him. He was going to think she was completely unhinged. Maybe she was. She looked up at the ceiling.

Way to go, Stevie. This is going to look great on your college applications.

Movement in the cell opposite her caught her attention.

It was her. The girl. And she was directly opposite. Sitting on the floor of cell 3A, a blanket on her lap, staring at the floor. She looked up at Stevie, blinked, clearly surprised to see her there. Quickly, she dropped her head again.

Had Oliver helped Stevie by putting her in the cell opposite on purpose? A sudden rush of affection swelled in her, caught her off guard. She pushed it away. It was a coincidence—she'd clocked him one on the nose, for god's sake—he was hardly going to do her a favor after that. And she really shouldn't be thinking about Officer Oliver Dean; she was in the middle of a murder investigation. *Get a grip, Baker,* she said in her head, or at least she thought she'd said it in her head, but as the girl in the cell opposite looked up, it was possible she had said it out loud. Great. She was a crazy woman in a prison cell talking to herself.

"I'm not crazy," Stevie called over, then realized that was probably quite a crazy way to introduce herself. "I'm Stevie, Stevie Baker. You chucked a banana milkshake at me earlier."

The girl didn't react—other than an almost imperceptible tensing of her shoulders, she kept looking at the floor, her long dark hair hanging over her face.

Stevie sat down on the floor too—better to be on her level— and leaned against the bars. She kept her tone light. "I'm not going to press charges, by the way."

Still nothing.

"Heard you made an eight-hour bus drive for Blair's vigil. Got to be a good reason you did that?"

"I just really like buses." Still she didn't look up.

"It seemed like you're really angry with Blair. And I think you came to her vigil because you had something important to say, so I'm here, ready to listen if you want to say it."

"You sound just like her." The girl's voice came out sharp, accusing.

"Like who? Blair?"

She looked up, eyes narrow. "No, the queen of England. Of course Blair."

"So you knew her, then?"

The girl let out a hollow laugh. "I know she was a lying bitch."

Stevie swallowed, pushed down the urge to defend her sister, and tried to keep her voice steady. "Did Blair do something to hurt you?"

"Look, I don't know what you want from me, but I'm *really* not up for some jail-cell heart-to-heart. So if you wouldn't mind shutting the hell up, that would be great."

For a moment Stevie wondered if she'd made a mistake. This girl seemed impenetrable—and was clearly angry. But Stevie knew about anger. She'd worn it like a cloak for a while after Mia disappeared. It was all she had for protection against the pain. She could see the hurt behind the fury in the girl's eyes. Simply being nice to her wasn't going to work.

"So you didn't know Blair, then? You chucked a banana milkshake at me for some other reason?" Stevie nodded at the girl's phone. "To get more followers on your social media?" She nodded slowly to herself. "Yeah, I guess that might make sense in some messed-up way."

God, she felt bad about doing this.

The girl glowered at her. "That's not what it was about at all."

"Sure it wasn't." Stevie rolled her eyes. "And *of course* you know Blair—she was always making friends with angry teenage girls."

The girl got to her feet, grabbed on to the bars of the cell.

"I did know Blair! Well, I thought I did. I thought she cared. I thought she was kind. But she was a liar."

Stevie got to her feet too. "A liar—*really*? What did she lie about?"

"She promised she was going to help me, and I believed her," the girl shot back.

"Help you with what?"

Stevie's words hung in the space between them. The girl's chin began to wobble, and her eyes started to fill. Guilt bloomed in Stevie's chest at having pushed her.

"What's your name?" Stevie said softly.

The girl sniffed. "Melissa."

"Melissa, what did Blair promise to help you with?" Stevie spoke every word gently—she couldn't risk her shutting down.

Melissa took so long to respond that it didn't look like she would, but then she said, "I told her what he was doing, and she said she'd make him stop."

Stevie's chest tightened. "Who are you talking about, Melissa?"

"Her manager, Kirk Tyler."

Twenty-Six

Stevie leaned against the door to her cell and listened to Melissa tell her everything about Blair's manager. She told her how Kirk lured her in with promises that she could meet Blair. How he'd invited her around to hear early plays of Blair's new songs, paid for cars to pick her up, given her free clothes and meals and VIP tickets and sometimes alcohol. How he'd made her think she was special. Important to Blair. Part of the inner circle. How it was fun for her to begin with. How she'd been dazzled by a glimpse of celebrity life. How lucky she felt. And then how he'd gotten her on her own and abused her.

Kirk Tyler was a monster. A groomer. It turned Stevie's stomach, sent her blood rushing hot through her veins. But when she heard about the part Blair had played, her heart froze, and her insides turned stone-cold. What Melissa was saying about Blair couldn't be true. It just couldn't.

Stevie listened to how her sister had walked in on Kirk and Melissa. How she'd stopped it and shouted at Kirk, "No! No more!" How she had comforted Melissa, sent her home in a taxi, and pressed her phone number into her hand. How Melissa had called. How they'd met up in a café, where Blair had sworn to her that she would deal with it. How she promised to expose Kirk for who he really was. How Melissa had believed her and how Blair had given her hope. Only for Blair to turn into a ghost.

Melissa drew her legs up to her chest. "A woman named Bex Lyons showed up at our house three weeks ago—a week after I'd last heard from Blair. Offered one hundred thousand dollars to keep my mouth shut. I guess that's what Blair meant by *dealing with it*."

A voice in the back of Stevie's head whispered, *Blair wouldn't abandon her like that—she just wouldn't*. But then a doubt flickered into life. The Blair that Stevie had known—the one who looked out for her when she was little, the one who stood up to bullies in the schoolyard—would never have turned her back on Melissa. But Blair the superstar? Could she have changed that much?

"My mom and stepdad didn't have to think about it—they took the money and tried not to look too happy about it. They said they believed me, but they also said that I didn't have any proof of what Kirk had done. That it was his word against mine. Besides, hadn't I gone there willingly? Weren't there photos of me backstage—didn't I brag about all the freebies on my socials—didn't I tell the world how lucky I was? Then they said that with all that money, they could pay for counseling, if I needed it."

"What happened to you was awful. I'm so, so sorry." Stevie heard the words—knew they weren't enough.

Melissa shrugged but her face was tight. She tipped her head back until it touched the wall of the cell. "I don't know what I was thinking, coming here. What answers I thought I'd find. I was just so angry listening to everyone talking about how great Blair was . . ."

A long, weighted silence. Stevie ran over everything Melissa had said. But she kept coming back to the same question—how could Blair have walked away from this?

A stone settled in Stevie's chest, sank deep down. Maybe she didn't. Maybe that was what had gotten her killed. Blair had told Hilton Moore that she had a story for him. A story about *someone important*. If that story was about Kirk Tyler and he had found out . . . well, that would be a pretty strong motive for wanting her dead.

Anger seeped into Stevie's bones and the spaces in between. Had Kirk killed Blair? He was now certainly Stevie's number one suspect.

"He can't get away with what he's done to you."

"Who's going to see to that? You?" Melissa said bitterly.

Yes, she sure as hell was. "I don't think Blair did walk away. Hilton Moore told me that a month ago, Blair went to him about a story. I think that story was about Kirk, and if he found out, he might have killed her so she couldn't talk."

Melissa lifted her head from the wall, frowned hard at Stevie. "You're telling me that a month ago, Kirk finds out that Blair's going to expose him, so he decides to kill her on the opening night of her homecoming tour? Why would he wait?"

The question slammed into her. Melissa was right—why would he? Unless . . . Stevie's heart tripped, climbed back up double time. "Maybe he'd convinced Blair not to talk, but then she changed her mind. She'd realized she'd done the wrong thing. Blair was arguing with someone in her dressing room on the day she was murdered. Maybe it was Kirk, and she was telling him that she was going to go public."

It was all slotting together. Kirk had access. He could have easily waited for Blair below the stage. Stevie clenched her jaw so hard that it ached. "Kirk shot Blair—then he sat in the audience and watched her body rise up on that platform, knowing what he'd—"

"Stop, please stop." Melissa looked up, cheeks wet with tears. "I can't listen to you telling me Blair was killed because of me."

"I . . . I . . . didn't mean . . . I'm just thinking out loud. Melissa, none of this is your fault. Kirk Tyler needs to be in jail for what he's done to you. You need to tell the police what you've told me. Then maybe the truth about Blair might come out too—"

"No, I just can't!" Melissa cut her off, shook her head violently.

"Melissa—"

Melissa jumped to her feet, started pacing the cell. "I won't do it. You've just told me you think Kirk Tyler's a murderer. He'll come after me. I know he will. He knows where I live!" Melissa's voice was frantic, eyes darting.

Stevie stood up, clutched hold of the bars. "But the police will protect you. You could speak to Officer Dean—we could get him right now and—"

"No!" Melissa stopped short, jaw set. "Stevie, I mean it. I'm not talking, and you have to promise me you won't tell anyone either. If you do, I'll deny it all. I am not standing up in a courtroom with only my word against his. We all know how that will go."

"Maybe it doesn't have to just be your word. Did anyone else know what Kirk did to you other than Blair? Other fans? Could someone from Satellite Entertainment have seen something?" Stevie's voice was fast, desperate.

"I don't know. I can't see how people wouldn't question why a man in his fifties was entertaining a teenage girl." Melissa's eyebrows drew together, a sudden flicker of irritation. "I guess they're all just too scared to lose their jobs."

"What about physical evidence?" Stevie rattled through the possibilities in her mind. "Do you have any texts from Kirk? Any inappropriate messages?"

"No, nothing like that. He was careful."

"Okay . . . but he paid you off. Did your parents have to sign anything?"

"I have no idea. Bex Lyons just showed up at the house, spoke to my parents, and transferred the money electronically."

"The money! That's it! If we can prove Kirk Tyler gave one hundred thousand dollars to the family of a fifteen-year-old girl, it's going to raise suspicion. Do you have any evidence of the payment? An account number? A screenshot of money going into an account? Anything that could tie him to a payoff?"

Melissa let out a puff of air. "I guess . . . but, Stevie, you're not listening, I don't want to be involved. If Kirk killed Blair, what's to stop him coming after me?" She paused, took a breath. "And what if you're wrong? What if Kirk didn't kill Blair, you stir all this up, and it's back to his word against mine?"

A ripple of doubt. Stevie turned over what she knew. She had a motive for Kirk, and opportunity, but no actual evidence. "Melissa, Kirk Tyler belongs in prison, whether he killed Blair or not, and I want to be a part of making that happen."

"Then you're going to have to do it without me."

Stevie remembered the girl that Kirk had been with at the concert—the one she had thought was his daughter. Her stomach twisted. "What if there are other girls? Don't you want to stop it happening to them?"

Melissa closed her eyes, exhaled heavily. "Please, don't put that on me. I'm sorry—I wish I could help you, but I can't."

Stevie nodded. If Melissa wasn't willing to talk, she wasn't going to make her.

"I won't ask you to say anything, but if you could *please* just get me that proof of payment . . ." Stevie paused. Was she pushing too much?

Melissa turned to face her, exhaled through her nose. "I'll see what I can do."

Before Stevie could thank her, the door at the end of the corridor burst open. Then a shout of "Stevie, I'm here!"

Stevie blinked twice. What. The. Actual. Hell. Was that . . . ?

"It's me!"

Colby.

She was being escorted by the same two cops who had brought in Stevie.

"You don't need to hold on to me! I can walk thirty feet on

my own!" Colby scowled at the hand that was clamped on to her shoulder.

Stevie stood, open-mouthed, as Colby stepped into cell 2A and the door was closed behind her. "Colby . . . I mean . . . how?"

"Let's just say, poor Oliver will have two matching black eyes in the morning."

Stevie pinched the bridge of her nose. "Tell me you didn't."

"I cannot do that, Stevie, because I absolutely did."

Poor, kind Oliver! The guy was just trying to do his job, and he'd been socked in the face twice.

"I had to!" Colby jerked her thumb toward the exit. "Nobody out there was telling me anything. And in my defense, I did try to topple the vending machine first—but those things are freakin' heavy, so I really had no choice but to land one on your boyfriend."

"He is not my boyfriend!"

Colby grabbed hold of the cell bars. "So, tell me, have you gotten that little milkshake-hurling lunatic to tell you what the hell she was thinking?"

Stevie closed her eyes, pressed her forehead against the bars.

"What?" Colby said. "What? Oh. She's next door to me right now, isn't she?"

"Colby, meet Melissa. Melissa, Colby."

Twenty-Seven

Stevie's dad slammed the passenger-side door. He'd arrived at the police station to pick her up not long after Colby had turned up in the cells. He'd barely spoken to her, hardly been able to look at her.

Frank got into the driver's seat. Started the engine. Then turned it off again. Grabbed hold of the steering wheel, knuckles whitening. He kept his eyes forward as he spoke—his voice trembling with anger.

"You assaulted a police officer, Stevie."

Stevie stared at the footwell. "I know."

He turned to look at her now. "You *know*? That's all you have to say for yourself? Do you know how humiliating it was for me to have to come down here? You're lucky Officer Dean isn't taking this any further. What were you thinking?"

"I . . . I don't know." Telling him she'd wanted to get arrested wasn't the right course of action.

"Marge said you were hassling her for information about the girl who turned up at the vigil."

"I just wanted to know why she did it."

"Stevie, it is not your place to find out!" Frank thumped the steering wheel with the heel of his hand.

"Dad, please, your heart," Stevie said.

"This is not about me. This is about what you did! And punching Officer Dean because he won't speak to you is unforgivable. Your mother can't know about this. It would send her over the edge."

"I think Kirk . . . I mean, there's a chance that Kirk Tyler killed Blair, Dad." The words were out of her mouth before she had a chance to think.

His eyes flicked across her face, his fury replaced by confusion. "What are you talking about? Why would you think that?"

"Kirk Tyler is a bad person, Dad, and I think Blair knew it and was going to tell the world what he'd done. Which would give him a motive to kill her."

"Where are you getting this from?" He knew the answer as soon as he'd asked the question. "You spoke to her? Stevie, if that girl in there told you something important, you need to tell someone."

"I can't tell you what she said—I promised Melissa I wouldn't."

"Stevie, this is a murder investigation! You can't make promises like that! If you know something, you need to tell Jimmy."

"I can't—"

"Oh, Stevie, you *will*," Frank said, steel in his words.

"No. I swore I wouldn't. She's not willing to talk and I don't think it's right to make her."

Frank ground his back teeth together. "I knew we should never have had anything to do with that guy."

"Will you tell Jimmy to look at him? Check over Kirk's alibi again? But please, tell him to keep Melissa out of it—she's just a kid."

Frank wasn't listening—his grip on the wheel was so tight now that his knuckles were almost translucent. His chest rising and falling, nostrils flared, air hissing out of them.

Stevie placed her hand on her dad's arm. "Call Uncle Jimmy. Get him to look over his alibi again."

Frank found her eyes, then nodded and took out his phone.

"Jimmy, sorry it's late—I need you to do something for me. I want you to take a close look at Kirk Tyler, check if his alibi holds."

Stevie strained to hear what Jimmy was saying but couldn't make out the words.

"I know . . . I know—just do me this favor. Check it again. And another thing, the girl that threw the shake at the vigil—ask her what she knows about Kirk . . . *Yes*, you can."

Stevie's mouth dropped open, anger sparking in her.

As soon as Frank ended the call, she said, "Melissa is going to know I've said something! I gave her my word I wouldn't!"

"This isn't a game, Stevie. Your sister was murdered. You've just been arrested! You need to stay out the way and let the police do their jobs. Right now, I don't want to hear another word out of you, except for 'yes, Dad,'—have I made myself clear?"

Stevie bit down on her anger, hardened her voice. "Yes, Dad."

"Now, I'm taking you home. We keep this to ourselves, okay?"

She turned away, looked out the window. "Yes, Dad."

Frank turned on the engine, drove to the exit of the parking lot, then swerved to avoid the car that was pulling in, straddling both lanes. He swore under his breath and the driver slammed her fist on the horn, then flicked them the bird.

Faith Green. A worse driver than Colby, apparently. She spotted Stevie, swapped her middle finger for a wave and a smile.

The road was clear, but Frank didn't pull out. "You know that woman?"

"That was Colby's mom." Stevie was actually pleased to see her. Colby hadn't been sure whether she'd bother to turn up.

Frank took a moment to process the information, then said, "Stevie, I don't want you hanging around Colby anymore."

Stevie wasn't about to *yes, Dad* to that. "What? Why?"

"Let's just say her mother is no stranger to Honeyville PD. Been in a few times for drunk and disorderly conduct. I don't want you around her."

"Colby's not at fault for her mom's actions! I thought you

cared about kids from difficult home situations. You volunteer at the Aaron Taylor Community Center!" Stevie paused, then said, "Besides, Colby is my friend. I need her." It was something Stevie could never have imagined saying when she'd first shown up on Colby's doorstep, but it was true. There weren't many people who'd be willing to put themselves in jail for her.

Frank let out a long sigh. "Fine, but don't let her lead you astray."

Astray? She wasn't some lost puppy. Really, if anyone was doing any leading, it was Stevie. Colby only punched Oliver because she had.

"And I want you to give me your word that you won't do any more investigating into your sister's case. We're all hanging on by a thread, Stevie, and today you've pushed it too far. It ends now— do you understand me?" He locked eyes with her, steel hard.

Stevie turned away, stared out the window. "Fine." Her dad had already made her break her word once that evening. She may as well do it again. If Kirk Tyler had killed her sister, she was going to find the evidence to get him put away, not just for murder but for what he'd done to Melissa too. Melissa wouldn't talk, but maybe she wouldn't need to if Stevie could find some other way to prove Blair knew about what Kirk had done.

Stevie went straight up to her room. She was going to rewatch the video of the argument in Blair's dressing room on her laptop, see if she could spot something in the footage that would confirm it was Kirk.

She opened the door, heard the scratching and meowing immediately. She ran over to her closet and pulled open the doors. "Catsy?"

Catsy bolted out, ran to the corner of the room where she sat all puffed up and shaking.

Stevie picked her up gently, held her to her chest. "How did you get stuck in there, you poor thing?" She kissed the top of Catsy's head and went to take her onto the bed.

And then she saw it.

A package on her pillow. Shoebox-sized, wrapped in brown paper. Holy shit. He'd been there. The stalker—in her room.

She moved to her desk, placed Catsy in her lap, and opened her laptop. "Let's find out who the hell you are," she said, logging in to the doorcam app and opening up the recording for June 4.

There were over forty motions captured for the day. Damn reporters were probably triggering it. But maybe that was a good thing—it increased the chances of it capturing something.

She clicked through, scouring each recording, starting with Annie arriving early that morning and ending with her and Frank returning that evening. But she didn't see anything. She rubbed her eyes and went back through again. There had to be something there.

And then she saw it. At six thirty p.m., her parents opened the door, headed for the vigil. The reporters started shouting and taking pictures, but behind them there was a flash of something down by the side of the house. It was so quick, she was lucky to catch it.

She moved closer to the screen and slowly scrolled back, one frame at a time. A breath escaped her. It was a grainy smudge only just visible, but unmistakably the back of a long coat.

"Got you, asshole," Stevie breathed. "Now, let's see what you left me."

She placed Catsy on the floor, moved toward the package—legs shaking, heart pounding.

She reached for the package. Then snapped her arm back. She shouldn't touch it.

She should call Jimmy. He'd send for forensics. She took out her phone, dialed the number. Her finger hovered over the Call button. Would it hurt if she had a quick look? If she was careful? She shouldn't mess with the evidence. Jimmy would be furious. But she could wear gloves—preserve any fingerprints. She rooted through her drawers, trying to find some. They'd be in storage in the basement with the rest of her winter clothes. She grabbed a pair of socks. They'd have to do.

Catsy mewed at her.

"It's okay, girl—I'm just going to have a quick look, that's all."

It wasn't easy to peel back the paper—her hands were shaking, and the stupid socks didn't make things any easier, but she would not screw up the forensic evidence this time. Eventually, she got it all off and lifted the lid.

A picture frame was lying face down, a black envelope on top of it—the same as the last one.

She picked up the envelope. She'd open it from the bottom. There may be DNA from the sender's spit on the flap. She found some nail scissors. Tried to slice it open. Using scissors while wearing hand socks was harder than getting the paper off.

She pulled out the card.

My princess, beautiful even in death. Do you miss her, Stevie? I do.

Stevie's stomach twisted at the sight of her name. She placed the card on the lid of the box and picked up the photo frame. She steeled herself and closed her eyes before turning it over. She gave herself a countdown.

Three.

Two.

One.

She opened her eyes.

The initials *BB* had been created out of a collage of photos. Photos of Blair lying dead on the stage, mixed in with photos of her body parts. Her arms—her legs—her breasts. They stood out—so bronzed and vibrant against the grainy pictures of her corpse. Stevie wanted to throw it, smash it against the wall. Disgust surged through her, hot and thick. Whoever had done this had butchered her sister. He'd butchered her and he'd found it beautiful.

Stevie placed the frame back in the box. Turned away from it. Pulled off the socks, threw them in her wastebasket, then put her hands on her head and started pacing the room. He must have come to the house when they were all at the vigil. He'd have known they'd all be there. She'd provided him with an opportunity, and he had taken it to show off about what he'd done. But how had he gotten in? The back door? A window?

Her stomach twisted again—tighter. She stood over her wastebasket, swallowed once, twice, three times, waited for the urge to throw up to pass. Her mind splintered—thoughts rebounding between the stalker and Kirk Tyler. She'd been so sure Kirk had killed Blair. But now? She glanced over at the box. He hardly seemed the type to break into her house and leave such a messed-up gift. Besides, he was at the vigil. Damn it. Maybe she'd gotten it wrong.

She grabbed her bag, put her laptop, toiletries, contact lenses, and a change of clothes into it. Then, with Catsy in her arms, she headed to her parents' room and knocked lightly on the door.

"Dad?"

Stevie heard a sigh, the sound of sheets being thrown back, then her dad's footsteps heading toward the door.

"Stevie, I was asleep." His voice was hard—he was still angry with her, then.

Her chin started wobbling. He couldn't be angry. Not when she was scared. "Dad, he's sent another package. The stalker"— her voice hitched—"he's been in my room."

Twenty-Eight

Stevie woke to the sound of her mom and dad snoring in unison. They'd arrived at the Holiday Inn just before four in the morning and booked a family room free of charge, thanks to the manager, Bob Baxley, being one of Frank's golfing buddies. Jimmy had insisted that they couldn't stay at home while they processed the scene and Marnie had insisted it was too late to wake up Hal and Annie. They needed their sleep, and she didn't want to worry them. She'd made Frank call Bob, who she was certain would understand.

When they arrived, the tired-looking receptionist had told them that cats were not permitted on the premises, but before Stevie even got a chance to argue, Marnie had pulled herself up to her full height of five foot nothing, and unleashed both barrels. She informed the woman that they were special guests of Bob and she would not allow Catsy to be separated from her daughter at her time of need. It wasn't clear to Stevie whose time of need Marnie was referring to—hers or Catsy's—but, either way, Stevie hadn't minded when Catsy had chosen to sleep at Marnie's feet instead of hers.

Stevie checked the time on her phone. It was eight a.m. Four hours of broken sleep was not enough. Every time she'd come close to drifting off, her mind had jolted her awake again with visions of body parts—Blair's and then hers—sealed behind glass. She stared up at the slow rotations of the ceiling fan from the sofa bed. With each turn of its blade, her mind switched between Blair's stalker and Kirk Tyler. Both could have killed her. When she'd spoken to Melissa, she'd begun to believe it was Kirk. But then she'd found that picture and now didn't know what to think.

Hopefully, one of the paparazzi would have gotten a photo of the guy—Jimmy seemed pretty hopeful they'd get an ID and, thanks to the doorcam footage, they had an accurate time frame.

She quietly slid her laptop out of her bag and put her headphones on. She brought up the video Colby took outside Blair's dressing room again, hoping that this time she'd notice something new.

She played it again and again on full volume, so the static hissed and made her ears itch. Whatever was being said behind that door, she couldn't hear it. She paused the video when the man emerged from Blair's room, studied the blurry image of the back of his head. It *could* be Kirk Tyler, but was she just willing it to be him? The still image was of no use, but if she could find some way of enhancing the audio, hear their voices, she might be able to prove who it was. She'd need special audio equipment for that. But where would she find that sort of thing? She sat up.

She knew exactly where. The Aaron Taylor Community Center.

She grabbed her phone, sent Colby a text.

I'm @ the Holiday Inn. Can u swing by & pick me up?

Sure. All ok?

Will explain when I c u

As she closed her laptop, she noticed an unread email. The sender was fghjj143@buzzmail.com. Her stomach dipped, not from shock, but from the awful certainty it was going to be bad.

Digging up secrets is a quick way to end up buried with them.

Stevie sucked in a breath, pulled back from the screen, the sudden spike of adrenaline causing her palms and scalp to sweat. Seriously? The photo frame and now this? She blinked at the screen. Secrets? What secrets? Kirk's? Blair's? Somebody else's?

Were they worth putting herself in danger for? Dying for?

You know what? Screw them. Whoever they were, she wouldn't let an email stop her from finding out. And this was more evidence, wasn't it? And evidence was a good thing.

She read the email again. It had been sent at 8:20 that morning. She must have missed it when she was going over the video. It had the same tone as the last one she'd received. Even used the word *digging* again. @BBWill_be_mine on another account? Had to be.

Were they responsible for the tiara and the framed picture, too? Her gut was telling her it was two different people. The language—the purpose—were completely different. The emailer wanted her to stop investigating, whereas the gift-giver wanted her attention. Well, he had it. They both had it.

"We've only been apart a few hours, and you've had a creepy picture *and* an email." Colby pulled out of the Holiday Inn parking lot, clipping the reception sign as she swung out of reverse. "You, girl, are an overachiever."

It was only coming up on nine o'clock, but the heat was already rising with the June sun. Stevie had crept out, leaving her parents and Catsy sleeping. She left a note telling them she was going for a walk and not to worry, knowing they would.

"It has been eventful," Stevie said. Understatement of the century.

"Poor you and poor Catsy!" Colby turned, locked eyes with her. "Are you sure you're okay?"

"I'd be more okay if you kept your eyes on the road."

"So, the email and the picture—you think they're from two different people?"

"I do. Why would anyone leave a package and then send an email telling me to stop investigating?"

"Because they might be insane. Ooh! They could have a split personality!"

"Yeah, I don't think that's it. It's two people. I'm sure. We just have to work out if one of them killed Blair."

"Okay, so working on the theory that one of them did, whoever sent you the email has to know that you're investigating her murder."

"That could be anybody, thanks to our front-page story in the paper."

"True, but maybe we should try and narrow it down a little."

"Yes, I think narrowing it down from the whole world might be helpful," Stevie said flatly.

"So there's Hilton Moore, Gunner Trip, Officer Dean, Melissa . . ."

Stevie winked. "You."

Colby scowled, stepped over the joke. "And then there's Kirk Tyler. Hey, do you think that he might know you talked to Melissa?"

Stevie breathed in deeply. "It's possible, I suppose. But that would have to mean Uncle Jimmy contacted him last night and I don't think he would have mentioned my name. But say Kirk did know—that's a strong motive to want me to stop digging."

"Especially if he's our killer. But—and hear me out while I try and put this delicately because it's a bit out there—what about someone in your family?"

She meant Hal, obviously.

"Real delicate, Colbs."

"You've said they don't want you to look into Blair's murder."

Stevie let out a hollow laugh. "You think someone in my family is sending me threatening emails? Honestly, they're perfectly happy to be threatening to my face. Take a left off Moreland Avenue."

"I know my way to the east side, Stevie. We lived on Ryland Drive before my mom won the lottery." Colby pulled up to the junction, tapped her fingers on the steering wheel. "So, who do we think is our gift-giver? That can't have been Kirk. He and Bex arrived at the vigil around that time, and there wouldn't have been an opportunity for him to get to your house, sneak in, and get back while you were out."

"What time did Gunner get there?"

"A couple of minutes after Kirk."

"So I suppose we're back to looking at the stalker?"

"And Blair told Gunner that she had figured out the stalker's identity, right? So maybe the stalker was who she was arguing with in her dressing room and he's our culprit!"

"Possibly, although I don't want to rule out Kirk Tyler. I just don't believe Blair would have kept quiet about what he did to Melissa unless she was threatened in some way. I think she was going to go public and that caused the argument. If it's Kirk Tyler on that tape, we'll have enough evidence to prove a motive. We might even get enough to secure a conviction."

"Yeah, I think the smart money is on Kirk." Colby pulled up and slipped into park. "Let's see if the video can help us bust his ass."

Marvin Thompson was opening up the center when Colby bumped her car up onto the sidewalk outside. The Aaron Taylor Community Center had been running for almost four years, and thanks to various Marnie-and-Frank-Baker-led fundraising initiatives, what was once a run-down hardware store was now a thriving community hub on the east side of Honeyville. When it first opened, Stevie had been a couple of times, but after Mia disappeared, she hadn't wanted to socialize. Besides, it was her dad's thing.

Stevie didn't know the east side that well. Marnie had never been enthusiastic about the area. According to her, the bars were seedier, the schools inferior, the sidewalks filthier, and the grocery stores dismal in regard to the organic produce that was for sale. Thanks to her warnings that Stevie should never go to the east side alone, Stevie had been a bit scared of the place when she was younger. When she was old enough to figure things out for herself, she realized that just because you couldn't buy smoked burrata, didn't mean the east side was the hell pit Marnie had led her to believe it was.

"I refuse to believe that anyone gave you a driver's license," Stevie said as she climbed out and surveyed Colby's parking. Her car was half on the sidewalk, half on the street.

"Got you here, didn't I?" Colby nodded at Marvin. "So that's the poor guy who fostered the boy who was shot on Independence Day a few years back?"

"Yeah, Marvin's the nicest man—must be in his seventies now. Dad told me that he and his wife, Gloria, took Aaron in after his parents died when he was twelve. It was supposed to be short-term, but he ended up becoming part of the family." Stevie sighed. "Aaron's was the last case my dad worked on. It really tore him up that they never caught who did it."

"I remember it happening. They said he'd broken in there to steal tools, right?"

"Dad said it made people care less—I guess, in some warped way, they thought Aaron deserved it for robbing the place. People thought he was just some foster kid who had gone down the wrong path. Dad didn't see it like that though. He was really upset about it. When Marvin and Gloria set up this center in Aaron's memory, Dad volunteered to give back to the community. To start with, I think he did it to ease his guilt at not being able to give the Thompsons any answers. Now I think he just likes helping out, especially since Gloria passed away a year ago."

Colby linked her arm through Stevie's. "Guess it helps to do something good after something bad has happened."

"Yeah, I guess it does."

Marvin smiled widely when he saw Stevie, his brown eyes crinkling at the edges, a little sadness in them. "Stevie Baker—it's been a while! Bring it in here for a hug."

Stevie beamed back and let him hold her. There were more flecks of gray in his black hair since she'd last seen him. "Mr. Thompson, it's good to see you. I was so sorry to hear about Gloria." Stevie hadn't gone to the funeral with her dad; it was family and close friends only, and she didn't know Gloria well.

Marvin held her by the shoulders, looked her in the eye, and Stevie didn't see pity, but understanding. "And I am so sorry about Blair."

"Thank you," Stevie said.

Marvin gave her shoulders a gentle squeeze, then turned to Colby. "And who is this you have with you?" Marvin asked.

Colby stepped forward, offered her hand. "I'm Colby Green, Stevie's friend."

Marvin shook it. "Pleasure to meet you, Colby Green."

"Excellent work you are doing here, sir," Colby said.

"Thank you." Marvin glanced up at the sign above the center. "Aaron was a great kid. Gloria and I loved him very much and we wanted to do something good in his name. We didn't want him to be forgotten."

Marvin's eyes drifted off for a moment, lost in a memory, but he gave himself a shake and rubbed his hands together. "So what can I do for you two ladies? We've got a new Ping-Pong table, and I'm getting pretty good if I do say so myself."

"We were hoping we might be able to use your sound equipment," Stevie said.

"You thinking of recording an album?" Marvin asked.

"God, no, nothing like that," Stevie said with a grimace. "We want to try and enhance the audio on a video we have."

Marvin whistled through his teeth. "I'm sure as hell not going to be able to help you with that, but Terence will be along in a minute. He's a bit of a whizz on that equipment. I could ask him to lend you a hand?"

"Thank you, but we've got this," Stevie said.

After half an hour fiddling around with the computer and sliding various buttons up and down on the soundboard, Stevie flopped onto the stool and said, "Nope, we don't got this."

Colby, who had grown bored after about ten minutes, sailed across the room on her wheely chair and called over to Marvin. "Mr. Thompson, we're going to need Terence!" Then she looked over at Stevie. "Who *is* Terence?"

The door to the center opened and a tall guy in a basketball vest walked in. His face split into a wide smile, showing a perfect set of teeth, when he saw Marvin hitting Ping-Pong balls over the table into a bucket. "Getting good, Gramps!"

Colby's eyes widened—then she pressed her hands together and repeated, "Let that be Terence. Let that be Terence."

Marvin put his bat down. "Terence! Girls, this is my grandson."

"Our father, amen, hallelujah!" Colby muttered.

Stevie rolled her eyes and hissed, "You are a liability."

"Would you believe I used to look just like him when I was his age?" Marvin said, looking at Terence fondly.

"I would." Stevie knew Marvin had a grandson, but she'd never met him. Terence had slightly lighter skin, but standing next to his grandfather, she could see how similar they would have looked at the same age.

"Terence!" Colby yelled. "Come here—I need you!"

Terence frowned but his smile didn't falter.

"Okay," he said slowly, brown eyes twinkling in the same way Marvin's did.

"We hear you know how to work this audio equipment," Colby said.

Terence walked over, peered around Stevie's shoulder. "What is it you're trying to do?"

"We want to enhance the audio on a video, but I can't even get it to load," Stevie said.

"May I?" Terence said, gesturing to the stool.

"Yes, you *may*," Colby said quietly to herself.

Stevie shot Colby a look to tell her to quit it, and got up so Terence could take her place at the computer. "Be my guest."

Terence sat down, started humming as he clicked on a few buttons.

"You're a very good hummer," Colby said.

A very good *hummer*? Stevie raised her eyebrows at her. Colby shrugged, leaned a little closer to Terence.

"Thanks? Aha . . . here we go." An image of Colby dressed as half a teddy bear appeared on the screen. Colby gasped, then sprang forward, putting herself in between the screen and Terence.

Terence grinned at her, a mischievous look in his eyes. "That you?"

"Nope," Colby said.

He leaned to the side, peered around her. "Sure looks like you."

"Colby, would you get out the way?!" Stevie said.

Colby held up a finger. "Just so you know, I do not usually dress up as a teddy bear mascot."

"Noted," Terence said.

Colby slid to the side and Terence picked up the mouse. "Which part of the video do you want to hear?"

"Further on from here," Stevie said.

"Okay, I'll track through the frames—say stop when I reach the right part."

Terence dragged the cursor along, and screen-Colby flashed up in various unflattering poses as she ran down the corridor.

"Can you just get to the right part already?" Colby groaned.

"Here! Stop it here!" Stevie said. "Is there any way you can make it so we can hear what's being said behind that door?"

"That's Blair Baker's dressing room?" Terence said, reading the sign on the door. The color drained from his face. "She was just killed, right?"

"I'm her sister, and I really need to know who she was talking to in her dressing room the day she was murdered."

Terence blinked, his eyes making the connection. "You're Frank's other daughter?"

"Yeah, and I *really* need to find out who she was talking to."

"Okay," Terence said slowly, "but shouldn't you take this to the police?"

"They already have it. Please, Terence, can you help?"

Terence ran his hand over his buzz cut. "Sure, why not?"

"Attaboy!" Colby said.

Terence shook his head, managed a small smile for Colby, then turned back to the screen. "I should be able to isolate the sound and boost that part of the audio track."

Colby leaned over Terence's shoulder, her face near his. "Hear that, Stevie? He can isolate the sound and boost that part of the audio track."

"I did hear that, because I have ears." Stevie gave her a gentle thump on the shoulder and mouthed, *Stop it!*

Colby rolled her eyes and turned back to the screen.

"It might take a bit of adjusting." Terence clicked through a few options on the computer, then started sliding buttons up and down on the sound system.

"Okay, let's try now." Terence clicked a Play button on the screen. The speakers popped, then hissed into life, and Stevie's heart clenched when she heard Blair's voice over the crackle of static.

"But I do know. I do know."

"That's Blair!" Colby said.

"Shhh," Stevie hissed. She leaned forward, ready to hear Kirk's voice, or even Blair naming her stalker.

"Whatever you think you know, hasn't Kirk always been there for you? He has always had your best interests at heart. After all the things he's done for you, you must know that. All you have to do is stop acting like a little bitch and keep singing. Let us handle the rest."

"That's not Kirk Tyler," Colby said. "That's not even a man."

Stevie kept her eyes on the screen, looking at the blurry image of the person coming out of the room. "That's because it's Bex Lyons."

Twenty-Nine

Stevie stormed out of the center—took out her frustration on a Coke can, booting it down the sidewalk.

Colby came running out after her. "I know it's not the result we were hoping for."

"Is it too much to ask that we could have heard Kirk threatening to kill Blair because of what she knew? Or Blair naming her stalker?"

"That would have been, like, *super* helpful," Colby said, "but let's just look at this as a tiny speed bump in our investigation."

"A speed bump?"

"Yup, and what do we do when we see a speed bump?"

"If it's you, ram your foot on the gas and fly over them."

"Exactly."

The tension in Stevie's body eased slightly. She sat down on the curb. "I really thought we were going to find something incriminating. The only thing that tape shows is Bex trying to convince Blair that Kirk Tyler was looking out for her. And that Blair was being difficult somehow."

Colby sat down next to her. "I know, but it's not the only thing. We have another lead—Bex Lyons. We need to speak to her. She may dish the dirt on Kirk Tyler. She was definitely talking to Blair about something. Maybe Kirk had sent her to tell Blair to keep her mouth shut. Well, she actually told her to keep her mouth open and sing, but you know what I mean."

"And if Bex won't talk?"

"We could speak to Melissa again. See if we can persuade her to go to the police? Even if Kirk didn't kill Blair, he deserves to go to jail for what he's done."

"Is it right to put that pressure on her?"

Colby shrugged. "I think *maybe* . . . men like him don't stop until someone makes them."

Stevie's phone started ringing. "It's my dad. I'd better answer."

"Stevie, we got your note—I wanted to check you were okay."

"I'm good—I'm just with Colby, trying to take my mind off things."

"I'm looking after her, Mr. Baker," Colby shouted.

"I'd rather you were with me, but if you want to be with your friend, you go be with your friend."

"Thanks, Dad. Have you heard anything from Jimmy about the stalker?"

"He's still processing the house. It takes a little time to get DNA back from the lab."

"Did any of the reporters get him on camera?"

"No one has turned in anything yet, but they're still looking. Don't give up hope."

Stevie sighed. "Okay, look, I'd better go."

"Love you, Little Bear."

"Love you, too."

Colby paused before putting the key in the lock. The plan was that they'd head back to her place so she could put a notice on the chat forum to see if any girls had stories like Melissa's about Kirk Tyler. But it sounded like the granddaddy of all arguments was blowing up inside.

"What now?" Colby said wearily. Then looked down at her boots, cheeks reddening. "Maybe this wasn't such a good idea."

The shouting grew louder.

"I told you, he said there's no more!"

"And I told you that he's bluffing!"

Stevie flinched at the sound of glass breaking.

The door burst open, sending Colby jumping back, key still in her hand. A man wearing a black tanktop and jeans, his hair in a straggly ponytail, stormed past them.

Faith Green appeared in the doorway, bathrobe undone, her *Simpsons* T-shirt on show. "Mike, get back here! I'm sorry!"

Without giving Colby or Stevie a second glance, Faith ran outside, bare feet slapping on the driveway.

"Mike! Wait!"

Mike stopped, hands on hips. "I don't see what the problem is!"

Faith reached up, put her hands on his face, made him look at her. "Okay, okay, I'll do it. You're right. You're right."

Mike leaned forward, stuck his tongue in Faith's mouth, and they started making out on the front lawn.

Stevie raised her eyebrows at Colby. "Well, that pivoted quickly."

Colby sighed. "They're always like this. Fighting, then making up." She glanced over at her mom and scrunched up her nose. "The making up is worse."

Stevie followed Colby inside and up to her room. "What do you think they were fighting about?"

"Honestly, it could be *anything* with them." Colby stopped at the top of the stairs. The carpet was covered in broken glass and the remains of a picture frame. "Looks like this one was a doozy. I'll go get a dustpan and broom."

Colby ran back down and Stevie started putting the larger bits of glass on the windowsill. Carefully, she picked up the broken frame—the photo of Faith holding her enormous check hadn't been damaged. Stevie placed it back on the windowsill but then picked it up again. What the hell?

Colby came thundering up the stairs. "Move out the way—the cleanup operation is here!"

Stevie turned around, mouth open, eyes questioning. "Colby, why is your mom's lottery check from Satellite Entertainment?"

Colby's face clouded over with confusion. "What?"

Stevie turned the picture around. "It's been signed by Kirk Tyler."

Faith suddenly appeared at the bottom of the stairs.

"Out the way, girls!" She took the steps two at a time, then shoved her way past Colby.

"Careful, Mom—there's glass," Colby said.

Faith tiptoed over the shards, disappeared into her room, then hollered, "Colby, have you seen my black-lace blouse?"

"It's hanging up in your closet," Colby called back, voice distant, eyes locked on the photo.

"Colby, your mom knows Kirk Tyler," Stevie whispered. "She must have been lying when we saw them together in the parking lot. Ask her how she got the check."

Faith burst back out of her room, buttoning up her blouse. "I'm off with Mike."

"Mom, why is your lottery check signed by Kirk Tyler?" Colby said, voice uncertain.

Faith stopped, lip curled, almost a snarl. "What are you talking about?"

"You said you didn't know him."

"I don't."

Colby took the photo from Stevie's hands, held it up for Faith to see. "But the check—it's from Satellite Entertainment."

"Well, Satellite Entertainment must have something to do with the lottery, then, kiddo."

"But does it?" Colby said.

Irritation set into Faith's face. "How the hell should I know? When people give me checks, I'm not asking where the money is coming from. Now, are we done here? Mike's waiting."

Colby stepped to the side and Faith disappeared down the

stairs. The front door slammed—an engine revved—then car wheels screeched off into the distance.

Colby shook her head, made for her room. "She's lying."

Thirty

Colby was right—Faith Green *was* lying. According to Google, the state lottery was run by the Mega Millions Group, and as far as Stevie could tell, they had no links with Satellite Entertainment.

"I just don't understand it," Colby said. "Why did she get eight hundred thousand dollars from Kirk Tyler?"

They were sitting cross-legged on the floor, backs against Colby's bed, the laptop between them.

"Did she ever work for Satellite?" Stevie asked.

"'Work'?" Colby laughed a hollow laugh. "She's never really *worked* for anyone."

"Kirk must have paid her for something . . ." Stevie trailed off. How could she ask what she needed to ask?

Colby raised her eyebrows. "What?"

"Colby, did anything ever happen to you at one of Blair's concerts?"

"If you're asking if Kirk-the-perv-Tyler did something to me and my mom accepted a payoff to keep quiet, the answer's no, Stevie. I would have told you *and* Melissa."

"Okay, then, good," Stevie said. "But why the hell would he give her money? Maybe she knew what he was doing and was blackmailing him?"

"That would make sense, but how would my mom know about that?"

"Or maybe your mom saw him kill Blair?"

"Stevie, Mom got that money years ago."

Of course she did. Stevie covered her face with her hands. She couldn't think straight. There was too much spinning around in her head. Kirk, the emails, the stalker, Gunner Trip, Bex Lyons, and now Faith Green. She needed to get her thoughts in order. Work through it all methodically.

"Let's set out what we know. Run through our key suspects."

"Ooh! I bought some string and sticky tack when I was getting supplies for the vigil, just in case we wanted to make a crime-investigation bulletin board! And I have flash cards!" Colby pulled them out of her desk drawer and waved them around triumphantly.

Stevie looked from Colby to the cards. "That's actually not a bad idea."

Colby pulled the lid off a pink Sharpie and wrote *List of Suspects* on one card.

Stevie raised an eyebrow. "You think the little heart for the dot of the *i* is needed?"

Colby shrugged. "Sorry, force of habit. Shall I do a separate card for each suspect and write down what makes them look guilty?"

"Yes, each suspect gets a card. Let's start with Gunner, as he was the first person we interrogated. He was lying to the world about the nature of his relationship with Blair, and he also lied about when he arrived in Honeyville."

Colby pointed her Sharpie at Stevie. "And he might be insanely hot, but I don't buy his whole 'I had a nap' line. But the police corroborated his alibi, and I also can't see why he would want Blair dead. He seemed like he cared about her."

Stevie pursed her lips and frowned. "Maybe the story Blair was going to tell Hilton was about him. Could he be considered 'someone important'?"

"Maybe to football fans. I just don't get killer vibes from him."

"Let's keep to facts rather than vibes," Stevie said.

Colby shrugged and stuck the card up on her wall. "Fair enough, but don't discount the power of the vibes."

Gunner Trip

- Motive: Unknown—seemed to genuinely care for Blair.

- Lied about when he came to Honeyville. Was here three days earlier.

- Blair must have trusted him as she was going to tell him who her stalker was.

- Has alibi.

Questions regarding Gunner:

- Why did he lie about when he arrived in Honeyville?

- Was Blair going to leak a story about him?

Stevie handed Colby another card. "Kirk's up next. He's a predator and Blair knew about it, which could be why she ended up dead. He paid off Melissa and it looks like he's paid your mom for something too. If Faith knows something about him, we need to find out what that is. She could be the key to establishing a case against him."

"I hear what you're saying, but I just don't understand how my mom could possibly know anything about Kirk. I'll do some digging—see if I can get anything out of her."

From what Stevie had seen of Faith Green, she wasn't hopeful.

Kirk Tyler

- *Motive: To stop Blair revealing that he is a groomer and abuser.*
- *Stopped Blair from talking to Hilton Moore about a story.*
- *Paid off Melissa $100,000.*

Questions regarding Kirk:

- *Why did he give Faith Green $800,000?*
- *Is he @BBWill_be_mine and is he behind the threatening emails?*

Colby clicked her tongue. "Okay, so Melissa told us that Bex Lyons is the one who came to her house. We also know for a fact that she was the one who was arguing with Blair in the dressing room. Should we be looking at her?"

"What, so Kirk tells Bex to bump Blair off, like some hired killer?"

"In my opinion she has a hairstyle befitting of a hired assassin."

"Again, let's also not base our theories on hairstyles, but she *must* know what he's been doing. I don't think we can rule her out."

Colby held up a card and an orange marker. "She *so* gets a card."

"Agreed."

Bex Lyons

- *Motive: Instructed by Kirk Tyler.*
- *Argued with Blair the day of her murder.*
- *Probably knows about Kirk's abuse.*
- *Blair's security so knows all Blair's movements.*
- *Has an alibi.*

Questions regarding Bex:

- *Was Blair going to expose Kirk?*
- *What was their argument about?*

Colby grabbed another card and selected a purple Sharpie. "Let's look at this whole stalker situation we have going on. We have your man in the long coat, the gift-giver, and BB-will-be-mine on the email, *and* those horrible emails to Blair that Hilton Moore printed on his site. They could all be different people?"

Stevie sat down on the beanbag and wiggled around until she found a comfortable position. "Split the card into three sections."

Unknown Stalker(s)

Motive: Crazy obsessive?

@BBWill_be_mine
- Identified through messages to Blair (@DollyPurrton_14) on Blair Baker fan site.
- He knew who Blair was and seemed to be aware of her movements.
- Sent threatening emails to Stevie through the wbm12345@buzzmail.com email and another account.
- Does not want Blair's death investigated.

Gift-giver
- Tiara.
- Creepy framed picture.
- First seen loitering outside Clover Lane.
- Has gotten into Stevie's room— caught on doorcam.

Creepy guy seen outside Stevie's
- Big guy.
- Wears long coat and baseball cap.
- Carries knife.

Questions:

- Who are they?

- Are they three separate people?

- Had Blair found out who they are? One, two, all of them?

- Did one of them send the deranged emails to Blair?

Colby pulled out another card and switched to a green Sharpie. "We also have this secret boyfriend Blair could have been meeting up with. Maybe something happened between them that led to him killing her. It would have been challenging keeping a love interest secret right here in Honeyville, but it doesn't mean Blair didn't manage it."

Stevie nodded. "Write it up."

Secret Lover

- Motive: Relationship broke down?

- Blair was seen in Honeyville—she must have been meeting someone.

Question:

- Who was Blair meeting?

"Is that it?" Colby asked.

"We need one for Hilton. I don't think he did it—he was outside filming when Blair was shot—but she wanted to tell him a story about 'someone important,' and that could be a motive for killing her."

Hilton Moore

- Who wanted to sell him a story on the Baker family and what was the story?

- Was Blair going to tell him about Kirk Tyler?

- Or was Blair going to reveal who her stalker was?

- Something about Gunner Trip?

Stevie pushed herself out of the beanbag and studied the cards while Colby used string to connect them all together.

Stevie ran her hand through her hair. "We have so many questions."

Colby stuck down the final string. "I truly believe that if we stand here and look at the cards long enough, the answer will come. It always does in crime shows."

"Here's a question you can answer for me—did you just randomly put string up there? You've just linked every card to every other card."

Colby tilted her head. "*Maybeeee*. Looks professional though. Legitimately feel like a real detective now."

Stevie stuck out her lip. It looked like a middle-school art project. "We need a plan of action. For me, Kirk is still the prime suspect so I think we should focus on him. We need evidence that he's a groomer. We need to find out if there are other girls out there."

"I can post something on the chat forum to see if anyone else comes forward. But I think you should see if you can get Melissa to change her mind. She might have had time to think. I think you should text her."

"Now?"

"No, wait until Thanksgiving—of course now!"

Stevie didn't hold out much hope. Melissa had been clear—she didn't want to be involved. But still, it was worth a shot, wasn't it, to get something concrete on Kirk? She took out her phone. Typed a message. Deleted it. Retyped another. Deleted that. She finally decided to keep it fairly short and to the point.

Melissa, hope ur ok. Been thinking about u a lot. If u change ur mind & want to speak to the police let me know. I know it's scary but I don't want him to hurt anyone else. Will support u whatever

Stevie sent the message. Colby leaned in and Stevie held her breath as she waited for Melissa's reply.

"She's reading it," Stevie said. "She's typing!"

U said u wouldn't tell

Stevie swore. Uncle Jimmy must have spoken to her. She quickly typed out a reply.

I'm sorry. I was worried about u. Pls can I call?

The message came up as not delivered.

"Do you think she's blocked you?" Colby said.

"Ugh. Probably." Stevie tipped her head back, stared at the ceiling. She'd messed it up. Maybe she should have phoned. Or sent her a few *how are you?* messages before mentioning the police. Maybe she shouldn't have said anything to her dad.

"She might change her mind," Colby said, too much doubt in her words.

"I don't think she will," Stevie said, but then her phone pinged. She grabbed it, pulse quickening.

"Melissa?" Colby said.

Stevie shook her head, pushed herself to her feet. "It's my dad. We're going to have to come back to this later. I need to go home. They've finished in my room and Uncle Jimmy wants to give an update on the case. Can you give me a ride?"

Thirty-One

Uncle Jimmy was already at the house by the time Colby dropped Stevie off. She closed the front door, gave Catsy's belly a scratch, and shouted, "I'm home!"

Marnie yelled from the kitchen, "Stevie, is that you? We're all in here!"

Stevie slung her bag over the banister and made her way through.

She found herself face-to-face with the aftermath of the night before—Oliver was standing in the kitchen doorway, sporting two black eyes. So much had happened since then, she'd almost forgotten she'd socked him one. Could she pull him aside—explain why? She glanced into the kitchen. Not the best idea with Jimmy and the rest of her family there. So she'd just have to ignore him forever and pretend it never happened, then. She could do that.

"Sorry, excuse me." She kept her eyes down as she tried to pass him, but he stepped to the same side as her and they ended up bumping into each other.

"Sorry," Oliver said, and stepped the other way, but Stevie did too and—oh god, somebody save her—she was stuck in some awkward never-ending dance of bumps and apologies.

She grew more and more flustered and embarrassed and, in the end, shouted, "Just stand still!"

"Right, yes, sorry, so sorry," Oliver said.

Stevie hurried into the kitchen and slipped into the seat next to Hal, cheeks hot.

Hal looked at her, raised an eyebrow.

"Don't even start," she growled under her breath.

Jimmy, who was at the head of the table, a laptop closed in front of him, cleared his throat. "So, now that everyone is here, I think we had better get started." He placed his elbows on the table, clasped his hands together. "As you know, we are pursuing many different leads."

"But you still have no idea who did it," Hal said—sharp, to the point, correct.

Annie placed her hand on top of Hal's. "Let's hear what Jimmy has to say, honey."

The *SportsCenter* theme song began blaring from Frank's pocket.

"Frank, your phone. Who's calling you *now*?" Marnie said, lips pursed in annoyance, as though the caller should have known better.

"Unknown number," he said, fumbling to switch it off. "Sorry, Jimmy, go on."

"There's a lot to discuss, the first being the picture frame that was left on Stevie's bed. We've sent it to the lab, and we have a DNA sample. It hasn't matched with anyone on the police database, but it does mean that when we find them, we can nail their ass."

"Did any of the reporters get a photo?" Stevie asked.

"I'm afraid we're drawing a blank on that—all the images we have from the time frame are close-ups of Frank and Marnie leaving the house."

"Still, the DNA evidence is good, isn't it?" Marnie asked.

"We think so. But we can't ignore the fact that someone has been in Stevie's room, mentioned her by name. We've had all the locks changed, and we're going to keep a police presence outside the house twenty-four seven."

Marnie clutched her hand to her chest. "Do you think Stevie's in danger?"

"We have no reason to think anyone wants to harm her, but this is a murder investigation, so we're not taking any chances. I don't want anyone to worry, okay?"

Stevie laughed, coughed to cover it up. *Not worry—yeah, sure!*

"Officer Dean will take the first shift."

Oliver nodded dutifully from the doorway—like he was ready to do some top-notch serving and protecting. Stevie caught his eye, and her cheeks flushed again. Stupid things had a mind of their own. She stared down at her lap. Could she just stop whatever it was she was doing already? Jimmy had basically implied she needed protection and here she was thinking about how Oliver looked kind of cute.

"I also have some good news," Jimmy continued. "Blair has been released by the coroner, so you can start planning the date of her funeral now."

Stevie's insides tensed. That word again—*funeral*.

Marnie reached over, touched his hand. "Thank you, Jimmy." She started crying. "I can finally put my baby to rest."

"Yes, thank you, Jimmy," Frank said.

Jimmy nodded. "You okay to continue, Marn?"

She sniffed and, hands shaking, pulled a tissue from the box on the table and nodded back.

Jimmy set his eyes on Stevie. "The next thing I want to discuss involves you, Stevie, and I'm sure we can clear it up very quickly."

"Me?" Stevie shifted in her seat. Was this about Melissa—had she told him about Kirk Tyler?

"Where were you the hour preceding Blair's show?"

Stevie did a double take. *What? No, seriously . . . what?*

"Oh, for God's sake!" Hal said.

"Why are you asking Stevie that?" Marnie said.

"Something has come to light—I'm sure it's nothing, but I just need to check."

"I was at the gym—I went straight from there to the concert. Why?" Stevie narrowed her eyes.

"We've had information that suggests you signed in to the concert twice. Once with Frank and Marnie at 8:02 p.m., but also half an hour before at 7:36, prior to when Blair was murdered."

Before Stevie could answer, Marnie banged her fists on the table. "Oh, this is ridiculous! First you accused Hal, now Stevie!"

"I'm not accusing her—I'm asking her why she signed in twice. I'm sure she can straighten things out. Stevie?" Jimmy raised an eyebrow.

"Surely, there must be some mistake?" Annie said. "I'm sorry—Marnie is right—you can't seriously be suggesting Stevie had anything to do with it."

"I didn't go in twice," Stevie said, her voice firm. "I was at the gym—Burton's—you can check; I have to buzz in with my phone, so there'll be a record."

"See, didn't I say we'd straighten it out?" Jimmy said. "It's probably just an admin error. Okay, let's move on to—"

"Hang on"—Stevie sat up straight in her chair—"that woman who checked our VIP passes, Janet—no, Janie—she asked for my ID when I gave my name. Do you remember, Mom?"

Marnie exhaled. "I don't know—things are hazy—possibly?"

"Maybe Blair's killer used my name to get in."

"But, Stevie, I thought you said this stalker was a man?" Marnie said.

"They could have easily said their name was Steve or something," Annie said.

"You need to speak to that Janie to see if she remembers anyone else using my name."

"We have," Jimmy sighed, "and unfortunately, Janie doesn't remember if any of the two hundred VIPs she checked in gave Stevie's name."

"So we're saying this Janie might have seen Blair's killer, but she can't remember what they looked like?" Hal said.

"We're not saying that at all. She could have just marked Stevie off by mistake. Which, in my opinion, having met Janie, is the most likely explanation. I really didn't mean for us to head down this path—all I needed to do was confirm Stevie only entered the concert once, which I've done, so could we move on to the next point of business?"

Stevie glowered at her uncle. It was like he was chairing a board meeting, not investigating her sister's death.

"Frank, you asked me to look into Kirk Tyler's alibi."

Stevie inched forward in her seat, hope rising.

Frank's phone began vibrating in his pocket. "Sorry, sorry," he said as he took it out.

"Just turn the damn thing off," Marnie said.

"I'm trying!"

"Hold down the side button!" Marnie said. "No, longer than that! Oh, for goodness' sake, hold it down!"

"I'm trying, but it won't turn off!"

"Stevie, help him," Marnie said, exasperated.

Stevie reached over and took the phone. She must have pressed the Answer button, because a tinny female voice said, "Is that you?"

Frank snatched the phone back, hung up, and held the button down until the screen went blank. "There, it's off. Sorry, Jimmy, you were telling us about Kirk Tyler's alibi."

Jimmy waved a hand dismissively, spoke quickly. "It's watertight. He's not Blair's killer."

Stevie's stomach dropped, her hope with it. "Are you sure?"

"He was in the control room with about fifteen other people at the time Blair died—Bex Lyons, the whole tech team—so, yes, Stevie, I'd say we're pretty sure."

Stevie slumped back in her seat. So Bex wasn't a hired killer, either—despite what Colby thought of her haircut. Unless . . . "Those people work for him—could they be lying?"

"What? All of them? You want me to keep looking into an innocent man, Stevie?" Uncle Jimmy's words came out brusque. "Or do you want me to keep looking for the person who killed Blair? You've had someone in your room, leaving depraved notes, and yet you won't let it go."

"But he's a predator!" Stevie fumed.

"Stevie?" Marnie said. She turned to Frank. "What's she talking about?"

"I'm investigating a murder, Stevie," Jimmy said, "and I'm telling you, Kirk Tyler is not our guy. But if you have evidence of any other criminal activity by Kirk Tyler, you need to tell me now, because I've had a long chat with your friend Melissa Carter and her folks, and they didn't have anything but good things to say about Kirk."

Stevie closed her eyes. Imagined how hard that must have been for Melissa to go through.

"Jimmy, what's going on? Who's Melissa Carter?" Marnie asked.

"I'm doing my job, Marnie," Jimmy said, eyes on Stevie. "That's what's going on. And it's not easy when Stevie keeps interfering with the case! So *do* you have any evidence, Stevie?"

Stevie slunk back in her chair, bit her lip, anger flaring hot inside her. There was no way Melissa would speak, and if Blair had wanted to do a story with Hilton Moore on Kirk Tyler, she hadn't told him what it was about. So, no, she didn't have any evidence.

"Okay, then," Jimmy said, satisfied.

Annie took a sip of her water, tried to bring the conversation back. "What lines of investigation are you currently working on? Do you have a prime suspect?"

"With the DNA evidence from the photo, we're currently focusing on getting an ID on Blair's stalker. We're trawling though all the emails, but they were sent from so many different addresses—IPs all over the country—so it's going to take some time to go through, but we're making progress."

Annie said, "I read those emails on the Hilton Moore website and they sounded so deranged. Only someone truly unhinged could have sent them."

"We've received the metadata from AT&T. We have a log of calls and messages made by and to Blair prior to her murder."

"How? You don't have her phone," Stevie said.

Oliver took a step forward into the kitchen. "We don't need her phone—we can still get the dates, times, durations, and the numbers involved."

Hal scoffed. "Can you read them—know what was said?"

"Well, no, but—"

"Then how much use is that?"

"Hal, give him a chance to explain," Annie said a little crossly.

"We can't read them, but we can look at patterns," Oliver said, excitement in his voice. "There's one number that is of particular interest to us. It has only ever made three calls—two of which were to Blair's number. We believe it to be a prepaid burner phone."

"So there's no way of tracing it?" Stevie asked.

"No, but we—"

"Thank you, Officer Dean," Jimmy said, cutting him off. "I think as lead investigator, it should be me who disseminates any information."

Oliver took a step back. "Of course. My apologies."

Jimmy spoke, voice rising, just in case anyone wasn't clear who was running the show. "On the day Blair was killed, a call was made to her from the phone at 7:02 p.m., then again at 7:34. This is right before the established time of death—somewhere between 7:40 and 8:25. Cell tower puts that phone right near Honeyville High Stadium at those times. What's interesting is that the phone was first used three days prior, also in the Honeyville area, then not used again until the day of Blair's murder. It was deactivated immediately after."

"So you think someone from Honeyville killed her?" Marnie said.

"It's likely, but not necessarily. Someone could have traveled here three days before the concert, possibly with the intention of murdering her."

Three days before? Wasn't that when Gunner Trip arrived?

Stevie looked over at Oliver. "Did you find out when Gunner Trip got into town?"

Jimmy stared over at him too, eyes dark. "Do not tell me she's the reason that I've had the Titans' lawyer's breathing down my neck! Tell me Stevie wasn't your tip-off!"

"She wasn't," Oliver said quickly. Maybe he was saving his skin. Or maybe he was saving hers—either way, Stevie was grateful, even if Jimmy didn't look like he believed a word of it. "Unfortunately, the witness was rather inebriated when I spoke to him and wasn't able to provide any clarity as to when Gunner arrived. The motel had no record of Gunner Trip staying there."

"Then maybe he checked in under a different name," Stevie said.

"This is all irrelevant," Jimmy barked, eyes now on Stevie. "He passed the polygraph, we have no sightings of him at the arena, only him leaving the Sable and Stone exactly when he said he left, and we can't place him in Honeyville when the first call was made from the burner phone."

Stevie chewed her lip to stop herself from blurting out that not being able to place Gunner in Honeyville wasn't the same as him actually not being there.

"But you don't know the caller is Blair's killer—it could have been anybody phoning her," Hal said.

"If people would stop interrupting me, I can explain," Jimmy said.

Stevie folded her arms, turned away from the table, anger rising in her.

"What is it, Jimmy?" Marnie said. "What have you found?"

Jimmy waited until everyone was looking at him, until Stevie was looking at him. His eyes were twinkling. He had a lead, and he was pretty pleased with himself about it. He leaned forward, the excitement in his voice clear. "We had a call from the *At Night with the Stars* production company—"

A phone started ringing and irritation flashed across Jimmy's face again. "Jesus Christ!"

Marnie looked at Frank accusingly. He held up his hands. "Not me this time."

"It's mine, sorry." Oliver pulled his phone from his pocket and hurried out to take the call in the other room.

"As I was saying," Jimmy continued, "the *At Night with the Stars* producer called Honeyville PD because they thought we should see something."

"That's the show Blair was supposed to appear on," Stevie said, "but what's that got to do with the burner phone?"

Jimmy leaned forward, looked at each of the Bakers in turn, checking he had their attention. "She did appear on the show. It was prerecorded three days before the concert."

"I still don't see what this has to do with the burner phone," Marnie said.

"There's this section in the show where Blair answers

questions from her fans—those in the audience and others who have called in. There was some post on Blair's social media giving the time of the pre-recording. Now, this one caller dials in, doesn't say much before hanging up. They were going to cut it from the show—the producers thought it was some oddball, you know, a prank caller—but Blair's death sheds another light on what was said."

Stevie straightened up. "What do you mean, 'what was said'?"

"The caller said"—Jimmy lowered his voice—"'I know what you did.'"

Stevie's skin prickled and Annie jolted forward, almost knocking her glass over. Did Jimmy really need to add the dramatics? It wasn't like the whole situation wasn't dramatic enough as it was.

"You think it was her killer?" Stevie asked.

"We're not jumping to any conclusions," Jimmy said, although it was clear that was exactly what he was doing, "but the call was made from the burner phone that called Blair just before she was shot." Jimmy sat back, watched how it landed.

No one said anything for a moment. Jimmy was right to be excited. It was an actual lead.

"What type of person would call up a TV show and do that?" Marnie said.

"A sicko, that's who," Hal said. "I'm guessing the same person who wrote those emails to Blair, left the packages for Stevie—Blair's stalker, right?"

"It's a very strong possibility—it certainly fits the profile," Jimmy said.

"Tell me the show isn't going to put that out," Marnie said.

"We've asked them to," Jimmy said.

"You've done what?" Marnie cried. "No. I won't allow it. I don't want all those ghouls out there watching my daughter's killer threaten her for their entertainment."

"*Seriously*, Jimmy? Why would you ask that?" Hal said.

"Listen, whoever the killer is, they must have friends, family, people around them who have noticed them acting strangely. It's likely they've shown an unhealthy interest in Blair both before and after her death. I think if we put the show out, it might convince someone to come forward." Jimmy spoke with such confidence that Stevie began to think that it might work.

"You've listened to the recording though," Annie said, "and you don't know who it is?"

"I have," Jimmy said. "It's short—there's not a lot to go on. Whoever it is sounds like they're disguising their voice—using some sort of voice app—but I really think it's worth a shot."

Stevie nodded at his laptop. "Go on, then—let's see it."

Jimmy turned the laptop around and hit Play.

Blair was sitting onstage, wearing a black catsuit with rhinestones in the shape of a guitar, the neck running down her left leg. Red lips split in a wide smile, so many perfect white teeth. Marnie closed her eyes, looked away, forced herself to look back when the caller came on the line. Avery Rose, the host, said, *"Now, I do believe the next caller, Riley, has a question about the inspiration for your hit 'Broken Roots and Burnt Bridges.'"*

Blair clutched her hand to her chest. *"Hi, Riley, thanks so much for calling! That song will always be so precious to me. What's your question?"*

The caller took a moment to respond. Stevie could just make out the sound of their breathing.

"I think our caller might be a little starstruck!" Avery said. *"Come on, now—don't be shy!"*

"I know what you did." The tone deep, unnatural, a robotic quality to it.

"Who . . . who is this? I . . . I . . ." Blair said, her voice trembling.

The hairs on Stevie's arms rose. On the screen, Avery laughed,

261

uncertain, but Blair was stock-still—eyes filled with fear.

"Riley, do you have a question . . . ? Riley . . . ? Riley, are you still there?" Avery smiled at the camera, pulled back control. *"Our caller seems to have hung up, but I think we all know what Blair did was make an album that has sold over ten million copies worldwide!"*

The audience broke into applause, and Blair smiled, but it wasn't as wide. Not so many teeth. Fear still in her eyes. Stevie wanted to reach out and touch the screen, ask her, *What did you do?*

The footage ended. Marnie started to cry. "That was them, wasn't it?"

Annie reached shakily for Marnie's hand and slumped down in her seat. Hal put his head in his hands.

"Put it out," Frank said, the first words he'd spoken for a while. "Air the show and find out who that bastard is."

Jimmy nodded, pleased he'd gotten his way, and closed the laptop. "One more thing, Marnie, we'd love for you to film a message that we could play at the end of the show, appealing for information."

Marnie sniffed, wiped her eyes. "Oh, I don't know, Jimmy."

"I'd like you to do it this evening at the PPN studio."

"This evening? I just don't know if I could."

Jimmy reached over, put his hand on Marnie's. "I think you'd do a great job, Marn. If you were to—"

Oliver appeared in the doorway, cleared his throat. "Sorry to interrupt, but we've got ballistics back from the bullet."

"And?" Jimmy said.

"We've had a match for a gun." Oliver ran his hand over his head, let out a puff of air. "I don't know what to make of it."

"Just spit it out," Jimmy said.

"The bullet that killed Blair was fired from the same gun that killed Aaron Taylor."

Thirty-Two

The same gun? Stevie couldn't wrap her brain around how that could be possible. What did Blair's death have to do with a boy who was killed almost half a decade ago?

Uncle Jimmy didn't move, didn't say anything. All the confidence that had been radiating out of him drained in a moment.

Frank stood up, knocking his chair over, and stormed out of the kitchen.

Marnie went to follow him, but Jimmy held up his hand. "No, I'll go." His voice was so commanding, Marnie sank back down in her seat.

"What's gotten into Dad?" Hal said.

Stevie bit her lip. Surely, a match was a good thing?

Oliver took a step forward. "I think I understand."

"You do?" Stevie doubted Oliver knew her dad better than she did.

"I imagine when a gun from a case you didn't solve is involved in the murder of your own daughter, it could be possible for someone to blame themselves."

Stevie looked at the upturned chair. Oliver was right. Her dad would blame himself for this. Already was.

Annie put her head in her hands. "I . . . I . . . can't believe this is happening. Poor Frank."

Stevie went over to the kitchen window. Her dad and uncle were at the end of the garden. Frank was gesticulating wildly, Jimmy nodding, then shaking his head in response. He put his hand on Frank's shoulder, trying to calm him down. All this stress wasn't going to be good for his heart.

"How on earth could the gun that was used to kill that poor Taylor boy be the same one that shot Blair?" Marnie asked.

"I guess one of three things could have happened," Oliver began, even though Stevie didn't think her mom had been expecting an answer. "One, whoever killed Aaron Taylor sold the gun, and it was subsequently bought by the killer. Two, it could have been dumped, and somebody found it, and three—"

Stevie turned around, her eyes catching Oliver's. "Whoever killed Aaron Taylor also killed Blair."

"Exactly," Oliver said.

Stevie's mind seemed to stutter. She couldn't work out how there could be a connection. "But how would some crazed stalker be linked to Aaron Taylor? It just doesn't make sense," Stevie said.

"It does throw a new light on the case. My instinct is that whoever shot Blair bought the gun not knowing it had been used in a previous murder. We're getting the old Taylor files out to look through down at the station," Oliver continued. "Maybe there's something that was missed."

Stevie made the next link quickly—both the burner phone and the gun were linked to Honeyville, which made it likely that Blair's killer was too. God—she'd been wrong about Kirk Tyler. Everything was pointing at the stalker—but who was he? BB-will? The guy in the long coat? The one who kept leaving gifts? Was it all the same guy? Could it be the secret boyfriend? Were they one and the same?

"Did Blair know Aaron?" Oliver asked. "I know Frank works at the center."

"Frank only met the Thompsons—that poor boy's foster parents—after Aaron had been shot," Marnie said. "I don't think

Blair ever mentioned him before that. Stevie, do you know if she knew him?"

Stevie turned around, leaned against the sink. "No, I'm, like, ninety-eight percent sure she didn't." She frowned—she sounded like Colby.

"Are you sure about the gun?" Annie asked. "Could it be a mistake?"

"It was a full match." Oliver's jaw was set and there was no doubt in his eyes.

Annie swallowed, looked out the window. "This is going to devastate Frank. You know how the Taylor case affected him, and he's right"—she pointed at Oliver—"Frank's going to blame himself . . . and what if it pushes him to the edge again? This is all just so awful."

Hal stood up, went to wrap his arms around her, but Annie stepped away. "No, don't. I'm okay. I'm sorry. I think I'm going to go home. This has all been . . . a lot."

"I'll come with you."

Annie took another step back, like she didn't want him near her. "No, you stay here."

"Annie, love," Marnie said, but Annie turned and ran out the door.

"Is she okay?" Stevie had never seen Annie like that before. Or the way she'd looked at Hal, like she was accusing him of something.

"You know Annie, she really feels things, and you know how much she loves Dad. This case is also bringing up a lot of feelings about Mia," Hal said. "She hasn't been sleeping well. She was up till the early hours pressing flowers."

"Flowers?" Marnie said.

"Oh. That was supposed to be a surprise. She's making a book of that bouquet Blair sent. Act like you don't know when she gives it to you."

"How thoughtful." Marnie touched her hand to her chest. "She's a good girl. You make sure you look after her."

"I always do." Hal nodded toward the window. "It's Dad I'm worried about. After how bad he got . . ."

Marnie shook her head, her eyes quickly slipping to Stevie, and Hal trailed off.

"What?" Stevie said. She knew the Aaron Taylor case had affected him, but she could tell this was something more. "What aren't you telling me?"

"Your brother just means the strain it put on his heart," Marnie said, standing up. "Officer Dean, can we offer you a drink? Some sweet tea? Coffee, perhaps?"

"No, thank you." He glanced out the window. "I should leave the chief to it. I need to get back to the station and see if I can find out anything else about the gun. I'll call Officer Dwight to cover my shift watching the house."

"Didn't Jimmy drive you here?" Stevie said.

"I don't mind walking."

Hal patted Stevie on the shoulder. "Don't worry—Stevie will give you a ride."

Stevie unlocked her car, and Oliver opened the driver's door for her. The smile he gave her stopped her from saying she was perfectly capable of opening a door herself.

Oliver climbed into the passenger seat, and she started the car engine. The radio blared at full volume and Oliver jumped at the sudden noise. Stevie laughed, turned it off, and pulled out of the driveway.

"Whoa, what a racket!"

Stevie looked at him and smirked. "A racket?"

Oliver closed his eyes, tipped his head back on the headrest. "That was your sister, wasn't it?"

"Uh-huh."

"In my defense, I was referring to the sound level, not her voice."

Stevie smiled—any awkwardness she'd worried about, being alone in the car with him made it melt away. Being this close, she couldn't help but notice how good he smelled—a warm, woodsy aroma, like cedar and sandalwood, rich and grounding.

They drove in silence for a while, Stevie playing the clip from *At Night with the Stars* over in her head.

"Can I ask you a question?" she said.

"You can—whether I can answer it is another thing."

She gave him a look—she wasn't sure if he was teasing or telling the truth. Perhaps both. "Do you think Blair knew her killer? The call coming from Honeyville—the gun. And in that clip the caller said, 'I know what you did.' You've gotta know someone to know what they did, right?"

"Or you could be a massive fantasist—either is possible." Oliver scratched the back of his neck like he was thinking. "Do you think Blair did something?"

"Something that made someone want to kill her? I don't know. It's possible. She certainly knew things."

"About Kirk Tyler?"

"You know what he did?" Stevie asked.

"I do. I was with Jimmy when he spoke to Melissa."

"How did she seem?"

"Nervous—like she wasn't telling the whole truth."

"But Jimmy says Kirk couldn't have killed Blair."

"It's like Jimmy said—his alibi checks out. Honestly, Blair's stalker seems like our strongest suspect. Someone who can make a picture like the one he left you can't be right in the head. Doesn't mean that Kirk Tyler isn't a POS though."

A smile flickered across her lips. Stevie kind of liked that he couldn't come out and say *piece of shit* in front of her. "He shouldn't get away with what he did to Melissa Carter."

"No. He shouldn't. He will though, if nobody comes forward. No evidence, no case."

When she'd been a little kid, Stevie thought the bad guys always got found, got punished. Frank would leave for work and say, *I'm off to put away the bad guys!* She thought he was some kind of superhero. Maybe he did too. Maybe that was why Aaron Taylor's case had affected him so much.

"What made you want to be a cop?" Stevie asked.

"The chicks and the fast cars," Oliver said and gave her a wink.

Stevie spluttered a laugh, kept her eyes on the road. "And how's that working out for you?"

"Not great. Jimmy doesn't really let me drive."

Stevie smiled, pressed her lips together. She would *not* ask about the chicks. "But I suppose having a job where you feel like you're trying to do something good makes up for it?"

"I guess it does. It's all I've ever wanted to do. Started my fourteen weeks of basic training on the day I turned twenty-one. In a couple of months, all going well, I should finish field training and be fully certified."

She stole a glance at him. He had a great profile. Like, maybe the best nose she'd ever seen. How had she not noticed it before? Boy, was she glad she hadn't broken it when she'd hit him. She stared at the road—what was she doing? Could she just focus on the conversation and say something?!

"Must be nice to know what you want to do with your life. My dad was the same. He would never have retired if it hadn't been for his heart. I think he lost a little bit of himself when he handed in his badge."

"His heart?"

"I know—he looks as strong as an ox. He's got pericarditis— stress makes it worse."

"Right." Oliver nodded, shifted in his seat. "Yes. I suppose it would."

He fell silent for a moment, and Stevie wondered what he was thinking, but then he said, "You ever think about following in his footsteps?"

"Me, a cop? I don't think so."

"I can see it—you do like asking a lot of questions."

Stevie laughed. "I wouldn't want to be in charge of a gun. But I have thought about maybe going into law."

She'd never told anyone that before. She was surprised that she'd said it out loud, as she hadn't really considered it as a realistic option.

"I think you'd make a great lawyer. I'll arrest 'em and you send 'em down!"

Stevie pulled into the parking lot of the station and killed the engine. She suddenly felt nervous. Probably because she now had to navigate through the process of saying goodbye, and she really ought to apologize for socking him in the face.

"Thanks for the ride," Oliver said, ready with the handle.

"I'm sorry I hit you," Stevie blurted out. "I had a reason."

He turned around, fixed his poor bruised eyes on hers. "I know why you did it, Stevie."

Stevie felt herself shrink under his gaze. "You do? I wasn't sure . . ."

"You don't have to be a detective to work out that you wanted to speak to the girl."

"You put me opposite her on purpose?"

"No, I just thought that the chief's niece ought to have the nicest cell."

"3B was particularly lovely," Stevie said.

"Your friend though, her reasoning is a little harder to understand."

Stevie laughed. "That's Colby."

"I should go." He opened the door, climbed out. "Bye, Stevie."

She kept her eyes on him until he disappeared through the station doors. Then she slumped back in her seat. *No, Stevie, do not do this. Do NOT do this.*

But she knew it was too late. She liked Officer-flaming-Dean.

Thirty-Three

Colby slid along the booth opposite Stevie.

"Man, have I got some stuff to fill you in on."

"Me too, actually," Stevie said.

"Okay, but me first." Colby grabbed one of Stevie's fries from her plate, chewed, screwed up her nose, then picked up the salt and shook enough to season all the fries Stevie may eat in her whole life.

Stevie grabbed the saltshaker. "Sheesh, Colby! Think of your arteries!"

"Sorry, Mom," Colby said, swiping another fry.

"If you want, you can order some food." Stevie said.

"Nah, I'm not hungry." Colby leaned forward, hands on the table, eyes flashing with excitement. "So, I received a response to my Kirk Tyler post."

"What did they say?"

"Not much, she was mainly asking me questions about Kirk—I kept it vague—said there were concerns about inappropriate behavior involving young girls. I thought she was trying to check that she was in a safe space. Got that wrong though."

"What do you mean?"

Colby helped herself to some more fries. "I don't think it was a genuine response, because a few hours later Bex Lyons is at the door, waving some cease-and-desist letter in my face."

"Bex Lyons came to your house? *No!*"

"I think she must have been signed up to the chat room and it was her who'd been messaging me. She told me that if I continued to spread malicious rumors about Kirk Tyler that she'd have my site shut down and they'd take me to court for defamation of character."

Stevie dropped the fry she was holding on to her plate. "What did you say to that?"

"I said that if she tried any of that, I'd take her to court for covering up a creepy, old pervert."

"You didn't."

"I did, but only after she'd gone. What I actually said was 'yes, ma'am.'"

"So that's it, then? We can't use your site to ask if there's anyone else out there that Kirk groomed?"

"No, because I am incredibly smart and as soon as she left, I blocked the account she was using, posted a message to ask if anyone has information about Kirk's behavior to DM me privately. I also asked if anyone knew if Blair had a secret lover, too. Then I left it half an hour, deleted the posts, and unblocked the account Bex was using so she would be none the wiser." Colby placed her hands under her chin and fluttered her eyelashes. "Am I smart? Tell me I'm smart!"

"You are very smart, but half an hour isn't very long."

"It's long enough. Since Blair's death, the traffic on my site has been huge."

"So, I guess we just wait and hope someone comes forward with some information," Stevie said.

"Yeah, and then hopefully we can nail Kirk Tyler's potentially murderous ass."

"Oh, about that. On to my news: Kirk's definitely not the murderer."

Colby's eyes widened. "What?"

Stevie told Colby about Kirk's apparently watertight alibi and the stalker and the burner phone and the *At Night with the Stars* phone-in, and then, when Colby had stopped *oh my god*ding, she told her about the gun.

"Wait. I don't understand what you're telling me right now."

"The same gun that killed Blair was also used to murder Aaron Taylor. Oliver says they're going to look back over the case and see if they can find anything to connect it to Blair's."

"*Oliver* said that, did he?" Colby said, tilting her head.

"I'm not going there with you."

"Going where?" Colby said, mock innocence to her voice.

Stevie ignored her. "I think that if the cops are revisiting the Taylor case, we should too."

"How are we going to do that?"

"My dad worked that case. He probably shouldn't have, but he's got the files at home in the attic. He brought them home to look through after he left the police force, but Mom told him to take them back to the station. He didn't though—he put them up in the attic—I think he always hoped he might be able to go through them and one day solve the case."

"You've got to admire his dedication. Must be where you get it from. But didn't Honeyville PD want them back?" Colby said.

"I'm sure they have copies."

"Hey, maybe I should talk to Terence. He might know something that could help."

Stevie raised an eyebrow, spoke flatly. "I can't imagine why you're volunteering to do that."

"For the investigation, of course." Colby grabbed a couple more fries, chewed them open-mouthed as she continued to speak. "Terence is kind of Aaron's cousin, right? I know they're not biologically related, but from what you've told me, Aaron was properly part of the Thompson family, and I think Terence might be able to tell us something."

Stevie had to concede that it wasn't the worst idea. "Okay, you speak to Terence, see what you can find out about Aaron and if he had any connections to Blair. I'll go through my dad's files. I'll call you later to discuss what we've found—if we find anything, that is." Stevie stood up, ready to leave.

Colby looked at her plate. "You done with that?"

Stevie pushed it toward her. "Thought you weren't hungry."

Stevie sat cross-legged with the files spread out on the attic floor and a notebook in her lap. It was hot under the eaves, and the dust was making her sneeze. She was fourteen when Aaron Taylor had been found murdered in Cranford's Lumberyard. She remembered some things about it, but the truth had gotten mixed up with the stories that had flown through the halls of Honeyville High. Casey Jones had told her that a madman had done it, and that Aaron hadn't been shot but cut into little pieces with a chain saw. Another story was that Old Man Cranford was the culprit, and his sons had covered it up and provided him with an alibi. Stevie even remembered a rumor about Aaron being involved in satanic worship. She hadn't believed any of the tales at the time, and she didn't believe them now.

She picked up the case summary and started reading.

Case Summary
Incident Type: Shooting
Case Number: 2022-1181-0341
Date/Time: July 4th 2022 23:50
Location: 145 Ellison Rd
Reporting Officer: Frank Baker, badge #1289, James Baker, badge #1427
Summary: On 07/04/22 officers were dispatched to Cranford's Lumberyard, Ellison Road, in response to a telephone call at 23:33 from a member of the public who reported seeing two men with

flashlights, possibly armed, climbing over the fence. Upon arrival at 23:50, officers located a Caucasian male, later identified as Aaron Taylor (aged 17 years), lying in the yard with a gunshot wound to the abdomen. The scene was secured. Aaron Taylor's car was found about 600 feet from the lumberyard.

Stevie wrote down *witness* in her notebook, underlined it twice. She stuck her pen in her bun, then pulled it out again, and changed her note to *two witnesses*—the person who saw Aaron climbing into the lumberyard, and the person he was with.

Behind the summary was the final police report her dad had filed to close the case.

Final Police Report and Investigation Overview
Case Number: 2022-1181-0341
Date: September 16
Investigating Officer: Frank Baker, badge #1289
Scene Examination: Aaron Taylor was discovered to be deceased from a gunshot wound on the grounds of Cranford's Lumberyard. He was found lying next to a nail gun and several planks of wood. It is believed that Mr. Taylor had the intention of stealing these items for a building project. A second police team discovered one single bullet casing the morning following the shooting. It must have been missed in the initial search due to the lack of light.

Witness Interviews: Miss Shiralee Rogers, Hollingdale Drive, reported the initial incident. She was returning home after a night shift as a nurse in Honeyville ER. She spotted two individuals breaking into the lumberyard. She phoned emergency services and returned home. No other witnesses have come forward. This is most likely due to the time of the incident and the remote location of the lumberyard. Miss Rogers was not able to give a description of the second person she saw at the scene.

Surveillance Review: The camera at the lumberyard was out of action. Last surveillance footage was the month prior to the incident. The cameras had been vandalized at the start of June and Mr. Cranford had not gotten around to getting them fixed.

Forensic Analysis: No DNA evidence was recovered from the scene other than that of the deceased. One bullet casing was discovered and believed to be from a Smith & Wesson M&P9 series 9 mm handgun. Footprints were not identifiable due to the footfall of the attending officers.

Public Assistance Efforts: A community bulletin was issued requesting information, but no credible leads emerged. All employees of Cranford's have confirmed alibis.

Challenges and Limitations: Lack of direct witness accounts. Lack of surveillance footage. No forensics to link to police databases.

Closure Justification: After a comprehensive review of all available evidence, leads, and investigative avenues, the case remains unsolved. With no new information or actionable leads, the decision has been made to close the case at this time. This decision aligns with department policy for inactive cases exceeding 12 months without progress.

It is believed that an altercation occurred between the two individuals, which resulted in the shooting and death of Aaron Taylor. All attempts to locate this person have been unsuccessful.

The case may be reopened if new evidence or credible information becomes available.

So it looked like her dad thought that the person who had gone to the lumberyard with Aaron had shot him and fled the scene. Which meant that seventeen minutes after Shiralee Rogers had made the call, Aaron and his accomplice had gone from breaking into the lumberyard together, to having a disagreement that led to Aaron being shot. Stevie scratched her head with the end of her pen. Was it possible for a fight to spiral so quickly that it led to murder? Possible, perhaps, but unlikely. Maybe Aaron's murder was premeditated. The person with Aaron had gotten him to the lumberyard with the purpose of killing him. But why? And what did any of this have to do with Blair? Stevie wondered if she was wasting her time—if she should be looking into the stalker instead, but the fact that the same gun was used in both murders was too compelling to ignore.

Stevie turned to the interviews that had been conducted with the workers from the yard. They were all quite short, all responding to the same questions—no, they didn't know Aaron Taylor; yes, they had alibis for the time of the murder. Had they noticed anything strange leading up to Aaron's death? Ira Davis (thirty-four) had noticed a hand drill had gone missing two weeks prior. Bert Howard thought that some wood had disappeared, though he couldn't be certain. Old Mr. Cranford had been interviewed too. He'd been in Vegas for his brother's seventieth. So the rumors he'd done it were just that, rumors.

There were also statements from Marvin and his late wife, Gloria. They both said that Aaron must have snuck out, because neither of them realized that he wasn't in his room until the police arrived at four in the morning. They told police that Aaron was in the process of building a tree house for their granddaughter, Zoe, who was five at the time, and they now believed Aaron had gone to the lumberyard to steal supplies. Neither Marvin nor Gloria knew who Aaron might have gone with. Marvin described Aaron as a kind, hardworking boy who they had come to think of as a son. No, he couldn't think of any reason why somebody might want him dead. Gloria could suggest no reason either.

The Thompsons' were the last statements in the file. Stevie closed it and placed it on the floor. Where was the statement from Shiralee Rogers? She flicked through the paperwork again, thinking it might have been put in the wrong folder, but it wasn't there. Maybe her dad hadn't brought it home. Odd, considering he seemed to have everything else. Shiralee had seen Aaron and the other person climbing over the fence. It would have been dark, but she might have seen something useful to the investigation—her statement should be in the file. Stevie clicked her pen, wrote down *Shiralee Rogers, Hollingdale Drive*. If Shiralee had seen the person who shot Aaron, she might have seen the person who had also killed Blair. Stevie decided it was time to pay Shiralee a little visit.

Thirty-Four

"I'll tell you what I told the cops at the time: that it was dark, and I didn't see much."

Shiralee poured Stevie a glass of iced tea and slid it across the table. Stevie was grateful for the drink—the lazy rotations of the ceiling fan did little to relieve the stuffiness in Shiralee's kitchen. It was coming up on seven in the evening, but Shiralee's house had retained the heat of the day.

Stevie had closed up the attic and texted Colby to tell her she was off to speak to a witness involved in the Aaron Taylor case. Colby hadn't responded, Stevie supposed she was too busy with Terence.

She'd almost missed the turn to Hollingdale Drive. It was on the outskirts of town and hidden among the red oak trees. Shiralee's was the only occupied house—the one opposite had been boarded up, the yard overgrown with weeds. Was showing up on her own in a remote place like this a good idea? Perhaps she should have brought Colby with her. But she was there now—it would be stupid to turn back.

The moment Shiralee opened the door and greeted her with a brilliant smile, any worries Stevie had immediately vanished. Shiralee was just getting ready for her shift at the ER. She had her scrubs on, black hair pulled back in a low, tight bun. She said she had an hour to spare before she needed to leave. Stevie told her it wouldn't take too long. She'd stretched the truth a little and said she was Aaron's friend.

Stevie took a sip of the iced tea. It was good—not too sweet. "Could you maybe start by telling me what you saw that night?"

"I was coming back from my shift when my car broke down. I had to pull to the side of the road. I don't have insurance and knew I wouldn't get anyone out to help at that time on July fourth, so I had to walk the rest of the way. It was only a few hundred feet, but I was tired and cranky." Shiralee slapped her hands on her knees. "Man, I was pissed! Anyway, I had to walk past the entrance to the yard, and that's when I saw the flashlight beam."

"How far were you from the yard?"

Shiralee shrugged. "No more than a hundred and fifty feet. I went down the track a little to see if I could work out what was going on. That's when I spotted the kid at the top of the fence, one leg dangling down either side. I thought about going over or shouting at him, but I didn't want the aggravation—not after the shift I'd just had. There'd been some bar brawl in Lacey's and I had to patch up this woman's head before they took her down to the station, and she was not the easiest. Anyway, I did not have the energy for another altercation, so I phoned the police."

"This was at 23:33?"

Shiralee gave a deep laugh. "I couldn't be so precise, but it would have been around then."

"Can you tell me anything about Aaron or the person he was with? I know it was dark, but anything at all may help—height, hair color, which one was holding the gun . . . anything at all?" Stevie knew it was a long shot, but she had to ask.

Shiralee frowned. "I didn't see another person. There was just the one kid, dangling over the top of the fence—the Taylor boy. And he was holding a flashlight, not a gun."

"But in the police report it says you saw two people breaking into the lumberyard and that you thought they might have been armed."

"I don't know what the police report says, but I know what I saw. One person holding a flashlight, not a gun."

She seemed so certain, but the report had clearly said *two men*. "You're sure?"

Shiralee folded her arms and leaned back in her chair. "You ever mistake one person for being two?"

"No." Of course she hadn't. "Can you remember who interviewed you?"

"Frank Baker—nice guy, I remember his name because my brother's called Frank. He came around the day after the shooting and took my statement."

Stevie's heart thudded in her chest. Her dad had taken the statement? "And nobody else spoke to you?"

"I kept thinking they'd call again, but no, the police spoke to me once and that was it. Honestly, I feel bad about it all. Maybe I should have gone over and spoken to the kid when I saw him up on that fence," Shiralee began, "but I thought he was just goofing around. I didn't think he'd end up dead. I was mainly worried about him hurting himself in there. Lumberyards are dangerous places."

Stevie stood up, mind whirring, while somewhere in the distance Shiralee talked about the injuries she'd seen in the ER from saws and drills. Stevie grabbed hold of the table, light-headed, hands clammy.

Aaron Taylor hadn't hurt himself—somebody had shot him. And her dad had lied about what had happened in his police report.

She heard Shiralee say, "Girl, you don't look so good."

"Thank you." Stevie's mouth was dry—her words came out croaky. "I should go."

"You okay? You don't want to sit down for a moment?"

"No, thank you," Stevie said—she needed to get out of there. "You've been very kind."

"I'll show you out." Shiralee got up, but Stevie was already heading for the front door, walking on legs that didn't feel like hers. Sweat ran over her scalp, causing her ponytail to stick to the back of her neck. She stumbled out onto the porch and pulled in a deep lungful of air. Too loud, the raspy staccato of cicadas collided with the rhythmic chirrup of crickets, making it impossible to think. Stevie clawed through her mind. There had to be a reasonable explanation. Frank had worked so hard on the Aaron Taylor case; there was no way he would have written down false information. Her dad was a good cop—an honest cop.

Stevie pulled out her key, blipped open the door of her car. She sat behind the steering wheel, heard herself say out loud, "Dad wouldn't lie."

But then a thought pushed through, and a sudden chill swept over her, despite the heat of the day. The note Hilton had showed her.

They're nothing but a bunch of criminals.

Thirty-Five

Stevie checked her phone—it was coming up on eight in the evening. Colby had left her a voicemail half an hour earlier. She pressed Play, waited to hear how her chat with Terence had gone.

"This is Colby of the Stevie-and-Colby detective duo, reporting in at 7:37 on June fifth."

Stevie rolled her eyes at Colby's attempt at professionalism.

"So, I had a good meeting with TT. I'm literally obsessed with his dimples! Did you see them? They are just the cutest!"

Oh. Not that professional, then. "You were supposed to be asking about Aaron's connection to Blair!" Stevie yelled at the phone.

It was as though Colby had heard her, because she said, *"Anyway, enough about dimples, on to my interrogation! TT said . . . Hang on, am I going with TT? Do I like that? Maybe Terence is better. Stronger . . ."*

"You are killing me here, Colby!" Stevie cried, then heard Shiralee opening her car to leave for work. Probably not the best look to be shouting at her phone. She slunk down in her seat, tried to listen to the rest of the message calmly.

"So Terence and Aaron were close, but he said that Aaron had never mentioned Blair to him. Couldn't think of why there'd be a connection. I asked him about Aaron's background. Real sad story, actually—did you know both his parents died of cancer?"

Stevie nodded to herself. She did know—it was so sad.

"His mom first, then his dad a year later, which is why he ended

up moving to Honeyville to live with Marvin and Gloria. Terence said that, to start, Aaron was really quiet and sad—occasionally angry, which is totally understandable. But Marvin and Gloria loved him like one of their own. They cared for him and helped him through his grief. Aaron did well with the Thompsons, too—he studied diligently, made the varsity football team, and was always polite. Terence thinks that part of the reason he tried so hard was that he was worried they might send him away. Terence said that would never have happened. Marvin and Gloria adored Aaron, but I guess when you've already lost so much, it's hard not to think you could lose everything again."

Stevie swallowed. The poor kid.

"Terence said that Aaron could sometimes be a risk-taker. He'd do reckless things—a late-night joyride, an aggressive tackle on the football field—like the hurt hidden inside him was finding a way out. But when I asked, Terence said he didn't know anyone who would want to shoot him. He said Aaron had no enemies he knew about—he had friends, but not really any close ones other than him."

There was a hiss of a soda can being opened, followed by the sound of Colby gulping.

"Sorry—all this talking is making me thirsty. Anyway, I asked Terence about the night Aaron was shot, and he told me that Aaron had skipped out on the Fourth of July celebrations to go to the lumberyard and pick up some wood and some tools he needed—he knew the place would be deserted. He was building a tree house or a playhouse or some den thing for Terence's little sister. Terence said Aaron was always doing things to show his gratitude to the Thompsons—but he wished Aaron hadn't felt the need. Terence thinks Aaron had been sneaking into the lumberyard for about a month, taking the occasional piece of wood and borrowing the tools he needed. Which he would take back." Colby let out a sigh.

"Okay, that's about it. Let me know how you did. I'm at my place if you want to drop by. Okay, bye!"

Stevie put her phone in the jack and left Colby a voicemail before she drove away.

"Good job with Terence. I'm tired so going to head home. Will catch up with you tomorrow." She didn't want to tell her any more than that by message. She wasn't even sure if she wanted to tell her what she'd found out face-to-face.

She set off for Clover Lane, but when she got to the intersection, a surge of dread flooded through her, and she found herself driving straight through. She wasn't ready to see her dad yet. What was she going to say? *Hey, Dad, you know that case that almost broke you? You didn't happen to make a mistake or lie on the report, by any chance?* Was she even ready to hear him if he had an answer for her? There were only seventeen minutes between the time Shiraleee made the call and the time her dad and Jimmy had arrived at the lumberyard to find Aaron Taylor dead.

If he was dead when they got there.

The thought clawed at Stevie's mind like a barb, caused her heart to beat double time. A car on the opposite side of the road blasted its horn. She jumped, realized she was straddling the central marking, and swung back into her lane.

What was she thinking? Her dad—Frank, dependable, loyal Frank, who'd worked so tirelessly on the Taylor case that it had made him sick—was involved in Aaron Taylor's death? It made no sense. It couldn't be true, because the gun used to kill Aaron had also killed Blair. There was no way in the world Frank would have killed his own daughter. That was simply unthinkable. And besides, he was with Marnie the whole time. Her heart rate started to slow. She was overthinking, looking for connections that weren't there.

She was driving around aimlessly, wondering what she should do, when Annie called.

"Stevie, I just wanted to check how you are. That meeting with Jimmy was a lot."

It was good to hear her voice—Annie's genuine concern. And instead of saying, *I'm okay*, she said, "Can I come over?"

Annie opened the door, then opened her arms for a hug. "Have you eaten?"

"Eaten?" Stevie hadn't even thought about food.

"I'll put a pizza in." Annie led the way to the kitchen. "Hal's taken Marnie to the TV studio to film her appeal for information on Blair. It's a four-hour drive—they're staying in a hotel overnight, so it's just us."

Stevie sat down at the breakfast bar. "I completely forgot. Did you watch it? How did she do?"

Annie picked up her iPad from the side. "You can watch—it's all over the internet."

Marnie sat beneath the pale studio lights, her voice trembling as she leaned into the microphone, eyes red-rimmed and unblinking. *"Please,"* she whispered, *"if you know who called in to* At Night with the Stars . . ." Her words snagged in her throat, grief swallowing her whole as the screen behind her flickered to a clip of Blair, sitting in her rhinestone catsuit with Avery Rose from when the anonymous call came through. In the studio, Marnie collapsed into quiet sobs.

Then Hal stepped into frame, his arm sliding around his mother's shoulders. His voice faltered as he faced the camera, his jaw taut, eyes shining with held-back tears. *"She was more than the spotlight, more than the songs; she was a daughter and a sister, and she was so loved. Please, if you know anything, tell someone."*

Stevie pressed Pause, freezing Hal in his moment of pain. She touched his face. How could she have ever thought he'd done it?

"You think it will work?"

Annie slid a pizza into the oven, a long, tired breath escaping from her lips. "Do those things ever? They certainly didn't for Mia." Annie seemed to catch the bitterness in her voice, shook her head. "I'm sorry—I don't mean to be pessimistic."

"Annie, I understand—I really do."

Annie leaned against the oven. "Every single lead we had from the appeals turned out to be a nut job or a money grabber."

"I know, but I guess it's worth a try?"

"Best not to get your hopes up though. The hope cuts the deepest in the end. When Mia went missing, everybody kept telling me to have hope and keep faith, but I think I knew she was dead from the start. I could sense my baby wasn't here anymore, but no one would allow that. I suppose I wouldn't allow myself to admit it either. So I had to keep believing she would come back."

"I'm so sorry, Annie."

"I know you are." Annie took Stevie's hands. "And I just want you to know that whether we find out who killed Blair or not, it won't change the fact that she's not coming back, but we'll work through it together. I'm here for you."

"I know," Stevie said, tears pricking her eyes. "You know, sometimes I forget Blair's actually dead. Is that awful?"

"Not at all."

"It's not like I saw her much, and it doesn't feel that different. But then I remember, and I get this jolt that I won't ever see her again, and I don't even know where to start with that thought."

"I think you have to do whatever you need to do to move on," Annie said.

Stevie nodded, but how could she move on, knowing that Blair's killer was out there?

"I need to know what happened, Annie."

"I understand that, but sometimes life just doesn't give us the answers."

"And what happens then?"

"What happens then is that we'll be here for you. Me and Hal, your mom, Frank—all of us."

Stevie choked down a sob. "Do you think Dad was a good cop?"

Annie frowned. "Where's this coming from?"

"What if I told you I think he might have made a mistake on the Aaron Taylor case?"

The lines on Annie's forehead deepened. "Your dad is a good man, Stevie. I couldn't possibly say whether he made a mistake or not. But Frank is someone who has always done the right thing."

The words tumbled out of her. "It's just he never found who killed Aaron and the gun never showed up and the whole investigation focused on tracking down the person who Aaron was with, but I don't think Aaron was with anyone."

"Stevie, slow down. I know this is all so confusing and I'm not quite sure what you're suggesting. You don't really think Frank is involved?"

Stevie rubbed the tears from her eyes with the heel of her hand. "No, of course he has nothing to do with Blair." She sniffed. "It's just that it was the same gun and—"

Annie cut her off, such pain in her eyes. "Stevie, please don't do this to yourself. Listen to me: This has nothing to do with your dad. Officer Dean said that the gun was probably sold. Anyone could have it. I understand what it's like, how your head can take you to awful, dark places, but you have to keep hold of what you know to be true. And you know that Frank is a good man."

Stevie's chin began to tremble. She hated herself for where she'd allowed her mind to go. She let her tears fall. "Is there something wrong with me?"

Annie moved toward her, held her by the shoulders. "There

is nothing wrong with you. It's natural to want to know what happened, but, Stevie, you really need to leave it to the police. Jimmy has the stalker lead he's following—he has their DNA—let's see if anything comes from that."

Stevie covered her face with her hands. The stalker—that's who she should be focusing on. She looked up at Annie, a wash of shame rolling through her. "You're right. Of course you're right. Please don't tell anybody what I said about Dad."

Annie stroked her cheek. "I won't say anything to anyone, honey."

The oven timer dinged. Annie gave her shoulder a squeeze, then went to take out the pizza.

"Only slightly burned. I'd say that was a win, by my standards!" Annie said brightly.

Stevie managed a smile.

"How about we eat pizza, watch some garbage TV, and then you can stay over in the spare room?"

"What about Dad? He'll be on his own." After what Stevie had thought—what she'd said—she had a sudden and overwhelming urge to see him. She didn't like to think of him at home on his own. One of his bear hugs might force away the guilt. Might make her feel better.

"I'll call." Annie picked up her phone, put it on speaker.

"Hello, Annie, love."

"Hi, Frank, I've got Stevie with me."

"Hi, Dad," Stevie said.

"Hi, Little Bear."

"I've asked her to stay the night, but she's worried about leaving you on your own."

"She's a good kid, that daughter of mine."

Stevie suppressed the urge to tell him she really wasn't, as the guilt swirled in her stomach.

"It's nice of you two girls to worry about me, but I'll be fine.

Jimmy's here—we're going over the Aaron Taylor case—seeing if we can find anything new."

"You are?" Stevie said, voice pitching up slightly. "Will you take a look over the witness statements?"

"We'll look over everything, Stevie—don't you worry. If there's anything here, we'll find it. Gotta go—I've left Jimmy up in the attic."

"Okay, Frank, good luck," Annie said.

"Bye, you two."

"Love you, Dad," Stevie said.

"You too, Little Bear."

Annie hung up, gave Stevie a small smile, and raised her eyebrows. "See, didn't I tell you—he's a good man."

Thirty-Six

Stevie woke early, pulled back the curtains, and opened the window to let some air into the room. The night before, she and Annie had binge-watched some awful show where celebrities had to try to make hyperrealistic cakes. It was stupid and corny and just what Stevie needed. For a few hours she'd been able to switch off and look away from her thoughts of motives and suspects and guns and emails and phone calls.

She left Annie a note, thanking her, and headed back home to find Catsy sprawled out on the porch, warming her tummy in the morning sun. Stevie crouched down and gave her a belly rub, then went inside, ready to see her dad.

Frank was sitting at the kitchen table, staring into space. His hair was stuck up at all angles and his eyes were ringed with tiredness.

"Hey, Dad." Stevie gave his shoulder a squeeze. "Did you find anything in your case file?" she said hopefully.

Frank shook his head. His jaw tightened for a moment, as though he were biting back words, then he forced his gaze back to the table. The silence stretched. Stevie couldn't tell if he was feeling frustrated or something else entirely.

"Nothing at all?" Stevie pressed. He must have read his report—he must have seen the mistake. "Did you go over all the witness statements?"

"Yes, Stevie." He sounded irritated. He must have realized, because he rubbed his face with his hands and said, "Sorry, didn't get much sleep last night."

Stevie wanted to press further but decided that it probably wasn't a good idea to push him. She'd try again, when he wasn't so exhausted. She opened a cabinet door. "You look like you could use some coffee. I know where Mom hides the good pods, but don't tell her."

"Have you been up in the attic?" Frank asked.

Stevie turned back, holding the cabinet door half open. "The attic? Why?" She tried to sound surprised—knew she'd overplayed it.

"Just answer the question." His voice trembled, like he was trying to control his anger.

Stevie's hand dropped to her side. "After Uncle Jimmy told us about the gun, I went through the case notes."

"And what did you find?"

Stevie chewed her lip, forced herself to say the words. "I think you made a mistake on your report. Shiralee Rogers only saw one person at the lumberyard."

Stevie waited for him to explode, waited for him to tell her she had no business reading police files, that she shouldn't be investigating the case, that she had no right to question his professionalism. But he didn't.

"Did you find anything else?" Frank's eyes fixed on hers. "Didn't take anything out of the box that you shouldn't have?"

She frowned—she had no idea what he was getting at. "Like what?"

Frank studied her face, like he was trying to work out if she was telling the truth.

"Like what, Dad?"

Frank nodded, and his whole demeanor shifted in a moment. "Nothing, love, it doesn't matter." He rubbed his hands together, smiled. "Now, did someone say coffee?"

Stevie stared at him. What the hell had just happened? "Like *what*, Dad?"

"I thought there might be some notes missing from the file; that's all," he said casually. He got up and took out two mugs from the cabinet.

"Shiralee's statement?" Stevie said.

Frank frowned, and Stevie wondered if he was about to get annoyed at her for suggesting he'd made a mistake, but he looked away and said, "Yeah, her statement."

Right . . . but was it that?

"It's no big deal—there'll be copies at the station. So where does your mother hide the good coffee?"

Stevie pointed to the top shelf of the cabinet. "Inside the massive casserole pot—can you reach it?"

He pulled the packet of pods out and grinned. "Bingo. You having some?"

Stevie stared at him, confused. "You aren't going to call me out for looking through the case file?"

"Do I need to?" Frank said. "You know what you did was wrong."

"No, you don't need to," Stevie said slowly. Although it might have been less disconcerting if he did.

"So . . . coffee?"

Stevie was about to ask him why he was behaving so strangely, when his phone buzzed on the kitchen countertop. He lunged for it, grabbed it quickly, but Stevie saw the notification on the screen: a text from Number, Unknown.

"Sorry, it's Jimmy—I should give him a call back," he said, heading into the hallway.

A lie. Clear and blatant.

Stevie leaned back against the cupboards, sweat suddenly slicking the back of her neck. The weird behavior—the phone calls and messages—her dad was hiding something. She needed to go. Get out of there. Talk to someone.

She took out her phone, called Colby. "Hey, can I come over?"

"I was literally about to call you!" Colby said. "I've received a message—well, two actually—from girls who might be willing to go on the record about Kirk Tyler."

Stevie's heart thudded double time. "I'll head straight over."

She ran out to her car, blipped the door, but realized it was already open. *What a dumbass.* Sure, she was distracted by everything that was going on with her dad, but she'd had an actual stalker in her bedroom and still couldn't remember to lock her stupid car.

Thirty-Seven

Stevie sat at Colby's laptop and read the messages again. One was from a girl in Idaho—she'd just turned fifteen when she went to a Blair Baker concert and had been spotted in the crowd by Kirk. The other girl was in California, age fourteen. She'd won a competition to see Blair live. Kirk Tyler had taken her and her mom out for dinner, and when her mom had gone to use the restroom, Kirk had assaulted her under the table. She hadn't told anybody.

"Even if he didn't kill Blair, the guy deserves to rot in jail," Colby said.

Stevie grabbed a Sharpie from the desk, walked over to their investigation bulletin board and pointed at Kirk's card. "Jimmy says he has an alibi. And I know the stalker looks like the prime suspect . . . but I still can't shake the feeling that he's involved. In my opinion, he has the strongest motive to kill Blair. Maybe his staff all lied for him. Maybe he had someone else do it?"

"Maybe that Bex Lyons," Colby said, eyes widening. She walked to the board and pointed at Bex's card. "She was arguing with Blair, *and* she was not happy when I posted on my site."

"She has an alibi for the time of the murder too. But we need to speak to her. If we show her the video of her coming out of Blair's dressing room and tell her we have girls willing to come forward, she may start talking."

"What I don't get is how Kirk Tyler, or even Bex Lyons, could have gotten their hands on the Aaron Taylor gun. Don't you think it makes it more likely that a stalker or someone else from Honeyville did it?"

Stevie ran her eyes over the cards. "We haven't really gotten anywhere with a possible secret lover."

"Oh, I forgot! I got a reply to my post—don't think there's anything in it though. A user called Blair-babe-six has a sister in the fourth grade. Apparently, a girl in her class, Tiffany, thinks her brother was dating Blair."

"Why don't you think there's anything in that?"

"Tiffany is only nine and is known for telling tall tales. Said she had an ice rink in her backyard too."

Stevie let out a frustrated sigh. "So the secret-lover line doesn't look like it's going anywhere."

"Should I take down that card?" Colby asked.

"No, leave it up. Did you get anywhere with your mom? Did she tell you why she got that money?"

Colby crinkled her nose. "All she's said is 'what does it matter why I got it?' And I know it looks suspicious, but I don't see how my mom could be involved. She got that money years ago."

"If Kirk has given her money, there must be a reason," Stevie said. "I'm not saying that it's relevant to Blair's murder, but maybe she knows something about Kirk that might help bring him down. Can you keep trying?"

"I can, but I don't think she's going to tell me anything."

Stevie sighed. She was sure Faith Green knew more than she was letting on. But for now, she had to sort out exactly what they did know. "Okay, I'm going to add any new findings to the cards."

Kirk Tyler

- Motive: To stop Blair revealing that he is a groomer and abuser.
- Stopped Blair from talking to Hilton Moore about a story.
- Paid off Melissa $100,000.
- More girls have come forward.
- Has an alibi.

Questions regarding Kirk:

- Why did he give Faith Green $800,000?
- Could he be @BBWill_be_mine and be behind the threatening emails?

Bex Lyons

- Motive: Instructed by Kirk Tyler.
- Argued with Blair the day of her murder.
- Probably knows about Kirk's abuse.
- Blair's security so knows all Blair's movements.
- Has an alibi.

Questions regarding Bex:

- Was Blair going to expose Kirk?
- What was their argument about?

Unknown Stalker(s)

Motive: Crazy obsessive?

@BBWill_be_mine

- Identified through messages to Blair (@DollyPurrton_14) on Blair Baker fan site.
- He knew who Blair was and seemed to be aware of her movements.
- Sent threatening emails to Stevie through the wbm12345@buzzmail.com email and another account.
- Does not want Blair's death investigated.

Gift-giver

- Tiara.
- Creepy framed picture.
- First seen loitering outside Clover Lane.
- Has gotten into Stevie's room—caught on doorcam.

Creepy guy seen outside Stevie's

- Big guy.
- Wears long coat and baseball cap.
- Carries knife.

Questions:

- Who are they?

- Are they three separate people?

- Had Blair found out who they are? One, two, all of them?

- Did one of them send the deranged emails to Blair?

- Did they call Blair on <u>At Night with the Stars</u> on the burner phone?

- Did they call Blair just before the concert?

"Okay, on another card can you write 'Aaron Taylor case'?" Stevie said.

"What color marker? Maybe red?"

"Whatever you want," Stevie said. "Just write down what I tell you."

Colby saluted. "Yes, ma'am."

Stevie took a breath; she wasn't sure if she could actually bring herself to say it.

"Stevie?"

"Put down, 'Why did Frank Baker misreport that Shiralee Rogers saw two people breaking into the lumberyard?'" She rushed the words out quickly before she could change her mind.

Colby stared at Stevie, red Sharpie hovering above the card. "Seriously?"

"I don't know if it means anything yet. Just write it down. Then underneath it add, 'Who keeps calling Frank Baker from an unknown number?'"

Colby blinked. "Stevie, you don't think your dad's involved, do you?"

"No, not really, but there's something about the Aaron Taylor case that doesn't add up, and the gun was used to kill Blair, so I'm thinking there could be a connection."

"Okay, then. I'll add that, too."

Aaron Taylor case

Questions

- Why did Frank Baker misreport that Shiralee Rogers saw two people breaking into the lumberyard?

- Who keeps calling Frank Baker from an unknown number?

- How did the gun that killed Aaron Taylor end up being used in Blair's murder?

Stevie stuck the final flash card to the wall and stood back, arms folded. "Even more questions."

Colby exhaled. "Yup."

Stevie clicked her tongue. Where to even start? Her eyes scanned across each name. "I guess we just have to work through them?"

"It's got to be a stalker, right? The call to the show, then calling Blair again just before her murder?" Colby said.

"That's what Uncle Jimmy and Oliver think."

Stevie knew everything was pointing toward a stalker being responsible for Blair's death, so why wasn't she able to close the book on Kirk Tyler? In her opinion, he had the most to lose—his whole career—if Blair exposed him for being a groomer.

"Look, I know Kirk has an alibi, and even if he didn't do it, I want to take him down. We owe it to those girls who were brave enough to message you. I truly believe Blair was going to expose him. She can't now, but we still can."

"I am totally here for taking down Kirk-the-perv-Tyler."

Stevie steepled her hands under her chin. "So we start with Bex Lyons. There's a chance she might give a statement about Blair. She must know what's going on. She also might be able to tell us more about who was stalking Blair. *And* she might even know why your mom was paid eight hundred grand. Besides, we know where she is."

"All very good points," Colby said.

Stevie took out her phone. "No time like the present."

It's Stevie Baker. I would like to talk to you about some information that has come to light regarding Kirk Tyler.

Bex texted back immediately.

Jefferson Suite Sable & Stone 1:00.

Thirty-Eight

Stevie jumped behind the wheel, threw her bag on the passenger seat, and slammed her car door shut. She began drumming her fingers on the steering wheel and waited for Colby to emerge from her house. She'd decided she needed to pee. *Can't interrogate Bex Lyons with a full bladder, Stevie.*

Her mind drifted to her dad. He was hiding something. But what?

"I brought you a present."

Shittttt!

Her heart threw itself against her rib cage and her entire body tensed. Her eyes flashed to the rearview mirror.

Fuck. Fuck. Fuck.

It was him.

The man in the long coat.

On the back seat of her car.

He looked up at her from under his baseball cap. Dark eyes shining, a smile on his lips.

"It's for Blair, really." His voice was soft, almost sweet.

She should get out of the car. She should scream. Why couldn't she move? Where was her voice?

Do something! Do something!

He held a box up, pulled out a silky white dress, and ran it against his jowly cheek.

Stevie's breath grew faster and faster, thinner and thinner.

The same thoughts throwing themselves against her skull.

Scream! Run! Do something!

Her eyes ran down to his side. Did he have a knife there, hidden under his coat? Her heart surged again. She really needed to do something. Her eyes darted to her bag. The pepper spray! Her hands wouldn't cooperate, kept gripping the wheel—refusing to let go.

Let go of the steering wheel and use the goddamn pepper spray!

He leaned forward, pushed the dress toward her. "Blair was going to wear this when I married her. I loved her, you see. But you know that already, don't you, Stevie? You got my other gifts. Would you see to it that my princess is buried in this? It's what she would have wanted."

Like hell it was.

Stevie grabbed the dress, threw it at him, then lunged for her bag. Hands shaking, she pulled out the pepper spray and pointed it at him, pressed down on the nozzle. The spray shot out sideways, covering the driver's-side window with a fine mist. Crap! How had she messed that up?

She coughed, lungs protesting, eyes stinging. Idiot. Idiot. Idiot. She turned the can around, pushed down on the nozzle and shouted, "This is for Catsy!"

Her second shot hit the target. He recoiled, howling, clutching his fists to his eyes.

Stevie yanked the door handle and gasped in a lungful of air. Tried to throw herself out of the car. Her seat belt tightened across her chest. She turned around, fumbled to unbuckle it, and tumbled out onto the road. She pulled herself onto all fours, gulped at the air, each breath scraping her lungs.

"Stevie?!"

She caught a glimpse of movement—Colby's boots—swift and determined, charging toward her.

"Call the cops! He's in the car!" she rasped, her eyes and nose streaming. "I pepper-sprayed him."

"Who? The stalker?"

"Yes!" Stevie coughed, rolled onto her back, dragged in another lungful of air. Her eyes were swelling up, closing shut.

"Oh. My. God!" Colby loomed over her, phone at her ear. "112 Oak Crescent! Send all available units! There's a stalker on the rampage! No, I'm not kidding! This is an actual emergency!"

She dropped her phone, crouched next to Stevie, her eyes running over her—wide and wild. "Are you okay?"

Okay was a stretch—her lungs were on fire and her eyes were burning, but Stevie nodded.

"Wait there! He's trying to get out!" Colby stood up, pulled her own can of pepper spray out of her bag, gave it a shake. "I think it's time for a second helping."

She ran toward the car, stuck her arm through the driver's door, and unloaded another can in his face. She slammed the door shut, did a triumphant nod, but then the back door opened.

He fell out onto the road, gasping for air, eyes ringed with angry red blotches, a knife falling from his coat, clattering to the ground.

"Shit on the sidewalk! He's out!" Colby cried.

Stevie pushed herself onto her knees, tried to pry her eyes open. "Stay back!" She coughed again, lungs screaming.

Colby took off—fast boots clacking on the road.

"Colby!"

The man staggered to his feet, doubled over, coughing and choking. He stumbled forward, lurching to the left, then to the right. Eyes fixing on the knife. Colby got to it first, kicked it and sent it skittering under the car. Then she charged at him, launching herself through the air and landing on his back. He reeled around, trying to shake her off.

"You're not going anywhere, you creep!" Colby wrapped her arms and legs around him, clung on to him like an angry koala. "You killed Blair Baker!"

"No!" He staggered sideways. "I loved her!"

Half bent, Stevie staggered toward them.

"You shot her!" Colby cried.

"I didn't shoot her. I loved her!" He spun around, twisting and writhing.

Colby clung on harder. "Save it for the cops, you freak!"

"Don't call me that!" Rage rippled across his face, his voice lower, louder. He bucked, sudden and violent.

Colby hit the ground. She reacted quickly, grabbing his ankle before he could get away, bringing him down too. Stevie hurled herself at him, elbow first. He grunted—air forced from his lungs.

"I didn't do it!" he cried, voice hitching and snagging in his throat.

Colby wrapped her arms around one of his legs, held on to it tight as he tried to crawl away. "We don't believe you!"

"It wasn't me!" He kicked back with his free leg. Stevie caught it, wrapped her arms around it, too, as he tried to pull himself forward. Stevie and Colby pulled back, using their body weight to stop his movement.

The sound of sirens. Not too far—maybe a couple of streets away.

He heard it and struggled harder, belly scraping across the ground, dragging Colby and Stevie with him. They must have looked like some ridiculous human wheelbarrow.

"Don't. Let. Go!" Colby said.

Like Stevie needed telling.

"I didn't do it! I couldn't have done it!"

The sirens were louder now. Stevie looked behind her, the flash of blue lights at the end of the street blurred by her streaming eyes.

"I couldn't have done it because I was in jail when Blair was shot!"

In jail? Stevie's mind tripped over itself.

Colby gave his leg a yank. "He's lying."

He coughed, tried to catch his voice. "I'm not! I didn't do it!"

The screech of tires, the sound of car doors being thrown open, feet pounding the path toward them.

Finally, a shout. "Back away from the suspect! We can take it from here!"

Thirty-Nine

Stevie leaned against the trunk of the police car—a cold compress held to her eyes.

He had gone with them willingly. As they pushed his head down into the back seat of the car, he looked at Stevie and said, "I didn't do it. I didn't kill Blair."

There was a sincerity to his voice that Stevie couldn't ignore. Sure, he was clearly crazy, but it didn't mean he was a killer. She'd gone over to him, told the concerned policewoman that she just wanted to ask a couple of questions, that it wouldn't take long. She'd told Stevie it wasn't procedure, but when Colby had pointed out that they had caught the guy, and she'd have to arrest them, too, if she was going to stop them, she pressed her lips together and said, "One minute."

He was sitting, shoulders slumped, hands in cuffs resting on his paunch, looking down at the footwell in the back of the cop car. He looked up when Stevie approached. His whole face was covered in red blotches that ran all the way up to his receding hairline. Stevie struggled to age him. Could have been anywhere between late twenties and early forties. She cleared her throat, cut to the chase. "You said you were in jail the day Blair died—is that true?"

He nodded.

Stevie believed him. What would be the point in lying when it could be so easily checked?

"Are you BB-will-be-mine? Did you send me emails from the

address wbm12345@buzzmail.com, telling me to stop looking into Blair's murder?"

"No," he said, "I didn't."

"They'll check your laptop, your phone, so if you're lying, you may as well tell me now."

"They can check all they want. I didn't send any emails."

Stevie nodded. So there *were* two stalkers. Her hunch had been right.

The policewoman shut the door then and said, "That's enough."

Colby finished telling her version of events, which involved a lot of physical demonstrations—a full reenactment to a startled-looking cop—and joined Stevie leaning on the trunk of the cop car.

"He said he didn't kill Blair," Stevie said.

"Of course he's going to say he didn't do it! If I killed someone, I'd lie about it too!"

Stevie raised her eyebrows. "Oh, you would, would you?!"

Colby rolled her eyes. "You know what I mean."

"I think he's telling the truth."

Colby gave her a nudge. "You got him, Stevie. You found Blair's killer. Gave yourself a face full of pepper spray in the process, but you did it."

Stevie forced a smile. She wasn't so sure.

"Out of peas." Marnie handed Stevie a pack of frozen homemade bolognese. "For your eyes—to help the swelling go down."

Stevie placed it on her face, let out an *ahhh* of appreciation.

She was lying head to toe with Colby, legs entangled, Catsy draped over them, watching *Friends* reruns and waiting for news from the police station. Faith Green hadn't answered the calls or messages the police had left for her, so, in the end, it was decided that Colby should go to the Bakers' to recover from their ordeal. For Colby, recovering had mainly involved eating an entire pack of OREOs while delivering lines a fraction earlier than the *Friends* cast. More than a little annoying, but as she'd helped save Stevie from a psycho stalker, she let it go.

Marnie perched on the arm of the sofa, started stroking Stevie's hair. "You must have been so scared."

She had been—when she'd first realized he was in the car. But she wasn't anymore. Not now that she knew who he was. Eric Corder, thirty-two, lived at home with his mom. Unemployed. A deeply troubled fantasist who hadn't been able to fight off two teenage girls.

"I don't know what I would have done if I'd lost you, too," Marnie said, her voice breaking.

Stevie took the rapidly thawing bolognese off her eyes—saw her mom was crying. "It's okay, Mom—I'm okay."

Marnie stroked her hair again. "I can't believe you caught him."

"It was Colby, really." Stevie smiled at her. "She was the one who ran toward him, kicked the knife away."

Colby waved her arm dismissively, finished her mouthful of OREO. "Fast boots never let me down. And to think Coach Tranmore said I was useless at soccer!"

"I am so grateful to you, Colby," Marnie said, her voice full of affection, her eyes filling with tears. "Thank god it's over. Blair's killer is going to go to jail, and we're going to be able to finally lay our daughter to rest and start trying to heal."

Stevie dropped her eyes from her mom's, bit the inside of her lip. She couldn't bring herself to say that although Eric Corder might be unhinged, a fantasist, mentally unwell, that she wasn't convinced he was Blair's killer.

Marnie turned at the sound of tires crunching on the driveway.

She stood up, dabbed at her eyes with the cuff of her blouse. "That'll be your father back from the police station. Frank, we're in here! Did he confess?"

Frank walked in, face gray, and chucked his keys on the coffee table. "No, love, it wasn't him."

"I really thought we had him," Colby said. She was lying on the floor, her legs up on Stevie's bed. "Your pal Eric was giving off such strong murder vibes."

Stevie rocked back on her chair, looked at the ceiling. "Well, it wasn't him because he was in a jail cell in Saluda Police Department when Blair was shot."

It was about as watertight an alibi as anybody could have. Five days earlier, on June 1, Eric had stolen a necklace from a department store and been caught by security. He'd gotten agitated and hit the guard, and they kept him in for the night. He'd spent the whole night crying that he would miss the concert and wouldn't be able to give the necklace to his princess.

He'd admitted to a whole bunch of stuff when Jimmy had questioned him—the gifts he'd left for Stevie and a good portion of the emails Hilton Moore printed on his site—but not all of them.

"And he didn't make the call to *At Night with the Stars,* either?" Colby asked.

"You heard what my dad said. He wasn't even in Honeyville then."

"So you were right—there wasn't just one stalker?"

"I think so. He told me he wasn't BB-will-be-mine. He could be lying, I guess, but what would be the point? Why admit to some things but not others?"

"So what now?"

Stevie put her feet up on her desk, pinched the bridge of her nose. "BB-will-be-mine doesn't want us looking into the case—doesn't want me digging up secrets. So I guess we need to find out what those secrets are. Because if we do, we'll know who had a reason to want Blair dead."

"And how do we do that?"

"I guess we go back to the original plan: work through the suspects and our list of questions, starting with Bex Lyons." Stevie looked at her wall clock—it was just past seven p.m. "I think six hours could still be considered fashionably late."

Forty

Stevie knocked on the door of the Jefferson Suite in the Sable and Stone hotel.

The plan was to be up front. Tell Bex they had witnesses who could testify that Kirk Tyler had sexually assaulted minors. Show her the video footage of her leaving Blair's dressing room and see what she said about that—see if they could get anything else out of her. It had seemed like a good plan back in Stevie's bedroom, but now, standing outside Bex's hotel room, Stevie was having doubts.

Bex opened the door, looked them both up and down, with her cold gray eyes. She was dressed in a white shirt and black suit pants, the creases sharp and precise. "I didn't think you were going to show."

"Yes, sorry, we had a run-in with a guy called Eric Corder. He was stalking Blair, but he isn't the killer," Stevie said. She watched Bex closely, checking her reaction to see if the name rang a bell.

Bex remained impassive. "You'd better come in."

Stevie and Colby exchanged glances as they followed her into the lounge area.

Bex gestured at the sofa. "Sit."

Stevie and Colby sat down at the same time. Bex sat opposite, eyes locked on Stevie's. "So this *Eric Corder* didn't shoot Blair?"

"No, he has an alibi."

Bex's jaw muscles tightened. "Shame."

Stevie waited for her to say something else. She didn't, just kept staring at Stevie.

She shrank under Bex's gaze and shifted in her seat. What was the best way to bring up the fact that Kirk Tyler was an abuser?

"We wanted to ask if you . . . perhaps . . . might be aware of some . . . activities Kirk Tyler may have partaken in and that Blair was aware of? Activities that were a bit . . . no, *wholly* inappropriate."

Yeah, that was not it. A lot of words but none of the right ones.

"What *are* you talking about?" Bex said.

Stevie tugged at her collar, tried again. "It's just that we think it is possible that maybe Blair knew what Kirk had been doing. And it is therefore possible that her knowing may have possibly led to her death. Possibly."

"I'm sorry—I don't have the first idea what you're saying," Bex said.

"Your boss is a dirty pervert, and we think he shot Blair because she was going to tell everyone. That clear enough?" Colby said.

Stevie swallowed, actually heard her throat make a gulping sound.

Bex leaned back in her seat, draped her arm over the back of the couch, voice slow and considered. "Those are some very serious accusations."

"You bet your ass, they are," Colby said. "And we've got girls who are willing to go on the record to say exactly what Kirk did to them."

"And these girls have physical evidence, do they? Proof of what supposedly happened?"

"Yes, well, not physical evidence . . ." Colby looked flustered, shot Stevie a panicked look. "They have their voices and the truth!"

"Their voices and the truth?" Bex let the words hang in the air. She cocked her head. "Not exactly damning, is it?" She smirked at Stevie, but her eyes were hard. "Perhaps I don't need to inform the lawyers just yet."

Stevie's throat tightened as her confidence drained away. Had they really thought they could waltz in here and get Bex Lyons to talk? She must have been covering up for Kirk Tyler for years.

"What do you mean?" Colby pressed. "Didn't you hear what I just said?"

Bex clasped her hands together, steepled her fingers under her chin. "Colby, isn't it? Can I give you a bit of advice?"

Colby looked daggers at her. "Go on."

"You've been lied to."

"Lied to?" Colby said, confusion in her eyes.

"Your voice isn't important. I know that you've been told that your opinion matters. It's not your fault—you've been duped by the influencers, the life coaches, the education system. They tell you to speak up and speak out! But the reality is, your voice is irrelevant, insignificant. And it means nothing in a court of law if you don't have any proof. So unless one of these girls you have managed to drag out of the woodwork has video evidence of Kirk Tyler engaging in—what was it you called it?" She looked at Stevie, that smirk on her lips again. "Ah yes, 'activities,' which may have been 'a bit, no, wholly inappropriate,' then I suggest you girls go back to your bedrooms and play with your dolls, or you are going to find yourselves in a whole world of trouble. Kirk Tyler is a powerful man. You do not want to cross him."

Stevie blinked. Bex knew what Kirk Tyler had done—the kind of man he was—and she didn't care.

"I think we might be done here." Bex rose to her feet.

"Not quite," Stevie said, her voice quiet, unsure.

"Excuse me?"

"You mentioned video evidence."

Bex cocked her head. "And?"

"It's just, we do have some. Not of Kirk, but of you." Stevie nodded at Colby. "Show her."

"Show me what?" Bex said. Her voice was still sharp, but Stevie saw a flicker of concern in her eyes, and she felt her confidence returning.

Colby held up her phone, put her hand on her hip, and pressed Play.

"That's you, coming out of Blair's dressing room on the day she died. You were arguing with her," Stevie said.

Bex scoffed. "You can't tell that's me! It could be anybody!"

"We had the audio enhanced. It's you, all right."

"So what if it is? Blair was difficult. She was always having arguments with the crew."

"But you didn't tell the police about it. In fact, when you were shown the video, you said you had no idea who it was."

Bex folded her arms, defensive. *"And?"*

"And I think that's just a little bit suspicious, don't you, Colby?"

"You bet your ass, I do!" Colby said. "Pretty sure lying to the police is frowned upon."

"That video isn't proof of anything."

Stevie shrugged. "Maybe. Maybe not. Depends on what you were arguing about."

"I don't even remember. Blair was always agitating about something."

"I think Blair is telling you she's going to expose Kirk as an abuser. And then a few hours later she winds up being shot. I wonder what people would think if we put that on the internet? People sure do love a new theory."

"I'd be very careful who you're threatening if I was you." Bex narrowed her eyes. "If that video sees the light of day, I'll make sure that the whole world knows what type of family Blair Baker came from." She leaned forward, cupped her hand around her mouth, and whispered. "And it's bad, Stevie. Really bad."

Stevie faltered. "Wh-what do you mean?"

Bex laughed, relaxed back in her chair—in charge again. "I don't think poor Marnie could take another shock, do you? And your dad, what with his bad heart . . . Oh!" Bex bit her finger, inclined her head. "Did I get that right? He does have a bad heart, doesn't he? I mean, that's not something he would lie about?"

"No, he . . . he wouldn't!"

"Okay, whatever you say!" Bex said brightly. "Now, this has been lovely, but I take it we're done here?" She nodded at the door. "You can show yourselves out."

Stevie didn't move, couldn't move.

Colby grabbed hold of Stevie's hand, pulled her toward the door, then stopped and jabbed her finger at Bex. "Just for the record, I do not have dolls! I have *one* doll. A Blair Baker figurine, and it is ornamental, not for playing with! And I think you, *lady*, are a truly terrible person, but seeing as you said my opinion doesn't matter, how do you feel about this?!" She tried to turn over the hallway table in some kind of protest, but it was far too heavy so she pulled a painting from the wall, eyeballed Bex, and dropped it on the floor.

"I don't feel much, actually," Bex said.

"Not listening!" Colby yelled, and pulled Stevie out of the suite and slammed the door.

Outside, Colby leaned against the wall. "Soooo, that didn't go quite as we'd hoped. We didn't even get to ask her about the eight hundred grand. Probably can't go back in now."

"No, probably not." Stevie was only half listening, her mind trapped by what Bex had said about her family. First Hilton had suggested there might be some secret she didn't know about, and now Bex. And what did she mean about her dad's heart?

"She's not going to rat out Kirk—that's for sure. I say we send the video to Hilton Moore anyway—put the theory that Blair's management team were involved in her death out there. See if she's more willing to talk when she's feeling some heat."

"But she said—"

Colby cut her off. "She has to be bluffing about having something on your family."

Stevie looked at the door to the suite, spoke more to herself. "What if she isn't?"

Forty-One

Stevie parked under the neon lights that read "sin Motel" and cut the engine.

"I'm all for interrogating Gunner Trip again," Colby said, applying some lip gloss in the vanity mirror, "but are you sure you're okay? You've barely spoken since we left the hotel."

"I'm fine." It was another lie. Stevie had been telling so many lately. She'd spent the drive chewing over what Bex had said. It was clear she knew something about her family, and it was also clear that she was suggesting her dad had made up his heart condition. Stevie would never have thought it possible, but then she would never have thought he would lie on a police report, either. Maybe she should have gone home and asked him, but when Colby had asked her what they should do next, she'd suggested they should visit Gunner Trip. It was an act of avoidance, but she couldn't face finding out whether her dad had lied again. Not yet.

They ran into Gunner on the metal staircase that led down from his room. He had his earphones in and a bag on his back.

"Oh, it's you two," he said, turning off his music. "I'm just off to catch a flight. Finally."

"We wondered if you could clear something up for us," Stevie said, straight to the point. She didn't wait for him to respond. "You got into Honeyville three days earlier than you said you did."

Gunner opened his mouth, but Colby was too quick. "There's no point in lying. We have actual concrete evidence."

They had the word of a guy in a dirty white vest, briefs and socks and slides, who appeared to have disappeared, according to Officer Dean, but sure, concrete evidence.

"We spoke to someone who saw you," Stevie said.

Gunner sighed, tipped his head back, and looked up at the sky. "If I tell you, you have to promise not to say why."

"That depends on whether it was because you showed up early to kill Blair or not," Colby said.

"No! Nothing like that."

"So what, then?" Stevie said.

"I had a tip-off that there was going to be an off-season drug test, and I thought it would be best if I was out of town when that happened."

Colby glanced at his biceps. "You're a drugs cheat? I thought your body was a temple."

"You don't understand, the pressures of playing in the NFL, it's—"

"Yes, very difficult, I'm sure." Stevie didn't want to get into his excuses there and then so she moved on quickly. "Our source tells us that you had guests while you were here. Who were they?"

"I was bored, so I invited a couple of girls I found on Tinder over. I needed some form of entertainment."

Stevie grimaced. *Some form of entertainment*—real nice. "So what was Blair doing that meant she couldn't meet you?"

"The first day I was here, she was filming a TV show—"

"Did you phone in?"

Gunner blinked. "Phone in the show? No, why would I do that?"

Stevie studied his face—he looked like he was telling the truth. "And after she got to Honeyville?"

"After she flew in, I guess she was getting ready for the concert. Oh, and she said she was meeting up with someone about pulling a new track she'd recorded. She'd been excited about it. Said it was going to be her most important, explosive song to date, but for some reason she'd gotten cold feet about it. And before you ask me, no, she didn't say why."

"She was meeting someone in Honeyville about a new track?" Stevie said. "Why didn't you tell us this before?"

"I didn't even think about it. Her voicemail about knowing who her stalker was seemed more relevant."

Stevie supposed that was fair. "So who was she meeting?"

"I'm guessing it was the new producer I told you about. She sent me an early demo a while ago, told me to keep it top secret—you can listen if you don't believe me. She wasn't sure of a title; either 'Breaking the Silence' or 'Serenade for a Scumbag.'"

A chill ran through Stevie as she repeated the titles in her head.

"A new Blair Baker track?" Colby said. "Errr, yes!"

Gunner disconnected his Bluetooth and played the song on loudspeaker.

Behind the curtain, you played your part,
A predator hiding in the dark.
No strings to hold me, I've clipped your crown,
The king of sleaze is going down.
The walls are closing in on you;
What you've hidden comes into view.
I'm not the prey, I'm not afraid;
The hunter's now the one betrayed.

Gunner pressed Pause. "Dark, but I kind of like it." He looked from Stevie to Colby. "What's wrong? You both look like you've seen a ghost."

Not seen one. Heard one.

"Holy mother of music," Colby whispered. "Blair wrote a song about Kirk Tyler."

"That's not all," Stevie said. "I've heard that tune before. And so have you."

"Where?" Colby asked.

"Terence Thompson."

Forty-Two

"Oh my god, oh my god, oh my god!" Colby repeated. "How the hell would Terence Thompson know Blair's song? Are you sure he was humming it?"

Stevie and Colby were sitting in the car in the motel parking lot—Colby was freaking out and Stevie was trying her best not to. Why had Terence Thompson failed to mention he knew Blair?

"Yes," Stevie said. "I'm, like, ninety-nine percent certain. I think he might be the hip young producer Blair was working with. Maybe it was him she was seeing each time she came back to Honeyville."

Colby closed her eyes. "You have to be kidding! It's going to turn out that Terence is the murderer, isn't it?" She threw her arms in the air. "I have the worst luck with boys! Of course it was going to be him!"

"It might not be him," Stevie said. "Although it does look pretty sus that he didn't tell us he knew Blair. Maybe he killed her because she was going to stop working with him. Gunner said she'd gotten cold feet over the song." Her brain fired through all the connections. "Also, I know Shiralee said she only saw one person, but Terence could have gone with Aaron to the lumberyard—they were close, after all, and it was dark—maybe he was hiding."

"Why would Terence shoot Aaron if they were close?"

"I don't know—maybe they had a falling-out—maybe it was an accident. But if someone was with him, then it makes sense that it was Terence."

"Oh my god, it *is* him, isn't it?" Colby shook her head and sighed mournfully. "As if a murderer could have dimples like that."

Stevie looked at her, incredulous. "What?"

"I'm just saying, dimples like that—unexpected on a murderer."

"Can you hear the words that are coming out of your mouth right now?" Stevie said, but Colby had a point—well, sort of. Terence really didn't seem like the murdering type. Not in comparison to Kirk Tyler at least. "If . . ." Stevie began, thinking aloud, "if Kirk thought Blair was going to leave him and put out a song like 'Serenade for a Scumbag,' it could end his career."

"Yes!" Colby shouted, so loudly Stevie jumped. "He would definitely want to kill her for that! He's way more likely to have done it than Terence!"

"I don't think we can rule either of them out, especially if the main thrust of your argument is based on dimples."

"Okay, fine, you make a fair point. But what do we do now? Send the song to the police? Confront Terence?"

They probably ought to tell the authorities what they'd discovered, but Stevie wanted to speak to Terence first, find out if she was right before she sent the cops around there. Marvin had suffered enough—she'd made an incorrect accusation about one of Mia's teachers and the fallout had been awful. She had to be certain. She checked the time on her dash. "It's nine thirty. I say we go home, and then tomorrow we head back over to the Aaron Taylor Community Center and ask Terence why he lied about working with Blair. Then we can decide what to do about the song."

Stevie dropped Colby off, then swung by the drive-through. Her parents were already in bed when she got home. Honestly, she was relieved; if Frank had been awake, she'd have to ask him about what Bex Lyons had said about his heart—about what Bex had meant when she said the *type of family* they were.

She kicked off her shoes in the hall. She had to focus on one thing at a time. And right then, her focus was on her stomach. After that, it was Terence Thompson. Maybe she might be able to find some paparazzi shots of him and Blair together to prove their connection. Now that she knew it was him Blair had been meeting, he might be easier to spot. She went into the kitchen and unwrapped her burrito. She took a bite, closed her eyes, and let out a satisfied moan. Can't beat Crispy Chicken Supreme.

She'd demolished half the wrap when she noticed a package on the kitchen counter. Her heart flipped. Another Eric Corder gift? No, it couldn't be—he was still at the police station. And his packages never had labels, whereas this one did. Not everything was to do with Blair's murder. She needed to calm the hell down.

It was addressed to her. She hadn't ordered anything—wasn't expecting anything. She licked the sour cream off her hands, and used her car key to cut open the tape.

She pulled out a load of red tissue paper.

"What the f—"

At the bottom of the box was a Blair Baker doll. Its head was lying next to the body—its eyes gouged out.

There was also a card with the words *Stop investigating or you're next* printed in bold type.

She picked the head up by its hair. Maybe @BBWill_be_mine had progressed beyond emails. It sounded like him. But then her mind latched on to something else. Something Bex Lyons had said, just a few hours ago.

I suggest you girls go back to your bedrooms and play with your dolls.

Not exactly subtle. It was her. It had to be. Had she followed them to the motel? Did she know about the song, too?

Stevie picked up the box and tried to see if there were any clues as to where it had come from. No postmark—it must have been hand delivered. She was going to check the doorcam when her phone started ringing and Colby's name flashed up on the screen.

"Colby, have you been sent a—"

Colby spoke over her. "Stevie, something terrible's happened."

Stevie stuck the phone under her chin, turned the box over. "You got one too?"

Colby sniffed into the phone. She sounded like she was crying. "Got one what? Stevie, it's my mom." Colby's voice hitched. "She's in the hospital."

It took a moment for Stevie to understand what she was saying. "The hospital? Is she okay?"

"She had a car accident. It's bad, Stevie—it's really bad."

"Where are you?"

"I'm at home."

Stevie put the box down. It would have to wait. "Stay there—I'm coming over. I'll drive you there."

Stevie hung back in the corridor while the doctor spoke to Colby outside Faith's room. Was it wrong to listen in? Perhaps, but she needed to know what Colby was about to face on the other side of that door. The doctor told Colby what she should expect. That Faith was unconscious but comfortable. They'd had to rush her in and had already operated on her spleen. It had gone well but it may be a little while before Faith would come around. She'd also suffered a blow to the head—either from the tree or part of the car. They hadn't been able to assess the impact of that yet. The doctor told her that Faith was hooked up to machines and that Colby would see tubes and wires and that it could look frightening, but they were helping to keep Faith alive. Stevie could tell by the look on the doctor's face, by how gently she was speaking to Colby, that things weren't good.

Colby looked so small and scared, Stevie wanted to run over

and hug her and tell her it would be okay, but she didn't know if it was the truth.

Stevie sat down in the waiting room, closed her eyes, and rubbed her temples. What would Colby do if her mom died? She didn't have anyone else. She wondered if Frank and Marnie would take her in. They had the room. She pulled that thought back—the poor woman wasn't even dead, and Stevie was already putting plans in place.

"Stevie, what are you doing here?"

She looked up to see Uncle Jimmy walking toward her. She checked behind him to see if Oliver was there too—her heart dipped a little when she realized he wasn't. She told herself off for being pathetic.

"Colby's mom was in a car accident," Stevie said.

"That was your friend's mom? I was the attending officer."

"Do you know what happened?"

"Probably driving too fast. They overshot that bend on Westville Drive. That time of day when the sun is setting makes visibility really tricky."

She knew exactly where he meant. "That's where Hal crashed."

"Yup, but they went over the edge of the road and down the hill through the wood; only stopped when they wrapped themselves around a tree."

"They?"

"Her boyfriend was in the car too." Uncle Jimmy stiffened his jaw. "I'm afraid he didn't make it."

Stevie cupped her hands over her face. "Mike *died*?" She didn't know the man at all and the little she had seen of him hadn't exactly turned her into a fan, but still, *dead*? It was awful.

"I was first on the scene, and I can tell you Colby's mom is lucky to be alive." He shook his head, sucked in through his teeth. "It's going to be a tricky job getting that car back up that hill. Have you heard how she's doing?"

"Colby's in with her now. I don't think Faith's conscious at the moment. It sounds pretty bad."

Jimmy gave Stevie's shoulder a squeeze. "I'm going to leave them my number so I can take a statement if she comes around."

Jimmy went over to speak to someone at the desk. A moment later a doctor appeared and took Jimmy off to a side room. Stevie leaned her head back against the wall and closed her eyes. Should she go home, check the doorcam on her laptop? She wanted to, but she needed to make sure Colby was okay first. She wished she still had the app, but her counselor had urged her to delete it after she'd grown fixated on scrolling through the endless loops of footage after Mia went missing.

"If you're tired, you should head home."

Stevie opened her eyes, saw Jimmy standing there. "I will, just as soon as I know Colby's all right."

Just as she said that Colby came out of her mom's room. Jimmy saw her and said, "I'll leave you to it."

Stevie stood up—eyes full of concern. Colby chewed her lip, and her chin started to tremble. Stevie darted over to her, pulled her into a hug. Colby sank onto her shoulder and sobbed. "It's my fault—it's all my fault."

Stevie held her tight. "No, it's not. How can it be?"

Colby pulled her phone out of her pocket, held it up for Stevie to see.

There was a message from Bex Lyons.

I told you not to post anything about Kirk Tyler or there'd be consequences.

Stevie's mouth went dry. "When did you get that?"

"She must have sent it when we were on our way over here. Stevie, I don't think Mom's crash was an accident."

Forty-Three

Stevie took the phone from Colby's trembling hands, read the message again. She tried to think clearly. "If Bex Lyons was responsible for your mom's crash, do you think she'd send a message like this? It's almost like she's sticking her hand up in the air and saying she did it."

Colby's forehead furrowed. "I don't know. I don't know anything anymore."

Stevie spoke gently. "This isn't your fault, Colby. That part of Westville Drive is a nightmare and Uncle Jimmy said he thinks your mom and Mike may have been driving too fast—"

Colby looked up from her phone. "Mike was in the car?"

"They didn't tell you?"

"Is he here?"

Stevie bit her lip. "He didn't make it. I'm sorry, Colby—Uncle Jimmy said he died at the scene."

Colby slumped back against the wall. Closed her eyes. "How am I going to tell Mom that?"

Stevie didn't have an answer. She didn't think Colby was really asking for one.

"This is an awful thing, Colby, but it wasn't your fault—you have to believe that. It was an accident. It's not linked to Bex Lyons or the case."

"On the phone earlier, you asked me if I got one. Got one *what*? Did Bex Lyons text you, too?"

"It doesn't matter—you need to focus on your mom right now."

"Got one *what*?" Colby said again, voice forceful.

"I think she sent me a doll."

"A doll?"

"It was a Blair Baker doll. Its head had been pulled off."

"Stevie, you need to tell the police."

"I know. I will. But—"

"But nothing! Stevie, your sister was murdered!" Colby shouted. Stevie jumped and the woman at the desk looked over. Colby lowered her voice: "This is serious. I know you think my mom's crash was an accident, but what if I'm right? What if it wasn't? You could be in danger—we both could."

"Jimmy already left the hospital."

"So call him."

Stevie pulled her phone out of her back pocket and pulled up Jimmy's number. She listened to it ring through to the voicemail. "Jimmy, it's Stevie. I know you were just here, but could you give me a call back? There's something I need to tell you. It's important."

"Thank you," Colby said, then looked toward her mom's room. "I should go back in, sit with her in case she comes around. You should go. I'll call you if anything happens."

"Okay, but let me know if you need anything, and I mean *anything*."

Colby gave her a hug, then headed toward her mom's room. She stopped, fingers wrapped around the doorknob. She looked over at Stevie, eyes glistening, a tremble in her bottom lip. "Stevie, would you—"

"I was literally just about to say I am an excellent bedside companion."

Stevie sensed someone standing over her, which caused her to stir. She lifted her head, blinked. The lights in the room too white, too bright. She squinted at the white coat, heard the beeps of the hospital equipment, and remembered where she was. She tried to move but realized she was pinned under Colby. The armchair was only meant for one, but they'd squished in together—Stevie underneath, Colby with her legs draped over her and hanging over the side. Now her legs were dead and her neck was stiff. They must have both been exhausted to fall asleep in that position.

"Good morning, I'm Dr. D'Arby."

Stevie gave Colby a shake—she groaned, opened her eyes. "You're not the doctor from last night."

"No, Dr. Hernandez's shift finished a couple of hours ago. I have your mom's bag—it was recovered from the crash." Dr. D'Arby handed over a beat-up leather purse.

Colby peeled herself off Stevie and took the bag, clutched it to her chest.

"The good news is that your mom is doing well. We've kept her sedated postoperation so we can monitor her, but I'm happy with how she's doing, so we're going to stop administering the sedatives."

"How long will it take her to come around?" Colby asked.

"Anything from a few hours to a whole day."

"And her head injury . . ." Colby swallowed. "Does she have any brain damage?"

"We'll know more when she wakes up, but we have every reason to be optimistic." The doctor paused. "Do you have any other questions?"

"Not at the moment, thank you, doctor," Colby said.

"You have some time if you want to go home, grab a shower, get something to eat. We'll call you if anything here changes," Dr. D'Arby said, giving them a smile as she left the room.

Once the door was closed, Colby started rooting through her mom's purse, gave up, and dumped the contents on the floor. "My mom's lived here her whole life. She's driven that route countless times and she knows to be careful."

"Colby, that bend is tricky . . . What are you looking for?"

"Her phone's not here," Colby said. "I thought I might see if Kirk Tyler or Bex Lyons had messaged her, too. I understand that there's a chance that it was a genuine accident. But what if it's not? Shouldn't we find out for sure?"

"Maybe it's still at the crash site."

"That's what I'm thinking too."

"All right." Stevie stood up, put her hands on her hips. "Then maybe we ought to take a trip out there."

Forty-Four

Stevie parked behind some trees on the shoulder a few hundred feet from the bend on Westville. She and Colby walked one behind the other along the side of the road, Stevie up front. It was still early, the sun not yet too hot.

Stevie stopped when they reached the tire marks that led from the road, through a broken guardrail, and down the hill through the loblolly pine and red oak trees. "Are you sure you want to see it?"

"I'll be fine. It's just a car."

Stevie peered down. "I think I see it." She pointed. "There—it's quite far down."

Colby put her hands on her hips. "Sheesh, I can't believe they got all that way through the trees."

Stevie glanced down at her shoes. "Are you going to be okay in those fast boots of yours?"

"Of course!"

"I'll go first. Just take it slow, okay?" Stevie set off, edging down the hill, sneakers slipping in the bone-dry dirt. She grabbed a tree for support, then swung around it and grabbed another. "Try and keep your feet sideways—that way you won't fall."

Colby trotted down past her. "Okay, Grandma."

"What are you, some kind of mountain goat?" Stevie said, trying to keep up with her.

Colby bleated, then pushed a branch out of her way. It flipped back and whacked Stevie in the face.

"Argh! Colby!"

She turned around. "What? Oh, whoops, sorry!"

Stevie ducked under the branch and hung back a bit. Carefully, she inched her way down and had to resort to sliding on her butt for a particularly steep part. By the time she reached the car, Colby was already rummaging around in the footwell on the passenger side.

The car was a total wreck. The windshield was smashed, all four tires blown—the roof had caved in from a tree that was still lying on top of it. Jimmy was right—Faith had been lucky to survive.

"Be careful of all that glass," Stevie said.

"I can't see her phone."

"I'll try the trunk," Stevie said.

"Why would her phone be in the trunk?"

"I don't know, but shall I take a look in case?"

"You go for it."

The trunk was pretty beaten-up—Stevie picked up a stick and used it to jimmy it open. "It's not in the trunk."

Colby put her head out the back window. "Consider me shocked. Try the driver's side. I can't reach it from here because the roof is in the way."

Stevie opened the front car door and took out her phone flashlight and shined it on the floor, then moved the mats and checked underneath. No phone there.

"What do you make of these tires?" Colby called out, crouching down by the front wheel arch.

"What about the tires?"

"They're slashed up real bad . . . like they've all got loads of puncture marks."

Stevie looked in the door pocket, pulled out a hairbrush, a pack of Trojan, a bottle of cheap perfume. "Could have come from rocks and stuff, I guess?"

"They're too uniform for that. Have a look."

"One sec, I'm just checking down the side of the seat." Stevie's fingers found something hard and rectangular. She shined her flashlight down the gap. Bingo.

"I think I've found it!"

She strained to get a hold, just managing to grab an edge and pull it free. "Okay, I've got it!"

"Great work!"

Stevie climbed out, straightened up. Colby snatched it from her hands. "Crap. The battery's dead."

"We can charge it in my car." Stevie brushed some glass from her shorts. "Let's have a look at these tires first though."

She bent down, worked her way around the car. Each tire had a series of puncture holes around its circumference. They were uniform in shape and size—no rock could have done that.

"Weird, right?" Colby said.

Stevie straightened up. "Yeah, it's like—" She stopped short at the sound of a car pulling up, then its door slamming. "Someone's here."

"We should probably *not* be here, then," Colby said. "Tampering with a crash site is probably not the best look."

"Run and hide?" Stevie said.

"Yeah, run and hide." Colby tore off through the trees, running downward on a diagonal.

Stevie chased after her, her sneakers struggling to gain purchase. She stumbled, threw her arms out, and tried to grab a tree to stop herself from falling. She missed, hit the ground, her knee striking a rock. The pain shot through her like a bolt and ran all the way up to her jawbone. When she looked, she realized she hadn't landed on a rock at all. Beneath her was a crisscross of metal spikes, one of which was stuck in her patella. Was that . . . ? Damn, it was. She'd landed on a spike strip—a *stinger*, as Frank called them—a tire deflation device to stop fleeing vehicles. Her stomach spasmed. She thought she might vomit. She closed her eyes and yanked her leg free. Let out a moan, swallowed the feeling of nausea that rushed through her as the blood started pouring down her shin bone. She got up and limped toward Colby, wincing with every step. Colby was hunkered down behind some shrub, staring at her wide-eyed, her hand over her mouth.

Stevie threw herself onto the ground.

"Oh my god, are you okay?"

It hurt like hell. "I'm fine."

"Stevie, you have a massive hole in your knee!" Colby closed her eyes. "I can't look at it. I feel like I might throw up."

"Not really helping!" Stevie hissed. Her knee was throbbing. Grinding when she bent it. Had she chipped the bone? "Can you see who it is?"

Colby lay down on her front, peeked around the bush. "It's your uncle."

Stevie peered around too, flinching when she moved her leg. Jimmy was going through the car, pulling out the floor mats. He moved on to the glove box. Then out to the trunk.

"What's he doing?" Colby asked.

"I guess he's processing the crime scene," Stevie said. But something was off. Shouldn't he have someone else with him? Wasn't that protocol? And the way he was moving so frantically, he almost looked angry.

He slammed down the trunk, kicked a tire, and let out a yell.

"What's gotten into him?" Colby whispered.

Stevie sucked in a breath then let it out slowly. The pain was hot now, running up and down her whole leg, up through her spine. "I don't know. Just stay very quiet so he doesn't know we're here."

Stevie's phone started ringing in her pocket. Colby's eyes widened in panic as Stevie scrambled to turn it to silent, but Jimmy must have heard, because he stopped dead still and looked straight in their direction.

"Who's there?"

The fury in his voice made Stevie and Colby duck back behind the bush.

"Do you think he saw us?" Colby whispered.

"I don't know." Stevie's heart was racing. Jimmy was her uncle, but right then, she was scared of him and she wasn't sure why.

"Hello? Who's there?"

"I think he's coming this way," Colby said. "Should we run?"

Stevie looked at her knee. "I can't."

"I could carry you? You're tiny."

"Just stay down and stay quiet."

"Who's there?" Jimmy called out again—the sound of dirt skittering down the hill and the snapping of twigs as he drew closer.

Stevie squeezed her eyes shut, tried to stay calm. He couldn't have been more than twenty feet away. Colby elbowed her in the ribs, then nodded toward the forest and mouthed, *Oh. My. God!*

There was a goddamn wild turkey strutting toward them. Were they seriously going to be given away by a *turkey*? Colby started flapping her arms at it, but the bird seemed unbothered and just sauntered right on past them, letting out a low gobbling sound.

"Who's th—oh." The footsteps halted. A huff. "Jesus, Jimmy, you're losing it."

Stevie and Colby looked at each other, wide-eyed. Jimmy was on the move again, but his footsteps were growing fainter. Then the sound of a car engine and wheels on asphalt.

They waited a few minutes, then, carefully, Colby peered around the bush again.

"Yup, he's gone."

They both let out long blasts of air.

Colby shook her head. "Can you believe he showed up at the same time as us? What are the chances of that?"

Stevie shrugged. "What are the chances of being saved by a frickin' turkey?"

"I know, right!" Colby grinned. "Does that mean we'll have to have meat loaf for Thanksgiving now?"

Stevie managed a half-laugh, winced again.

Colby looked at her knee, breathed in through her teeth. "Ewwww. That looks bad."

Stevie's stomach lurched. The wound was deep, still oozing blood. "I landed on a police spike strip."

"A what?"

"Those spikes police use to take down cars in chases. It must have been what caused those punctures in the tires."

Colby's mouth dropped open. "You think that's what caused my mom's crash?"

"It can't just be a coincidence."

Colby's eyes widened. "So you're saying the police are involved?"

Stevie considered it, couldn't make that scenario fit. "No, I bet anyone could pick a stinger up from eBay."

Colby's jaw set. "Anyone like Bex Lyons."

Would Bex Lyons really send a text that could implicate her? "She'd have to have some balls to threaten you and then take out your mom's car."

"Maybe she's using . . . what's it called?" Colby clicked her fingers. "Reverse psychology? Is that right? I bet she's banking on us ruling her out because it's too obvious."

Stevie wrinkled up her nose. That seemed like a bit of a reach. "Yeah, I don't know."

"And what the hell was your uncle doing out here? Talk about timing."

A ripple of unease threaded through Stevie's veins. Jimmy's mood had felt so off. "He was looking for something and he didn't look happy that he couldn't find it."

"Mom's phone?"

"That, or maybe he was looking for evidence of what caused the crash?" Both seemed reasonable—Jimmy was a cop. But why had he been so angry? Stevie placed her hands on the ground, bracing to push herself to her feet. "We need to get that phone charged and see what's on it. Let's get back to the car."

"Do you need help getting up?"

"I can manage." Stevie tried to put weight on her foot to stand, but the pain shot through her again.

Colby wriggled under her arm, helped pull her to her feet. "We should see about getting you some cowboy boots like mine next time we're running through a forest. Those sneakers of yours don't have the necessary grip."

Forty-Five

Stevie started the engine and a minute later, Faith's phone pinged into life. Colby put in the PIN. When it didn't work, she tried again.

"She must have changed her code."

"Think. Could it be a birthday? An important date?" Stevie said. She took her own phone out, saw it was Frank who had called her when they were hiding from Jimmy. He'd followed up with a message when she didn't answer.

Please come home now. Very worried about you. Your mother almost passed out when she saw the doll in the kitchen.

Stevie hammered out a quick reply to say she was fine and not to worry—she'd be on her way ASAP.

She leaned back against the headrest. Damn it. She'd left the doll on the counter when she dashed over to take Colby to the hospital.

Colby threw Faith's phone on the dash. "Locked out for fifteen minutes. What if I can't figure it out?"

"Could we use face recognition?"

"We could, but neither of us have my mom's face."

"How's this for a plan: I drop you at the hospital and you can wave the phone in front of your mom's face. I'll go back to my place—there's some things I need to sort out at home. I'll check the doorcam to see who dropped off the death doll, and then I'll head over to the center and see if I can find Terence and ask him why he lied about knowing Blair?"

"You don't need me there for that?"

"I'll manage."

"What about your knee? Don't you think you should get that looked at? You'll probably need a tetanus shot."

"I'll stick a Band-Aid on it, take some Tylenol, and deal with it later."

Stevie let herself into the house, shouted that she was home, then raced up to the main bathroom to see if she could clean up her knee before her parents saw and started asking questions. The doll was going to be hard enough to explain away. They were all out of Band-Aids, so she snuck into her parents' en-suite to try their cabinet.

Her mom hollered up the stairs, "Stevie? What are you doing up there? Are you okay? We need to talk about this horrific doll!"

"I know! Using the bathroom! I'll be down in a sec!" Right after she'd finished up there and then checked the doorcam footage.

Stevie tried the bottom shelf first and moved the anti-dandruff shampoo, Marnie's Veet facial strips, and five boxes of toothpaste out the way. Clearly, there'd been a sale at the store. No sign of any Band-Aids though. She went up on her tiptoes and scanned the top shelf. Bingo. There was a box behind a row of pill bottles. Frank's meds.

She took the bottles down. The first was labeled propranolol. A beta-blocker. That must be for his heart—Bex Lyons had been lying. She really was a total bitch. The second bottle was Paxil. Stevie took out her phone. "Siri, what is Paxil used to treat?"

"Paxil, or paroxetine, is used in the treatment of several mental health disorders related to anxiety and depression."

Stevie blinked. Depression? Her dad wasn't depressed, was he? She took the third bottle.

"Siri, what is bupropion used for?"

"Bupropion may be paired with some antidepressants to counteract sexual side effects or address energy levels and motivation."

Stevie kind of wished she hadn't checked that one out. She looked back at the propranolol. Asked one more question. "Siri, is propranolol used in the treatment of pericarditis?"

"No, beta-blockers are not typically a primary treatment for pericarditis, a condition characterized by inflammation of the pericardium. Treatments usually focus on reducing inflammation through the use of NSAIDs, nonsteroidal anti-inflammatory drugs."

The bottle slipped from her hand and landed on the bathroom tiles. Not typically a treatment for pericarditis? Her dad had been lying this whole time?

"Stevie, what are you doing in here?"

Stevie turned around. Marnie was in the doorway, a questioning look on her face.

"I was getting Band-Aids."

Marnie's hand shot to her mouth. "What on earth have you done to your knee?"

"I fell."

"It must have been quite some fall. You need to get that cleaned up. It could need stitches."

Marnie closed the toilet seat, lowered Stevie onto it. "I'll do it."

Marnie grabbed some cotton balls and ointment from the cabinet and filled the sink.

Had her mom known? How could she not?

Marnie knelt down in front of Stevie and tutted. "There's so much dirt. Where were you when you fell?"

Marnie pressed a wet cotton ball on the wound. Stevie didn't even wince.

"Mom, does Dad really have pericarditis?"

Marnie paused for a moment, the cotton ball still. She knew.

"Why would you ask that?"

"I looked at his meds. He has depression, right? Why didn't you tell me? Is that why he left the police force?"

Marnie rocked back on her heels. Took a moment to consider her response. "Your father is a proud man, Stevie. He didn't want anyone to think less of him. For *you* to think less of him."

Stevie remained silent, left room for her mom to speak.

"He suffered a great deal mentally after the Aaron Taylor case." Marnie picked up a clean cotton ball and began cleaning the wound again. "I don't know whether it was his failure to secure a conviction, or the fact that it was a kid who'd died, but he wasn't the same after. He knew he was making mistakes at work. He couldn't sleep, was barely eating. In the end, he had no choice but to leave on mental-health grounds."

"How didn't I realize?" Stevie said quietly—her heart ached at the thought of her dad suffering like that.

"Because you were young! And he hid it from you. He hid it from everyone for a while. There was a time when I was very worried about him. But he's on the right med regimen now and he's doing so well. I'm really so proud of him."

"Did Blair know?"

"I think when she started to go off the rails, Frank talked to her about his own struggles to see if he could get through to her."

"And Hal?"

"Yes, Hal knew too."

"So it was only me who didn't know?" Little Stevie, left in the dark as usual.

"I think it's because your opinion mattered the most."

Stevie nodded, bit her lip. It would have been hard for her dad to admit any weakness to anyone, but she was his Little Bear. He knew she looked up to him more than anyone. She wished he'd known that she wouldn't have thought any less of him.

Marnie chucked the cotton balls in the trash can, then gently rubbed some Neosporin onto the wound. Stevie clenched her teeth, tried not to squeal.

"I think I'm all done here, take some Tylenol to help with the pain, but you really need to go to the ER and check if you need stitches."

Stevie stuck her head under the faucet and swallowed a couple of pills. "I'll head over there soon. I need to see Colby anyway."

"Before you go, we still need to discuss the doll. Stevie, why didn't you tell us Eric Corder sent you another package?"

She didn't correct Marnie on her assumption. "I forgot."

Marnie's eyes widened. "You *forgot?*"

"Colby's mom was in a car accident—I had to drive her to the hospital."

"Oh my goodness! Is she okay?"

"I'm not sure. I hope so."

"If there's anything Colby needs, tell her to ask."

"I will," Stevie said.

"But anyway, this doll. Your father's spoken to Jimmy. He's going to come and pick it up and take it for forensics. He thinks Eric Corder sent it before he was arrested."

"He does?" Stevie screwed up her face. This package was different from the others. Eric left gifts for Blair. The doll was a warning for Stevie.

"I would never have brought it in off the doorstep if I'd known that monstrosity was in it," Marnie said.

"It was on the doorstep?" That was different from Corder too. He'd left packages in Stevie's car, in her room—he'd invaded her privacy. Leaving a package on the doorstep felt out of character for him—less personal.

"I brought it inside after your father and I got back from Annie and Hal's last night."

"What time was that?"

"We went over about seven thirty and got back just after ten." Marnie's voice grew quieter—her eyes drifted far away. "We were going through plans for the funeral." She leaned against the sink. "A morning service or afternoon? Maple, cherry, oak for the casket? What flowers? What music? All these questions to answer and all I want to shout is *No.* No to the time. No to the casket. No to the flowers, no music. No. No. No! I don't want any of it. I don't want to think about any of it. Because none of it should be happening. I shouldn't be burying my daughter. I shouldn't have to answer these questions."

Pain bloomed across Stevie's chest. Her sister was dead and there was only one question she cared about—who had killed her. She needed to check the doorcam.

Marnie buried her face in her hands. Breathed in deeply.

Stevie reached for her. "Mom?"

"I just need a moment."

Stevie waited—watched her mom battling to hold herself together.

Marnie raised her head, sniffed, smoothed down her blouse. She placed her hand on Stevie's cheek. "Why don't you go and change out of those filthy shorts. Are you hungry? You must be hungry. There are some waffles left over from breakfast."

"Waffles sound great, Mom."

Stevie chucked her shorts in the laundry basket and sat at her desk in her underwear, her heart too heavy in her chest. She hated seeing her mom's pain. Hated how it drew out her own and forced her to look at it. She wasn't ready for that. Not yet.

She put her head in her hands. Her dad had hidden his illness from her, and now she was sure he was hiding something else. And what about Jimmy? Why had he been acting so strangely at the crash site? What was she not seeing? She raised her head and pulled her laptop toward her. And who the hell had sent her that doll?

She logged in to the Baker family doorcam account and opened up the recordings for June 6 the night before. Any footage of someone dropping off the package would be sometime between seven, when her folks left for Hal and Annie's, and when Stevie arrived home, around nine thirty.

The motion sensor had been triggered three times. The first two were Catsy and the third was at 7:56 p.m. She clicked on it and watched as someone walked up the steps to the front door, rang the bell, and waited for a moment before leaving the package on the step.

The blood drained from Stevie's head and a coldness surged through her body.

She heard herself whisper his name. "Oliver."

Forty-Six

She slammed the laptop shut. Started pacing the room, ignoring the pain from her knee. She couldn't sit still, not when her mind and heart were racing so fast. Oliver was behind the package. It had been a police stinger that had caused Colby's mom's accident. He hadn't been with Jimmy when it happened because Jimmy had arrived at the scene alone. But why? Why would Oliver want to kill Faith Green and why would he want to kill Blair? And what link could he have with the gun from the Aaron Taylor case? Was Oliver Aaron's friend? Did *he* go with him to the lumberyard? It was possible—Aaron would have been twenty-one now, so he and Oliver would have been around the same age.

There was a gentle knock at the door. "Stevie?" Frank poked his head in, then covered his eyes and ducked back out.

Stevie grabbed a pair of shorts from her drawer and quickly put them on. "You can come in."

Frank tentatively entered the room. "Is everything okay, love?"

Okay? Stevie might have laughed if she wasn't so close to tears. "Do you have Officer Dean's number?"

"His number? Is something wrong?"

Yes, something was really fucking wrong. "No, I just think it's about time I apologized for punching him the other night."

"It probably is." Frank got out his phone, pulled up the contacts. "How do I share?"

"Can you air-drop it?"

Frank held the phone at arm's length. "Hmmm, do I press this?"

"The weather in South Carolina is expected to be warm and summerlike. The daytime highs are forecast to reach around 86°F (30°C), with nighttime lows around 79°F (26°C)."

"Let me do it."

Stevie took his phone and scrolled down through the contacts until she reached Oliver's number. She was about to hand the phone back, when the contact above caught her eye.

Number, Unknown.

Why the hell had her dad entered a contact in his phone as Number, Unknown? Stevie's mind quickly locked on to the answer. He was hiding someone's identity. Her heart picked up, beat double time.

"Done?" Frank asked, taking a step toward her.

"Almost." She fought to keep her face neutral, her fingers steady as she tapped on the contact. She didn't recognize the phone number.

"Give it to me. I'll read it out," Frank said, reaching for his phone, a sudden tightness to his voice.

Stevie quickly repeated the last four digits of the number in her head as she'd never remember them all—4276, 4276, 4276. Then she swiped back to Officer Dean and AirDropped his contact details just as Frank took the phone from her. Her phone pinged and she smiled. "Done."

Frank slipped the phone in his pocket, made to go, then turned back to face her. He looked at the floor and swallowed. "Your mother told me that you know . . . about my health issues."

"I'm so sorry you didn't feel like you could tell me, Dad." They were supposed to be close, but now there seemed to be an invisible wall between them, and Stevie didn't know how to find a way through.

Frank pursed his lips. "It's not always easy to admit the truth to the people you love."

"Know that you can tell me anything, Dad. If there is anything that's bothering you or worrying you, you can tell me." Stevie looked at him hopefully, expectantly. He caught her eyes, looked away quickly, and pulled her into a hug.

"That's a deal, kiddo. Same goes for you—if there's anything going on with you, you need to tell me."

"So there's nothing?" Stevie asked.

Frank rested his chin on her head. "I just miss her; that's all. I wish we could have seen her more. I wish we could have known her more."

"Nothing else?"

"No. How about you? Anything going on with my Little Bear?"

"No, I'm okay." Stevie leaned into his chest—a heavy feeling in her own.

They were both liars.

After Frank had gone, Stevie looked at Officer Dean's number. What was she actually going to do with it? She didn't think she'd get the truth from him over the phone, so she sent him a text.

It's Stevie. Are u free to meet?

Sure, in 1/2hr. Where?

Founder's Park. Bench by the swings.

Somewhere public. She grabbed her bag, just in case she needed to pepper-spray Officer Dean in the face.

Her house keys weren't on the hallway table. Marnie must have tidied them into the drawer. She opened it up, grabbed her keys, then paused. The passes to Blair's concert were in there, *Homecoming* printed above a bold *VIP*. She hadn't come home though, had she? And she never would. Stevie was hit by a sudden sense of loss so devastating it took her breath away. She clutched the hall table, fought to drag a lungful of air. Then another. And another, until the pain eased.

She closed her eyes, shut the drawer.

Then she opened it again.

One, two, three, four passes. But they'd been sent five by Satellite Entertainment. Annie and Hal hadn't taken theirs—neither of them had gone to the concert.

Where was the fifth pass?

Stevie started searching through the drawer. There was a lot of crap in there. Maybe she just hadn't seen it.

But no, there were only four passes.

She closed the drawer again.

Maybe they'd only received four passes in the first place. She hadn't actually counted them herself. She'd only been told that Blair would be sending one for each of them.

Hal could have chucked his away in protest. It seemed like something he'd do.

Or perhaps her mom had put one into the *special box*, which contained mementos of all Blair's achievements. She did keep everything after all. Marnie had made boxes for Hal and Stevie, too—both considerably smaller than Blair's.

Stevie covered her face with her hands. What was she doing? Why was she fretting over nothing when she had Oliver to question?

She decided to walk to Founder's Park. The Tylenol had kicked in, and her knee wasn't hurting too badly. It would be good to get some fresh air and focus her thoughts. It wasn't far, twenty minutes at most, if she cut down the alleyway by Millbrook Street. She didn't like using that route normally—the place where Mia went missing. The mural that had been painted by Mia's classmates had faded, and the orange-red cross-vine bushes had grown so rapidly of late that they had covered half her face. Stevie used to think their flowers were beautiful. Now she thought they had no business growing where something so awful had happened.

She hurried along the path, head down, fists in her shorts' pockets, going over the questions she would ask Officer Dean. Well, one question, mainly. Did he kill Blair? She stood to the side to let a car pass. Then carried on to the end where she made a left, barely registered the black SUV that was parked by the sidewalk. Or the quiet hiss of its running engine.

A rush of feet from behind her. She turned. A jolt of awareness coming too late.

Darkness slammed down on her.

Coarse fabric closed over her head.

Forty-Seven

It happened so fast she didn't even have time to scream. Hands grabbed hold of her wrists. Another pair around her waist. She kicked out, tried to rip her hands free, but the grip was too strong. She thrashed from side to side, breath coming out in ragged gasps. She was lifted upward, shoved hard.

Now she screamed.

She landed on her side. The smell of leather. A door slamming. The sound of an engine. A car—she'd been thrown into the back of a car. She screamed harder, kicked at the door with her feet. She tried to pull her hands apart—couldn't. Her wrists were bound tight, plastic cutting into them.

"Shut up or I'll cut your throat." A voice, gruff and low.

Stevie kept her screams inside, where they bloomed in her chest, then burst back out of her, as sobs. This couldn't be happening. She wouldn't let it happen. She fought against the helplessness— kicked at the door, tried to find the handle with her feet. The car turned a corner.

"Stay still!" A different voice this time? She wasn't sure. Thoughts ran wild through her head.

"Why are you doing this?"

"I told you to shut up. I have a message for you."

Something about the voice. The gruffness—it wasn't real. They were disguising their voice. Stevie's heart jerked at the realization. She knew them. Oliver? Only he knew she was going to be near the park. "Oliver?" she said, then louder. "Oliver!"

Stevie rolled forward in the seat as the car turned a corner, then came to a stop.

"Final warning. Stay out of business that doesn't concern you, or next time you won't be so lucky."

Hands on her again—pulling her out of the car. Pushing her down onto the ground, onto her knees. A jolt of pain. Then a snip at her wrists. The biting plastic released. Screeching tires. The sound of the engine growing quieter.

She grabbed at the sack. Pulled it off her head, blinked back the brightness, took a deep lungful of air. She was back at the start of the alleyway. Mia's alleyway. She'd been driven in a circle around the park. She turned in the direction of the car, saw it disappear around a corner. She tried to stand, but her legs wouldn't cooperate—too heavy, or not even there. She dragged herself backward and rested her shoulders against the wall. Trembling, she closed her eyes, tears pushing at the corners, as she realized how easy it could be to make someone disappear.

Forty-Eight

"Stevie? What are you doing down there? I was waiting for you—"

Stevie's eyes shot open. She was lying against a brick wall. It felt hot against her back. She saw the sack next to her and jumped to her feet, fists shaking but ready—clenched in balls.

Oliver took a step toward her—hands out, palms open, voice full of concern. "Stevie, are you okay?"

Stevie looked around, guard up. "How did you get here?"

Oliver's brow furrowed. "I drove. I'm parked a couple streets away, why?"

"How did you find me *here*?" Stevie glared at him, her breathing fast and loud from her nose.

"Stevie—"

Stevie shouted over him, grabbed the pepper spray from her bag. "How did you find me *here*, Oliver?!"

His eyes ran over the can, flared with recognition. He attempted an easy smile. "What's with the pepper spray?"

"Just answer the question!"

Oliver gestured at the park. "I was waiting by the swings. When you didn't show, I decided to leave . . ." He paused. He looked puzzled, sounded puzzled. "Stevie, you know you've got the nozzle pointed toward you?"

Again? Seriously?

Stevie scowled, turned the pepper spray around.

Oliver spoke gently. "You're worrying me—what's wrong?"

She came straight out with it, wanting to see his reaction.

"Somebody put a sack over my head, bundled me into a car, and threatened me—that's what's wrong. And now here you are." Her eyes bore into his face, pushing him for an explanation.

Oliver's eyebrows pulled together—his lips parted, like he was genuinely concerned. "Are you hurt?"

Stevie didn't know whether to buy it. "No."

"Someone *threatened* you?"

"Yeah, crazy, right?" she said, voice thick with sarcasm. "I guess they want me to stop looking into Blair's murder. And do you know what else is crazy? This all happened right after I got your little present."

"Present?" Oliver's eyes darted across her face. "What are you talking about?"

"Cut the crap, Oliver—I saw you on the doorcam. You delivered a package to my house at 7:56 last night."

"I don't understand how that's at all relevant right now. Stevie, if someone tried to kidnap you, I need to take you to the station, make a report. You should really speak to someone—"

"You don't know how it's *relevant*?!" Stevie spat. "Did you do it? Did you kill Blair?"

"Of course not!" It was almost a shout. Oliver checked himself, rubbed his forehead, found a more even tone. "Stevie, I'm really sorry—I'm trying to understand what you're saying but you're making no—"

Stevie cut him off, couldn't listen to him lie any longer. "You sent me a Blair doll with no head and the message 'you're next.' Then, after I arrange to meet you, someone kidnaps me. So, yeah, it seems pretty relevant to me!"

Oliver stared at her, slack-jawed. "Stevie, I promise—I didn't try to kidnap you and I didn't send you that doll—I would never. But you need to report—"

"I *saw* you, Oliver."

"Stevie, please, think about it for a moment. Do you seriously think I'd go right up to the doorcam if I knew what was in there? Do you think I'd ring the bell? You're in shock, which is completely understandable considering what's just happened, but none of this has anything to do with me."

"But . . ." Stevie faltered, her mind struggling to stitch her thoughts together. "I saw you."

"I didn't know what was in the package when I dropped it off—I promise."

"Where did you get it, then?" Stevie's voice trembled—she wiped a stray tear from her cheek. Wanted to trust him, didn't know if she could.

"If I tell you, I don't want you to jump to conclusions. I'm sure there's a perfectly reasonable explanation. I saw it and thought I'd be helpful and bring it around. Honestly, I thought it might be nice to see you and check in on how you were doing."

She shook the can at him. "Where did you get the package, Oliver?"

He swallowed.

"Oliver!"

"I found it in the back of Jimmy's cruiser. I took it into the station to ask him if I should drop it over to you, but he wasn't there, and when I got outside, the car was gone. So I drove around to your place myself."

"Uncle Jimmy had it?" She lowered the can, her arm a deadweight at her side.

"He was probably taking it into evidence so you wouldn't see it. Protecting you. I should have checked with him before I brought it over."

Stevie sniffed. Was that it? Was that the reason? "You think he was protecting me?"

"I'm certain that's what happened. I bet it was from Eric Corder."

She shook her head. "No, the doll is different from Corder's other packages."

"What are you saying? You think Jimmy's behind it?" Oliver laughed.

Stevie didn't answer. Could Jimmy be behind it? Could it have been him in the car? Was it his voice? She couldn't be certain it wasn't.

"Stevie, come on, *Jimmy*? You know him—he wouldn't hurt you."

Did she know him? She hadn't recognized him in the forest— the way he behaved, how angry he was. But it had been Bex Lyons who had warned her and Colby away from looking into Kirk and told them to go and play with their dolls. She had to be behind the doll. Not Jimmy.

"We're still looking to ID Blair's other stalker—the one who phoned the show—but this doll, the threat abduction—it's all very in line with the profile we're building," Oliver said, watching her closely. He probably thought she was going crazy.

"I think it was Kirk Tyler. I think he killed Blair because—"

Oliver cut her off. "Stevie, he has an alibi. I've gone over all the witness statements again because I knew you had doubts, but it wasn't him."

"But Bex Lyons warned me away from looking into him and—"

Oliver exhaled deeply, ran a hand over his hair. "When did you speak to Bex Lyons?"

"Colby and I went around there yesterday and then I get that doll and Colby's mom is in a car accident, and I just think—"

He put his hands on her shoulders, looked her in the eye. "Stevie, take a moment. Breathe. You've just been through a lot. And I understand your compulsion to look into your sister's death, I really do, but I think you need to stop now. It clearly isn't safe, and it isn't good for you. You can't go around questioning people—you need to leave it to the professionals."

She stared at him, a flash of anger surging through her. "You think I'm losing it."

"No, not at all, but you've put yourself in danger. If what you're telling me is true about being thrown into the back of a car—"

Stevie pushed his hands from her shoulders. Took a step back. "What do you mean, 'if'? You don't believe me?"

"Of course I believe you. Which is why I think I should take you home. You're in shock—look, you're shaking."

"I'm shaking because I'm angry." It was shock, too, but she wasn't going to admit that. "I think Kirk knew Blair was thinking of releasing this song and—"

"Stevie, please, enough. You have to stop." He sounded like he was pleading now. "You can tell me everything that is concerning you later—once you've had a chance to recover."

Everything that was *concerning* her? She wasn't complaining about a frickin' hotel stay. She wanted to tell him about the song, and that Colby's mom's crash hadn't been an accident, and how Kirk had abused more girls than just Melissa Carter, but she could see he'd shut himself off. Well, she could do that too.

Her face hardened. "Fine. Take me home."

"Stevie, don't be like that. Listen, I'll speak to Jimmy, find out where he got the package from. And I'll also do some more digging into Kirk, but I really think this person who phoned *At Night with the Stars*, the one who called Blair from Honeyville right before she was killed, has to be the prime suspect for the murder, and maybe we can link him to the doll, too."

"The stalker? You really think it's him?"

Oliver nodded emphatically—his eyes earnest. "Yes, Stevie, I do. Don't you?"

Maybe he was right. Maybe it was.

Oliver opened the passenger-side door to let Stevie out. He'd radioed Jimmy, hadn't got an answer, so had decided he'd wait at Clover Lane and keep an eye on her until Jimmy got in touch. Stevie didn't want his eyes anywhere near her. Sure, whatever, he seemed genuinely concerned about her. But she didn't need concern—she needed to find out who had killed Blair, and at that moment Oliver was more of an obstruction than a help.

Stevie looked up at him from her seat. "Could I wait in the car and you go in first? Tell them what happened so I don't have to?"

"Of course." His face softened—his eyes held hers. "I promise you—I'll find out who did this to you, and who murdered your sister."

Stevie gave a small nod, watched him walk up her driveway. Then, when he rang the doorbell, she pulled her car keys out of her pocket and bolted for her car.

Nice of him to offer, but *she* was going to find out who'd put that sack over her head, and who had killed Blair. And as he hadn't been ready to listen to what she had to say, she was off to speak to a possible stalker—a possible lover, even—about a song.

Forty-Nine

Terence was the only one in the center. Stevie found him sitting at the sound system, headphones on, running sliders up and down, nodding away to the music. He smiled and held up a finger, telling Stevie to wait. She pulled up the wheely chair, sat down, considered how she should play it. There was only one way really. Direct.

Terence flicked a couple of switches, then pulled his headphones down onto his neck. "Stevie, how are you doing?" He picked up a glass of water and took a sip.

"Why didn't you tell me you were working with Blair?"

He coughed on the water, then looked at her like she was crazy. "Excuse me?"

"You were working on a song with Blair, 'Breaking the Silence' or 'Serenade for a Scumbag'?"

His eyes widened for a fraction of a second, but it was enough for Stevie to know he knew exactly what she was talking about.

He set the glass down and leaned back in his chair, clearly trying to look casual. "Me, working with Blair Baker?" He folded his arms over his chest, forced a smile. "Girl, you're dreaming."

"Terence, I heard you humming it, and I bet the police would be able to find it on that sound system of yours. She also gave a copy to Gunner Trip, which I'm sure could be traced back to you. So what happened? Did Blair decide to go with some other producer? Did you get mad, kill her?"

"No, nothing like that! She would never. *I* would never—" He stopped, closed his eyes.

"So you *were* working with her, then."

Terence opened his eyes and gave a small nod.

Stevie took a long breath. She'd known she was right about their music connection, but now that Terence had confirmed it, she wasn't sure what it meant. She didn't think he was the killer, but if she was wrong about that, she was now all alone with him. Her adrenaline spiked and she had to work to keep her voice steady.

"When did it start?"

Terence ran his hands over his head. "A year or so after Aaron died. She was the one who bought the sound system."

Stevie blinked. "That was Blair?"

"She came around here with Frank one day to look at the place. I told her I was into music, and she said she'd like to help me with that. I'd send her my stuff—she'd critique it, make it better. Then after your niece disappeared, she went quiet on me. I didn't think I'd hear from her again. Until, out of the blue, she asked me if I wanted to work on something new, but it had to be on the down-low. She said it would be explosive when it came out, but it would make my name."

"The song's about her manager Kirk Tyler," Stevie said.

"It wasn't too tricky to figure that one out. She told me she wanted to work with me because I was the best, but really it was because I'm an unknown. If Blair used some other producer, it would have gotten back to Kirk. When she had a gap in her schedule, she'd fly here, and we'd come to the center after it had closed and work through the mixes."

"But she wanted to pull the song?"

"She was having doubts. But the evening before the concert, she came to see me. She told me that whatever happened, she wanted to put it out."

So Blair bailed on the family dinner to see Terence. It fit

with the message Blair had sent about having to do something important. A rush of emotion surged through Stevie. Blair was going to do the right thing. She tried to stay focused. What if Blair *hadn't* told him she wanted to put the song out? What if she'd actually told him it was never going to happen—snatched his big break from him?

"Where were you around seven p.m. the night Blair was murdered?"

Terence gave a cold, bitter laugh. "You can't think—"

Stevie rounded on him. "Just answer the question."

His jaw tensed. "I was at the concert. I took my sister, Zoe, and her friend Tiffany."

"Tiffany? She doesn't happen to think she has an ice rink in her backyard, does she?"

Terence frowned. "What?"

"Nothing, carry on."

"Anyway, Blair had sent me some tickets. She said she was going to do a tribute to Aaron at the beginning. I was touched. Zoe, Tiffany, and I spent the afternoon at the mall. I took them for a pizza—then we went to the show. I have receipts."

He sounded truthful. "Was your relationship with Blair more than just work?"

"No. Don't get me wrong, I liked Blair. She did a lot for me, but it wasn't like that. I don't know—she seemed troubled. Maybe all celebrities are like that, but she seemed to walk around in a cloud of sadness."

Stevie took his words in, showed no reaction, though it hurt to know how right he was. "Why didn't you tell me you knew her?"

"I guess because I figured people would start asking questions . . . like you are now."

She nodded, couldn't work out if that made sense or not.

"And where were you on the night Aaron was killed?"

Terence glared, his voice edged with anger. "Tell me you did not ask that."

"The gun that shot Blair also shot your Aaron." Stevie watched him carefully, waiting to see how her words would land.

Terence didn't move for a moment. Then he picked up his water and took a sip, his hands shaking slightly. "The same gun?"

"Yes, and considering there's a link between you and them both, you can understand why I ask."

Terence shook his head and looked up at the ceiling. "This is why Colby was asking all those questions about Aaron. Great. There I was thinking something might be happening between us, and she was thinking I might be a murderer?"

"I think Colby is very much rooting for you not to be."

A brief smile formed on Terence's lips. "That's nice of her." Then his face became serious. "I was at home with my sister and my mom. You can check with them, but I'd rather you didn't go around stirring things up."

"I'd rather my sister wasn't dead," Stevie shot back.

Terence held his hands up. "Fine, check if you have to. You'll see I'm telling you the truth."

Stevie held his gaze, couldn't tell if he was lying or not. It didn't matter if he was—she'd be able to find out. She moved on to her next question. "Do you know if Blair saw anybody else when she visited Honeyville?"

"As far as I knew, only you."

"She didn't see me."

"What can I say—she said she was meeting her sister. She could have been lying, of course."

Was there someone else Blair was meeting in Honeyville? Someone else who wanted her dead?

Stevie stood up. She'd heard enough. Terence appeared to be telling the truth.

"So is that it? You believe I didn't kill your sister or Aaron?"

"You've just told me you have alibis, so I guess I'm going to have to." Stevie made for the door, but paused before opening it. "What are you going to do with the song?"

Terence shrugged. "I don't know what I *can* do, now that Blair's not here."

"I think you should release it."

He tilted his head, eyes narrowing. "You do?"

"Blair made it for a reason—she wanted people to hear it."

Fifty

Stevie took her phone out to call Colby on her way to the hospital. There were fourteen missed calls from her mom and dad, and from Oliver. A bunch of texts, too, pleading for her to call them all back. Then Oliver saying he had to go, that he was going to try to find Jimmy. Stevie didn't reply, dialed Colby's number instead.

"Hey, Stevie!"

"I'm on my way to you from the Aaron Taylor Community Center."

"Great!" Colby said enthusiastically.

"Terence has given me alibis for Blair's and Aaron's murders. I think he might be in the clear."

"Wonderful news!" Colby's voice was unusually upbeat, even for her.

"Why are you being weird? How are things at the hospital? Did you get into your mom's phone?"

"She's awake and showing no signs of brain damage," Colby replied brightly.

"That's great. Colby, I'm so relieved."

Stevie heard the sound of a door opening and closing.

"Stevie, I haven't been able to get her to open the phone," Colby whispered. "Your uncle is in her room asking her questions about the crash. He's been in there for a long time."

"What's she saying happened?"

"Well, listen to this. When she first came around, she said that all she could remember is that she hit the bend and suddenly lost control."

"Okay, that makes sense."

"Then Jimmy points out to her that she could be facing vehicular homicide charges—dangerous driving—the speed she was traveling. She glares right at him and says, 'And I suppose that arrest from 2022 isn't going to help my case.' Which I don't think is the smartest thing to bring up, and at this point I'm thinking she probably isn't in the right state of mind to be talking to a cop, but Jimmy sort of shifts in his seat and says, 'Colby, why don't you go and get us all some coffees?'"

"Why was she arrested in 2022?"

"She got into a bar brawl at Lacey's. Anyway, I don't think I should go and get some coffees—there's this weird atmosphere in the room, but Mom is all like, 'Yeah, go and get some coffees, Colby.' So I go and get the damn coffees and when I get back, her whole story had changed. She's now saying that Mike was at the wheel and driving erratically."

Stevie bit her lip. What the hell? "But Jimmy said she was the one driving and he would know—he was the one who found them."

"The thing is, he seemed to be buying her new version of events. Which I suppose is good because she won't face charges. But, Stevie, we both saw those punctures in the tires. Jimmy's taking down notes and he says, 'So you were just out for a drive?' And Mom says yeah, like going out for a drive is the most normal thing in the world for her to do. Then Jimmy asks her about her phone, and she says she doesn't know where it is and he gets all agitated and I'm sitting there with it in my pocket and to be honest, I don't know what the hell is going on but *something* is and I really think I need to see what's in my mom's phone, but I can't do that with Jimmy hanging around."

"Okay, I'll try and get rid of him—I'll be with you in five."

Stevie hung up and dialed Jimmy's number. He let it ring, so she tried again. He answered on the fourth try.

"Stevie, I'm at work right now."

Stevie sobbed into the phone. "Jimmy, this is really important. Officer Dean left you a message, but you haven't called back."

"One second."

Stevie listened to his footsteps as he went out into the corridor.

"Okay, Stevie, what's wrong?"

"Someone abducted and threatened me by the park. I think it was Blair's killer."

"Jesus. When did this happen?"

"A couple of hours ago. I'm scared, Jimmy. Mom and Dad can't understand why you're not here and everyone's really upset, and can you just come around?"

"Okay, try and stay calm. I'll head straight over."

Stevie hung up and pulled up on a road opposite the hospital entrance and waited until she saw Jimmy pull out.

Then she texted Colby.

Did u get into the phone?

👍 Be out in 1 sec!

Stevie swung her car into the parking lot just as Colby burst out through the automatic doors. Stevie gave a short blast on the horn and Colby ran over and climbed into the passenger seat.

"Did she give you the code?"

"Nope. I held the phone up to mom's face, then made a dash for it. She's probably wondering what the hell I'm doing. I'll just tell her she was hallucinating from all the drugs she's on if she questions me about it. How was Terence?"

"Understandably not that happy that we suspected he might be a murderer."

"I hope this hasn't ruined my chances with him."

Stevie blinked. "I think it may be kind of hard to find an inroad now."

Colby grinned. "We'll see."

Stevie elbowed her. "Can we focus on the task at hand?"

Colby saluted, then opened up the messages. Started scrolling through. "Where shall I start? There are hundreds."

"Start with the ones from Mike. If they were heading somewhere, maybe they arranged it in advance."

"Good thinking." Colby clicked on a message from Big Boy Mike. An image popped up. Colby tilted her head. "What *is* that?"

Stevie leaned over. She knew exactly what it was. "Oh my god! Close it! Close it!"

Colby froze, eyes going round—then she yelped and threw her mom's phone into Stevie's lap.

"Colby!" Stevie screwed up her eyes, swiped the message away. "Did we just see a dead man's penis?"

Colby blinked hard. "Yes, I think we did."

So disturbing. Stevie held up the phone away from her. "I will proceed with extreme caution going forward."

"Ironic nickname—*Big Boy* Mike, if you consider the evidence," Colby mused.

"I do not wish to consider the evidence, Colby. I'm one second away from wanting to scrub my eyeballs with bleach."

"Fair point." Colby shuddered. "Hard to unsee it though, isn't it?"

"Let's just focus on what we're supposed to be doing."

Stevie scrolled through the texts from Mike, bracing herself each time for a visual assault. She paused when she got to a message from the evening of the accident that Mike had sent at 6:01 p.m.

They have money. They'll pay.

"Who do you think *they* is?" Stevie asked.

Colby shrugged. "Dunno. Scroll to the top of the message thread."

Stevie scrolled up. Then glanced at Colby. "I've found something!"

Have u heard anything?

Not yet

Phone again

I've tried—not answering

Keep trying...

So?

Nothing yet

Remind him what u know

He wants to meet at Kavannagh's 8:00 tonight

Didn't I tell u! We're in the $$$, baby!

I'll pick u up 7:30

"Mom was blackmailing someone." Colby looked up from the message, blinking. "She knew something, and she was blackmailing them."

"Kirk Tyler?" Stevie said, pulse quickening. "She's gotten money from him before. We saw her talking to him in the parking lot after Blair's vigil. She must know something about him. And whatever she knows almost got her killed."

Colby pressed her palms to her face. "I really thought it was my fault," she said. "That she was targeted because I was looking into Kirk."

"If your mom has been blackmailing dangerous people, Colby, that is not your fault." Stevie drummed her fingers on her chin. "Kavannagh's is that dive just outside of town, right? You take Westville Drive to get there."

"So someone, most likely Kirk or Bex, knew Mike and my mom were going to be heading that way at that time?" Colby said. "Did he contact her at all?"

Stevie scrolled through the phone, felt a rush of adrenaline when she saw the initials *KT*. "KT—that must be Kirk Tyler, right?"

Colby nodded, chewed a nail. "Did he send a message to arrange the meetup at Kavannagh's?"

Stevie shook her head. "There's only one message thread on the morning of Blair's vigil between your mom and KT."

We need to talk

We already reached an agreement

I need more

Blair's dead. Tell the world for all I care

Stevie stared at the phone, her eyes fixed on the words *Blair's dead*. So blunt. So final.

She made herself focus—try to make sense of the message. "What does that mean, 'tell the world for all I care'?"

"She was trying to get money from him," Colby said, "but he wasn't having any of it."

"Maybe he changed his mind? I'll do a search for Kavannagh's, see if it comes up in any other messages."

One message thread with a contact named Safety Net came up.

070422 If u want me to keep quiet u need to pay

Kavannagh's 8:00 tonight

"What do those numbers mean?" Colby asked. "And who the hell is Safety Net?"

Stevie shot Colby a look. "I don't know, but I think they were responsible for putting your mom in the hospital."

"It could be Bex Lyons, just put in under a different name," Colby said.

"I have her number stored in my phone. Read the number for this Safety Net person and I'll type it in and see if her name comes up."

"803-555 . . ."

Stevie punched the numbers in. "Go on."

"0134."

Stevie's heart lurched in her chest—her fingers froze.

"Stevie, 0134 . . . why aren't you typing it in?"

Her throat tightened. "I don't need to type it in because I already have it."

"It's Bex Lyon's?"

Stevie could barely find her voice. "No, it's someone else's."

Fifty-One

"Stevie, whose is it?" Colby pressed again.

Stevie's hands trembled. "Colby, what's your mom's number?" Her voice came out small and shaky.

"What's my mom's number got to do with it?"

Stevie took a breath. "Does it end with 4276?"

Colby cocked her head. "Yeah, how do you know that?"

Stevie looked at her lap. "He's Safety Net."

"Who?"

Stevie swallowed, her throat too tight. "My dad."

"What?!"

Stevie raised her eyes to meet Colby's, saw her disbelief reflected back at her. "It was my dad who told your mom to meet at Kavannagh's."

"Mom was blackmailing your dad? Why?"

"I know what those numbers mean. It's a date: Fourth of July 2022."

"That was the Fourth of July Mom got herself arrested for fighting in Lacey's. Why would she be messaging him about that?"

"Because it's also the day that Aaron Taylor was shot in the lumberyard."

"What's that got to do with her?"

"I think she must know something. My dad worked that case, but he lied in his report, and he had a breakdown after, and now your mom has a crash on the way to a place he arranged to meet her."

Colby shook her head. "No, not your dad, Stevie."

"He knew about that corner. It's where Hal had his accident, and it wouldn't be hard for him to get his hands on a stinger. He had your mom's number in his phone under Number, Unknown. She'd been calling him." Stevie shook her head as she pieced it all together—the connections now so clear. "My mom's card was declined in the store the other day. I thought she was just a bit shaken, had messed the payment up or something. But . . . I think there was no money in the account because my dad's been paying your mom to keep quiet about what she knows."

"What do you think she knows, Stevie?"

"I think she knows exactly what happened to Aaron Taylor, and I think it has something to do with my dad."

"You think your dad killed Aaron? But . . . does that mean that you think he killed your sister, too?"

"I don't know," Stevie said. "But I think I need to speak to your mom."

Colby held the straw up to Faith Green's dry lips. She sucked down three gulps, then nodded that she'd had enough. She turned her eyes to Stevie, voice rasping. "So ask your questions."

"What do you know about the murder of Aaron Taylor?"

Faith looked away. "Now, why would you think I'd know anything about that?"

"Cut the crap, Mom. We've read the messages. You were blackmailing Frank Baker because you know something about what went on on the Fourth of July."

Faith lay back on her pillow. "'Spose I always knew it would come out one day. Should never have told Mike, really. I wanted to leave it—I'd gotten enough from Kirk—but Mike, well, he insisted."

"Could you start from the beginning?" Stevie asked. "What exactly do you know about Aaron Taylor?"

"That Fourth of July I'd been drinking at Lacey's. The guy I was seeing at the time, Jason, he got into it with some other dude over a game of pool. Things got heated—we both got arrested. I had to go to the ER room to patch up my head, and then I was taken to the station."

Stevie edged forward in her seat. She didn't understand how any of this could be related to Aaron Taylor.

"They kept Jason in for further questioning, but I got out early that morning. I was sitting around the back of the station, having a smoke, when your dad and his partner, your uncle, appeared out of nowhere. They didn't see me. I was sitting behind some dumpsters, but I could hear every damn word those two said."

Stevie gripped hold of the end of Faith's bed. "What did they say?"

"Your uncle was real upset. Crying and wailing about his career, how he was screwed. He kept repeating, 'It wasn't a gun—it wasn't a gun.' Your dad was trying to calm him down. He took his gun from him and said to him, 'Jimmy, we can make this go away. No one needs to know. We'll just say that the witness saw two people climbing over that fence, that they were armed, that he was probably killed by the person he was with.' Then Jimmy said, 'Will people believe that—what about the missing bullet casing?' and your dad said, 'We're the police—we can make them.' Jimmy said, 'But I shot him, Frank.' And your dad grabs him by the shoulders and said, 'No, Jimmy, you didn't.' It was later that evening, thanks to Colby's obsession with all things Blair Baker, that I realized who Frank was and understood that what I'd witnessed could be worth money. A lot of money."

Uncle Jimmy killed Aaron Taylor, and her dad had covered it up.

Stevie tried to swallow, but her throat had closed, locked tight against the surge of nausea rising from her stomach. No wonder her dad had broken down after the case. It was from the guilt of living a lie. And it had been guilt that had made him volunteer at the center. Like giving a few woodshop lessons could make up for the loss of a life.

"Holy shit," Colby said, voice breathy. "But why would Kirk Tyler pay you to keep that quiet?"

"I'd gone to that Hilton Moore guy first. Told him I had a story to sell him about the Baker family not being as straight as they'd have people believe. But then I realized he wasn't where the big money was. That was Blair. So I called her up, outlined the situation, and the next thing I know, Kirk's waving a check from Satellite Entertainment in my face and demanding that I tell him everything I had on Blair's family. So I told him what I knew, took the money, and swore I'd keep quiet. I knew folks would start asking questions if I was suddenly rolling in cash, so I made out that I'd won the lottery. Got that check blown up big and everything."

"I can't believe I thought you actually won the lottery," Colby muttered.

"Then that woman Bex Lyons shows up at the house saying she wants to reinforce the terms of the deal. Let's say she makes it real clear that if I don't keep my mouth shut, things are going to get ugly real quick."

"So Blair knew everything," Stevie said. "She knew what Jimmy did, how Dad covered it up, and she paid up to protect them, offering Hilton the story about Hal in the deal. No wonder she couldn't leave—couldn't speak out about Kirk—he had something over her." Something awful.

Stevie stared into space. So had Blair gotten involved with Terence Thompson out of guilt?

"But then Blair was killed and you went back for more," Colby said.

"As I said, that was all Mike. He thought a story like that was worth millions. I told him we shouldn't mess with the likes of Kirk Tyler. As it turned out, Kirk wasn't interested, so Mike pivoted. He went and spoke to your dad. Frank wouldn't see sense to start with, and it ended up in a bit of a fight and he gave your dad a black eye. Still, Frank wouldn't budge. But then, after Blair's death and the interest in her got even more intense, so did Mike. I think your dad realized he wouldn't leave it, and he ended up giving Mike a few grand."

Stevie pinched the bridge of her nose. She was right about why Marnie's card was declined at the store, then.

"Guess your old man got even though."

"What do you mean?"

"Well, Mike's dead, isn't he? Guess your uncle is repaying the favor to your dad and covering it up."

"That's why he bought your story about Mike driving," Colby said.

"He didn't buy it—he suggested it. Told me if I kept my mouth shut, he'd get me off and write it up as an accident. If I didn't, he'd see to it that I went down for Mike's death."

Stevie stood up, legs hollow. She sniffed back the tears. She'd heard everything she needed to hear.

"Where are you going?" Colby asked.

"I'm going home. I need to ask my dad what he did with the gun."

"Shall I come?"

"No. Call Oliver. Tell him everything."

Fifty-Two

Jimmy's cruiser was parked outside the Baker house.

Shit. He was there to talk about the abduction.

To hell with it. He needed to hear what she had to say.

Stevie walked in through the front door, the bile rising in her stomach. Her mom, dad, and Jimmy were sitting around the kitchen table. Jimmy in his uniform, legs stretched out, feet crossed. Frank was staring blankly into space and Marnie was sitting bolt upright, anxiously twisting her wedding band.

Marnie jumped up when Stevie walked in. Her face ashen, her eyes blotchy. "Stevie, where have you been? We've been so worried!"

Stevie's chin began to tremble uncontrollably. Tears spilled from her eyes, ran hot down her cheeks. She was about to blow her family apart. She'd say the words and everything would change forever.

Frank rose from his chair, concern etched across his face. "Oh, Little Bear, you must have been so scared. Officer Dean told us what happened at the park. You need to tell Jimmy everything so we can catch the bastard that did it."

Stevie didn't think she'd be able to find her voice, to say the words she was about to say. She was splitting in two—the truth hacking her down her center. One half still believed that her dad was the best man in the entire world—the person she had trusted to do the right thing more than anyone she had ever met. The other needed to know the truth about what he had done.

"Where did you put the gun, Dad?"

The question hung between them, filled the room, pressed at the walls.

Frank swallowed—his voice came out quiet and unsteady. "What are you talking about? What gun?"

Stevie's voice hitched in her throat. "The gun Jimmy shot Aaron Taylor with."

Frank looked at her, the concern in his eyes shifting to something else.

"Stevie, what are you talking about?" Marnie gestured toward Stevie's uncle. "Jimmy's here to speak to you about what happened to you today."

Stevie's insides trembled, but she kept her eyes on her dad. "Where is the gun that Jimmy used to kill Aaron Taylor?"

"Enough of this nonsense!" Jimmy got to his feet, his chair screeching on the floor tiles. "Why would your dad know where the gun is?"

"You know why!" Stevie blasted, a molten anger surging through her. "And Dad tried to kill Faith Green because she did too!"

"Tried to *what*?" Frank said, head snapping to Jimmy.

"She doesn't know what she's talking about. I don't know where she's getting any of this!"

Jimmy's face was growing red and his hands twitched at his sides.

Stevie narrowed her eyes at Frank. "I know it was you who sent Faith Green along Westville Drive, blew out her tires with a spike strip."

"What? No ... Oh god." Frank's eyes filled with understanding. He breathed slowly, deliberately. "Jimmy, you didn't. Say it isn't true."

For just a second, Stevie's mind scrambled to catch up. Then the truth slammed into her.

Jimmy? It was Jimmy? She swung around and looked at her uncle.

He threw up his arms. "Of course it isn't true. Frank, it was an accident."

He was lying. Her dad hadn't lured Faith onto that road—Jimmy had. Relief fluttered in Stevie's chest, fragile and fleeting.

"The boyfriend was driving recklessly! That bend—it's a nightmare—he's had a bunch of traffic violations and . . ." Jimmy trailed off, his eyes finding Frank's.

Frank shook his head—his shoulders dropped. "Oh, Jimmy, what did you do?"

"Nothing! Your daughter is losing it again!" Jimmy tried to laugh—it came out hollow.

"I have proof," Stevie said, voice cut with steel. "I've seen the messages. I saw you at the crash site looking for Faith's phone."

Marnie looked from Stevie to Frank, eyes desperate. "Frank, what is she talking about?"

"She doesn't *know* what she's talking about!" Jimmy yelled back, spittle flying from his lips. "Stupid little bitch has been poking her nose into things again. You can't ever believe what she's saying!"

Marnie seemed to grow about a foot taller—her eyes flashed with rage. "Don't you dare speak to my daughter like that!" She pulled Stevie toward her, cupped her hands around Stevie's face, searched Stevie's eyes like she might find the answers there. "Stevie, honey, tell me what's going on."

Stevie struggled to get a breath, her words bursting out between sobs. "Jimmy . . . shot Aaron . . . Dad knew and covered it up."

Marnie looked over to Frank. He didn't raise his head, just stared at the floor, shoulders slumped.

Marnie's chin began to wobble. She swallowed, blinked back her tears, brushed the ones from Stevie's cheeks with her thumb.

She kept her eyes on Stevie's, searching them for the truth. "Are you sure, honey?" Stevie nodded, saw the understanding reach her mom, saw the pain it brought with it.

"She's lying! Or confused at least!" Jimmy cried, desperation now mixing with the anger in his voice.

Marnie swung around, eyes blazing. "Frank, is what Stevie is saying true? Did you have anything to do with Faith Green's crash?"

"Jimmy asked me to message her." Frank didn't look up when he spoke, his voice quiet, heavy. "He told me he was going to meet her at Kavannagh's to talk to her about the situation, see if we could come to some arrangement."

Jimmy took a step toward him, the color draining from his face. "Frank, don't say any more."

Frank raised his head, eyes filled with tears. "Jimmy, I'm done with not speaking. This needs to end."

"And Jimmy shot Aaron Taylor?" Marnie pressed, her eyes fixed on her husband.

"This is ridiculous!" Jimmy shouted, a vein pulsing in his neck as the rage rushed up in him again. "Can you hear yourself, Marnie? You can't believe this? Frank, tell her."

"Jimmy shot him," Stevie said, "and Faith Green knew and was blackmailing them."

Marnie's voice tremored when she spoke. "Frank, did Jimmy shoot the Taylor boy?"

Frank looked down at the floor again, nodded.

Marnie swallowed, her body stiffening as she took the confession in. "Where's the gun?"

"I don't know," Frank said, voice pitiful.

Marnie turned her fire on her husband. "Where's the goddamn gun?!"

Stevie jumped, heart hammering in her chest, and Frank slumped back down in the chair, hung his head. "I don't know where the gun is. After Aaron was shot, I wiped all records at the station that linked it to Jimmy—then I hid it in the attic. But it's gone, and I don't know where it is. Jimmy and I searched the whole place."

"That's what you were doing in the attic? You weren't looking over the case at all." Stevie's brain tripped to the next realization. "But if you were looking for the gun, that means you didn't kill Blair."

Frank looked at his daughter, tears running down his cheeks. "Oh, Little Bear, of course I didn't kill Blair. Stevie, I know you think you might not know who I am right now, but kill my own daughter?"

"I . . . I . . ." Seeing the heartbreak in her father's eyes, feeling it deep within herself, made the words Stevie wanted to say twist into nothing.

"The attic?" Marnie staggered forward, grabbed hold of the edge of the table. "The gun in the attic?"

"Mom, what is it?" Stevie put her arm around her, helped her onto the chair.

"I . . . I never made the connection," Marnie said, face paling.

"What connection?"

"That the gun I found in the attic could be the one that shot Blair. I thought it was Frank's. I found it one Christmas, a few years ago, when I was putting the decorations away." She nodded over at Frank, voice bitter. "I thought *he* was going to kill himself with it. So I got rid of it."

Stevie gripped hold of Marnie's hand. "Mom, this is very important. What did you do with the gun?"

Marnie's voice came out more as breath. "I wasn't sure what to do with it. I just knew I had to get it out of the house."

Stevie's pulse thudded in her ears, loud and slow.

Marnie's eyes clouded over. "I gave it to your brother, Stevie. I gave it to Hal."

Fifty-Three

The kitchen tilted, then seemed to spin around her. Stevie lowered herself onto a stool, tried to slow her breathing.

Hal has the gun. Hal has the gun. Hal has the gun.

"Hal was with Annie," Frank said.

Stevie held on to that. Hal had an alibi. He had the gun, but it didn't mean he'd killed Blair. He could have dumped it. Sold it. Anything.

The missing pass snapped into her thoughts like a flare.

No. He didn't go to the concert. He was with Annie.

"Hal didn't kill Blair," Marnie said. "I'm his mother and I know he isn't capable of such a thing."

Stevie clung to her words, desperate for them to be true.

"Still," Jimmy said, "I should get someone over to the house."

Marnie banged her fists on the table. "No! Don't you dare start playing policeman now! You killed that poor Taylor boy! You do not get to say what goes on here!"

"It was an accident, Marnie! It was dark. I thought he had a gun . . ."

"Those are all the things you could have said at an inquest, if you both hadn't covered it up," Marnie shot back. Her face twisted in disgust, and she turned to her husband, took her aim at him. "Frank, how could you?"

"I was looking out for Jimmy. He's family. Family comes first. The poor boy was dead—Jimmy going to jail wouldn't bring him back. It was a terrible, terrible accident, and I am haunted by it every day."

"Good," Marnie spat. "You should be. Covering for Jimmy is unforgivable—but continuing to do so after Mia vanished is incomprehensible. This family knows what it's like to live in the dark, and yet you chose to inflict that same pain on another family!"

Frank hung his head, his body shuddering as he sobbed. Stevie wanted to go over to him, comfort him like he always had for her when she was crying, but she couldn't do it.

"It's not the same pain though, is it?" Jimmy said. "The boy wasn't really theirs."

A flood of revulsion rushed through Stevie, and she spat, "*What?* You think that because Aaron was fostered, the Thompsons weren't as devastated by his loss?! Aaron Taylor wasn't just *some kid with a difficult past* like you once called him. He was loved. His life mattered."

"Stevie, honestly, it wasn't my fault," Jimmy said. "I'm trying to make amends, be a good cop."

"A good cop?" Stevie could have laughed. "You were going to send me a headless doll of Blair!"

"That wasn't me," Jimmy said, not enough conviction in his words.

"Oliver found it in your car."

Marnie shook her head, eyes unblinking. "Jimmy, why would you do such a thing?"

"He didn't want me looking into the case." A thought jabbed at Stevie's mind. Holy shit. Her uncle was off the rails. "It was you, wasn't it—in the park? You put that bag over my head and threatened me!"

"I swear to god, Jimmy, you better not have!" Marnie yelled.

Frank was by Jimmy in two strides, held him by his collar,

tears replaced by rage. "Don't lie to me. Not now. Was it you? Did you threaten Stevie?"

Jimmy struggled to get his footing, face reddening. "It wasn't my idea."

Marnie threw her arms in the air. "It wasn't his idea, he says!"

Frank shoved him into the wall. Held him there. "I should have let you rot in jail!"

"I did it for you, Frank! Bex Lyons wanted me to stop Stevie looking into Kirk Tyler's activities or she'd go to the station and tell them everything she knew about the Aaron Taylor case. And we'd both go down. We just wanted to scare her a little—Stevie was never in any real danger."

"His activities?!" Stevie cried. "He's abusing young girls, Jimmy. Young girls that, as a police officer, you are supposed to protect."

"I didn't have a choice!" Jimmy's nostrils flared in frustration.

"But you did have a choice, Jimmy!" Stevie cried. "You could have told the truth! Those girls' statements could provide a motive for why Kirk or Bex killed Blair."

"Jesus Christ, Stevie! It wasn't them. They have alibis. They didn't call that show—they didn't call Blair from a burner phone. The chances that they could have gotten ahold of the same gun as the one that killed Aaron are so small, it's almost impossible."

"Your gun, you mean?" Stevie spat.

"Yes, and we all know who has it now," Jimmy fired back. "So rather than yell at me, why don't you let me go so we can figure out how we can protect him!"

Frank glared at Jimmy, chest heaving, and released him from the wall.

Stevie clenched her fists. "Hal has an alibi."

Jimmy scoffed. "You don't think Annie would have lied for him?"

Stevie opened her mouth, but no words would come out.

"You might not understand this, but families protect each other. So maybe it's time to drop this whole thing. Wrap up the investigation into Blair, forget about what happened with Aaron Taylor and to Faith Green, before you end up destroying your brother's life too."

The pounding of fists sounded at the door, followed by a shout of "James Baker, are you in there?"

Jimmy looked up, worried.

"I can't do that," Stevie said, her words split with sobs.

Jimmy glared at Stevie, his whole body trembling with anger. "Who is that?"

"It's the police—they already know."

"I am the police!" Jimmy shouted.

Frank stood up, straightened his shirt. "Not anymore, Jimmy. Come on—let's do what we should have done a long time ago."

Marnie, bent over the kitchen table, let out a wail.

Jimmy glared at Stevie. "I guess for some Bakers, family doesn't come first."

Tears streamed down Stevie's face, her breath catching in jagged hiccups.

Frank placed his hands on Stevie's cheeks. "I am so sorry."

She looked up at him. "What have I done?"

He bent down and kissed the top of her head "You've done the right thing, Little Bear. You were being true to yourself. Your wild, wonderful, perfect self."

And then he was gone.

Fifty-Four

Stevie stood at the window in the living room. The car doors slammed, one and then the other, as Frank and Uncle Jimmy were driven off in the back of two separate police cars. She closed her eyes, let out the howl that had been waiting in the pit of her stomach, and sobbed, her body shaking from the effort. She slid down the wall to the carpet, put her head between her knees, and rocked back and forth. How could this be the right thing? Maybe Jimmy was right—maybe the truth would have been better hidden.

She heard footsteps on the carpet. She looked up, wiped her face—the snot and the tears. Oliver, standing there with his kind, sympathetic eyes. "Stevie, I'm so sorry." He exhaled, slow and deep. "Jesus, what a mess. I don't know what to say."

What could he say? What could anyone say?

"Can I get you something? Tea? Coffee? A new Band-Aid for your knee, maybe?"

Stevie shook her head. She didn't want anything. Except for her whole life to be different. "Your mom is giving her preliminary statement. Are you okay to speak once she's done?"

She nodded, turned her head away.

He hovered there a while—she could feel him watching her. She wished he would leave.

He must have sensed it. "I should probably go." His feet padded across the carpet again.

Her heart heaved in her chest. Surprised her. She turned her eyes to him, suddenly desperate for him to stay. "Did I do the right thing?" The tears came again, chasing each other down her cheeks. "Because right now I really don't know if I did."

Oliver moved to sit down next to her, back against the wall, his shoulder touching hers. That comforting smell of cedar and sandalwood. "A boy died, Stevie." He spoke the words so gently. "Of course you did the right thing."

"Do you think my dad will forgive me?" Stevie kept her eyes forward, unable to look at him.

"I think it's him who should be seeking your forgiveness."

Perhaps Oliver was right, but it didn't make her feel any better—any less guilty.

"Stevie, you're not the guilty party here."

Could he read her mind? Or maybe her guilt was written all over her face. Maybe it always would be.

"What you did was incredibly brave, and I can't imagine how hard it must have been, but you've helped to bring closure— justice—for Aaron and the Thompson family." His voice was so firm, yet so gentle.

She sobbed, heart cracked open. "But what about my family?" She looked at him now, searched his eyes, hoping for an answer.

"Stevie, when people do wrong—cause other people harm, like your dad and Jimmy have—they need to be held accountable. There's a price that has to be paid. And man, does it suck that that price is going to affect you. But you can't let what your family has done ruin your whole life. You are your own person, and I know you can't see it now but you'll find a way through this."

He was right. Stevie couldn't see it now though. She wondered if she ever would.

He was looking at her now too, really looking at her. Her gaze glided over the gentle angles of his face, his lips, those eyes that seemed to see right into her. Could he see how broken she was?

How damaged? She was in pieces, and he was so together.

Self-conscious, she pulled away, closed herself back up. "Has someone asked Hal about the gun?"

Oliver's eyes registered the change in her and his gaze slipped from her face. He stood up—Stevie did too. Awkward to be sitting on the floor, so close to each other.

He cleared his throat, checked back in to cop mode, voice formal. "They're over there now."

"What's Hal said?"

"I don't know yet."

"I think one of the VIP passes is missing. There's only four in the drawer in the hall table."

"You think?"

"I don't know. It could have been put somewhere else. Maybe we only received four. Maybe it got lost in the mayhem at the concert. Or maybe . . ." Stevie swallowed the lump in her throat. "Maybe Hal took it."

Oliver nodded. "That's a lot of maybes. So maybe it's nothing. But thank you for telling me. I'll look into it." He paused, cleared his throat again. "Do you mind if I ask you a question about Hal?"

Stevie managed a half-smile. "I think it's probably your job to ask questions."

"Do you think your brother could have killed Blair?"

He had to ask it, but the question still hurt. And it hurt because she didn't know the answer. Jimmy was right—Annie would lie to protect her husband. But that didn't mean Hal had done it. She couldn't imagine a world where that was possible. But she also couldn't imagine a world where her father had covered up a murder either.

It couldn't be Hal though. It just couldn't.

"I can't see what reason he would have. Sure, he was pissed about her going to the papers about his DUI, but he'd been pissed with her about that for years. He loved Blair. Honestly, I think all the animosity came from missing her. He was hurt, but he loved her."

"Okay, thank you, Stevie." That formal voice again. She'd closed herself off—now he had too.

"If you find the gun at his house, it won't look good for him, will it?"

"No, it won't."

A police officer came in from the kitchen. "I've finished taking Mrs. Baker's statement."

"I guess that means I'm up," Stevie said.

Tiredness throbbed in her bones. She checked the clock in the hallway; eleven p.m. She'd been talking for hours. Feet heavy, Stevie headed up to her room above the garage. Turned the opposite way at the top of the stairs and found herself outside her parents' door. She knocked lightly. "Mom? Are you awake?"

"Stevie?"

Stevie pushed the door open a crack, peered in. Her mom was sitting up in bed, eyes red from crying, holding a picture frame in her hands.

"Can I sleep with you tonight, Mom?" Even when she was little, Stevie hadn't ever needed the comfort of her parents' bed. She did now though.

Marnie pulled back the covers, patted the empty space where Frank should have been. "I think I'd love that."

Stevie climbed in and Marnie ran her fingers across the three faces in the picture frame. "Such beautiful girls."

It was the last photo taken of Stevie, Blair, and Mia all together. It had been Mia's twelfth birthday and Blair and Hal had just started talking again. Mia was in the center, her arms wrapped around Stevie's and Blair's necks, pulling them all closer together.

Mia's bracelet was glinting in the sunlight, casting little stars over her face and Blair's. Mia was grinning, staring straight ahead— Stevie and Blair were both looking at her.

"They really were," Stevie said.

"And you still are. Brave and beautiful."

Stevie's heart ached—she didn't feel either of those things right then.

Marnie placed the picture back on the nightstand and took hold of Stevie's hand.

Stevie laid her head next to her, stared up at the ceiling. "They wouldn't tell me anything about Hal," Stevie whispered. "Mom, what if it was him?"

"You know your brother, Stevie. He could never."

She'd known her dad, too, though, hadn't she? If Hal had killed Blair, did she even want to know?

"I'm so sorry," Stevie whispered.

"Stevie, this is not your fault." Marnie's voice was firm. "Don't think for one second that it is."

"I'm so sad, Mom." Stevie's tears ran down her cheeks, fell onto her dad's pillow.

"Me too, honey."

"Are we going to be all right?" Such a small sentence, so hard to say. Weighed down by impossibility. Or maybe it was hope.

"I think we are both going to have to try very hard for that— for a while at least. But we need to try, for ourselves, and each other. Stevie, you have your whole life ahead of you, and I'm going to make damn sure that it's a happy one."

Stevie squeezed her mom's hand. "I love you, Mom."

Marnie squeezed back. "I love you, too. So very much. Now, let's try and get some sleep." She reached over, switched off the bedside lamp.

Stevie lay in the dark, thoughts chasing around her head.

Thoughts of Jimmy. Her dad. Of Aaron Taylor and of Mia and Blair.

But one cut through them all.

Hal had the gun.

Fifty-Five

The ping of Marnie's phone pierced through the dark.

Stevie's eyes flicked to the bedside clock. It was just after midnight.

Marnie reached for the lamp, squinted at the phone screen, then handed the phone to Stevie. "I left my reading glasses downstairs."

"It's Annie." A rush of adrenaline. "The police have left. Should I call her?"

"Yes, do—see how they are."

Stevie dialed the number—Annie picked up after the first ring.

"Hi, Annie, it's Stevie. What's going on?" It took all her will not to ask about the gun.

"I'm here with Stevie," Marnie called out, then nudged Stevie. "Put it on speaker—I want to hear what she says."

"Hi, Marnie, I'm afraid we've had a rough night here. Hal's been through quite an interrogation—to be honest, we both have."

"Are you both okay?" Stevie asked.

"I'm fine, and I'm sure Hal will be. They've taken him to the station to take his statement formally."

The station? Shit. What did that mean?

"Couldn't they have waited until morning?" Marnie said.

"He wanted to get it done." Annie let out a long sigh. "Honestly, it's been a lot to process. We were trying to get our heads around the fact that Frank and Jimmy were involved in the Aaron Taylor murder, and all the cops wanted to talk about was the gun. I told them that I had no idea there was ever a gun in the house."

"But . . . did you have the gun in the house?" Stevie asked.

"Apparently so. Hal explained how Marnie had asked him to get rid of it, so he put it in a lockable case in our basement. The police searched, but they couldn't find it down there. I think it must have been taken by mistake during one of my decluttering sprees. I remember Goodwill sent a truck around to pick up a load of boxes and our old dryer. I vaguely remember a locked case down there. I guess I must have thought it was another box of old electronics and told them to take it too. You know how Hal loves to keep every cord and cable in case he needs it someday."

Stevie's body relaxed. It wasn't Hal. Thank god, it wasn't Hal. But then a wave of despair rolled through her. She might never find out who had killed Blair. "So anyone could have it?"

"I suppose they could. If I'd have known it was there, I would have handed it in. But enough about the gun. How are you both doing? What's happened with Frank and Jimmy . . . ? It's such a lot to process."

"One minute I refuse to believe it's happening—then I'm furious, then I'm overcome with despair," Marnie said. "But this family has been through worse. We can get through this, too."

"Yes, we have been through much worse." Annie fell silent. Mia's name unsaid. Blair's, too. She cleared her throat, her tone shifting. "I should probably go. You two try and get some sleep. I'll come and see you tomorrow afternoon."

"Love you lots, honey," Marnie said.

Stevie ended the call, switched off the bedside lamp, and lay back on the pillow. "Do you think you'll be able to sleep?"

Marnie found Stevie's hand under the blanket. "I think I stand a much better chance with you here."

"Same."

They both fell silent, but sleep felt too far out of reach. Stevie rolled over, then back again. Her mind was too full, too restless. Blair's killer was still out there.

"How's the knee?" Marnie whispered.

"Throbbing."

"There's some Advil in the cabinet. Take a couple of those now and we'll find time to go to the doctor's in the morning."

Did people go to the doctor's when their dads were being charged for covering up a murder? She supposed they must.

She climbed out of bed and switched on the light in the en-suite. She popped a couple of pills into her mouth and stuck her head under the faucet.

She looked into the mirror. A pale, broken girl stared back at her. She turned away, couldn't bear to look at herself, but a glint of light in the mirror caught her eye. The light from the silver feather.

She held the necklace, let the chain slip through her fingers.

Something stirred right at the edge of her awareness. An idea, a connection, a flicker of meaning, but it slipped away before she could catch it.

"Are you okay in there?" Marnie called out.

"Yes," Stevie said distractedly.

She turned off the bathroom light and lay next to her mom. What was it that was tugging at her—pulling her—to make the connection? It was like trying to remember a dream already half forgotten. Marnie's breathing fell into a slow rhythm and she started snoring gently, but Stevie couldn't sleep.

And then, in a rush, it came to her. Made her bolt upright.

Mia's bracelet. The one in Marnie's photo. It was a charm bracelet—Stevie remembered her wearing it.

There was a heart—she remembered that. An apple? A horseshoe. Definitely a horseshoe. But was there a feather?

Stevie pulled back the covers, grabbed the picture frame, and quickly tiptoed out into the hallway. Was there a feather? She turned on the hall light, studied the photo. It was no good. The bracelet was obscured by the glare of the sun.

She ran to her room, threw open her closet, and stood on her chair so she could reach the top shelf. She yanked out her winter sweaters. There it was, right at the back. The box she had promised her family she had gotten rid of.

She sat down on the carpet, her bad leg out straight, and lifted the lid. She took out the heavy notebook, ran her hands over the front, fingers tracing the bubble writing.

Finding Mia.

For a moment everything slowed. She hadn't looked at the book for two years—the writing seemed alien, yet familiar at the same time. Her counselor had encouraged her to focus on Mia's life and celebrate that, not agonize over every tiny detail of her disappearance. She told Stevie she had to let go of the case. Stevie had told her to go to hell. But eventually even she knew she needed to, to get better. She'd pushed the details away to protect herself. But now, she needed them back.

Furiously, she flicked through the pages, past the newspaper cuttings about Mia's disappearance, the missing poster that she'd put up all around town. Photos from the vigils. Details of suspected sightings. Copies of her letters to Uncle Jimmy asking to see the police files. The replies, saying he was unable to give her the information.

And finally, to the last photo ever taken of Mia. The photo Stevie had taken at her own sixteenth birthday party.

Mia's head was resting on her hands. And around her wrist was the bracelet. Several charms were hanging from it.

A horseshoe, a heart with a diamond in the center, a star, a butterfly.

And a feather.

The exact same feather that was hanging from Stevie's neck.

She turned it over in her hands. Every cell in Stevie's body fired off a small charge at once.

It wasn't a **B** engraved on the back. It was an **m**.

Fifty-Six

Stevie's hand fell to her side. Mia was wearing that bracelet on the night she went missing. How could Blair have a charm from her bracelet?

The only way was if she had been there. If she was somehow involved. But that was impossible. Blair would never hurt Mia. She loved her. There had to be another explanation.

Stevie paced her room.

Maybe she saw something. Maybe Blair had been in that alleyway with Mia. But if she'd seen what happened, why didn't she tell the cops? If she knew who'd hurt Mia, Blair would have screamed it from the rooftops. She would never have stayed silent and watched her family go through all that pain—it was unthinkable. Why would she? What would stop her from speaking up?

The answer hit her like a sledgehammer to the chest.

Not what. Who.

Kirk Tyler.

He was the only one with the power to keep Blair quiet. The one who knew about Aaron Taylor and the cover-up. If Blair was in Honeyville, Kirk could have been too. Maybe he was watching the house. Saw Mia leave alone—after all, he liked young girls. Stevie's stomach twisted as the pieces slotted into place. It was him.

Kirk Tyler had killed Mia.

And when Jimmy had murdered Aaron Taylor and her dad had covered it up, they had not only denied the Thompson family answers—they had also ensured that no one would ever know what happened to Mia.

Because Blair could never, ever risk speaking out.

But Blair knew staying silent was wrong. It must have been what made her so messed up. She understood that she was the only one who could tell the world what Kirk was like. Maybe she was finally ready to speak out, about Melissa and the other girls, about Mia, about everything.

Then, when Blair told Bex she was finally going to expose him on the day of her concert, Kirk must have picked up the gun from somewhere in Honeyville. A gun that turned out to be the one Annie had chucked. He'd made certain she'd be silent forever.

Stevie's heart blazed, fury coursing through her, making her hands shake.

Blair might not be able to speak out. But she could.

Stevie grabbed her phone, quickly hammered out a text to Colby. It was past one in the morning. She wouldn't respond, but Stevie needed to tell someone.

Kirk killed Blair and he killed Mia.

Stevie stared at the words, knew with every fiber of her body she was right, and pressed Send. Then she stuck her feet into her sneakers and left a note for Marnie on the hall table.

She would go to the police, tell them what she knew. But first, she had to talk to Hal and Annie.

Annie opened the door, a mug in her hands. "Stevie?" She was still dressed—wearing jeans and a black top. Her curls piled up in a bun on top of her head. Annie looked Stevie up and down and she realized she was still wearing her pajamas. "What are you doing here at this time? Is everything okay?"

Stevie swallowed, let out a shaky breath. "Can I come in?"

"Of course." Annie stood to the side to let Stevie in, a look of worry in her eyes.

Stevie followed her through to the living room, sat down on the couch.

"Hal's still at the police station. I wanted to wait up for him. It will be nice to have some company. Do you want something to drink? I'm having a hot chocolate . . ." Her voice trailed off. "Stevie, what's going on? You look . . . I don't know . . . kind of wild."

"I need to tell you something. Something I think might be important."

Annie pressed her lips together. "Go on."

A wave of nausea washed over her. "It has to do with Mia's bracelet."

"Mia's bracelet?" Annie lowered herself down onto the armchair opposite Stevie.

"The one she was wearing when she went missing. There was a charm on it—a feather." Stevie pulled the chain out from under her pajama top, and Annie's eyes widened. "Blair, she had it—"

Annie cut her off, voice trembling. "Don't, Stevie."

She had to—

She had to tell Annie what she knew. "I know it's hard to talk about Mia's case, but I think Blair was there when—"

"Stevie, please don't do this." Annie's hands were gripping her mug so tightly her knuckles were almost translucent. "Please, leave this alone."

"But, Annie! Don't you see what I'm trying to tell you? If Blair had Mia's charm, she must have been there when Mia disappeared."

Stevie looked at Annie, waiting for some kind of response, but she didn't speak, didn't even move.

"Annie? Did you hear what I said? I think Blair knew what happened to Mia and I think she was killed for it."

"Blair knew, all right." Annie stared at the wall behind Stevie's head, eyes unfocused.

It was as though all the air had surged out of the room. Stevie shifted on the couch. "What do you mean?"

"I know about Blair." Annie set her mug down on the coffee table. "About the bracelet. How she came to have it. Hal and I gave that feather charm to Mia for her eighth birthday, got it engraved with an *M* on the back. An inexpensive thing—not much more than fifty dollars. I'd almost forgotten about it. We bought her a few different charms over the years." Annie sighed at the memory. "But then, about a month ago, I thought I saw it again. I was watching an interview with Blair about the homecoming tour, and she was fiddling with this feather pendant hanging around her neck. And something jolted in me."

Stevie waited for her to continue, waited for what Annie was saying to make sense. If she knew Blair had Mia's charm, why hadn't she said anything before?

"I paused the video, took a closer look, and I thought, 'That looks just like the charm we gave Mia.' So I called Blair and asked about it. She said it was hers, that she'd had it since she was little, and she was so convincing—made me feel awful for even asking. And I wanted to believe her, I really did, but something in me knew she was lying."

Unease flooded through Stevie's body.

"I couldn't let go of the feeling that she was hiding something, and that feeling grew and twisted, and it took over. For weeks, I went back over every video of Blair, every photo, every social media post, like a woman possessed. And you know what I found? She'd worn that necklace every day since Mia went missing. But there was not a single photo, not one video, *nothing*, that shows she ever wore it before. And I came to the same conclusion that you seem to have reached. That Blair was there when Mia disappeared. So, when I heard she was recording that show, I phoned in, used an app to hide my voice, to see how she'd react. I could tell by the fear in her voice that she'd been lying. That she knew something."

Stevie's mind tripped over itself. "That was you?"

"Yes, that was me." Annie drew a deep breath. "After that, I had to decide what to do. I knew she wouldn't tell me the truth about what happened to Mia on her own. So I had to find a way to make her."

Ice prickled at Stevie's neck. "What do you mean, 'find a way to make her'?"

"You have to understand that she didn't give me any choice." Annie stood up, turned her back to Stevie. "You know Blair used to come back here and see just me? I used to think that was because she cared, maybe even liked me the most. Now I know it was to ease her guilt." Annie turned back around, swallowed down her tears.

"All those visits, all those opportunities to come clean—but she never did."

"Annie, what did you do?" Stevie said, voice low, heavy with fear.

"After the call in to the TV show, I had three days until the concert, so I came up with a plan to get her to talk. I played the loving aunt. I started checking in with her, asking her how she was doing. Asking all about the concert—her entrance, the timings. She thought I was genuinely interested."

Stevie sat frozen, her mind caught somewhere between disbelief and horror at what she was hearing.

"I sent her a message to tell her I had a new phone, then called her on the night of the concert using the burner phone, to tell her I was dropping by to wish her luck. I waited outside the venue until I knew she'd be waiting in the platform below. She liked to be on her own then—to get in the right zone, apparently. I called her again to apologize for being late and asked if I could just say a quick hello before the show. I used the VIP pass to get in."

"It was *you* who gave my name? Why . . . why did you choose me?"

"It wasn't personal, Stevie. I had to get in there and I knew your name was on the list. I didn't think it would matter, that they'd probably just think they'd made an error when you turned up later—which they did. They checked my bag—I was worried they might pat me down—that they'd feel the gun at my hip. But it seems that's not necessary if you're a VIP. The things you can get away with if people think you're important! And for a while I thought I'd get away with it. But then that officer of yours announces that it was the same gun that killed Aaron Taylor."

"Get away with what?" Stevie said, her voice barely a whisper. The whole time she'd been listening to Annie speak, Stevie had tried to convince herself that it wouldn't end like this. That Annie wouldn't say what she feared she would say. The room started to spin, and Stevie gripped hold of the arm of the sofa.

"No. You can't have shot her." Stevie shook her head, refusing Annie's words, forcing them away. "Why are you saying this? Why would you kill Blair? I . . . I don't believe you."

Annie's chin started to tremble. "I'm sorry, Stevie, but I did."

Stevie jumped to her feet. "No! It doesn't make sense! Didn't she tell you that Kirk Tyler killed Mia?"

Annie's eyes broke from the wall and found Stevie, tears building at the corners. "I wish she had, Stevie. And, god knows, blame lies with that man too."

"Then what—" Stevie sniffed, voice hitching in her throat. "What did she say? What could Blair have possibly said to make you kill her?"

Annie's face screwed up with pain as tears flowed down her cheeks. Her voice tremored. "I . . . I don't know if I can tell you, Stevie."

"Tell me!" Stevie screamed the words. Her chest heaved, each breath sharp and ragged. She waited, heart pounding, as Annie didn't move. Then, finally, Annie slumped down into the chair and closed her eyes. She swallowed, opened her eyes again, and nodded. "Okay, then. I'll tell you everything." Voice different—steadier.

"I'm sure you remember how Blair turned up at your party a mess—she was high on something—or some things—out of her head, whatever."

Stevie's pulse throbbed at her temples. "I remember," she said, and dropped onto the couch.

Annie shook her head, disdain curling her lip. "That's what Blair led with, when she finally started to speak. Like her being on drugs might somehow absent her from any culpability. She told me how she'd been in a dark place, how there was a stalker—you've seen the emails. She was scared—terrified, even. Her manager had warned her that there was a very real threat to her life.

"After Blair leaves your party, and tears off in her car, Mia decides she wants to go after her aunt. You remember how much she loved Blair. How much she adored her. Of course she would—Blair was beautiful and talented and famous to boot. So Mia leaves the house, chases after her aunt, and finds her car parked in town outside Lacey's. Unaware that Blair, who is out of her mind, paranoid on god knows what, has convinced herself that her stalker is in Lacey's Bar."

Annie took a long breath; a tear ran down her cheek. Then another. "Blair comes tearing out of the bar, jumps into her car, and drives off, drugs and liquor flooding her system."

Stevie dropped her head in her hands. She didn't want to listen anymore. She knew the path Annie was taking her—the alleyway she was leading her down. Her heart was pounding so loudly in her ears now—a drumbeat counting down to an inevitable ending. Her sobs became jagged, desperate, like they might tear her in half.

"She told me she didn't see her. Didn't even know it was Mia until she got out of the car."

Annie's words echoed in Stevie's head—unreal and unbearable. *She didn't see her. Didn't even know it was Mia.* Stevie searched Annie's eyes, tried to find something to say she was lying, saw only the painful truth. She tipped her head forward. Blair had killed Mia. Stevie's whole body seemed to fold under the weight of the pain.

"And do you know what Blair does, now that my precious baby is lying on the ground, bleeding to death on the gravel? Does she call an ambulance?" Annie laughed, sad and hollow. Stevie wanted to tell her to stop, that she'd heard enough, but she couldn't speak.

"No, of course she doesn't, because she's a star. She calls her manager. And Kirk Tyler and that Lyons woman take my baby away and *poof*"—Annie flicked out her fingers—"they make her disappear."

Stevie looked up, her voice a howl in her throat. "Disappear . . . where?"

"Blair didn't know, and the fact that I had a gun to her head when I asked makes me think she was telling the truth. She did tell me that she'd learned that Kirk was the one who had been sending her those emails everyone thought were from a stalker. She said it was his fault that Mia was dead. He was the one who had terrified her—messed with her mind."

"Why would he do that?"

"Another form of control, I suspect. To keep Blair too terrified to leave him. She'd worked hard to discover he was responsible. She might have lived if she'd put as much effort into finding out where they'd buried Mia. Taken some ownership of her actions, done something to put them right. But no, even though she'd driven the car that killed Mia, even though she'd allowed her body to be taken away, then removed the evidence that had fallen from my daughter's wrist and wore it around her neck, she thought she wasn't to blame."

Fire burned in Stevie's veins. "And you killed her for it?"

"I didn't go to the concert meaning to kill her. I only wanted to find out where Mia was. But when I was below that stage, do you know what I heard?"

Stevie shook her head.

"I heard my daughter's name. Blair had used my Mia and Aaron Taylor as part of her show." Annie clicked her fingers. "Something flicked inside me like a switch. 'Lift them up in your hearts'—that voice-over filled the stadium. I asked her how she could do that, knowing that she'd killed Mia. I didn't even know about Aaron then. I could see the shame in her eyes. She said it wasn't her decision—that she'd argued against it, but that the production team had insisted. Nothing was ever her fault! And when I asked again where Mia was, and she couldn't even tell me, I felt such rage. Such rage at her for allowing all these things to happen, for being so weak, so self-centered, and the gun was in my hand . . . I didn't even hesitate. I just shot her. And it was no accident. I killed her completely and utterly on purpose. Your sister knew Mia was dead all along. She watched our pain and she did nothing." Annie's voice was quiet, almost calm. "The hope of the reward money, of the appeals, the sightings, every new lead, she sat back and watched that hope cut through us time and time again and still she did nothing. She said nothing. How could she do that?" Her eyes filled with tears.

"I don't know, Annie. But I also don't know how you could kill her."

"When your sister took Mia from me, I think she took away my heart—hollowed me out. Because I don't know how I did it either. But I'd do the same thing again." Annie clenched her jaw, sniffed back the tears. Then took a breath and closed her eyes. When she opened them again, the sadness had shifted into something else. Something hard.

"Hal . . ." Her brother's name caught in her throat. "Does Hal know?"

"No, he does not. He's like you, Stevie—too good. He would have turned me in, and then I would never find out where Mia is. But I will tell him. I'll tell him everything, after, when the time is right."

What did she mean, *when the time is right*? After what? An icy dread settled in Stevie's gut.

Annie rose to her feet, crossed over to the bookcase, then bent down and, with some effort, pulled off the wooden panel at the base. She reached underneath and felt around for something.

"Annie, what are you looking for?" Stevie asked. But she knew—of course she knew.

Annie got to her feet and turned around. In her hand was the gun.

Fifty-Seven

"Annie, what are you doing?" Stevie stood up from the couch, her mind throwing itself against her skull, eyes fixed on the gun.

"I'm going to go over to Kirk Tyler's hotel and hold a gun to his head until he tells me where my baby is."

"And if Kirk won't talk?"

"He'll talk." Grit in her voice. "And when he's finished talking, I'm going to kill him, too. Kirk Tyler deserves to die for everything he's done. To Mia, to those girls. Even for what he did to Blair and what that's done to me."

"Annie, please, don't do this." Stevie pulled out her phone, hands trembling. "We should go to the police. They can speak to Kirk, get him to confess. If you explain—"

Annie pointed the gun at Stevie. Her finger was on the trigger. "Put the phone down." Annie's voice was cold, detached.

"What are you going to do, shoot me?" Stevie laughed despite the panic building inside her.

"Yes, in the arm or the hand if I have to."

Stevie's eyes stretched as fear clawed at her chest. "You're crazy!"

"Grief can do that to a person."

"Annie, you're not thinking clearly—"

"I am, Stevie. I'm thinking very clearly. Kirk Tyler's not going to talk to the police. He'll lawyer up. Pay his way out of it. I'm too far in this now. I have already made peace with the fact that I am going to sit in a jail cell for the rest of my life for killing Blair.

But I know I will finally feel free if I can do that knowing where Mia is. My sweet, beautiful child deserves a proper burial. Surely you must understand that?"

"No, this isn't the way." Stevie scrolled through her phone, searching for Oliver's number. Fingers trembling too much to work.

The click of the safety. "Put the phone down."

Stevie looked up. Annie's eyes were trained on her.

"Down! I mean it."

Stevie leaned forward, dropped her phone on the coffee table.

"Good, now move." Annie gestured toward the door with the gun.

Stevie laughed. Couldn't believe what was happening. "Annie, you don't need to—"

"I'm serious. Into the hall."

Stevie glared at her, didn't move for a moment, but then she saw the frenzy in Annie's eyes. She was deadly serious.

Annie opened the door to the closet. "Get in."

"Annie, I'm not getting in the closet. We can speak to the police together."

"Stevie, you need to get in the closet. Hal will be home later and he'll let you out, but I have to do this. I won't let you stop me."

Stevie made to shove past her. "No, I won't let you kill again. This isn't you, Annie!"

"It is!"

The sound of the gun was deafening. Left Stevie's ears ringing, the hallway full of smoke.

Stevie's mouth fell open. Annie had blasted a chunk out of the banister.

"Get in the closet!" Annie screamed, nostrils flaring, tears flowing down her cheeks.

From inside, Stevie heard the sound of the key in the lock, then of Annie's car screeching away.

* * *

Stevie rattled the handle of the closet. Kirk Tyler was the worst of mankind, but she couldn't let Annie take his life. What good would come of it? Only more pain, more hurt. Her dad, Jimmy, Blair, Annie—they had all done terrible things. Did they all deserve to die too? Where would it end? One revenge bleeding into another. No more. She had to put an end to it.

She banged her shoulder against the door. Once. Twice. Harder on the third time. The door bounced on its hinges. And again. She lunged forward, throwing every ounce of her weight into the strike. A hollow, jarring crack at the hinges. Pain exploded through her shoulder. She drove her foot forward, slammed it into the wood— and the frame splintered. *One more, just one more.* She pressed her arms against the walls of the closet. Brought her leg up and kicked with her heel. The door gave way, one hinge busted. She squeezed through the gap, went to run to her car. She heard her phone ringing from the living room and she turned and ran to get it, answered on the way out to her car. "Colby," she said, breathless.

"Stevie! Are you okay? I was sleeping—"

Stevie stuck the phone in the jack, started the engine. "Colby—"

"And I just got this psychic sense that you needed me—"

"Colby, listen—"

"And I woke up and I saw your message about Kirk killing Blair and Mia?"

"I was wrong! Annie killed Blair!"

"What. The. Fuck?"

"She's gone to Sable and Stone now. She's going to kill Kirk Tyler."

"What the actual fuck?"

"I need you to call Oliver, tell him what's happening. I'm heading over there now."

"Wait. Stevie. Is that a good idea?"

"Just call Oliver and get the police over there as soon as you can." Stevie hung up, put her foot down on the gas.

Ten minutes later she pulled into the Sable and Stone parking lot, the gravel crunching beneath her tires. It was just after three in the morning, and it was still pitch-black. As she pulled into a space, her headlights swept across the lot. There was Annie's car, parked at the back. Stevie killed the engine and her eyes flashed up to Kirk's room on the top floor. The curtains were drawn. The lights were off.

Her eyes moved along to a sash window that was half open. Then the metal fire escape staircase that led to it, Annie on the top rung, disappearing inside.

Stevie reached for the car door, pulse hammering—she charged across the lot, then up the drive. She took the staircase steps two at a time, pausing at the top, trying to listen to what was going on inside. It was too quiet—her breathing too loud.

She hesitated a moment before ducking through the window— Annie wouldn't shoot her for following, surely? Inside, she waited for her eyes to adjust to the darkness. She was in the living area— she recognized it from before—the table, the sofas, where they had all sat the morning after Blair had died. She turned on her phone flashlight, saw a door ajar ahead of her. She tiptoed toward it, the sound of gentle snoring growing louder as she drew close. She held her breath and crossed the threshold of Kirk's bedroom.

It was dark but Stevie could see Annie's silhouette. She was by Kirk's bed, one hand on the bedside lamp cord, the other holding the gun to his head as his chest rose and fell in time with his snores.

With one swift action, Annie pulled down on the chain and the light switched on. Stevie flinched at its brightness. Kirk, lying on top of the sheets in navy, silk pajamas, snorted and stirred a little.

"Annie," Stevie hissed, heart thundering, stomach turning over.

Annie swung around, looking startled, but quickly regained her composure. "Stevie."

"Annie, don't do this, please. It's not too late."

Stevie's whole body was shaking, but the gun, which was still trained on Kirk, was so still in Annie's hands.

"I'm not leaving here until I find out what he's done with Mia's body. Don't you want to know too?"

She did. Desperately so. "This isn't the way."

"It's the only way."

Annie pushed the gun onto his temple, gave him a little tap.

Stevie's insides froze—her lungs stopped dead.

"Wakey-wakey, Mr. Tyler."

Kirk moaned slowly—his eyes flickered open.

Annie smiled at him, her gaze laser focused. "Ah, Mr. Tyler, you're awake."

Kirk's eyes widened, the color immediately draining from his cheeks. He wailed and tried to scurry to the other side of the bed, his feet getting tangled in the sheets.

"There's no need to panic," Annie said. "I'm only here to ask you one very simple question and all you need to do, to stay alive, is answer me."

"Help! Help me!" Kirk screamed, looking to Stevie.

Annie pressed the gun into Kirk's cheek, pushed against the flesh. She pulled a roll of duct tape from her bag and chucked it at Stevie. "Tape him."

"What?" Stevie looked down at the roll in her hands.

"Tape him. I need him quiet while I ask my questions, then we'll go, and nobody dies."

"Nobody dies?" Stevie said.

Kirk cried out for help again.

"Do it!" Annie yelled. "Before someone hears!"

Stevie hesitated. If she did it, would they finally find out where Mia was? Would Annie be satisfied and leave without killing him? Ignoring the bile rising in her stomach, she pulled out a line of tape, tore it off, and pressed it over his mouth. She turned away quickly, unable to look at the fear in his eyes.

"So, Mr. Tyler, I'm going to explain things to you very clearly," Annie said. "In a moment, I'm going to remove the tape that is currently covering your mouth. When I do that, you will have thirteen seconds to tell me what you did with my daughter's body after Blair Baker killed her. I've chosen thirteen because that was the age of my beautiful, kind, caring daughter when you stole her from me. If you do not have an answer for me in those thirteen seconds, I am afraid I'm going to have to blow your brains out on this one-thousand-thread Egyptian cotton. Do I make myself clear?"

Kirk's eyes were wide, so much white bulging from the sockets.

"Stevie, would you like to tell Mr. Tyler here how you know that I'm not lying about shooting him?"

"I know she's not lying, because she's the one who killed Blair." The truth, a stone in her gut.

Kirk's eyes widened farther, little red veins crisscrossing the whites, tears at the edges.

"So do you understand the terms of this agreement?" Annie said.

He began nodding his head furiously.

"I take the fact that you are nodding to be a very promising sign for your future, Mr. Tyler. I'm going to remove the tape now, and then I will start my countdown."

Annie ripped the tape off, one sharp pull. "Thirteen. Twelve—"

Kirk gasped a lungful of air and then the words rushed out of him. "She's in the forest! We buried her in the forest."

"The forest?" Annie said, eyes steady, voice cracking. "What forest?"

He sobbed, lines of snot joining his tears. "The forest on the route west out of Honeyville."

Mia was in the forest. In her darkest thoughts Stevie had visions of some landfill site or of Mia's body being trapped under concrete. She fought to keep her voice even. "Do you know where in the forest? You'd recognize the spot again if you saw it?"

"Yes, yes, I would. I could take you there." He looked at Annie, eyes desperate and pleading.

"No, you explain to me now," Annie snapped.

"But then you'll kill me." His face cracked open, a wail bursting out.

"I'll kill you if you don't, and then I'll go find Bex Lyons and offer her the same deal. I'm sure she won't be so stupid as to turn it down."

"Take Columbia Way off Westville. There's a picnic spot. Walk fifteen minutes due east, until you reach the stream—there are four red oaks standing in a circle—she's buried in the middle of them."

Annie turned to Stevie. "You get all that?"

Stevie nodded.

"I've told you what you wanted—now are you going to let me go?"

Annie's eyes grew darker. "Let you go? Why would I do that?"

"Enough, Annie," Stevie said, heart picking up. "He's told you what you need to know."

"He needs to pay for what he's done! To my Mia. To all those girls he abused. You see, I have Blair's phone, and there was quite a lot of evidence on that." Her eyes shot to Kirk. "Did you know she was recording you?"

"I'll pay! I'll pay whatever you want. Please, please don't kill me." His skin was waxy white, glistening with sweat.

Stevie's eyes flashed to the window. Where the hell was Oliver? Annie could do anything right now and she wasn't sure that she'd be able to stop her.

Annie tilted her head from side to side. "You want to pay for my silence? To keep quiet about the kind of man you are, the terrible things you've done? I think the price that comes for hiding a truth like that is too high even for you, Mr. Tyler." Annie put both hands on the gun, held it out straight.

"Annie, no!" Stevie said. "He needs to stand trial. He needs to face the people he's hurt."

"I'm afraid that's not enough," Annie said.

"Three million? Four million, then." A sob broke through him, causing his body to convulse. "Whatever you want! Name your price!"

"I'm sorry—there's only one price high enough for what you've done, and that's for you to rot in hell."

The click of the safety.

Stevie's heart threw itself against her rib cage. She turned, dived toward Annie. Toward the gun. Shouted her name. Her voice shattered in the crack of the blast.

Fifty-Eight

Her head struck something hard. She landed on the floor. Pain shooting through her knee, her skull. She rolled onto her side, ears ringing, vision split with light. The smell of smoke. She put her fingers to her head—the tips came away bloody. Had she been shot? She felt her skull, found a gash not a bullet hole. She reached out, found the hard edge of the nightstand, tried to pull herself up. Her legs were not compliant, her vision woozy.

In the distance she could hear screaming. Was it her? No, someone else. She forced her legs to straighten, pushed herself to her feet. She was by the bed. So much blood. She turned away. Couldn't bear to look . . .

Through the whooshing in her ears came the sound of splintering wood. Followed by someone shouting.

"Weapons . . . down . . . on head . . ."

She couldn't catch it all.

Something heavy thudded to the floor.

She heard a name. Her name.

A hand on her back. A voice she knew, telling her it was going to be okay. That it was over.

Oliver.

She turned around, fell into his chest, her body slack. His arms around her. Moving her to a chair. His face in front of hers now. Looking in her eyes. Her head, too heavy, wouldn't stay up. Another face—a light in her eyes, rolling to black.

* * *

Stevie's eyes flickered open—she squinted, the lights too bright above her. The gentle beep of machines. Her head was pounding—thunderclap feeding into thunderclap.

Colby's face loomed over her. "She's awake! She's awake!" She ran to the door. "SHE'S AWAKE!"

Stevie flinched. Her voice came out raspy. "Too loud."

"Drink." A straw was stuck into her mouth and Marnie's face came into view. "Stevie, sweetheart, you're in the hospital—you hit your head quite badly and it caused you to have a fit. You've been dipping in and out of consciousness for a while now."

She spat the straw away. "I had a fit?" Her mind was soupy—she couldn't piece together what happened. She remembered the click of the safety, the explosion of light and noise and then . . . nothing.

Colby's face appeared above her again, eyes wide. "Uh-huh, the full shebang."

Stevie's mind stretched back, tugged at her memory. Annie. The gun . . . "And Kirk Tyler? Is he—"

"Down a testicle," Colby said brightly, adding a triumphant nod of her head.

"A testicle?" Stevie fought against the tight hospital sheets to sit up.

"Here, let me." Colby pushed a button on the side of the bed, which slowly raised Stevie up.

Marnie sat down on the chair, inched it forward. "He'd be dead if you hadn't thrown yourself at Annie—at least, that's what she's saying. I doubt many would weep if he was."

"I'm glad he's alive."

Stevie looked over. Hal was sitting on a chair in the corner. His hands were clasped, elbows on his knees. He looked so broken. Stevie's heart ached for him.

"He needs to stand trial, be held accountable for what he did," Hal said.

"Do you know?" Stevie said, her eyes finding her brother's. "What happened—Blair, Mia . . . why Annie . . ." Stevie couldn't put the words together.

Marnie took her hand, her voice barely above a whisper. "We know. Annie has explained everything."

"She gave me an alibi," Hal said quietly. "When I asked her why she did that, she said she was protecting me—that because of what I'd said in the past, I might be a suspect. I told her that she shouldn't have—that I was innocent so it shouldn't matter." Hal shook his head. "When she came back after . . ." Hal gulped, took a breath. "She told me she'd gone to the evening church service, but no one was there, that even the pastor must have been at the concert. It never crossed my mind that she'd lied . . . that the alibi was to protect her . . ."

"I'm so sorry," Stevie said, her chin beginning to tremble. "How do we . . . ? After all this . . . it's too much . . ." Her voice hitched in her throat, gave way to a sob.

Hal strode over, tears running down his face. He took Stevie's other hand. "I don't know, Stevie. I don't know." His voice cracked and his body shook as he laid his head down on Stevie's shoulder and sobbed. "But you and Annie found Mia, Stevie. You found her."

Stevie stroked her brother's head, let her tears fall onto him, each one asking the question—was it worth it? Was the truth worth all the pain? Was it better than the not knowing? Stevie couldn't even begin to answer that.

Stevie was drifting in and out of a morphine haze when there was a knock on her hospital door. They were keeping her in for the night for observation. The bump on her head had been pretty bad and required several stitches, but the doctors didn't think that she'd suffered any significant damage. Colby had performed a cheer, involving a lot of leg kicks and bedpans in place of pom-poms when she'd found out. It had been cute to start—*Give me an* N, *give me an* O—but spelling out every letter of *no significant damage* had gone on for longer than either the performer had stamina for or the audience would have liked.

Another knock on her door. Stevie tried to shout, but her voice came out slurred. "Come in." She used the button to raise up the bed. She was a little woozy—No, maybe a lot woozy, but definitely nice woozy.

Oliver poked his head into her room. "Hi, I just wanted to check how you're doing."

He looked all soft around the edges. "Aw, you came to check on me!" Stevie heard herself saying. She tried to work out how she was doing, but her head was too fuzzy. "I think things are bad, like really, *really* bad. My family is a bunch of criminals, well, some of them. But all things considering, right now, I feel pretty swell."

Oliver smiled. "They got you on some strong meds?"

"Why do you say that?"

"No reason."

"I want to thank youuuu"—Stevie reached out and pressed his nose—"for showing up at the hotel when you did."

Oliver laughed. "You have Colby to thank for that. She turned up at my place, dragged me out of bed, and drove me to the hotel. I called for backup on the way. I wasn't sure I was going to make it there alive at one point. That girl drives fast. And badly. Very badly." He shook his head at the memory. "At least fourteen traffic violations before we'd even left my street."

Stevie grinned. "Sounds like Colby."

"She cares about you a lot. When that gun went off, an officer had to hold her back from charging into the room armed solely with a can of pepper spray."

"She is actually the best person," Stevie said. "The best."

"Takes one to know one, I suppose," Oliver said, then coughed and lowered his eyebrows. "I was also hoping to arrange a time to meet with you officially."

"You sound serious. Am I in any trouble?"

Oliver frowned. "For what?"

"I broke into Kirk Tyler's hotel room and duct-taped his mouth."

He pressed his lips together. "Hmmm, tiny bit criminal of you, but I don't see any substantial jail time." He winked and Stevie smiled. "When do you get out of here?"

"Tomorrow. What are you thinking if we're meeting officially? Swanky restaurant? Steakhouse?"

"I actually meant the station, to take your statement."

Stevie threw her arms in the air. "The station it is!"

"Say around three?"

"It's a date, Oliver Officer!" Stevie frowned. Tried again. "Oliver Officer Dean!"

Oliver cleared his throat and said, "Yes. Fine. Three o'clock. See you then."

He turned to leave, then turned back around.

"Hi again!" Stevie said.

"Look, when you're up to it, maybe we try the swanky restaurant or steakhouse thing." Oliver looked down at his hands, suddenly unsure of himself. "But only if you want. Sorry. What am I doing? You're as high as a kite and I'm—"

"No, it's okay. I am fine. So, *so* fine and I'd—"

Stevie was cut off by the sound of clanging bedpans and the door bursting open.

"Give me an *N*! Give me an *O*!"

"Not the bedpans!" Stevie pointed a wobbly finger at Colby. "I love you, Greeny Colb, but not again with the bedpans!"

Colby shrugged, handed the pans to Oliver, who looked at them with complete confusion, before eventually deciding to put them on the side table.

Colby sat down on the end of Stevie's bed. "I was only celebrating the fact that your brain's not broken!" She looked from Stevie to Oliver, lowered an eyebrow. "Did I interrupt something?"

"I am so, so fine," Stevie said. "Tell Ollie Boy I'm so, so fine."

Colby blinked. "I think we may need to talk to a nurse about your dosage."

One Year Later

Stevie grabbed the sweater out of her backpack and pulled it on over her head.

"That one of your jailbird knits?" Colby asked as she wriggled her skirt over her hips.

Stevie rolled her eyes. "*Yes*, Annie made this one." She pulled her hair up into a messy bun. "What time does the concert start?"

"Eight, but if you get a move on, we can get a drink in a bar I want to try out first." Colby pressed her hands together in prayer. "God bless the Brits and their low drinking age."

Stevie sat down on her bunk. "I still can't believe we're in London about to watch your boyfriend play at the Royal Albert Hall."

"I think it's very inconsiderate of him to crash our Europe trip, *actually*," Colby said as she applied her lip gloss in the hostel mirror. "And he might not be my boyfriend for long if there are some actual real-life royalty there."

"You love Terence, and you can pretend all you like, but I know you planned everything so you could see him here. You're not going to leave him for some earl."

Colby frowned at her reflection. "What even is an earl?"

"Not a clue."

Colby smacked her lips together, screwed the lid back on her gloss. "Terence is all right, I suppose. I'll probably keep him. You know 'Serenade for a Scumbag' went platinum?"

"Colby, I was there when he called you. Your screaming almost got us kicked out of the Louvre."

Colby laughed, gave her a playful punch on the arm. "It was exciting, okay? Let me have my moment—we can't all have boyfriends who fight to uphold truth and justice."

"I mean, Oliver did have to fine someone for persistent jaywalking yesterday. And without Terence the whole world wouldn't know what a rat Kirk Tyler is." Stevie chucked Colby her jacket from the bed. "Ready?"

"I am." Colby crouched down and took Stevie's hands, her expression serious. "But you're sure about this? It was a year ago today that—"

"I know. I'm sure."

"How are you feeling, *truthfully*?"

Truthfully? Over the past year Stevie had a lot of time to think about how she was feeling. And about the truth—and whether it was worth all the pain that it brought with it. The jury was still out on that. Her dad, Jimmy, Blair, had all tried to bury what they'd done. Each deceit spilling into another like a loaded gun passed from hand to hand. Hiding from the truth had been what had caused so much destruction. It had denied the Thompson family the answers and the justice Aaron deserved for too many years. So, yes, the truth was important. But how you dealt with it, how you lived with it, was even more so. Hal and Marnie said that knowing had brought some sense of peace. Stevie wasn't sure if she could claim that yet. But the truth enabled her to grieve what she had lost and to try to move on. Try to build a life—an honest life, a good life—with people she could trust. The people she loved.

She pulled on her cowboy boots. "*Truthfully?* Right now, I am feeling very lucky that I have you as a friend."

Colby grinned. "You bet your ass you are." Colby took out her phone for a selfie. "Now smile!"

"Not another one," Stevie said.

"Err, Miss I'm Not Photogenic when you really are, you did promise your dad when you visited him in the slammer that you would document this whole trip. So smile and say 'Colby and Stevie, BFFs forever!'"

"Do we have to say that every single time?"

"Yes, Stevie, we do." Colby took the photo, checked it passed her standards, then said, "Sending to Melissa."

"Did she tell you she smashed her sophomore year?"

Colby squealed. "Like, so many As!"

"I'm so glad she's doing well."

"I know she sees a counselor about what happened to her, but I genuinely think blasting a bullet into Kirk's balls was a massive help."

Stevie snorted. "Her achievements are down to the fact that she's intelligent and tough."

Colby slung her arm around Stevie's neck. "Promise you're not going to forget me when you go off to college to become some big, fancy defense lawyer."

"How could I? You're going to come visit me all the time. Besides"—Stevie gave her a wink—"we *are* Stevie and Colby, the detective duo!"

Colby beamed and clapped her hands. "Oh my god, you said it!"

"Well, it's probably not as cringey as I originally thought."

"We should get T-shirts! We could have a logo and everything. Ooh! Maybe there could be three magnifying glasses on the back to show we solved three murders?"

"Colby," Stevie said flatly.

"Too much?"

"Maybe just a little."

Acknowledgments

To my editor, Ali Dougal, thank you for your belief in this book and giving it a home at Simon and Schuster. It has been such a joy working with you and I am so grateful for your invaluable editorial guidance.

A special thanks to my American editor, Sarah Barley—your sharp and insightful comments strengthened the book immeasurably. To Tierney Holm for your thoughtful editing and constant help along the way and to Lauren Atherton, for her tireless work and remarkable attention to detail—I couldn't have asked for steadier pairs of hands.

I am also hugely grateful to Rachel Denwood for championing both me and this story.

To the stupendously talented David McDougall, I am indebted to you for creating such an exceptional cover. And also to Emma Quick for the incredible book trailer which I have watched far too many times.

I would also like to thank Sarah Mondello, my copy editor, who has taught me the power of the em dash—and so much more. And thanks to my US proofreader Kerry Johnson and UK proofreader, Jennie Roman.

I would also like to thank Theo Steen, Maud Sepult, Emma Martinez, and Tanya Hill for their incredible work in selling the foreign rights. Your enthusiasm and dedication have helped bring this story to readers far beyond home, and I am so grateful.

To everyone else at S&S UK and S&S US behind the scenes—your work is so appreciated, thank you.

My thanks also go to my great friend, Katya Balen, for reading my very messy first draft and reminding me to believe in it.
I would also like to thank my agent, Sam Copeland, for his unwavering faith in me. Without his support, I would never have had the confidence to write for young adults.

Finally, to Andrew, William, and Douglas—your love, patience, and support at home have meant more to me than I can ever put into words.

WATCH OUT FOR STEVIE AND COLBY'S RETURN

SPRING 2027

ABOUT THE AUTHOR

Jennifer Pearson has previously written as Jenny Pearson. Her novels for younger readers, including *The Super Miraculous Journey of Freddie Yates*, have been published in twenty languages. She has been shortlisted for UK awards including the Costa, Waterstones Prize, Branford Boase, UKLA and Lollies, and her books have been selected as Waterstones Book of the Month, the *Times* Book of the Year and *Sunday Times* Book of the Week. This is her YA debut.

lonely 🌐 planet

Amsterdam

Catherine Le Nevez, Mark Elliott, Barbara Woolsey